The box was dropped at the corner of Thirteenth and Main some-time around midnight. It was left open so the summer wind would blow the contents free. It was full of sheets of paper, and the wind carried them south, beneath the light of the lamps, where they were caught in doorways and phone booths, along with the other detritus of the night. Around dawn, the first curious readers gave them a cursory glance, and soon every piece of paper had been picked up and its message shared around the city.

Before long, everyone was talking about Whisper.

BY LUKE ARNOLD

Fetch Phillips Archive
The Last Smile in Sunder City
Dead Man in a Ditch
One Foot in the Fade
Whisper in the Wind

WHISPER IN THE WIND

LUKE ARNOLD

orbit

orbit-books.co.uk

ORBIT

First published in Great Britain in 2025 by Orbit

1 3 5 7 9 10 8 6 4 2

A CIP catalogue record for this book is available from the British Library.

ISBN 978-0-356-52162-6

Typeset in Garamond by Palimpsest Book Production Limited, Falkirk, Stirlingshire
Printed and bound in Great Britain by Clays Ltd, Elcograf, S.p.A.

Papers used by Orbit are from well-managed forests and other responsible sources.

Orbit
An imprint of
Little, Brown Book Group
Carmelite House
50 Victoria Embankment
London EC4Y 0DZ

The authorised representative
in the EEA is
Hachette Ireland
8 Castlecourt Centre, Dublin 15,
D15 XTP3, Ireland
(email: info@hbgi.ie)

An Hachette UK Company
www.hachette.co.uk

orbit-books.co.uk

For Laura, finally and forever

1

The cafe was quiet, the city was burning, and I was happy.

Unbothered by the sirens and black smoke wafting in from the west, the last of the lunchtime customers took off with their meals and bestowed me with compliments and coins on their exit. I cleared the tables, scraped the hotplates clean, and took the garbage out onto the street.

Fire. Down near the Rose Quarter. An orange haze to the low clouds that made my skin crackle in anticipation of some incoming excitement.

Lives were being changed or ended. The start of someone's adventure.

Not mine.

I still needed to deal with the dirty dishes and check the stock and prep the patties for the dinner rush . . . though a quick look from a higher vantage wouldn't hurt. I didn't need to get involved – my meddling days were in the past – but this was still my city and I'd feel left out if there was a mess being made without me.

I climbed the steel stairs of the fire escape, resenting every step. Those hideous eyesores were bolted to every building on Main Street like someone had wandered through a gallery and welded hunks of metal onto all the art. When I got to the top – and saw nothing of interest besides more black smoke – I decided that it was finally time to bust this damn thing up.

Though the steps were useful, the railing offended me. It obstructed the view out the Angel door with a stamped strip of metal that read "NILES COMPANY CONSTRUCTION". The Angel door was a remnant of better days, before the Coda, when flying creatures could leave from the fifth floor and launch straight into the air. It was a reminder of what we once took for granted and – during periods of unchecked optimism – what we hoped could be reclaimed. The railing was installed by men who wanted those days gone for good. It was a safeguard that made me feel like I'd been separated from the city. I didn't like that. I might have spent most of my life as the eternal outsider – an intruder in every room, and the odd one out of step and out of time at every turn – but not any more. I'd found my place. Worked out a way to do some good in this world gone sour. I'd become a proper, useful part of Sunder City, and I'd be damned if anyone was going to put a barrier between me and the streets that finally felt like home.

It wasn't the first time I'd made an unauthorized attempt at city deconstruction; the steel barrier was warped with dents and blowtorch burns from my previous efforts. Say what you want about the Niles Company (and I'll say more than most), but they sure know how to bolt a bunch of metal together.

The structure had stood strong against my side kicks and mallet attacks, so I'd made a few enquiries and procured something special.

Seven years ago, when the Coda froze the sacred river and turned down the lights on this once-majestic world, we'd believed that the magic had vanished from existence. That was technically true – no denying the fact that we were living in a faded, bloodstained copy of the life we once knew – but the memory of that power still echoes down these streets, sticking to the shadows, hoping to be heard one last time. That's what I found, again and again, in my fruitless attempts to turn back the clock. Not magic. Not a way back to that better world. Just the curdled residue of what once was. A sacred power gone to seed, sprouting warped versions of its old self: often surprising, always dangerous, but occasionally useful.

I took the vial of acid from my pocket. The out-of-town Dwarven dealer claimed that it came from a Basilisk. I was pretty sure that – like all the old beasts that survived the Coda – it would no longer be some wild titan but a poor invalid animal, perhaps the last of its kind, held in captivity and milked for this strange greenish liquid. Once upon a time, a few drops of this bile would have been a weapon to win wars with. Now it was just a useful tool for breaking down unwanted metal barriers.

I unscrewed the lid – sure to keep the open vial away from my nose – and poured a couple of drops onto the bolts that were holding up the steel beam. It worked slowly, but a faint hissing sound and a thin stream of silver smoke let me know I might be making progress.

For the record, I wasn't taking down the balustrade because I desired a clear path out the Angel door if I ever felt like nosediving into nothingness. I'd moved on from those dreary days when the thrill of a five-story drop onto Main Street was my daily fantasy, and I now had too many customers that relied on me for a cheap, calorie-filled meal every morning. I just didn't like the idea of anyone, especially Thurston Niles, telling me what to do.

I had my routine, a hard-earned sense of satisfaction, and no desire to get involved with anything outside the greasy little cafe that Georgio had left in my care. I filled my days with bacon, eggs and coffee, and other than a preference for milk or sugar, anyone else's business was no business of mine.

I tried to tell myself that when I saw a couple of ash-covered kids running up Main Street from the south.

Even without the soot and sweat, you would have guessed they were guilty of something: a duo of nervous teenagers who kept changing their pace, unsure whether they should be running for their lives or attempting to play it cool. When the sirens got louder, they panicked and turned into Tackle Place, unaware that it was nothing but an L-shaped, dead-end crack between the backsides of buildings without any fences to hop over or doors to kick in. If someone was on their tail, then the kids had just cornered themselves and given their pursuer plenty of time to catch up.

Goddammit.

I stepped through the Angel door and into my office. My plan wouldn't work if I was seen sprinting down the fire escape, so I dumped the vial of acid in my desk, went through the waiting room into the hall, then down the inside stairwell taking it five steps at a time.

I came out the revolving door – no sign of any pursuer yet – and back into the cafe. The kids re-emerged from their fruitless adventure in the alley, and before they could scamper, I rapped against the window loud enough for them to hear.

They were flushed-faced, youthful, and as skittish as rabbits after a whipcrack. The one who heard me first was a Half-Elf girl with curly black hair, wide eyes, and the mottled two-tone skin that many of her kind had developed after the Coda. She was expecting danger more than assistance so I needed to beckon her repeatedly before she got the message. She turned to her companion for hasty deliberation about the risks of accepting my offer, but when the distant sirens became noticeably less distant, they decided to take their chances with the stranger in the window.

As soon as I saw that they were playing along, I grabbed a pile of greasy plates from the kitchen and brought them back out into the dining area.

"Are you Georgio?" asked the girl, holding open the door while looking up at the sign that dangled above it. It was a question I'd learned to endure on a daily basis. No, I was not the ancient Shaman who'd guided lost souls through the old world and filled empty stomachs in the new one. I was just one of the lucky people who benefitted from his wisdom before he wandered out of Sunder in search of a dream.

"We're under new management. I'm Fetch Phillips: amateur fry cook. Now, come in, sit down, wipe your hands, and try to look innocent."

I set a table of dirty dishes for two then threw them each a damp dishcloth. The Half-Elf's friend was a stocky, blond Human whose hands bore the telltale marks of recent pyromania.

"Anyone get killed?" I asked.

The girl looked up, defensive.

"What?"

"Whatever stunt you just pulled. Anyone killed? Badly hurt?"

The sirens were getting louder. Cops would soon be coming up Main Street and the kids were visibly nervous.

"It wasn't even us," said the girl, wiping her hands. "We were sneaking around the Rose when this whole house went up in flames."

"It was bullshit anyway," said the boy, wiping soot from his face. "The firefighters were already there. Must have done it themselves."

"One of them pointed at us, trying to pin the blame. We got out of there, but—"

She was cut off by a police car blowing past the cafe in a blur of blue light and black exhaust. I didn't know if I believed her, but I didn't really care. The Sunder City Police Department weren't the lazy paper-pushers they used to be, and their treatment of ex-magical creatures who didn't fall into line was getting worse every week. I was happy to accept the kids' story without regard for its relationship to the truth.

"I think we lost them," said the Human boy. "Let's go."

Before they could get up, Constable Bath jogged up the sidewalk and stopped right outside the front window of the cafe. His uniform was soaked with sweat and his hair was slick and sticking out at all angles. It looked like he'd paused to catch his breath, but as he leaned against the cafe to settle himself, his focus shifted to the customers inside.

There was a clatter of metal against porcelain as the suspects picked up their cutlery and shoveled the last of their imaginary meals into their mouths. I snatched the sooty dishcloths from the table and shoved them into my pockets as Bath made his way around to the entrance.

"Ophelia," hissed the Human boy, "your hair!" He pointed to

a paper petal caught in her curls: a calling card of the Rose Quarter, thrown by sex workers on balconies to attract the attention of those walking below. These accidental souvenirs had revealed the lies of many a Rose Quarter patron in the past, so I plucked it out and crushed it in my fist as the bell above the door went "ding".

Bath stood at the threshold of the cafe, his expression a badly mixed cocktail of suspicion, trepidation and bewilderment. Our ruse was as thin as a Vampire on a hunger strike, but Bath was considerate to a fault and a lapsed believer in his own instincts, so he couldn't help but give us the benefit of the doubt.

"Fetch," he panted. "We're . . . we're looking for some vandals. Set fire to a cottage in the Rose Quarter." Out the window, more cops jogged into view. One was knocking on the door of the teahouse across the way while two others charged down Tackle Place.

"Is that what all the hubbub was about?" I remarked, pouring cold coffee into a dirty cup as if it were a refill. "We all thought we could smell something, didn't we?"

The double act played their part, nodding silently. The girl took an overly enthusiastic swig of coffee, almost spat it out when she registered the temperature, but managed to swallow it with an audible gulp.

Bath looked from the kids back to me, then back to the kids.

"Two suspects, apparently," he said, his high-pitched voice avoiding accusation. "Young. They'll probably be . . . sooty."

He had the unblinking stare of a dog at the kitchen table, waiting for somebody to slip up and drop a piece of their meal, as if any minute now, one of the kids was going to clumsily let fall a confession.

"I haven't seen anyone come past recently."

"And what about . . .?" He pointed at my two guests.

"Oh, this lot wouldn't have seen anything either. They've been back in the kitchen for the last hour learning the ropes. I've been teaching them how to use the fryer and we've just been tasting the results. You haven't seen anything out of the ordinary, have you, kids?"

The boy just shook his head but the Half-Elf with the big eyes found her voice.

"Nothing like that. Sorry. We'll keep a lookout though."

Bath's habitual civility caused him to thank her without meaning to. He looked back to me with a pleading expression on his face, hoping that I'd show him some sympathy by ending the charade.

"Golly, Fetch. It's a lot of damage. If we don't find the folks who did this, Company Men will be the next ones that come knocking."

At first, I thought it was a threat. But no. Not from Bath. It was a warning, sure, but one meant as a mercy. A chance to come clean with him before Thurston Niles sent out butcher boys in charcoal suits to ask the same questions without the strained civility.

I gave him a smile – to let him know I appreciated his care and his candor – but I wasn't worried about Niles Company goons or more city cops or the wrath of Thurston or Detective Simms or anyone. I was just a humble cafe owner taking care of his customers on an early-summer afternoon.

"Thanks, Bath. If I hear of any leads, you'll be the first person I call." I made my way to the kitchen, calling to the kids over my shoulder. "All right, team, lunch break's over. Next up, it's bacon butties – a cop favorite, as it happens – and we'll need three dozen for afternoon tea."

There was the scraping of chairs as they jumped to attention, leaving Bath to contemplate his options. It didn't take him long. He wasn't made for this kind of work. Backing up a superior officer was one thing – he had no problem following orders, no matter how inane, insane or immoral they were – but send him out on his own and he acted like a timid farm boy attempting to court a date.

In the kitchen, the fugitives gathered around me, holding their breath. We waited, and waited, until the bell jangled once more and the door slammed shut. The Half-Elf broke out in wild laughter, slapping both her friend and me on the back.

"Yes! Thanks, fella. We'll give the copper a couple of minutes to clear off then get out of your hair."

"Not a good plan," I said. "Bath may be too nervous to arrest you on his own, but that doesn't mean he won't bring his buddies back for another look."

Their smiles faded.

"So, we should go?" asked the boy.

"Cops will be all over the streets. Let's hope Bath is too embarrassed to confess that he walked away from the culprits, but if he *does* come back, we need to solidify your story." I took two aprons from the hook (perfectly clean, as I'd never used them myself) and held them out. "Come on. Three dozen bacon butties by four o'clock."

They made a show of thinking it over, but they were still buzzing from the thrill of getting away with arson and I think the novelty of the whole thing tickled them too much. They tied the aprons around their waists and stepped up to the stations.

"There's the rolls, fresh from the bakery this morning." The boy made a right mess of his first attempt, hacking at it with a butter knife. "Kid, serrated knives are in the block on the bench. I sell these for two bronze coins a piece so make them look worth it." He was about to argue back, but a look from his lady friend made him fall into line.

I turned my attention to the Half-Elf.

"Bacon's in the icebox. Bottom drawer, wrapped in butcher's paper. What are your names, anyway?"

"I'm Ophelia, that's Ashton."

She skipped across the room as I turned the knobs on the grill. A crackling whoosh brought a stream of heat from the pits below the city. They hit the underside of the hotplate, and I closed my eyes and breathed deep.

There was fire in the air, but unlike the black smoke outside, this was obedient, tame and contained. It was a good day. Coffee in the pot, meat on the grill, and a couple of kids safe off the street. I was finally doing something useful.

Bath didn't come back that day. Or ever. A few nights later, he was shot eight times in his own home. I can't say I cared all that much. He'd picked his side, hadn't he? One less cop to worry about. Why would I make that any of my business?

If only I had.

Maybe then the good days would have lasted a little longer.

2

The box was dropped at the corner of Thirteenth and Main sometime around midnight. It was left open so the summer wind would blow the contents free. It was full of sheets of paper, and the wind carried them south, beneath the light of the lamps, where they were caught in doorways and phone booths, along with the other detritus of the night. Around dawn, the first curious readers gave them a cursory glance, and soon every piece of paper had been picked up and its message shared around the city.

Before long, everyone was talking about Whisper.

Turn the bacon, crack the eggs, switch the pot, flip the bread. Get more . . . goddammit.

"Ophelia! Where did the cinnamon buns go?"

She popped into my periphery, wiping icing from her cheeks.

"Payment for taking orders. Put them on my tab."

"You don't have a . . . Forget it. What's the order?"

"Three breakfast specials, two black coffees, five biscuits, a butty and a big bowl of milk."

I made some modifications to the cafe after Georgio left on his quest, and Ophelia took great joy in reaching through the new window that linked the dining room to the kitchen and sticking each order to the cork board as it came in. It had only been a week since I'd met them, and though the wide-eyed Half-Elf and her Human companion had proved to be useless kitchenhands, that hadn't stopped them from making themselves at home. They deigned to take an order or two when things got busy. Which was nice, because ever since word got out that Georgio's cafe was a haven for maligned and misbegotten youth with a taste for trouble, the place had become as busy as a Succubus's bed.

The tables were so full that new arrivals were forced to take a lean, but that was no longer indicative of the place doing good business; the teenage rabble who'd decided to make the cafe their unofficial clubhouse hadn't got it through their heads that I might appreciate them paying for something once in a while. The rowdy mass of feral hormones had pushed all the tables on the north wall together, and there was barely an hour without at least a couple of kids hunched over it, scrawling in notepads or flicking bottle caps. These pint-sized rebels made up most of my visitors but only a small percentage of my income, spending plenty of time but little else. Most days, it didn't bother me, but they were louder than usual that morning. There were a number of new kids in attendance and the place was so packed that my other regulars couldn't reach the counter.

"Where's Richie?" I shouted to Ophelia (we'd gone past the pleasantries of please-and-thank-yous days ago). "His delivery's getting cold."

"Oi! Hand 'em over!" Richie's huge, olive face appeared above the pack. He may have once been a Shepherd of the Opus – and was still plenty of pounds of Half-Ogre muscle – but even he was having trouble moving through the crowd. "I've been trying to get inside for ten minutes."

I passed the basket of egg sandwiches over the heads of a few tea-drinking Dwarves, and Rich took it with both hands.

"Outta my way or I'm coming straight through ya!" he yelled, before parting the sea with his sizable belly. I was already back at the grill, plating up breakfast burgers and starting on the next set of specials. I poured coffees without thinking – two pots always on the go – and passed them through the window, trusting that the sound of jangling metal meant that someone was dropping the correct amount of coin into the till.

Check the mushrooms, slice more tomato, taste the sauce.

"Hey, Pheels," I called to my Half-Elven helper, "what's with the crowd today, huh?"

As a response, Ophelia pinned another piece of paper to the cork board. There were similar pamphlets in the hands of all the younger patrons, crumpled and dog-eared from being snatched back and forth. I'd noticed them being passed around but was too absorbed in the rotation of eggs and sausage to give them further thought.

"They've been blowing all over town," said Ophelia, handing out coffees while I perused the pamphlet. "Nobody knows where they came from."

It looked like a news article that had broken free of the paper and headed out on its own. The typeface was simple – blue/black with the occasional smear – and only ran for a couple of paragraphs.

YOUR LEADERS ARE LYING TO YOU

Friends, Rebels and Youngsters,

Brave Actors, True Hearts,

I see an afflicted city.

Doesn't everyone remember reading information not gossip?

Eloquently related, rational, even-handed, dispassionate, objective news?

Not a dictator editor's measly offering of regurgitated horse-shit, every night reciting yesterday's propaganda?

I seek truth.

Old news and Niles-designed tales have unprecedented reach, soiling their once-nuanced newspaper in lies.

Enter Sunder's herald: a voice every leader endeavored to shut up, not Derringer's erroneous rag, spreading unsafe falsities, fouling every reader.

Beware, your cops help only insidious criminal entities take hold.

Early tomorrow, read an investigation telling of real secret meetings using Sunder treasuries.

Delivered in earnest,

Mister Whisper.

I turned back to the fire. *Pour the coffee, refill the beans, pile the bacon, take the back row of eggs off the heat.* I could understand why the kids were excited – this was just the kind of big talk they liked to fill the place with instead of filling my pockets – but I was already putting it out of my head. So, the city was corrupt? What a surprise. The *Sunder Star* was selling goose shit as gospel? Whoop-de-do. It was nice to know that somebody was out there kicking up a stink, but the state of Sunder's four estates was less of a concern to me than working out how to get my hash browns crispy without giving the customer an instant heart attack. No Man for Hire here any more. No wannabe hero. You want anything other than a hot breakfast? Go bother someone else. *Plate the next row of eggs, crack another dozen, send out the coffee, get the next batch on the stove.*

Once the coffee was on, I added tomato and beans to the plates and lifted them up to the window.

"Order up!"

I'd been anticipating Ophelia's smiling face, but the one staring back was as far from a smile as a papercut to a pistol shot.

Detective Simms stared through the service window, golden eyes visible over her tightly wrapped black scarf. Summer had hit the city, and while everyone else was down to essential layers – even I had my top buttons undone and my sleeves rolled up to my elbows – Simms was wearing a wide-brimmed hat, a scarf around her mouth, and the collar of her trench coat popped up over her ears (or where her ears would be, if Reptilia were a species who sported them).

I sensed something off about Simms but put it down to her fluctuating appreciation of my friendship, her aversion to crowds, her dislike of young people, or her dislike of people in general.

"Here you go, Lena." I reached under the counter and pulled out a glass jar of bone-white cream.

"Fetch, I don't want that. I—"

"It's the last I have in stock," I said, turning my back on her. *Flip the eggs. Butter the toast. Pour the coffee.* "I'm still waiting on the ingredients to boil another vat."

It was a reduction of collagen, marrow and fat, a few easily obtained plants and herbs, and a generous dollop of something Portemus (Sunder's most enthusiastic mortician) called Reanicol. Portemus used the serum on his "clients" to preserve them for as long as possible, and together we'd created this cream: a milder version of his invention that worked as a topical lotion for ex-magical creatures whose skin had problems with this non-magical atmosphere. I didn't exactly know what Reanicol was – like a lot of things to do with Portemus, it's wise to stay oblivious to the details – but there was surely some magical element in it. Not active magic, of course (that had been dead for seven years), but a twisted remnant of the power that was kicked around the world in those glorious days before the Coda.

Knowing Portemus, the substance would have been something extracted from the unfortunate creatures who made their way through his mortuary, and if there was some magical power in it – no matter how dulled and disappointing it had become – that meant that it was now an outlawed substance in Sunder City. For that reason, the jar had no ingredients list and the label just read "skin cream".

The response from customers had been positive – nobody had reported any miraculous response to the ointment, but it apparently eased some of their discomfort – so Simms and others would sometimes drop by the cafe to refill their supply.

I assumed that's why Simms was paying me a visit, but she left the jar on the counter and cleared her throat.

"Fetch, I'm on my way to a crime scene. I want you to come with me." Her sibilant speech wasn't much above a whisper, but

I noticed one of the kids clock what she said. It was Ashton, the Human arsonist who'd hidden out here with Ophelia after fleeing from the Rose Quarter fire. He'd just been stepping up to the window to return a pile of plates, and looked us over with unmasked suspicion. Ashton was still cynical about the Man for Hire turned cafe owner who'd opened his place up to Sunder's growing counter-culture, and his sneering expression set me on edge.

"Sorry, Simms," I said, placing a black coffee beside her skin cream, "I'm a little busy." I dropped a Clayfield into her cup as a peace offering. They were harder to come by these days. The strips of bark worked as painkillers because the tree they were derived from was magical in origin, so a lot of stores had stopped stocking them for fear of repercussions.

There were now two pieces of contraband in front of Sunder's most scaly police detective and, though I hadn't accepted her proposition, she wasn't about to leave them behind. She pocketed the jar, pulled down her scarf and sipped the coffee, taking a long, strained breath.

More tomatoes in the oven. Drain the oil. Cut a string of sausages.

"It's Bath," she said, as I salted the potatoes. "He's dead."

I paused for as long as I could – maybe a second or two – then picked up the spatula and rotated the eggs.

"I'm sorry, Simms. What happened?"

"I'd rather not talk about it here."

"And I'd rather have a few extra hands who know how to fry an egg, but here we are." *Flip, slide, season, serve.* "If you need someone to talk to, Richie was just—"

"It happened in Bath's apartment. His home. There was someone waiting for him. A *lot* of someones, by the look of it. It's . . . well, you should see it for yourself."

I could only afford to glance up occasionally but, when I did, I saw Ashton standing over the large table, holding court. Kids leaned in to listen to him, all looking in my direction.

"Sorry," I told Simms. *Bacon, egg, brown sauce. Eight rolls ready to go.* "I can't leave. Why do you want me along anyway? You know I don't do that work any more."

"I want—"

"Hey! Copper! Read the paper this morning?" Ashton was standing at the head of the table with a smug look on his face. It was a match for the smug looks on the others sitting around him.

The grief and exhaustion that had been weighing Simms down took a back seat, and her narrow eyes became cold, golden slits. She attempted to ignore the provocation.

"Phillips, I can't make this an official request, but—"

"Didn't you see it, Detective?" It was Ophelia's turn to pipe up. The group didn't have a leader but, if they did, she would have been first in line. She was holding up one of the newsletters as if she was casually sharing a piece of amusing gossip. "Today's big story alleges that you and all your friends are on the Niles Company payroll. Not much of a scoop, right? You've been enforcing his rules since the day he arrived."

Ophelia wasn't wrong. It had been a year and a half since Thurston Niles turned up in Sunder, and ever since he'd started signing checks, Mayor Piston and the local police had become increasingly concerned with the dangers of unsanctioned magical practices.

Simms refused to take the bait, keeping her attention on me.

"He didn't deserve this, Fetch. He was a good kid."

"You excited about Mister Whisper sharing all your dirty laundry?" said a third kid – this one with blue hair and a piercing through his nose – and I wondered if each of them was going to try to have their moment.

Simms bit her lip to stop herself from snapping back.

"Bath was on to something. I need your help to find who did this to him."

A tear in her eye caught the warm light of the kitchen. At a different time in a different place, it might have persuaded me, but she wasn't the only one applying pressure.

"Fetch?" prompted Ophelia, as if I were an actor on opening night who'd forgotten his line.

Maybe all I did was serve up greasy eggs and better-than-average coffee, but in the months since Georgio had left and I'd taken over, the place had developed a certain reputation. It was a safe place, in a city where that was becoming hard to find. We had flexible hours, no cover charge, and furniture that was already so stained you couldn't add to it if you tried. The kids were only the latest lost souls who'd made it their second home. They were mostly full of hot air – spending their days celebrating petty vandalism and dreaming of a violent revolution – but I had more affection for their unruly brand of anarchy than I did for the shiny badge pinned to Simms's coat. I'd never had much luck aligning myself with other people's agendas, but if I was going to throw my lot in with anyone, these youngsters seemed a safer bet than any of the other groups who'd asked for my allegiance.

I'd helped Simms out before – I'd even sided with the cops over the people they'd vowed to protect – and I'd promised myself I wouldn't do it again. She wasn't here as a friend. She was here because she wanted justice for her fallen comrade, and it was time I made it clear that the police and I weren't on the same side.

"Sorry, Lena," I said. "You and your officers can sort this out on your own. My orders are piling up."

I turned my back before she could argue. One row of eggs was already overdone and as I dropped them into the scrap bucket, the crowd of kids erupted in jeers and cheers, applauding Simms's exit and my lackluster show of defiance.

"That's enough!" I called through the window, playing the role of beleaguered schoolteacher. "This is a cafe, not your clubhouse, so treat my customers with respect or get out."

Ashton led a round of "ooohs" but Ophelia cut them off.

"He's right," she told them. "Don't act like children."

An obedient silence followed. Ashton looked embarrassed and I hid a knowing smile. The kid was smitten. I tucked that ace up my sleeve so I'd have it ready the next time he tried to undercut me in front of his crew.

I put four specials on the counter – they weren't perfect, but they'd pass – and as some Elves rose from their seats to collect them, a paperboy stepped into the cafe, dinging the bell for the thousandth time that morning.

"Delivery of the *Sunder Star*."

He dumped a pile of tabloid papers by the door.

"HEY!" I yelled. "You get that filthy rag out of here. I never ordered it."

The "paperboy" was a few decades old for the job. He wore a tailored tweed three-piece despite the heat and sported a white beard that had been waxed and brushed to unnatural perfection. He raised his notepad to his squinting eyes and furrowed his brow.

"Ah, no, no, no. It says here I have a special delivery for Mr Fetch Phillips."

Great. I thought. *Some kind of prank*. Thurston Niles must have been missing my visits so much he'd decided to mess with me until I paid him some attention.

"Well, I don't want them. Take 'em with you."

The paperboy shrugged and looked down at the pile, then he leaned forward, as if something peculiar had caught his eye. He picked up the top paper and brought it to his nose. He blinked, then looked at me, then back to the paper, and back to me again. When he spoke, his voice was laced with warning.

"I dunno, mate; I reckon you might want to see this."

Despite the heat of the kitchen, my blood went cold. I beckoned him over and he put the paper on the counter.

There I was.

My own stupid face, eight years and an eternity younger, standing side by side with the leaders of the Human Army. General Taryn – the man who'd recruited me – had a fatherly hand on my shoulder, with more senior officers on either side. We were the men who'd put an end to the magical age and doomed the world to death and decay. Our actions had shared the burden of mortality with those who had never known it and dragged even the greatest of this world's wonders down to our level.

I was so stunned by what I saw that by the time I looked up, some customers had already retrieved other papers from the pile. Choking back panic, I dragged my eyes to the headline.

WAR CRIMINAL IN OUR MIDST
Local agitator, Fetch Phillips, catalyst for the Coda.

My old, wounded heart clenched like a streetfighter's fist. What the hell was going on? The Coda was the worst thing that had ever happened to the world. The attack on the sacred river severed its connection to magical creatures, making the Elves mortal, the Wizards powerless and the Fae extinct. My involvement wasn't common knowledge – only a few people knew the facts, and a few more knew a scrap or two – but I never thought it would warrant front-page news. I looked out to the large table, ready to watch in real time as more people who'd been dumb enough to put their faith in me tasted the inevitable disappointment.

But there were no shocked faces. No disbelieving stares. They were all just flipping through the various sections, remarking on the bullshit and bluster that was typical of every edition of the *Star*. Ophelia looked at me and shrugged, so I looked back to the paperboy.

He dropped the role of "confused delivery person" and stared back with the blank, uncaring eyes of a hired goon. The kind of look that had me mentally calculating the distance to the nearest sharp object.

"They're not reading what you are," he said, voice low and monotonous. "But they will tomorrow if you don't come with me. The editor wants to see you."

I had all kinds of insults lined up, but a look back at my personally designed newspaper smothered them. Things were finally going well. Every day, I went down to the cafe and did something that actually mattered. Sure, my life wasn't as exciting or as wild as it had been a few months before when I was actively trying to turn back time, but there was a lot less blood and broken bones (unless you counted what went into the mincer). I'd found my place and my purpose and fuck me if some prick at a typewriter was going to take that away.

I shoved the paper into the oven and watched it burn. Once the offending article had been turned to ash, I picked up a ladle and saucepan and banged them together until everyone shut up.

"Finish your meals and settle your bills. Kitchen's closing early!"

3

I was led outside to an illegally parked car. It would be illegally parked almost anywhere, because it was longer and wider than any parking space in the city. I tried not to look too impressed. On principle, I hated any modern contraption made by Niles or Mortales – especially the higher-priced pieces that would never be available to the common man – but the craftsmanship of this piece couldn't be denied.

"Where do you get something like this?" I blurted.

"*You* don't," said the paperboy/henchman/driver as he opened the back door for me. He'd changed his persona yet again, becoming a brash yet attentive steward. "Bespoke order, straight from Mira. A Mortales-made, one-of-a-kind motorcar. Ain't she a beauty?" I wanted to disagree, but there was something about the smooth angles of the paneling, the dark sheen to the windows and the curve of the hood that made you want to run your hands all over it. "Careful! Your greasy fingerprints will fuck up the chrome."

The interior was tan leather set within dark wooden framing, like I was stepping into an exclusive whiskey bar on wheels. The gearstick and handbrake were the same shiny chrome as the details on the exterior, and embedded in the center of the steering wheel was a glimmering, translucent gem that glistened with a silverish shade of purple.

Surely not.

"What's that?" I asked, my voice already shaking. The driver turned the key and pointed out the details like a proud parent.

"That's Buffalo leather from beyond The Su, very hard to come by. Grovan Mahogany. Dwarven silver mechanisms. Mr Derringer had to import that from—"

"The crystal. On the wheel."

If he registered my disgust, it didn't change his tone.

"Ooh, that. You won't believe it."

"Try me."

He plucked the silk handkerchief from his breast pocket and gave the crystal in question a little love.

"That's pure, bona fide Unicorn horn. You probably heard that the horn was more a kind of magical mist, right? Well, when the Coda crystalized the magical river, it also crystalized the horns in every Unicorn's head and . . ."

I let him ramble, but I needed no schooling on the subject. I'd encountered one of the rabid creatures in the wild. Killed it, I'm sad to say. It was self-defense, though I still felt shitty about it. I felt shittier still that I'd proceeded to break off the beast's horn to use as medicine, hoping to save the life of a friend. That hadn't worked. Instead, we'd ended up using its power to put down a rampaging Warlock.

I still wasn't sure if it was worth it. Who was I to take something so sacred and use it for my own means? Especially when those means might have squashed Sunder's last attempt at pushing back against Niles's occupation.

But whatever I'd done with that piece of pure magic, at least I hadn't stuck it into a fucking steering wheel.

I felt the indignant rage rise in my throat. I wanted to spit venom at the driver for marveling at the fact that a miracle had been shaped into a meaningless bauble. But I had no high ground. No greater insight. Not a leg to stand on. Besides, if I opened my mouth, nothing would change. So, I just stretched myself out on the luxuriously long back seat and closed my eyes. As a recent subscriber to the early-riser club, I'd also signed up to the fraternity of noontime nappers and liked to steal some slumber whenever the opportunity presented itself.

"SHIT!" The driver slammed on the brakes, and I bounced off the back of the passenger seat before landing on the floor. "This is a bloody road!"

It looked like someone had been drying out their sheets and the linen had made a run for it. A congregation of white robes was passing in front of us, each carrying a lit candle.

"What's that all about?" I asked, pulling myself back up.

"New church, apparently. It's been in the paper. Some priestess came to town a couple of months ago. I guess this is their way of drumming up constituents. Fine by me, as long as they STICK TO THE BLOODY SIDEWALK!"

The billowing sheets floated by, unperturbed by the driver's outburst. A smaller car could have gone around them, but this beast of a machine filled a whole lane of Main Street without an inch to spare.

"Is it true?" asked the driver when he got going again.

"Is *what* true?"

"What it said in the paper. That you caused the Coda." I kept my eyes closed and grumbled in the universal language of "let me sleep" but he'd wet his lips on a scandal and wanted a proper drink. "How's that even possible?" I felt the car come to a stop — not our final destination, just an intersection — and heard the creaking of leather as he turned around in his seat. "I mean, look at ya."

"I can't. My eyes are closed."

The leather squeaked again, the car rumbled on, and the man kept blabbering.

"You're a bum, right? I mean, no offense, but I've scraped more impressive specimens from between my toes. How the hell could you be so important?"

"Don't believe everything you read in the paper, pal."

He gave a snort of reluctant laughter.

"I'd get those jokes outta your system now, if I was you. The editor don't like wise guys."

"Yeah, I can tell from his articles. Does the *Star* even hire journalists these days, or do you dictate the stories straight from Niles himself?"

There was a meaner, deeper laugh from the driver this time.

"Oooh, the boss is gonna hate you."

There were many sides to the gray-bearded man. Long gone was the pleasant and polite paperboy, and as much as the grumbling manservant annoyed me, I preferred him to the unblinking henchman that occasionally took over his body.

He gave up questioning me about my past, but that didn't mean he was ready to drive in silence. Even with my eyes closed, I was fed enough commentary on the world outside that there was no need to see it for myself. Apparently, there was nothing out there but terrible drivers, and women so stunning a buttock and bosom could scarce go by without enthusiastic report.

"Wake up, sleepyhead," said the driver, slowing us down. "We're— Oi, you!" He slammed the brakes again, but this time I managed to catch myself. "GET OUTTA HERE, YOU FUCKING PEEPER!"

I looked out the window at the gates of a huge estate. Beside the fence, a short Cyclops in a brown suit and pork-pie hat was stumbling out of the shrubs, fiddling with a long-lens camera.

"Just doing my job, Carnegie. You know the deal."

The driver – Carnegie – jumped out. I thought he was going to rough up the photographer, but he went for one of the gateposts, inserted a key into a mechanism, and the gate began to open. Only then, did he turn on the Cyclops.

"Listen, Ward, you fuck."

He was back to playing the standover man, the intimidator. The exchange became too low to hear, but throughout it all, the brown-suited Cyclops kept smiling while Carnegie's face grew red. I heard them say something about sunbathing, then the driver came back towards the car, his voice returning to the attitude and accent of a long-suffering servant. "If you're still here when I come back, I'll give you a story worth telling!"

The Cyclops laughed and pointed his camera in our direction.

"Ooh, that was a good snarl, Carnegie. Give us another one,

just like that." He snapped the camera, and I hoped the tinted windows were dark enough to keep me hidden. Seeing myself in the *Star* was more than enough fame for one day. "Who you got in there? Another secret visitor for the missus? Careful, mate; Mr Derringer's still at home."

"Fuck off, Owen."

We went through the gates, up the drive, and I could see Carnegie's eyes burn in the mirror the whole way to the top of the hill.

"All right," he said when we came to a stop. "Out."

We were in the driveway of a colossal brownstone building with wrought-iron bars over huge arched windows. The path was pebbled with white stones that reflected the morning sun as if each of them had been individually polished. The gardens that surrounded the house would have dwarfed any other dwelling, made up of plants that weren't usually seen in Sunder: bamboo, palms and tropical trees with leaves the size of a Wyvern's wings.

"This way." Carnegie led me through a front door that was more than twice my height. I was deposited on a wooden bench and told to stay still, but as soon as the helper's head was turned, I got up and looked around.

The hall was sparsely decorated – no rugs, no art – but I opened the closest door and stepped into some kind of gallery. The high ceiling was broken up by skylights, illuminating the monumental pieces that filled the high walls. The paintings were of a scale and mastery I'd only seen in the Lopari throne room or the walls of the Sunder Museum (before Niles turned it into his personal house of propaganda).

I went in uninvited and turned to face the first piece on my left. I'd always been jealous of people who could identify the period, style or artist on sight. My old friend and mentor Hendricks could have. He knew his painting masters even better than his fencing masters, but he'd had a few hundred years head start.

The painting depicted a Gorgon – snake-headed and scaled,

with piercing silver eyes – writhing in ecstasy. Or perhaps in pain. The subject's body, partly concealed in murky shadow, was naked. A woman – both fearsome and enticing – with a feverous expression and blood pooling at her feet. The blood was dripping from the fangs of the serpents who grew out of her head, knotted and twisting with the same straining tension as their host. The woman's shoulders and arms were marked with bites – pairs of pinprick holes, some weeping – that punctured her pale skin. The longer I looked at it, the less fearsome and more tragic she became.

"It's fucking awful, isn't it?"

I spun, unable to hide my surprise. On the other side of the room, reclining on a red leather chaise, was a woman wearing a silk dressing gown, no shoes, long black gloves, platinum-blonde bed hair and dark sunglasses. Her pose was so perfectly sculptured – an artwork in itself – that I chose to believe she'd intentionally positioned herself that way before getting my attention.

"Sorry," I said. "Didn't see you there. I assume you're the lady of the house?"

"Trixie Derringer," she said, with a drawl that could have come from breeding, a bottle, or both. "I'm sorry, darling, this is usually the safest place for peace and quiet. Isaac's friends are more interested in courting his checkbook than appreciating his art. Especially those that smell like burnt toast and beef fat."

I cringed.

"Sorry about that."

I was wearing the same thing I'd been sporting in the sweatbox of a kitchen: gray slacks marked with oil and egg yolk, a white shirt painted with the same pattern, and my sleeves rolled up to expose the four tattooed rings that wrapped around my forearm. I felt the urge to cover them up, but resisted; she'd already got a good look at them and, as her husband had been the one to mock up that story, I assumed it would be too late to hide my history from anyone in this house.

I stepped forward and extended a hand.

"Nice to meet you, Ms Derringer."

There was an awkward pause as my hand just hovered there, the Gorgon making no move to touch it.

"Are you waiting for me to do something?" she asked. "If so, I can't see you."

The dark glasses suddenly made sense.

"Sorry. No, that's fine. Was just going to shake your hand, but—"

"Oh, how formal. Yes, let's." She held out a gloved hand, and I moved mine to find hers. Her shake was surprisingly strong. "There you go. What lovely manners, young man. Sorry I'm not getting up. I struggle in this interminable heat."

She ran her hand through her hair, and as the white strands flowed between her silk-covered fingers, I saw that they didn't move like hair at all. They were large, translucent locks that, once disturbed, floated around as if they weighed next to nothing.

Snakeskin.

Not the kind they make boots out of, but the kind that's left behind when a reptile shakes loose an old layer. Her head was covered in a pit of serpents, though their bodies were gone, leaving just the outlines of empty, bone-colored ghosts. The heads were still intact, so each strand ended in a hollow-eyed, open-mouthed scream. The skin was so light that they wafted around, creating the illusion that the snakes were still alive, reaching out from her scalp in search of something to sink their teeth into.

I looked back to the painting, then back to Trixie.

"It's not me, if that's what you're thinking," she said. "That's my great-aunt. Painted by a jilted lover who took her rejections as proof that she was filled with some inner, unchecked turmoil, rather than the fact he was a joyless turd with a drinking problem. Though, if I remember correctly, he did capture her eyes."

Playfully, she put a finger on top of her sunglasses and, at a painfully slow speed, began to push them down. My jaw clenched. Sure, the magic was gone, but there are certain rules that get drilled into you when you're being trained to fight magical creatures: only engage Werewolves when the moon is new, plug your ears before greeting a Banshee, and never look a Gorgon in the eye.

The sunglasses slid smoothly down her nose, revealing a set of polished peepers. There was no white, no discernible iris or pupil, just the dull, mottled gray of solid stone.

I knew there was no magic. I knew nothing would happen. But I couldn't help but look away.

"Phillips, where the hell are you?"

The bellowing voice bounced off every wall of the enormous house like the building itself was shouting at me. Ms Derringer pushed her glasses back up her nose and smiled, flashing a modest set of fangs.

"You'd better be running along. Isaac doesn't like to be kept waiting."

I was happy to take her advice, until I stepped back through the doorway and saw the monster I was here to meet.

4

The size of the house suddenly made sense. The colossal doors, the ridiculous car, the tropical plants stolen from rainforests and forced to endure Sunder's ever-changing climate. Isaac Derringer was a Sasquatch. Eight hundred pounds of simian muscle force-fed into a woolen suit that would have been unseasonable if the guy hadn't spent most of his life wrapped in a dense layer of fur. His natural coat had mostly fallen out, but a thick gray mane billowed out of his collar and merged smoothly with his bushy mustache.

He was standing in one of the doorways down the hall, his hand gripped to the wooden frame like he was ready to snap it into splinters.

"Here," he grunted, and turned without another word.

I found him in an expansive, well-lit room. Windows on two sides looked out on a lush garden that must have taken half the city's water supply to keep green. The other walls were decorated with framed articles from the *Sunder Star*'s lifetime: the installment of Governor Fenchurch (Lark's predecessor), construction of the stadium, Eliah Hendricks – High Chancellor of the Opus – making his first diplomatic visit, and plenty of buildings that had since been burned down due to mismanagement of the fire pits. The *Star* had a reputation for pitiless reporting, and it appeared that Derringer made that accusation a point of pride, displaying a double-page spread of Coda victims that was printed while the bodies were still warm. It usually only took a glance at a *Star* article to start me swearing, so I was proud of myself for being able to look upon so many at once without descending into a tantrum.

"You met my wife," stated Derringer, without inflection.

"Yeah. You're a lucky fella."

"I'm a hard worker, Mr Phillips. Nothing more."

It's always the guys with employees, wealth and well-connected friends who get defensive about their work ethic, because they so desperately want to believe that the only difference between them and the people who clean their toilets is their ability to apply the elbow grease. Your story must be pretty fragile if admitting to a bit of good fortune causes the whole ruse to come crashing down.

"Yeah, I bet. It's real backbreaking labor to play on people's fears every day. Or do you deliver the papers yourself?"

He huffed, and the hairs under his nose had a party.

"Let me show you."

Derringer approached a wooden plinth. There were a bunch of them around the room, staggered between the articles. Some held awards, others propped up pieces of machinery that must have held some historical importance. The largest of them, in the center of the space, had a great big hunk of metal on it. It looked like my sandwich grill but with a crank attached to the end.

"The Derringer desktop letterpress," he said, attempting to imbue his words with eminence. "When I arrived in Sunder City, this was all I had: a single-operator printing press of my own design. It took half a day to prepare a single plate, and the other half to print a couple hundred copies. That's how I started. Just me, my own words, and my grit."

I pushed the top plate of the letterpress and it swung smoothly down on a hinge to meet an identical plate below. There was no paper or type inserted into the machine, so all it did was leave a blue-black smudge on my hand to tell me to stop playing around.

"Stop playing around," barked the Sasquatch, ganging up on me. I wiped the ink on my shirt, which made a mess of the cloth without dulling the stain on my finger in the slightest. Derringer looked down with an expression of deep regret. Good. Anything I could do to have him rethink the benefits of bringing me here was a point in my favor. "You've read my paper?"

"I sometimes catch a few words before I wipe and flush."

He gave an exasperated sigh and made his way to a mahogany desk that could have been home to a Gnome and his extended family.

"How did you like my story?" he asked, taking a seat. I flexed what little independence I had by not immediately joining him. Instead, I wandered lazily back and forth, glancing at the archived pieces.

"Even less than your usual gimcrack hatchet jobs. Who's your source?"

"Don't play smart with me, Phillips; it's not your strong suit. I've had your number for years, I just never saw why it might interest my readership. Coda stories don't sell papers."

That made sense. Why pay for a depressing reminder of what's right outside your window?

"So, what changed? Slow news week?"

"Quite the opposite." He reached into his suit pocket, pulled out a piece of paper, and slammed it down on the desk. It was another copy of the newsletter the kids at the cafe had been waving around. "These were distributed—"

"I saw them." I stopped my wandering at a photo wall full of familiar faces. There was Derringer shaking hands with Demon Minister Baxter Thatch and Thurston Niles, and another of him drinking champagne with Mayor Piston at a sickeningly auspicious event. Even Simms was there, sporting a rare smile while standing with a Derringer on either side. This collection was the perfect supporting evidence for Whisper's story: every influential member of Sunder City rubbing shoulders and scratching backs. It was shameless. "So what's your issue with the newsletter? Don't like competition?"

"This isn't competition, it's propaganda." He ignored my incredulous snort. "This newsletter is not here to inform. Not even to entertain. It's made to unsettle. To provoke. Our readers trust us, and it's not good for the city when that trust is undermined."

"Your readers don't trust you; they just can't escape you. Your papers are piled in every corner store and tea shop in the city; even if they don't turn the front page, your headlines burrow in their brains for free."

"Catchy headlines are just good journalism."

"Come off it. You don't care about informing your readership any more than this Mister Whisper does. The *Star* stokes paranoia and prejudice, turning neighbors against each other for a few bucks a day. This is just about *Whisper* moving in on your turf."

He breathed faster, the hairs under his nose rising and falling like the hands of kids on a carnival ride.

"You don't like me, Mr Phillips."

"Ah, shit. You managed to pick that up? You media types really are perceptive."

"You don't like me, and yet you'll help me." I stopped wandering, put my hands in my pockets, and finally gave him my full attention. For a guy who could have got whatever he wanted by threatening to tear your ears off, I wondered why he'd hitched himself to the written word. Clearly he'd been successful at it, but maybe people are more willing to go along with your story if you can snap their bones like dry biscuits when they don't.

I had a lot of questions for the monkey-faced mogul, but I decided to go with the simplest one first.

"Why me?"

"Because you know the ones who are behind this. If I'm honest, I'm still not convinced that you aren't directly involved."

"I make cheap meals, not newsletters."

"Yes, but your little cafe is home to a specific kind of clientele." *Shit.* The kids. All my little revolutionary regulars.

"Come on, Derringer. That's . . ." Well, it was a fair assumption. The sentiments that Whisper put into print bore more than a passing similarity to the passionate rants that were shouted over bowls of fried potatoes every afternoon. And it's not like the kids wouldn't be up for it; handing out incendiary pamphlets was a step down from the rampant vandalism that typically filled their schedule.

So, he was right about one thing but very wrong about the other. I chuckled as I took a seat.

"Derringer, I wasn't going to work for you when I thought you just wanted my usual hired fool routine. But now you want me to rat on my customers? Hell, I've got more chance of sprouting snakes from my head and turning you to stone. How did that used to work, anyway? Did she always wear the glasses? Hell of a thing to marry a woman without ever making eye contact."

He pushed past my quips. The guy could push his way through a stampede without breaking stride.

"If you don't help me, I'll publish the story. All the gory details. The way you betrayed the Opus, how you led the army to the source of the sacred river, and how they doomed us all. Then, how you made your way to Sunder City in hopes of playing hero, but how all you've done in seven years is serve yourself. You're a traitor and a liar who talks a big game about being a man of the people but cuddles up to Thurston Niles when he thinks nobody's watching."

I couldn't see it under his furry facial hair, but it sounded like the old coot was smiling. Fine. Let him smile. His threats didn't matter if I knew for a fact that I'd never give him what he wanted.

"I'm not hiding who I am," I said, only half believing it myself. "I know what I did."

"But do your customers? What happens to your operation when everyone knows what you took from them?"

"I serve people coffee and burgers. If they don't want to come to my place any more, I'll be out of a gig, but I won't rat those kids out to save myself."

"Ahh. So, you *do* think they're responsible for the letter?"

He thought he'd tricked me. I wasn't sure he hadn't. Ophelia and her friends were likely suspects, but that was only because I hadn't considered any other options.

I grabbed the newsletter from the desk. It was the same as the one that Ophelia had pinned to my order board but with different imperfections in the print: small smudges and gaps in the letters where the plate didn't get enough ink.

"You're looking in the wrong place," I said. "The kids were all excited this morning, like this information came as a surprise."

"Not excited that they succeeded in spreading their nonsense?"

"I was busy in the kitchen, but I don't think so."

"Perhaps one – or a few – did it without telling the others."

"Maybe. Or maybe there are more than a handful of people who are sick of you and Niles and Piston treating the city like you own it. Whisper could be anyone."

A few printed newsletters dropped on a street corner. I could see why the kids were excited about it – the sentiments on the page so clearly aligned with their own – but why did Derringer care? Surely it wasn't the first time someone had accused him and his buddies of corruption.

"What's the big deal?" I asked. "This is a handful of flyers containing unsubstantiated accusations. I know you believe in the power of the written word, but this is a slingshot against your fortress full of soldiers and siege weapons. Why not just let Whisper talk? Unless . . ." It was my turn to be perceptive. "Unless there's some particular story that you're worried might get out." He said nothing, but that told me a whole lot. "Whisper hinted that this was just the beginning. What are you afraid he might say?"

There was a shiny wooden box on the corner of Derringer's desk. He opened it to reveal a bunch of thick, Boralo brand cigars. He prepared one for himself, and it was clear that I wouldn't be invited to join him.

"*You* are the man with something to hide, Mr Phillips. I'm just trying to keep this city stable. Do you have any idea what it would be like out there if the citizens stopped believing that they were in safe hands? If they realized how close they are to chaos? My paper frames the world in a way that they can comprehend. I let them choose to believe that someone is in control. Without the *Star*, how would anyone sleep at night?"

"That's a lovely story you tell yourself, Derringer. A finely edited tale to justify the lies." Finally, I saw a crack in his rock-hard demeanor, so I dug in my fingertips, hoping to prise up a piece of him like a loose floorboard. "When did you start taking orders from the men at the top?"

"I *am* the top."

"Oh, sure. But did your propaganda deal start with Piston? Or did you give Governor Lark the same thing? Favorable press for those in power, used to keep the common folk in line, right? Blame any issues on the latest wave of immigrants. Criticize any new ideas that threaten the status quo. It was always obvious but you kicked it up a few notches when Niles came to town. Did you just happen to fall head over heels in love with the new regime? Or does Thurston have something on you? I'm sure you like to tell yourself you hold all the cards, but Niles is the one who tells you what to play."

His fist hit the desk like it had been launched from a catapult.

"I was here a long time before Thurston Niles."

"I know. Must be a pain in the ass to have the new arrival calling the shots."

He curled his lip, snorting cigar smoke all over both of us.

"You mistake the order of things. I shaped this city into the jewel it is today. The way people see Sunder, the way they see themselves within it, that's all because of me." The floorboard was up and all manner of things were scurrying out: pride, anger and indignation. "I am the voice of Sunder City. I decide whose stories are told and whose are silenced. I have shouldered that responsibility from the moment I arrived here, and neither you nor Niles nor this ridiculous Mister Whisper understands what it takes. Find him, or your role in this city will be rewritten before your eyes."

"How the fuck do I do that? By searching for someone with an axe to grind against the *Sunder Star*? I could throw a rock down Main Street and hit a suspect on my first try."

"Then get throwing, Mr Phillips. If you don't unmask Whisper, you'll be front-page weekend news. But find out which one of your itty-bitty insurgents is responsible, or uncover an alternative culprit, and I promise you, your article will go back in the vault."

"I told you, I'm not gonna do it."

"And I told you, you will. I'm hard-working, ruthless, cunning and surprisingly charming when I want to be, but do you know what makes me such a good rag man, Mr Phillips?"

"You're so inconspicuous?"

He smiled wide. Between his whiskers, I saw a row of yellow teeth, each the size of a postage stamp.

"I'm an impeccable judge of character. You want to tell me to go fuck myself. You want to believe that you will act on principle, that you have such humble ambitions that you would leave your life at any moment, without worry, but you are lying to yourself as you are trying to lie to me. Like everyone else out there, you don't want to lose the life you've got. You know as well as I do that if this city casts you out, there will be nowhere else in this world where you can go."

The house was quiet. The plot of land was so big, so removed from the rest of the city, that I couldn't hear the sound of the streets. What an empty, awful fucking place. How could you write about Sunder from up here? How could you know anything at all about what made it move, made it sing, made it bleed? He was right. This was my city, and there was no way in hell I was going to let him and his sad excuse for a newspaper drive me out of it.

"I'll find Whisper," I said.

"I know you will."

He was already seeing the story in his head. Prepping the headlines and the captions, believing that this would all play out according to his plan. But *my* stories never went smoothly, and I wasn't about to start playing by his book.

"Just remember," he said, as I got to my feet, "plenty of things might happen in this town, but only what I print becomes the truth."

You gotta hand it to the guy, he knows how to get his way. Despite my initial reservations, I walked out of that office, firmly set on solving the case. Because if Whisper's newsletter was a knife in Derringer's side, then like all good stories, someone needed to give it a twist.

5

Refusing to be driven home in that man-cave on wheels, I wandered out the front gates to find myself in an unfamiliar part of the city. That didn't matter. It only took a few days in Sunder to realize that if you wanted to walk from a well-maintained estate to a drafty room on the wrong end of town, your journey would be from north to south. I faced the rising sun, turned right, and enjoyed the feeling of heat on my cheek and the Derringers at my back.

He'd been exactly the kind of hack I'd always expected to be behind the *Star*: so confident in his own intuition he'd hold up two convenient facts and fill the space between with his own imagination. Sure, I didn't want to leave this city, but not because I was worried I wouldn't have anywhere else to go. I had customers who relied on me. If I left, it would put an end to Richie's deliveries to the retirement home, and the under-the-counter contraband that people had come to count on. Georgio's cafe would close – or worse, be taken over by someone who didn't understand it. Who kicked people out if they didn't buy anything or told everyone to keep their voice down, not realizing that food and drink was only half of what the place offered.

If that story went to print, it was all over. A handful of people knew about my past but each of them relied on the fact that they were one of the few. Once everyone knew, even Sunder's more inscrutable citizens wouldn't be seen around me. Simms would keep her distance, the kids would clear out, and the customers who'd developed a taste for Georgio's style of coffee would have to make do with the muddy brew they boiled at the teahouse across the road.

I wasn't leaving, but there was no way I was ratting out those kids. If one of them was Whisper, I'd find a way to cover it up. If it wasn't them, and I didn't set the record straight, then we'd all lose. Derringer would drag those kids through the mud and trash my name along with anyone else who used my place as a hangout. He was right about one thing: these days, whatever the papers said was taken as the truth. The cops and the courts were all in cahoots, upholding the same bullshit stories and spreading them as far as they would stretch. As soon as Derringer named one of those kids, then Simms and her sergeants would come knocking. They'd dig up every bit of hooliganism the kids had ever committed (and plenty they hadn't) and use them as another example of what happened when you didn't dance to the city's new beat.

First, I needed to find out the truth. Then I could work out what to do with it.

I didn't like the idea of following Derringer's orders, but if I could keep Ophelia and her friends out of the papers, then this was a mystery worth mulling over for a couple of days. No point letting the *Star* ruin the last shreds of my reputation if Whisper turned out to be just another rich weirdo with plans for a rival paper, or some would-be-mayor trying to score political points. The kids at the cafe might be petty criminals with an acute lack of consideration, but they still had plenty of time to grow up and put that energy to good use. The last thing I wanted to do was step aside and let Derringer steal their futures just so he could continue to reign over his kingdom of misinformation. Niles, Piston and Derringer were already doing their best to dim the horizons of the next generation, funneling everyone into factories or turning them into foot-soldiers. Writing all our stories for us. Telling us what we were. What we wanted.

Fuck them. I know this city deeper than they ever will. I know its gutters and its back doors and the smell you only recognize if you've spent a night face down on the cobbles. You can't understand this city if you're so big and rich that people pin smiles to their faces whenever they see you. You need to know what it looks like naked and bleeding. You've gotta pick a fight with a park bench. Flirt with a lamppost. Run away with a drainpipe and buy the street signs a beer. This is my goddamn city, not theirs, and if anyone's gonna finally get me thrown out of it for good, it's sure as hell gonna be me.

I cut through an alley from Tenth Street to Meryl Ave and saw a gathering a few doors down: police tape, cop cars, reporters and rubberneckers. An apartment block had been closed off and there was enough excitement to suggest it was something out of the ordinary. Most crimes were lucky to be given the attention of a lone constable with a notepad and nightstick, but two types of incidents would push the cops into real action: if it looked like magic might be involved, or someone had attacked one of their own. When Detective Simms stepped out into the sun, I realized it might be both.

"Detective," called a reporter, "any statement for concerned Sunder citizens?" She was a lady Satyr in a loose-fitting linen suit. The fact that she was on my side of the tape meant that she wasn't with the *Star*. They wouldn't need to ask for statements or access, but would already be stomping over the crime scene and rewriting history to suit the week's agenda. Simms took a step towards the reporter but a Niles Company goon in a charcoal suit called out to her from a nearby convertible.

"Over here, Detective! I need to run a few things by you."

Simms gave the reporter an apologetic shrug and did as she was told. What a joke. Even Sunder's toughest cop had given up trying to fight back. The reporter shook her head – annoyed but unsurprised – but kept waiting in the vain hope that a more accommodating public servant would come down the stairs. Instead, she got me.

"Who you with?" I asked.

She spun on her hooves and extended her hand, clearly anticipating someone who might warrant a dose of professional politeness.

It only took a few seconds for her well-trained eyes to take in the state of my clothes, my stained fingers, my unshaven face and unbrushed hair, and realize that I would more likely be a local vagrant than a good lead.

"Tabatha Ratchet, Lamplighter Radio." Her eyes flicked back to the apartment block, not wanting to let a loiterer like me distract her from an opportunity.

"Nice to meet you, Ms Ratchet. I'm Fetch Phillips. Could I ask you a quick question?"

"You've got this all mixed about, Mr Phillips. Asking questions is *my* business, and I happen to be in the middle of that business right now. Excuse me." Two more cops came down the stairs, "Hello, officers! Up for a short report? Spare a highlight for the Lamplight?" But they were both uniformed constables and knew to leave the big responsibilities like talking and thinking to their superiors. When nothing else happened, Ms Tabatha Ratchet waited to see if I'd do her the favor of disappearing from her life, before sighing and turning to face me.

"You had a question?"

"You see the newsletter that dropped last night?"

"The early-morning warning of big news to come? Yeah, I saw it, but my mouth doesn't water until I know a meal's coming."

"Have you heard of this Mister Whisper before?"

"Course not. It's clearly some kind of alias."

"Yes, but could it be some existing journalist taking on a new name?"

"Just as getting hammered don't turn you into a nail, putting ink on paper don't make you a reporter."

"Sure, but the letters, the . . . I don't know what you call it. The . . ."

"The typeface."

"It was professionally printed, right?"

"Better than handwriting if you're hoping to keep anonymous, and the only sane choice if you want to mass produce, but no legitimate media outlet would launch their new product with a scrappy single-sheet print like that. It's a stunt. Or a warning. Probably political, but there's no way it's the work of a journalist with experience."

"So where would you start looking, if you wanted to track them down?"

"It seems to me you're searching for some kind of radical. Someone young, perhaps. I hear there's a cafe on Main Street that's become a hangout for those types of kids. I forget the address but—"

"That's fine. I know the place."

I was about to release her from my company when I looked up and made accidental eye contact with Detective Simms. Her expression chilled my blood. Not because she seemed angry – the usual boiling rage wouldn't have bothered me – but because her face softened, and I realized with horror that she was happy to see me.

Oh, no. She thinks I've had a change of heart.

"Detective," said Ms Ratchet, seeing that I'd captured Simms's attention, "there are rumors that this was some kind of execution. Can you confirm if—"

"Sorry, Ms Ratchet. Not now." Simms cocked her head to direct me down the line. I followed, leaving Tabatha to wonder how the clueless tramp had managed to cut in front of her. "Fetch, you're too late, the apartment is full of photographers and they're just about to move the body."

"Oh, right. Damn."

"You should have come when I came to collect you."

"Yeah. Sorry, Simms. I just couldn't step away."

I don't know what did it – my lackluster acting or her finely tuned intuition – but the penny finally dropped. She rolled her bottom lip into her mouth and bit down on it with her blunted fangs.

"You didn't come to help me."

"I . . . I was just passing by."

She took off her hat and crushed the brim in her fists. "They killed him, Fetch. Shot him eight times in his own home. Just because he wanted to protect people."

Sunder cops had always walked a dubious line between being punishers and protectors. The laws had been loose enough to allow each officer to define the role for themselves. When I'd first arrived, the culture was already toxic, but people now spoke of that era as a golden age for the Sunder PD because they'd at least kept up the illusion of honor. The bar had been low because we didn't dare imagine a world where corruption wasn't rife and the local sergeants didn't throw their weight around for personal gain. You took the beatings when they came and counted any lost coins as part of the city tax. But there were bright spots. Richie had been one. Simms had done her best. Bath, from what I saw, was just another constable who went wherever he was pointed, and that was the problem. Ever since Niles had moved in – bolstering the police presence with his own charcoal-suited goons – even the most conscientious cops couldn't balance out a broken force. The police were right there at Niles's side as he forced his future on Sunder's citizens, squashing any attempt to search for a lingering spark of magic. Thurston Niles and Mayor Piston had decided that Sunder was better without hope, and they'd etched that message into the boot-heels of every cop so they could stomp it into our thick skulls. That's why Richie quit. That's why I didn't want to help Simms. And that's why – while I don't believe that Bath got what he deserved – I had no interest in tracking down anyone who had the balls to fight back.

But Bath had been working under Simms, so she felt responsible, and I wasn't such a heartless prick that I couldn't understand that.

"It's a dangerous time," I said. "I'm sorry this happened to him. It isn't fair."

Simms breathed hard through the thin slits of her nostrils.

"No," she said. "It's not."

The door to the apartment block was kicked open by a Cyclops constable. He was carrying the front end of a stretcher while an orange-bearded Dwarf took up the rear. There was a body on top of it, wrapped in waterproofed cloth, and the sight of it sent nearby photographers into a frenzy.

"Have some fucking respect," snarled Simms, and left without a goodbye, walking beside the body to prevent the shutterbugs from getting a clean shot. A middle-aged Werewolf with patchy fur ran over to the door to check it for damage – clearly the landlord, already perturbed about losing a tenant without notice – and bumped into my old pal Portemus – the Necromancer mortician – who came out next, his eyes following the corpse like it was a precious artefact.

I slipped away while I could. I already had one unwanted case on my hands, and I had no interest in picking up another. I'd find Whisper, do my best to clear the kids from the suspect list, and get back to doing the one job I was good at.

What's a dead cop to a city that's already fighting for its life? Constable Bath had strapped a weapon to his side and marched out to do the bidding of terrible men. What's the right way to deal with a weak-willed boy like Bath whose dumb mistakes can do so much damage? Once you make the choice to follow through on a command, it becomes your decision, and you have no right to complain about the consequences.

I'd finally learned that lesson. So had Bath. Poor kid. Whatever his crimes were, they surely paled in comparison to mine, but I'd been allowed to grow up with my regrets and have a chance to amend them. He got eight bullets in his body and a swift trip into oblivion.

It wasn't fair. But nothing is. So, we say goodbye and move on.

I tried to do that. Might have succeeded.

If only the corpse of Corporal Bath hadn't been carrying so many secrets.

6

My impromptu trip to the Derringer house had cut short the breakfast rush, fucking up just about everything in my carefully curated life: less money in the register, unsold buttered rolls that wouldn't keep, and a curdled, crusted mess on the fryer that would need to be cleaned up before lunch. This kind of mess was exactly why I'd given myself a rule against leaving the cafe straight after service. The remaining bacon was trapped on the hotplate in a layer of congealed fat like ducks stuck in a frozen lake, and the filthy dishes left on tables welcomed flies like they had a reservation. I added heat to the hotplates to loosen everything up, grabbed my steel wool and spatula, and went on the attack. My first job in Sunder had been cleaning, and maybe it was the one I did best.

I usually worked in silence, appreciating the way that – after so many years juggling guilt, doubt and second-guesses – the simple work washed my mind into a comforting silence. But as I stacked the spices on the shelf, I noticed Georgio's radio for the first time.

I hadn't owned one since I was back in Weatherly. The magic-powered transmitters that were available in Sunder when I'd arrived were too expensive, and after the Coda I'd refused to purchase any Human-made appliances that weren't essential.

It had sat dormant so long that I was surprised how quickly it burst to life, and Elven horn music filled the cafe. I managed to turn down the volume and scan the channels. It was easy to cross the unwanted stations off the list; city-sanctioned propaganda all has a similar ring to it. There were countless voices singing the praises of the Mayor or warning listeners about breaking rules. I waited for songs to end, before smooth voices told me that I'd tuned into the Brisak Network or Hallow Air, until a pre-recorded jingle announced that I'd finally found the correct frequency.

"You're tuned to Lamplighter Radio. Yesterday's tunes. Tomorrow's news."

Tabatha would still be at the crime scene, so I had to make do with a couple of elderly Wizards droning on about budget cuts to the retirement village while I mopped the floor.

My mind kept drifting to the potential fallout which could follow Derringer publishing his story. Where would I go? For all its problems, Sunder protected me. A lone Human – especially one marked the way I was – would have a hard time being welcomed anywhere else. I'd have to go back to hiding my tattoos. Maybe change my name. Again. Could I bare another Human-run city like Braid or Mira? By the sound of it, the Mortales Corporation had an even tighter grip on those places than Niles did here. Maybe I could jump the walls of Weatherly and go back to my old life in a land where sheltered Humans pretended that the other species didn't exist. No Elves, no Wizards, no Dragons. Just us. I could return to my post as a city guard, protecting the inhabitants from non-existent enemies. Spend the rest of my days soldiering on in a sweet little bubble where nobody knew any better.

How long could I stand it? Fifteen minutes, maybe?

No. I needed to talk to the kids, see if they really were behind the newsletter, and protect my greasy little corner of the world.

Once the hotplates had been downgraded from unhygienic to merely mildly revolting, I turned my attention to the neglected dishes. When I spun the faucet, nothing happened, so I turned on the others. All that came out were a few weak drops. *Shit.* I followed the pipe under the sink, along the wall, checking for leaks and tapping for blockages, but everything seemed dry and clear.

Ding.

The door swung open, and a couple of unfamiliar voices entered the dining room. I looked at the clock on the wall to confirm that, yes, someone had ignored the sign and arrived before reopening.

"We're closed," I called out. "Come back in fifteen minutes."

The two men entered anyway. They were wearing matching uniforms: burgundy steel-capped boots, charcoal trousers, white T-shirts under black suspenders and three-quarter-length burgundy jackets made of a thin, glistening material with bronze buttons. Their jackets sat open to reveal polished pistols in low-slung leather holsters. The decision to wear their weapons so ostentatiously was surely supposed to be some kind of threat, but to me, it just made them look easy for someone to snatch.

They were Human – probably a little younger than I was – and they stood on the other side of the service window with their hands in their pockets, smiling and staring like I was an exhibit in a zoo.

The shorter one chewed gum with an open mouth. I turned the radio down and heard him say to his friend, "Told you it was him."

A cold breeze went through my body. The mallet on the counter was used for turning tough meat into mince patties, but it would do an equally good job of turning cocky smiles into bloody puddles. I grabbed the handle, held it out of sight, and pretended that I hadn't heard what he'd said.

"Hey, fellas, lunch doesn't start for another hour."

Their smiles only got wider. The friend of the gum-smacker stepped forward. He had a physique that would make a marble statue feel soft, and I was worried I might chip my mallet on the sharp edge of his jawline.

"Captain Fetch," he said, breaking into a grin that matched his companion's. "It's us!"

Captain? The only time I was ever called that was . . . Oh, hell no.

They were soldiers from the Human Army. We'd spent a year together clearing Wyverns and Griffins from towns down south, back when those creatures had enough magic in their bones to put up a fight against Human farmers. We'd also fought a wayward Wizard and a couple of other creatures who'd wandered too close to Human dwellings, before we were ordered up the mountain to fight the battle that ended the world.

It was no wonder I hadn't recognized them. They were just kids back then. Hell, so was I.

"Goddamn," I said, trying to sound pleasantly surprised. "Private Reeves," the taller, "and Gumption," the gum-smacker. Gumption's real name was Gunter or something, but he'd been bestowed with one of those nicknames that eradicated his previous title from existence.

They broke out laughing – tickled that I'd remembered them – so I dropped the mallet under the bench and came out of the kitchen to shake their hands. I couldn't remember if Reeves had always been this tall or if he'd kept growing while I hadn't.

"What the hell brings you two to Sunder?"

"We just signed up as firefighters," said Reeves, pulling open the lapels of his jacket to show off his shiny new attire. "Saw the recruitment ad back in New Lanfield and hopped a ride on the next truck out. Good salary, cheap rent, sweet get-up and a six-shooter; what's not to love?"

I looked them up and down, not bothering to hide my confusion. The shine on the jacket must be due to some heat-proof coating, but it wasn't the sort of outfit I'd want to wear if I spent my days running into burning buildings.

"I thought Sunder firefighters were volunteers."

"New initiative." Gumption looked proud at being able to sound out the four-syllable-word. "Mayor is committed to keeping y'all safe."

The Mayor? With that kind of funding, and the shine on those new firearms, I was pretty sure the initiative had started somewhere else.

"So, what? You supposed to shoot the fires to death?"

Reeves laughed and pulled up a stool, leaning his elbows on the counter. "Well, apparently there's all kinds of sabotage happening in this place. Pipes being burst and engines being messed with."

Gumption found his own stool and sat just the same way, following Reeves's lead just as he'd done all those years ago.

"We're here for the fires," said the sidekick, "but also for the people starting them. Can't forge a new future if people are fucking with the means of production, now can we? Only takes a few bad apples to spoil the broth."

Sabotage? Surely Ophelia and her friends hadn't taken their experiments in civil disobedience far enough to inspire a new Niles-funded taskforce.

"I just can't believe it." Reeves was still staring at me, smiling wider than ever. "One of the locals was giving us the lay of the land, telling us the best places to drink and where to meet girls, and they said that the best coffee in town comes from a grimy little cafe on Main Street manned by an old gumshoe named Fetch, and I turned to Gummy and said 'surely not' and he said 'sure-lee NOT'! So as soon as we'd dropped our bags and got into our new uniforms, we came down here, and look at what we find: Captain Fetch himself, cleaning his kitchen and making goddamn coffee! I know you're not officially open yet, Captain, but could we trouble you for a couple of cups? They really are the talk of the town."

"Well, I'd love to help you," I said, warming to their jovial mood, "but the water stopped running for some reason."

"Oh, everything south of Seventh is dry until noon," said Reeves. "They need to adjust the pipes to send water out to the new developments. Didn't you read it in the paper?"

"Must've missed it," I said, filling the pots from the bottles of drinking water that went out on the tables. "But it better come back on soon or I'll miss the lunch rush."

"Of course! Can't have the poor citizens of Sunder City going hungry, now can we?"

His tone was warm and celebratory, with that edge of playful, shit-stirring attitude that grows in any group of men who are supposed to fight on the same side but feel compelled to maintain an internal hierarchy.

"So that's where you two have been since I last saw you? New Lanfield?"

"Pretty much," said Gumption, daring to break tradition by speaking first.

"Wasn't worth exploring for a while there," added Reeves. "Everything outside the Human cities was gray and cold and . . . just sad, you know? But then we heard that Sunder got the fires back, and that Niles was sprucing the place up, so we thought it might be time to hit the road again. And boy, was it worth it. This is something else."

He might have been talking about the city, but he was staring at me as if I was the greatest wonder of all. I supposed it made sense. During these young men's formative years, I was in a position of power. I knew too well the whiplash of seeing an old mentor after many years. The people I'd worked for and served under – Amari, Hendricks, Tackman, Taryn, Graham – retained a mystical place in my memories: larger-than-life figures that – even after I witnessed their fallibility, mistakes and flaws – I had trouble removing from the pedestals I'd built beneath them. It was no wonder these kids were spun out to see the guy they'd taken orders from in their youth scrubbing away at old saucepans. Maybe it was a good thing. Maybe it would have helped me if I'd gained a better perspective on my heroes before I'd watched them fall.

I poured three coffees and set them out on the counter. My former subordinates each took a sip, then Reeves slapped his leg and hollered in glee.

"Well, holy shit! They weren't lying! That's the best cup of joe I've had in any city on the continent. Of course, nothing compares to a fireside pot at sunrise on a dusty trail, but everything tastes better on the road, now don't it? Hey, Captain, you remember that wild goat you cooked up one time?"

"Oh, damn that was good," agreed Gumption.

"*So* damn good that I can't resist ordering goat every time I see it on the menu. But it's never come close to tasting the way it did when we'd been out on the land for weeks on end, dreaming of a home-cooked meal."

I topped up the cups and upturned the pots to let them drain and cool, talking as I worked.

"Those were some wild times. Sorry to say I'm fresh out of goat, but I'll keep an eye out next time I'm down the markets."

That got them laughing.

"I'd appreciate that, Captain. See if you can't recapture the magic."

"I gotta say," mumbled Gumption in his brew, "this firefighter deal seems pretty cushy, but nothing compares to serving under Captain Fetch."

They laughed again, but this time it was more of a snicker. Something between themselves.

I wiped my hands on a dishcloth, confused that it wasn't coming clean, until I remembered that the stain on my fingers wasn't grease from the stove but ink from Derringer's press. Unable to shift it, I looked up, hoping to get in on the joke.

"What do you mean?"

Reeves's wide-as-a-horizon grin was going nowhere.

"Oh, c'mon, Captain. You know."

Gumption snickered again, and his smile had a nasty edge to it. I finally remembered how much that little prick had rubbed me the wrong way. Son of a minister or something. Liked to shoot beasts in their hindquarters and watch them struggle.

"*What* do I know?"

Reeves sipped his coffee, looking at me over the rim. Gumption snickered again.

"It was all a ruse, man. A joke. On you." Sip. Snicker, snicker. "General Taryn got a bunch of us together and told us we had an unusual mission. Serve under some Opus traitor and make him feel special. Remind him that all of us Humans should be on the same side. Fill him full of 'yes, sirs' and 'oorahs' until he thought he was one of us. Then, when we'd got him all buttered up and feeling self-important," snicker, snicker, "we'd let our superiors – our *real* superiors – know that it was time to finish the job."

"It was easy as hell," chuckled Gumption. "But man, it got tedious. A whole year hunting Gryphons and Wyverns on home ground. Damn embarrassing, really."

Reeves turned to him, remembering something.

"But remember that day some old coot of a Wizard went crazy and tried to fight us?"

"Oh yeah! I guess that one day was pretty hairy."

"After six months of *acting* like soldiers we'd almost forgotten how to fight!"

"Lucky for us, that mad bastard damn near blew his own dick off doing too many spells." When they'd had their fill of laughter, they looked back to me.

"Surely you worked it out," said Reeves, in a tone that could have been mistaken for sympathetic. "After everything went down. After you told them where to go, and we did what we did. Wasn't it obvious?"

It was. I had known it. I knew it the moment I gave up the information I'd learned from Hendricks and told the Human Army where they could find the source of magic. I'd known I'd been used, sure. I'd worked out – too late – that General Taryn had been milking me for information from the moment I'd been recruited. Didn't take a genius to put that together. But had I thought they were all in on it? The other soldiers? Other captains? My own squad? No. Even after it had all played out and the ash had fallen on this emaciated world of my own making, I hadn't gone back and re-examined that time in detail. Hadn't wanted to. Had known not to think too deeply in case I stumbled on the truth.

But now I knew. Now *they* knew I knew. I wanted to reach for a Clayfield but – with their eyes still fixed on me – any movement seemed like an admission. If I didn't answer, I would pretty much prove them right. But what answer could I give? Tell them I didn't know? That I'm as naïve now as I was back then? Or validate their story by agreeing to its truth?

There was no good answer, which was why I'd never been so relieved to hear the phone ring.

Their laughter followed me as I came out of the kitchen and lifted the receiver on the phone beside the till.

"Hello?"

Simms hissed down the line.

"Fetch. I just got down to Backlash and I think you should check something out."

"What the hell is Backlash?"

"The prison, Fetch. South of the river. Hell, you really have checked out."

I realized it must be the big construction site which had been dumping mud in the south river for the last year, but somehow its new moniker had escaped me.

"I told you, Simms, I can't help you with this case."

"This had nothing to do with Bath. The night patrol picked up a kid for thieving and it sounds like he knows you. Just come down here and see if you can help him out, otherwise I don't like where this is going."

I was reluctant to leave the cafe again, but any excuse to get my old war buddies out of here was welcome.

"All right. I'm on my way." I hung up. "Sorry, fellas. Duty calls."

Reeves finished his coffee and stood up straight.

"Don't let us stand in your way, Captain."

"Yeah," added his shadow. "Your skills must be in high demand."

I kept my hand on the phone, holding back the urge to drive it into the chump's crooked mouth.

Luckily Reeves stepped between us.

"Great to see you, Fetch. Really. What a treat."

"Yup," said Gumption. "A bona fide blast from the past."

They strode out, Gumption still snickering, and I slammed back the rest of my coffee.

What the fuck did they know? Little shits. Good luck trying

to embarrass a man who's been sleeping with his shame every night for seven years. Try to knock me off my high horse? Fat chance. I live under its hooves, taking kicks to the face for fun. I know I'm a fool, and I'm not trying to pretend I'm anything else. I make the coffee, you pay your couple of bucks and—

Oh, fuck. The bastards didn't even pay.

Now *that* made me angry. You don't drink Georgio's coffee and forget to pay. I stewed about that until I got all the way down to the far side of the river, where I found plenty of other things to be furious about.

7

"Would you believe that this is my doing?"

Simms met me by the riverside, just outside the open portcullis of Backlash's gates. The building was an expanse of black concrete and steel with only the tiniest, letterbox-slot windows to break up the high, flat, razor-wire-topped walls.

"Not intentionally," she added. "Last year, it was my idea to turn that old grain silo into that short-lived jailhouse we called the Gullet. We needed somewhere to throw unruly elements like Rick Tippity while they awaited trial. After Deamar destroyed that building, all we had left was the jail. Which is fine for the short term but it breeds trouble. Too close to the center of town, and you can only keep someone in there for a day or two before it causes problems. But this . . . well, come inside."

Two cops stood to attention at the entrance, with two more just inside. They were all heavily armed, projecting an aura of readiness like athletes at the starting line waiting for a signal. Only this time, they'd be the ones firing the pistols.

A wall of Mortales-made payphones stood as the last bastion of the real world – the connection between freedom and incarceration – before we entered the first dark hallway that led to many more dark hallways, all dripping with foreboding. Iron-barred doors looked in on tiny rooms not much bigger than the single beds and latrines they contained. The slit windows were spread out and useless, so clear tubes of pit-fueled firelight ran along the low roof, roiling and red, creating wavering shadows that danced at our feet.

So quiet. So many cramped rooms waiting to be filled. We passed a dozen empty cells before Simms stopped us outside a room that contained what might have been Backlash's only occupant.

"You seen him before?"

The young man was dressed as unseasonably as Simms – thick material covering his whole body – but in a style that was rarely seen in the city: a light brown, long-sleeved tunic covered by a forest-green poncho, worn sandals and a single glove made from heavy leather. The clothes were filthy and moth-bitten, and his long red hair tangled over his face.

His ungloved hand clutched nervously at the opposite sleeve. What was he? Elven? His pupils were pinpricks despite the darkness, and his ears were pointed to the sky. But his skin was still tight, unlike full-blooded Elves whose once-eternal skin lost its elasticity after the Coda. He looked like he'd been living rough for some time, and he gave me only a cursory glance before returning his gaze to the floor.

"I don't recognize him," I said. "Should I?"

Simms moved us out of earshot.

"He got picked up for stealing food from stalls at the Mess. I don't think he's been in the city long. Not enough street-smarts to stay out of trouble. He wouldn't give us an address or any other details, but when we pressed him for a contact, all he said was a man with four rings painted on his right arm."

"Well, I don't think he means me."

"You sure about that? Maybe word has got around that if you're on your last legs, the soft-hearted brute with the tattoos at Georgio's cafe might throw you a bone." I scrunched up my face. Why does hearing what other people think about you always make you feel like you have sand in your teeth? "When you set something in motion, Fetch, you don't always have a say in what it turns into." She put a hand on the concrete wall, perhaps weighing up the cost of her own actions, and what had been done off their back.

"What's with the get-up?" I asked.

"You've never encountered the Sect of Frondescence?" I shook my head. "They're Druids who reside in the Togul, restoring the woods after the great fires."

The Togul was the old Fae home, burned down in the Fifth War. I'd been there once before, accompanying Hendricks and Amari to a ceremonial dinner to pay our respects to that historic tragedy. I met a lot of Fae that night, but as all Faeries went extinct with the Coda, this kid certainly wasn't one of them.

"I visited there, briefly," I said. "But I don't remember any Druids."

"So no reason one of them would come looking for you?"

"Not that I can think of."

"Well, why don't you see if the kid can shed some light? He's barely said a word to the rest of us."

I wandered back down to the stranger's cell and stood there, waiting to see if a latent spark of familiarity would fire up, but got nothing. He only made eye contact in fleeting glances, probably thinking I was here to accuse him of more crimes or to administer his punishment.

"I'm Fetch Phillips."

He didn't respond immediately. When he did, it was just a sheepish, "Okay."

"Where you from?" He shrugged. "What's your name?"

"Inero."

"All right, Inero. What do you need?" He shrugged again. "You need a place to stay?"

He locked eyes then. Tried to read my intention.

"Why?"

"Why what?"

"Why would you help me?"

I reached out and grabbed hold of one of the bars. The light in the place was low, but he could now see the tattoos on my arm. Four rings, marking each time I'd been dumb enough to sign up to somebody else's way of doing things: the Weatherly Guards, the Opus Shepherds, the Human Army, and Sheertop Prison (that one I didn't have a say in).

Inero's eyes went wide.

"You're *him*."

Shit. Maybe I *had* garnered some kind of reputation on Sunder streets. I'd have to watch myself. I was barely making ends meet without being known as some good Samaritan who takes in strays. Still, this place was as sad as an undressed salad, so I wasn't about to leave the kid behind.

"Oh, right," I remarked, ever the bad actor. "Sorry, Simms. This is my second cousin, Onero."

"Inero," corrected my new ward.

"Yes, Inero. I was supposed to pick him up from the carriage station last night. My mistake. Any bail I need to pay for?"

Simms's scarf shifted, which I assumed was on account of a smile.

"I'll take care of it."

"Thanks, Lena. Now come on, Inero. Better get back to the cafe and call your mother. She'll be worried sick."

I accepted Simms's offer of a lift back to the cafe, sliding into the back seat with the boy.

"So, where did you hear about me?" I asked. The kid shrugged, eyes darting at Simms. "You don't have to worry about her. She's the one who wanted me to get you out. Did you hear it from some other kids on the street?" He nodded. Real chatterbox, this one.

"Where are you from?" asked Simms, putting on her kindest tone, which was still akin to a knife being sharpened.

"Woods," he replied.

"Ah," said Simms, as if there had been anything of interest in the kid's response. I remembered my adopted mother complaining of my single-word answers as a teenager and never understood her frustration until now.

"So, you're a Druid?" I asked.

"What?"

"A Druid. Your clothes."

He looked down, as if he hadn't even realized he was wearing anything.

"Oh. They're not mine."

And that was that. We made a couple more failed attempts at banter until the young man's conversation skills rubbed off on us and we rode the rest of the way in silence. Simms – as Sunder's most law-abiding serpent – wasn't the fastest driver, but I was happy to avoid another long walk in the heat. Until we approached the cafe and I saw Ashton and Ophelia sitting on the curb outside.

They glared at the police-issue sedan as it approached, and glared harder when they saw me step out of it. Simms pulled away, leaving Inero and I to face the ire of the idealistic teenagers.

"Told you he was a stooge," said Ashton to Ophelia. I was already behind on the lunchtime prep and couldn't be bothered explaining, but Ophelia jumped into my path.

"Fetch, what's going on? First that detective comes to you like you're her partner, then someone from the *Star* personally picks you up, now you're getting lifts in cop cars? Are you up to something?"

"What do you mean, up to something?"

"The gang are getting nervous. They're starting to think you're just like the rest of them. Maybe worse. That you're keeping tabs on us so that you can dob us in to Niles or the police or whoever else you're friends with."

"You really think I'd do that?" I was meant to say it flat and direct – play it off like it was a ridiculous accusation that didn't bother me – but even I could hear the hurt in my voice. Ophelia clearly could too, because she came at me with those wide and compassionate eyes.

"No," she said. "Of course not. But you're sure as hell sending some weird signals. And if I can't convince the others that you're not a rat, they're going to find somewhere else to hang."

That made me laugh.

"You mean I won't have a cafe full of poor teenagers who take up all my seats and barely buy a bowl of fries between them? What ever shall I do?"

I stepped around her, but Ashton's irritating voice made me stop.

"See. He's a fucking snitch."

I punched the window of the cafe so hard I was surprised I didn't break it. Didn't mean to. Wasn't quite sure where the anger came from, to be honest. Just too many people keeping me from my kitchen? Or was it the fact that he was putting a finger on the problem that I still didn't know how to solve? Rather than be embarrassed by my outburst, I took advantage of the fact that I'd put Ashton on the back foot.

"All right, you two. Here's the deal. Derringer, the editor of the *Star*, thinks you're responsible for that newsletter you were passing around this morning. Is he right?"

Ophelia was aghast.

"You *are* spying for them!"

"They *asked* me to spy on you. I told them to jump."

"Then why do you care?" demanded Ashton, getting to his feet.

"Because I'm trying to run a business here, and I need to know what trouble you're bringing in. So come on. Was it you?"

After mulling it over, Ophelia appeared flattered at the accusation.

"You know, we thought about doing something like that, but it would take a lot of coordination and we're not really there yet. I can't get everyone facing the same direction on anything more than a bit of random vandalism. I suppose one of us could have gone out on their own and done something like this, but I can't imagine who."

"Nah, we'd know about it," said Ashton. "The crew can't tag a park bench without bragging." Then he caught himself, frowned at me again. "But see! You're fucking grilling us for Derringer!"

"I'm not! But if I don't find a way to turn their attention elsewhere, then some other investigator will be down here to finish what I never started. Either that, or they decide to pin this on you anyway."

"Fine with me," shrugged Ophelia. "I don't mind the publicity."

"It could be a lot more than your picture in the paper. Whisper's newsletter was accusing the *Star*, the Mayor and Niles of corruption."

Ashton laughed.

"Yeah, what a scoop. Barely worth the ink."

"You know that all Mayor Piston cares about is perception. Look at how he's been treating harmless folk who try to whip up a bit of old magic in their spare time. He makes an example of them whether they're dangerous or not. If he decides he wants to make an example of you and your friends, then you could have the whole city coming down on your head for something you didn't do. I don't want that."

They mulled that over. Ophelia reluctantly nodded.

"Yeah, I guess. I mean, we've still got a lot of fun stuff on our to-do list, so if we're gonna get pinched, it should be for something proper rambunctious, not a boring bit of writing that's not even ours."

"Exactly."

It was a relief to be back on the same side. I'd argued with too many people that day already.

"But . . ." She squished up her face, struggling with the conundrum. "Does that mean you're going to help them catch the real Whisper? I don't like that."

"Me either. Maybe there's a way to do both: get Derringer looking away from you lot without helping him for real."

"How?"

"I was a Man for Hire, remember? I have a whole career of professional ineptitude to draw from. I can feed Derringer so many wrong turns and red herrings he won't know which way is up. That might give us enough time to see what Whisper does next. Perhaps anonymity isn't his long game."

Ashton mulled it over, still wary that I might be trying to bamboozle him.

"Yeah, maybe." Then his eyes moved to the redheaded young

man in the moth-bitten sweater. He'd kept his distance during the conversation so Ashton hadn't noticed him until now. "Who's this?"

"Oh, yeah. This is Inero. He's new in town . . . I think. I don't really know. But maybe you could—"

Ophelia interrupted.

"Uh, Fetch."

"I know you're busy but I need to get the kitchen fired up and—"

"No, Fetch, LOOK!"

She pointed down at my feet. The ground was wet.

"What the hell?"

There was a small river flowing out from under the cafe door. I fumbled for the keys, opened it up, and let loose a filthy wave of water.

The taps were back on. Of course. For once, city maintenance had kept to schedule.

I ran inside and turned off the faucets, but there wasn't an inch of the cafe that wasn't already flooded.

Fuck. Me.

I closed my eyes and stood there, hoping that somehow, when I opened them, this would all be undone. Instead, the only thing that changed was that my socks were soaked through.

"Fetch?"

Richie was at the door, pointing ever-so-helpfully at the indoor swimming pool that had appeared in the dining room. Ashton, Ophelia and Inero were tucked in behind him, using his ample body as protection from my inevitable outburst.

"I know!" I flicked off every switch in the fuse box and grabbed the mop. "Everyone, find somewhere else for lunch. Kitchen's fucking closed!"

It was only a small flood, but a few unfortunate factors turned it into a nightmare. The first – uneven flooring – wasn't my fault. It meant that the water flowed far and wide, into every corner of the kitchen, dining area and storeroom, seeking out cardboard boxes full of un-washable items like coasters, napkins and paper cups. I'd been waiting to buy better shelves until the cafe turned a profit, so the week's delivery of potatoes and cabbages got taken out too.

Why didn't I just wash them? Well, because of something that actually *was* my fault. Muck had been building up under the equipment – out of sight, out of mind – until the accident brought everything into the open. My less-than-thorough mopping meant that there was a lot more than tap water contaminating my stock. It took the rest of the day and some of the night to get rid of the ruined produce and mop the main floor dry, but I kept on working, determined not to make the same mistake twice. I searched every dark inch of the cafe for hidden puddles, getting down on my knees with towels and rags until there wasn't a single damp spot that would turn into mold or rot through the floor. When that was done, I filled in some of the more egregious holes, hoping to make the next mistake less disastrous. If anything like that happened again, at least the water wouldn't pick up as much filth.

Inero wandered back sometime after dark.

"How are your new friends? They look after you? Get you something to eat?"

He nodded. "Yeah."

There goes old blabbermouth, talking my ear off.

"Well, come on; I'll show you to your room."

We climbed the stairs, and I went into my office to retrieve a set of keys. Inero stood in the doorway, looking in dubiously.

"Don't worry, this is mine. You're next door." I grabbed the least offensive pillow from my bed and took him to the door down the hall. The lawyer had moved out a few months ago, and as far as I knew, nobody else had even looked at the place. I still had the spare keys from the time he'd gone into hospital and asked me to water his plants.

There were enough cracks in the wall to stop the place from getting too stuffy, and the carpet looked thick enough to lie on without too much discomfort.

I handed Inero the keys and the pillow.

"Not much, but it should keep you out of trouble. We'll get you some furniture and supplies in the morning. I'd give you my bed, but I haven't done laundry in a while so you probably—"

"This is good. Thank you."

"No problem. Get some sleep. I'm going to finish up downstairs."

It was long after sunset by the time I'd finished in the kitchen, and though the place was cleaner than ever, it still looked like a dump. Burn marks stained the floor, walls and benches, and some of the grease was so fused to the steel that there was no way of stripping it with anything less than liquid magma. I suppose that was its charm, though, and I would have felt out of place if the cafe had started looking too shiny.

It was a waste of a day – bad for business and bad for my bank account – but as I wiped down the pots and pans, I started thinking about how I was going to seize the morning and get the place back on track. I'd start by brewing a vat of that skin cream and sending some over to Simms as an apology. I didn't have to like her work, but I could still keep her as a friend. Simms had her way of trying to make the world a better place, and I had mine. We'd always struggled to stand on the same side of things, but now that I wasn't a Man for Hire, it was easier to look past her badge to the woman behind it, trying to make a difference. She chose to go out every day, knowing she'd only deal with people at their worst, and do her best to see the good in them. She tried to keep an open mind and a nuanced perspective. That ain't easy. Most people can't hack the mental strain of remaining in the gray area. Eventually, they all cave in to an us-and-them way of being, just so they can get through the day without tearing their hair out. Fighting against binary thinking was hard enough on a good day, but after your friend gets filled with bullets in his own home? The fact that she wasn't out there right now, taking out her grief on any potential suspects, was as close as the Sunder PD got to saintliness.

I'd been no good at seeing straight when my emotions were involved. That's why the cafe was a better place for me than out on the streets. Sure, there was spoiled food, faulty equipment, surly customers, a lack of sleep and the blisters and burns to consider, but all those issues were on the outside. I didn't lay awake at night considering the long-term effect of my short-crust pastry.

If I tried to weigh the possible ramifications of what would happen if I managed to track down Whisper, it made my chest hurt. I'd made that kind of call several times already, and I was pretty sure I'd never got it right. That's why I was so relieved when the phone rang, and the voice on the other end said, "Job's off, Phillips."

Derringer's breath came down the line like a thunderstorm forced through a rusty drainpipe.

"What do you mean?"

"I mean Whisper's no longer a concern."

All I could ask was, "Why?"

There was a long silence before he responded.

"What do you care? I'll call the editor, tell them to destroy your story."

What the hell is going on?

"Uh . . . thank you."

More silence. More heavy, tension-filled breaths.

"You think you're a good man, Mr Phillips?"

What? Things were getting even weirder, but at least it was a question I could answer.

"No, Mr Derringer. I am, without a doubt, not a good man."

He huffed, and I swear I felt the wind hit my face.

"Where are you?" he demanded, suddenly full of fire. "That cafe of yours?"

"Yeah. Why?"

"Stay there. I'm on my way."

"No! I'm—"

He hung up. Prick. What was he coming for? A fight? If so, I wouldn't stand a chance. He could break me into little pieces and scatter me on his soup like a salted cracker. I wasn't about to run away, though. All day people had been dragging me from my kitchen, and I was just thankful that someone finally had the courtesy to come to me.

I went out to the dining area, sat down, and closed my eyes while I waited.

I wish I hadn't. I wish I'd taken a moment to look around and breathe it all in. To appreciate the place and what I'd done with it.

While I still had a chance.

8

I must have nodded off almost immediately because I woke with a start, thinking I could hear the rumbling of Derringer's heavy breath.

I jumped to my feet, but I was still alone, and the rumbling sound was coming from outside. Up Main Street, the two glaring headlights of Derringer's monolithic automobile were heading my way. Not fast, but erratic, weaving from side to side.

My first thought was that Derringer had disturbed his chauffeur on his night off, and Carnegie had been forced to drive while inebriated. Then the car came towards the cafe, hit the curb with a violent jolt, and came to a screeching stop just outside the window.

It was Derringer himself behind the wheel.

That explained the car's erratic handling. The mogul was so big and so used to being chauffeured around, that he'd probably never driven before. Of course, a self-made genius like him wouldn't let a lack of experience, knowledge or common sense stand in his way.

I was about to applaud his effort when his face contorted into the strangest expression.

It wasn't fear. Not exactly. Well, not the fear of something in particular. Not fear of something seen or known. It was an expression I'd witnessed in abundance the night of the Coda, before anyone had worked out what was going on. Because it wasn't pain and loss that hit the magical creatures first, but the wild-eyed panic of not understanding what was happening to them or why. A tragic confusion and a sudden awareness that their fate was beyond their control. That was a tough ride for anyone to go on, but for a creature like Derringer – who had learned to control not only his own life, but the lives of everyone around him – you can hardly imagine the bedlam that would have been building in his brain.

He stared at me with disbelief, put a hand on the glass, and mouthed a single word.

Why?

Then he exploded in a ball of debris-filled fire.

I'm sure it happened in stages. I'm sure, if you could slow the explosion down with magic, there would have been the briefest of moments between the first spark and the expanding flame. You would see the car open up – metal, leather and rubber becoming deadly shrapnel – before the force reached the window of the cafe, shattered it, and blasted me off my feet.

For me, Derringer was transformed into an orange flare at the exact same time I felt my back go through the first of several wooden tables, glass embed itself in my face and the eyelashes burn from my blinded eyes. The air evaporated before I could get it into my lungs, and I was still a long way from comprehending what had happened when my head hit the tiles beneath the kitchen window and bent my neck to an angle that would cause me pain for months.

Things dropped onto my twisted body – bits of car, the street, dining chairs, probably pieces of Derringer himself – and I closed my eyes against the heat.

There are things I only remembered later: the scream of the tea-lady across the way as a sheet of metal – ripped from the door of the vehicle – sailed through her window; the brick that flew over my head, into the kitchen, where it punctured the ice box and blew up a gallon of milk; the subtle crash out the front door as the wooden sign – proudly announcing your arrival at Georgio's cafe – hit the cobbles.

I lay there, taking a rare guilt-free break, waiting for the pain. I pushed back any thoughts that dared to acknowledge what had happened. What would need to be fixed, and what might be broken for ever. I lay there for as long as I could, until the ground around me grew wet and cold. Water ran past my legs, filling the dining room and spilling out onto the street. A pipe had burst, and this time it would take more than turning off a faucet to stop the flow.

A crowd gathered on the street, bringing screams of horror with them, but I consoled myself with the only positive thought I could muster.

Hey, at least the water's clean.

9

"Gorgoramus Ottallus?"

The city official said it with too much attitude for it to come across as a real question. She must have known that Georgio's full name belonged to a famed magical adviser, and quickly assessed that the tenderized Human sitting in the gutter wasn't a wise and legendary figure from the old times.

After the blast, cops had dragged me out on the street and placed me on the curb. I leaned my back against a lamppost and tried to come to terms with the tragedy that had just unfolded. Everyone had been far more interested in the smoking shell of the car than the gutted cafe, and I'd thankfully been left alone until this sharp-featured Harpy with her overstuffed clipboard started firing her voice into my glass-filled face.

She repeated her non-question.

"Are you Gorgoramus Ottallus?"

"No."

"But you say it's your cafe?"

"It's still Georgio's. I'm just looking after it for him."

The official flicked through the sheaf of papers as if my answers were a rude inconvenience to her evening. I spat into the gutter. My saliva was dark with blood.

"Where is Mr Ottallus?"

"Saving the world or something."

"What?"

"I don't know. He hasn't called." Another shuffle. An exasperated sigh. "I'm sorry if this is a pain. Next time I get myself blown up, I'll try to do it during business hours."

"Do you have any paperwork from Mr Ottallus detailing the handover?"

"He didn't hand it over. I'm just looking after it until he comes back."

She pulled a pencil out of her jacket and readied it.

"And when is Mr Ottallus returning?"

"I don't know!" The shock had worn off and my head was trying to turn itself inside out.

"Well, along with the police investigation, a safety assessment will need to take place before anyone is allowed in the building. Does Mr Ottallus have insurance?"

"I have no idea."

"Of course you don't."

She scribbled away, and I knew that every word she wrote was another headache waiting to happen. Georgio had bought the place outright when he arrived in Sunder, but after a rogue Genie had restored a portion of his powers, he'd given me a brief lesson in brewing coffee before wandering into the night. I'm not sure if he'd expected me to make coffee for others, or if he just felt bad that he'd saddled me with a caffeine addiction and didn't want to cut off my supply. I'd taken it upon myself to keep his business going in his absence, staying on top of the levies and taxes, and I thought that was all anyone would care about. Turns out that – according to the city – I was nothing but a glorified squatter.

The official whipped a document from her pile and held it out like a drawn sword.

"Fill this out, front and back, and, if at all possible, get Mr Ottallus to sign it at his earliest convenience. Preferably in the next forty-eight hours. Otherwise the city may have to seize owner-ship of the establishment in order to conduct any repairs that—"

I was ready to scream when a familiar silhouette appeared by the smoldering automobile: a thin, jacketed figure in a wide-brimmed hat pulled down low.

"Simms!" I called, cutting off the official. "Can you give me a hand?"

Simms didn't move. She couldn't resist holding back, threatening to abandon me the way I'd abandoned her when she'd come seeking my assistance that morning. She looked from the shattered cafe to me, and shook her head as she approached.

The official grew even more irritated at the idea of being over-ruled.

"Detective, I'm trying to determine a chain of responsibility with the business in question, and—"

"Give us a moment, Phillis."

"Detective, I'm not one of your underlings. You can't—"

"I'm not giving you an order, I'm asking for compassion. Please."

Somehow, the request hit whatever small shred of kindness the Harpy's job hadn't ground down inside her heart, and she went back to examining the interior of the cafe.

"What happened?" asked Simms.

I told her what I remembered: the impromptu visit from Derringer and the spontaneous combustion of his vehicle.

"What caused the explosion?" she asked.

"How the hell should I know?"

"Don't yell at me, Fetch."

"Am I yelling?" I knew I was, but with the ringing in my ears, it was likely even louder than I realized. "Sorry."

She brushed my bad mood aside and turned to the huddle of cops.

"Meredith!" A Banshee with a medical bag came over to us. "Look him over, will you? See if there's anything wrong with his head, other than the usual."

The nurse knelt beside me, unzipped her bag, and took out a little white pill and a bottle of water. When she held them out, I raised an eyebrow.

"Come on," I said. "Where are the Clayfields?"

She shook her head. Simms answered for her.

"Can't dish them out any more. New regulations."

"Oh, fuck off. I've got some inside. Just—"

I pointed to the cafe just as the Harpy walked out with another tight-buttoned official, both of them carrying boxes: the ones that held my Clayfields and the ingredients I used to make Simms's skin cream.

"Hey! That's mine!"

I went to stand up but Meredith held me down. I was dizzy enough that it wasn't hard to do.

"Not your business, not your property," said the Harpy, trying to hide her smug smile.

"Simms, stop them! That's— OW!"

Meredith had found a shard of glass under my hair. Together, they made a convincing argument for me to stay still.

"Listen, Fetch," said Simms, "if you don't know *how* Derringer was killed, I want you to think about *why*."

"I don't care why. I don't care how. I don't care about any of this. I just want my cafe back so I can keep working."

"*Think*, Fetch. First Bath. Now Derringer. Stop being selfish and—"

"Selfish?!" I swatted Meredith's hand away. The piece of glass she'd removed from my dome bounced along the cobbles. "Sorry, Meredith, really, thanks, I didn't mean to . . ." The Banshee zipped up her bag and stepped back. Understandably, that was all the help I was getting from her tonight. "Simms, you're a detective, I'm not. I never was. But even when I was a Man for Hire, I tried to help those who were being stepped on, not those that wore the boots. I never would have worked for Derringer, and I won't be roped in to working for you."

Simms might be losing her scales, but her skin was still too thick to be hurt by such petty insults. She knelt close, and her cold, yellow eyes burned into mine.

"You spoke to Derringer. For some reason, he was here to visit you personally. I think you know why someone might want to kill him. If you work that out, please, come talk to me. Otherwise, I'm worried this is only the beginning."

There was a seriousness to her stare – one that was hard to snap back at – and before I could respond, an engine – high-pitched and squealing – stole everyone's attention. The noise gave us just enough time to scramble out of the way before a small truck came down Main Street at a reckless speed. Simms forgot me immediately, swearing under her breath and marching towards the new arrivals as they tumbled out of the truck like children arriving at a birthday party.

"All right, everyone, no need to panic. Help has arrived!"

Reeves. Followed closely by Gumption and two other uniformed men. All of them big and loud and taking up as much space as they could manage.

"Where's the fire, eh?" asked Gumption to nobody in particular (which was apt, because nobody in particular answered). There was no fire, and clearly no need for whatever brand of protection these brash young men were pretending to offer. There was also no need for me to hang around and watch their performance play out, so I went in through the revolving doors and climbed the stairs to my room on the top floor.

Inero's face peered around the corner.

"What's happening?" he asked.

"Too much to explain, too little for you to worry about. Go back to sleep and we'll sort it out tomorrow."

He nodded but neither of us moved.

"So, you're from the Togul."

He shrugged. "I don't think so. I just kind of . . . woke up there."

"Right." So many possible questions, I was surprised by the one that came out. "See any Fae there?"

The Fae were the most sacred of all the magical species. A collective term for a whole bunch of divine creatures – Sprites, Brownies, Boggarts, Pixies, Imps – that were more magic than mortal. They were so closely connected to the magical source that when the Coda crystalized the sacred river, the Fae froze up too. A whole population turned to organic statues of wood, ice or stone.

"Fae?" he repeated. "Aren't they all gone?"

"Yeah, but I wondered if . . ." Wondered what? If somehow things were different out there? If the great forest had kept some Fae alive and word just hadn't reached the city? "Sorry, I got knocked around and I'm talking shit. Get some sleep, kid."

The door to my office had once read "Fetch Phillips: Man for Hire", but now there was just a piece of old wood nailed over the space where the window had been. I went in and collapsed on the bed, appreciating how the ringing in my ears drowned out the commotion on the street. No need to lament the fact that I wouldn't get a full night's sleep, because I had no reason to ever get up again. Certainly not at any respectable hour. Everyone would have to get their coffee somewhere else. Maybe for a while. Maybe for ever.

Released from all obligations, I closed my eyes and slept a dreamless sleep. It lasted for about forty-five minutes, when I woke to cold metal being forced into my mouth, and somebody whispering the words, "Don't move."

10

A pair of cold green eyes hovered in the darkness above me.

"Where's your gun?" they asked.

It was hard to speak clearly. A pistol was pressing down my tongue.

"Don' 'ave one."

"Bullshit."

I shrugged. No point trying to quip back until I was able to pronounce consonants.

Then there was another voice, from somewhere in the room.

"What other weapons does he have?"

The green eyes repeated the question.

"What other weapons do you have?"

"Numbindadopdar," I mumbled.

They pulled the gun out of my mouth. I didn't get too excited; the dim light showed it still hovering in front of my nose. Close enough to stop me from lying. No matter how tough you think you are, it ain't easy to lie to a killing machine when it's pointed at your face.

"Knife. In the top drawer. Brass knuckles . . . I don't know. Somewhere."

There was a shuffling sound at the desk, then the other voice spoke again.

"Got the knife. Forget the knuckles." The second intruder turned on the desk lamp, but I'd already recognized him from his infuriatingly measured tone.

"What the hell are you doing here, Thurston?"

I looked past Yael – deadly Half-Elf henchwoman – to Thurston Niles, kingpin of Sunder City, sitting at my desk, spinning the tip of my knife into the wood with a look of irritated impatience, as if I was the one who'd broken into his home and disturbed his sleep instead of the other way around.

He'd been in the city for less than two years but he'd changed a lot in that time. The gray hairs had spread from above his ears, further up the sides of his head. His laugh lines had adjusted their attitude, joining up with his furrowed brow to give the impression of a man with a multitude of problems working their way through his mind. I vainly hoped that he'd wake up one day, sick of the pressure of keeping the city under his thumb, pack his bags, and let us get back to running Sunder without his insidious influence.

"Stay where you are," he said, not taking his eyes from the knife. "If you get up, we'll shoot you. Got it?"

"You think I *want* to get out of bed? Have you ever been in bed? It's fucking great. I bet you're the first person in history to wake someone up in the middle of the night and force them – at *gunpoint* – to stay under the covers. Hell, if you asked me to get *out* of bed I'd probably go with the bullet."

"Yael, go get him. It's safe."

She was reluctant to lower her weapon, but even more reluctant to question her employer's demands, so she went out through the waiting room.

"What's going on, Thurston? I've had a shitty enough night already."

"My friend wants to ask you some questions. He's just being cautious, considering recent events."

"Oh, like the fact that Derringer is covering the front of my building? I mean, not covering it for a story, covering it with his own—"

Thurston sneered. I'd rarely seen him this serious.

"I'd watch those cracks tonight, Fetch. Derringer and Henry were close."

"Who the fuck's Henry?"

Yael came back in with a pot-bellied Human in his sixties. The man was wearing a luxurious leisure suit, a look of haggard grief and a face that I'd seen printed on election posters for the last eight years.

It was Henry Piston, Mayor of Sunder City himself. I'd barely seen the guy at a distance, let alone met him, let alone had him walk into my home while I was still under the sheets.

"This place stinks," he said. It wasn't directed at me or anyone else, just a statement of fact.

He stood at the foot of the bed with his hands in his pockets, chewing on his bottom lip and – from the look of it – not liking the taste. "Why was Isaac here?"

No introductions? Fine by me. I wanted this over as soon as possible.

"I have no idea. He tried to hire me this morning then called to cancel the job. I agreed, but he decided to pay me a visit."

"He threatened you and you defended yourself? Is that your story?"

"I did nothing of the sort. I waited patiently for him. He crashed his car into the curb outside, and a few moments later it turned to shrapnel. I never said he threatened me, and I don't know why he wanted to see me face to face."

"What did you say to him? On the phone?"

"I asked him why he cancelled the job and he wouldn't tell me. He kept asking about whether I thought I was a good man. Not sure why."

The Mayor chewed harder. Seemed that question puzzled him too. Niles started wandering around, kicking piles of clothes and examining the dusty shelves.

"You haven't started drinking again, have you?" he asked.

"No, but there's some whiskey on the filing cabinet if that's what you're after."

He found it.

"A sober man who keeps alcohol in the home? I'm impressed."

"*Mostly* sober," I corrected.

"Even more impressive. Henry, you want some?"

Piston shook his head. Thurston found a glass and got to cleaning it in the basin. The Mayor barely moved, his head hung low, his face troubled.

"Was anyone else downstairs when you called Isaac? Any of your anarchic customers know he was coming?"

"It was midnight. I don't open till dawn, Mr Mayor. Apparently that's when most people want breakfast. You should come by sometime. I'll cook you up a— Oh, yeah, sorry, somebody blew up my business. We'll have to take a raincheck."

He wasn't listening. He was trying to make sense of the whole thing even though there was no sense to be found. Whatever had caused the accident – a fault in the vehicle or a weapon deployed from the shadows – finding out the cause wouldn't bring real comfort. His friend had vanished without warning, never to be heard from again. No goodbye. No body. Sudden death was always a shock, but the fact that Derringer had been an immovable slab of power and influence made it all the harder to comprehend. I had no answers for him, and though he was a man who was used to getting answers when he asked, I think he finally realized I had nothing to offer.

"Let's go," he said. "This place stinks."

Henry and Yael stepped outside, but Niles lingered at the foot of my bed.

"Good show," I grumbled, curling back up in anticipation of sleep. "You've let him think he's still in charge."

His head swiveled around, taking the place in.

"It's clean," he muttered. "Relatively. Cleaner than it was."

"Uh . . . thanks."

"Every man talks about pulling himself together. It's nice to see someone follow through." Then, just when I thought he was giving me an actual, unqualified compliment, he added, "Glad to see the modern Sunder is proving fruitful for you."

"Fruitful? Pretty sure your latest import just blew my place to pieces."

"Yes. Sorry about the cafe. You want me to—"

"No."

I had to say it hard and fast before I let myself be tempted to accept his offer. It would be nothing for him to fund the repairs. Have that city official lose track of my forms. Hell, I could have a whole new cafe by the end of the week. But some things cost more than money.

He took my refusal with a smile.

"Ah, yes. I understand. We must preserve the illusion of independence if we want to stay motivated." He went over to the desk and finished his whiskey. "Don't worry, Fetch. You can keep thinking you're still in charge."

He switched off the desk light and wandered out. Good riddance. I wasn't going to bother getting out of bed to check how they'd broken in. Probably lock-picks. Hopefully Yael was talented enough to crack the lock without damaging the mechanism, because I didn't have the money to pay for a new one. Hell, I might never make any money again. From a guard to a Shepherd to soldier to a gumshoe to a fry cook. Surely that was enough. Surely I didn't have to start over somewhere else. I wasn't sure I could handle being bad at some new stupid job all over again. Maybe it was time to lie down and let things move on without me.

That sounded pretty good, so I closed my eyes and slept until morning. I might have kept on sleeping, through the day and beyond, if I hadn't heard something slam against my door.

It was another copy of the *Sunder Star*, with another bile-inducing headline.

ISAAC DERRINGER: DEAD
YOUTH ACTIVISTS AND WAR CRIMINAL BEING
INVESTIGATED FOR MURDER

The death of Isaac Derringer has shaken Sunder City to its core. As we all come to grips with the loss of the city's most trusted voice, attention turns to finding those responsible. A source has informed the *Star* that the prime suspects are several young rebels who regularly frequent the business where the attack took place. It has been alleged that Isaac Derringer was lured to the location by cafe worker Fetch Phillips (known to some as Sunder's controversial *Man for Hire*) so that the agitators could commit their heinous act. Mr Phillips, as we've previously reported, was the Opus traitor who sold classified information to the Human Army, causing the event that we now know as the Coda.

The words "previously reported" gave me hope, but it was only after I'd run across the road to the teahouse and found a real copy of the day's news that I could take a proper breath. The actual paper opened with a soppy dedication to the newspaper's editor without any mention of me, the kids or possible suspects.

I'd received another false front page created solely to get under my skin. This one was made by someone other than Derringer (unless his first act in the afterlife was to find a way to fuck with me).

Derringer had said that he was going to cancel my story and release me from any obligation. Obviously, he hadn't passed that information on to his subordinates, and one of them had decided to carry out his dying wishes.

Were they really convinced that the kids and I killed Derringer? Knowing the *Star*, just because they said it in print it didn't mean they believed it. But it was a threat I couldn't ignore. They were accusing the kids of more than just printing provocative newsletters now, and if the cops and courts decided to jump on board, then being forced to drink sub-par coffee would be the least of their worries.

As I went to leave, old habits made me reach for my coat. I hadn't worn the beaten-up Opus uniform for over a month, as the Chimera fur stitched into the collar didn't mix with the summer heat. I decided to leave it behind. The day was already warm and there were too many uniforms in the city as it was: charcoal suits, burgundy boots, police badges and branded coveralls. Everybody needed to be on a team. Everybody but me. I'd learned a long time ago that any group who would want me on their side had to be up to some kind of bullshit.

I barely glanced at the cafe on my way out. Just enough to see the police tape that blocked every entrance and the city officials who were still snooping around inside. They could have it, for now. Just until I found out why the *Star* was fucking with me, and what I needed to do to get them off my back.

As I turned south – towards the Kirra Canal and the printing press beyond it – I almost felt like smiling. It had been a while since I had something worth fighting for. Those kids weren't responsible for Derringer's death, and I wasn't going to let the *Star* drag their names through the mud just to fill a few pages. Whoever had sent that paper didn't know what they were in for, because while Ophelia and Ashton might have their whole lives ahead of them, I now had nothing to lose.

11

Well, that was the dumbest fucking idea imaginable.

Here's a tip: if you've got the worst headache of your headache-filled life, and you have a choice between a woodpecker mistaking your skull for a tree trunk or stepping inside a working printing press, then I'd start growing leaves.

"I'M HERE TO SEE THE EDITOR!" I screamed at a Gnome in earmuffs.

He blinked a few times, shook his head, and ran a finger across his throat in the universal expression of "they're dead".

"THE NEW ONE! WHOEVER'S IN CHARGE!"

He scrunched up his face in confusion, and that was all the encouragement I needed to give up on my mission and get out of that echo chamber before I went deaf. I gave the Gnome a dismissive wave, turned around, and walked straight into a tall Kobold in a black suit and cap.

I bounced off his chest and prepared myself for the assault that usually followed when hired goons appeared out of nowhere. Instead, he jerked his head to the right and took his own directions. I followed. Anything to get away from those screeching, stamping machines that were spitting out the *Star*'s shallow brand of shitty news.

I was led into a reception area with nothing in it but a stylishly uncomfortable couch and a coffee table with the previous three days' editions of the *Star* laid out beside each other. The wall that separated it from the factory was thick enough to dull the painful clatter, but I could still feel the vibrations of the machines in the jelly of my eyes. There was a wooden door opposite the couch with a lock but no handle.

"Wait here. The boss will be with you shortly."

He went back out the way we'd come, and I began the impossible task of trying to get my ass comfortable on a couch with no armrests, a low back that would be lucky to support two vertebrae, and not a cushion to be seen.

With nothing else of interest in the room, the papers begged for my attention, baiting me to open the pages and poison myself. Because that's the thing about the bad-faith stories that papers like the *Star* love to peddle: even when you know they're lying, the lie still works. Your reason, logic and experience might know that they're beating up bullshit to sell a few subscriptions, but your fears and prejudices are far less rational. If you read a headline that says "All Goblins Want to Slap Your Bottom" you might laugh at its ridiculousness, but I bet you'll remember those words the next time you turn your back on one.

After ten minutes of uncomfortable boredom, I finally cracked and opened a paper. By page two, I was picking fights with headlines. The front page was the usual fearmongering about random people going missing out west. I was pretty sure all these tales that suggested we should be afraid to walk the streets were just a way for Niles to sell more firearms. But the one that really got me going read "Hero Cop Killed by Activists".

The story was a bunch of biased speculation about who might have committed Bath's murder. The only confirmed fact seemed to be that he was found in his apartment with multiple bullet wounds. Everything else was spin, with the *Star* spending most of its ink on wondering who might be motivated to kill a policeman loyal to Sunder's new regime. It was the usual hyperbole and rhetoric, opening the reader up with questions then prompting them to comb their own prejudices for an answer. I threw the rag across the room into the wooden door, and it opened a moment later.

A short Human with a pear-shaped head and small round spectacles looked me over. He wore an exaggerated frown that projected a dangerously short fuse; the kind of expression adopted by someone who is used to being in charge and wants anyone to think twice before bothering him. The first words out of his thin-lipped mouth made it clear that I'd already wasted too much of his time.

"Hello, Mr Phillips." He picked up the thrown paper and smoothed out the pages as if it was a precious garment to be presented to a king. "Before we start, know that I am familiar with your brand of boorish behavior, and I ask you to spare me as much pain as possible. This day need not be harder than it is."

I laughed at that. It hurt, but I tried not to show it.

"Aren't you the one that printed another bespoke newspaper just to rile me up? Don't poke the beehive then complain about getting stung."

He dropped the paper back on the table with the others.

"Fair. My name is Urik Volta, managing editor of the *Sunder Star* for the time being. As you can imagine, there is much to attend to."

He held the door open and waited for me to follow.

Volta's office was made from cement walls painted white, and as lacking in character as everything the *Star* put its name to.

"So this is life at the top, eh? They ever let you out into the yard for exercise?"

"For pity's sake. Just sit down and listen or I'll publish the article and be done with you." He dropped into his leather recliner, and I lowered myself onto a creaky wooden armchair. "I know the agreement you had with Isaac. I made the mock-up of your story myself, on his orders."

"How did you even get that information?" I asked.

He snorted. "I'm not here to answer your questions, Mr Phillips, but your story has been on file for years. Contacts in the Human Army gave us an account of your involvement in the Coda soon after it happened." I opened my mouth to ask a follow-up question, but he correctly guessed what I was going to say. "Why didn't we print it? Even though the *Star* is an unbiased and trusted news source" – I gave him a snort of my own – "we take the potential ramifications of our stories very seriously. A decision was made early on to . . . de-emphasize the connections between the Human Army and the Coda for fear of provoking violent action within the community."

"Oh, yeah. Your paper has always been so careful about inspiring resentment. Like that story you printed last year suggesting Witches used Elven blood in their spells. Tender piece of reporting, that one."

"That article was a freelance opinion piece, nothing more. The point is, we decided to suppress your story for fear that your personal actions would reflect unfavorably on the rest of Sunder's Human population."

"And now?"

He shrugged. "Now we feel that Sunder has reached suitable stability, so if your story were published today, the horror of your actions would mostly land on your own head. As long as the story is given the proper nuance, of course."

Suitable stability. He meant that Niles had such a strong hold on the city that any Magum who attacked a Human would be locked up without question.

"Derringer called me last night," I said, tired of listening to Volta's half-truths. "He called off his little blackmail plan. Said that Whisper was no longer a concern and that the article would be cancelled."

Volta raised an eyebrow.

"Why wouldn't Whisper be a concern?"

"He didn't tell me that. Maybe he uncovered Whisper's true identity."

"If he had, it would be in today's paper."

"Unless he died before he could tell you."

"The same way he died before he could tell me that you'd been released from our services? Sorry, Mr Phillips, but I find that story a little too convenient."

"Convenient my ass. If he'd stayed home and called you rather than coming to me, I'd be out of this mess and still have my cafe."

His nostrils flared. He was a man who mostly interacted with subordinates, and he wasn't good at handling an unbridled asshole with a poor sense of self-preservation.

"Isaac wanted your help and I intend to fulfil my friend's wishes."

"Fuck your friend. He was a self-serving monster who thought he knew better than everyone else. He took more than his share while he was alive, and he's not any more deserving now he's dead. Find Whisper on your own."

I went to stand, but Volta slammed his hands on his desk, shocking both of us.

"I don't care about Whisper. Not exactly. I want you to find Isaac's killer."

"I don't do that any more. I'm sure every cop and Niles goon will be happy for a chance to prove their loyalty to your little cabal. Let them do their duty, I'm out."

Volta leaned forward on his desk, attempting to push aside his annoyance in favor of finding common ground.

"You know that won't work. There is a cold war happening on these streets, and the rebels know how to keep quiet. For all your mess and all your mistakes, you're permitted to move in both worlds. You are welcome where journalists and police are not. You can find out who did this."

"Maybe. But I won't."

"Then it's not just *your* story that our readers will get to enjoy." *The kids.*

"They've done nothing wrong."

It was his turn to chuckle. One glimpse of his crooked, brown teeth made me hope it never happened again.

"They've done plenty wrong. We have proof of some of their misdeeds, and there are plenty of stories that – with some tactful insinuation – won't require it. The Mayor is passionate about any article that explores the damage done to our society by wayward citizens. It helps him justify his policy changes to an increasingly nervous population. Of course, if we had another person to pin Derringer's murder on, I could convince my partners to let your friends be. Otherwise, I'm painted into a corner, aren't I? I'm afraid I must offer up something."

He raised his hands, palms up, like he had no say in the matter. Just another humble worker trying to keep up with the modern world. I hated everything about him, but I didn't doubt he'd do what he said. The guy had all the integrity of a failed soufflé.

"What makes you think he was murdered?" I asked.

"Journalistic instinct."

"Not just a fault in that rolling behemoth of his?"

"I've already talked to the manufactures in Mira, and nothing in that car's construction could have caused an explosion like that."

"And you believe them?"

"I'm yet to be convinced. But this is exactly the kind of thing I'm expecting you to investigate."

"I'm not . . ."

I trailed off. I was going to say that I wouldn't be investigating anything. That I wasn't for hire and I wasn't going to come out of retirement to bring closure to the death of a diabolical prick like Derringer. But what else was I going to do? Go back to drinking all day and let the kids meet their fate unchallenged?

Fuck.

Volta saw my resolve fade, smiling like a builder who'd just placed his final brick. He wrote something on a piece of paper and pushed it over the desk.

"That's my personal number for when you have something to report. Don't take too long, Mr Phillips. The more practice I have at writing your story, the more excited I am to put it into print. If a slow news day hits soon, I might not be able to help myself."

12

So I was a fucking Man for Hire again.

But I had no intention of dropping Whisper – or whoever was responsible for Derringer's death – onto the front page of the *Star*. Not until I'd uncovered their identity and given them a chance to explain their motives. For now, I just knew that there was no way I was going to let Volta make my troublesome teens his story of the week, right when Piston and Niles were baying for blood.

I decided not to waste my day calling manufacturers in Mira. They'd keep me on hold for eternity, only to give me simpler answers than the ones they'd cough up for Niles, Volta, Piston and the police. Instead, I walked all the way up to Derringer's urban jungle and found the gates to the estate already open. There must have been so many cars coming and going – cops and commiserating friends – that it had been easier to leave it that way.

If there had been visitors, there weren't any now. It didn't take much to make the place feel empty. The driveway looked huge without the four-wheeled monstrosity filling it up, and now that the mighty Sasquatch had moved on, the size of the house went from practical to ridiculous. As far as I knew, nobody else in Sunder would need those giant doors and high hallways, so the whole place remained a monument to a man who had wielded more influence over our lives than most of us understood.

A bouquet of flowers had been left at the door. The first of many, I imagined. I rapped at the knocker.

Light footsteps tapped towards me, and the door opened a crack. "Hello?"

"Ms Derringer, it's Fetch Phillips. We met yesterday morning. I'm sorry to disturb you."

The crack got wider, but not enough to be an invitation. Trixie Derringer's face was covered in a black veil, obscuring everything but the polished shine of her stony eyes.

"I thought Isaac fired you."

She knew about that? It felt like the first piece of good news I'd had in forever.

"He did, but his employees at the *Star* have picked up his tab. Any chance you can tell them he let me go?"

"They still want you to find whoever wrote that newsletter?"

"That, and whoever killed your husband. The two cases could be connected, but it's too early to say."

"Well, I'm sorry to disappoint you but I have less sway than a steel beam down there. I could make a call, but I don't think it will help you any."

"No, that's all right. I feel bad enough for disturbing you." She sniffed, and reached under her veil to rub her eyes. I wondered what her tears were like. Maybe she was crying wet cement. "How are you doing?"

"Oh," she shook her head like she was shaking off a bad dream, "I don't really know yet. Doesn't seem real. Doesn't make sense." She snapped her head to me, suddenly remembering something. "You were there, weren't you? The police said he was outside your cafe."

"I'm afraid I was."

"Why was he there?"

"I don't really know. He seemed troubled. Were you with him last night?"

"I was out in the greenhouse. He was busy with phone calls and meetings and whatever else. He likes me to stay away while he's working. So I won't overhear anything delicate."

"Did he have any visitors? Anyone else here?"

"I don't think so. It was just the two of us. And Carnegie, of course. His driver."

"Yeah, I met him yesterday. He lives on the premises?"

"Mmm-hmm."

"Why didn't he drive Mr Derringer to my place?"

"Oh, poor Carnegie came down with some awful sickness. I tucked him in early with a bucket beside his bed."

"Lucky for him."

"Well, I suppose, but . . ." She paused, catching my suggestion, not liking it. "Oh, come now, Mr Phillips. I dare say Carnegie loved my husband more than I did."

"I'd like to speak to him anyway, if that's all right. Just a couple of questions."

She sighed as if the whole thing was just exhausting. Her languid, grief-filled body leaned against the door, still wearing those long, black gloves despite the heat.

"You know, most everyone wants to get their name *in* the paper, Mr Phillips. You're the first man I've met who runs around trying to get his name *out*."

"So you do know some of your husband's business."

"I catch a scandal or two. Yours is more interesting than most."

"It's not my story I'm worried about. If I don't find the real culprit, Volta's going to pin your husband's death on the kids who frequent my cafe."

"He's running a newspaper, not the courts."

"Trixie, you know better than I do that once the *Star* prints a story, most judges won't risk their career by going against the grain. These teenagers aren't dangerous, they're just overeager kids who hope to make the city a better place but haven't worked out how yet. They don't deserve to be accused of murder just so Volta can give your husband's important friends someone to blame."

"Murder?"

"Volta's theory, not mine. I know nothing about nothing, and I'm all ears if you have any better theories you're willing to share."

She sighed and leaned her head forward. The hollowed-out snakes rolled over her, floating out towards me, and I couldn't help but flinch.

"Fine," she said, "but you come to me first, whatever you find. I want to hear Isaac's story before Volta messes with it. He was my husband, and I should have a say in what gets said about him."

I had no problem with that. In fact, I liked that she saw Volta and the *Star* the way I did. It felt good to have a potential ally in high society when every other member wanted to mount my head as a hunting trophy.

"Deal," I said, and she stepped back from the door to let me in.

The place was quieter and emptier than it had been on the first visit. Trixie walked ahead, her gloved fingertips sliding along the wall, as she guided us through the house, out the back, to the door of a little worker's cottage.

"Oh, Ms Derringer, please don't come in," moaned Carnegie after she knocked and announced herself.

"Don't worry, Carnegie. I won't. But someone here wants to talk to you."

"I'm not really in the talking mood, Ms Derringer."

She pushed the door open, and the driver rolled over in his bed, squinting into the light. It was dark inside, and something smelt off. If the driver was faking his illness, he'd really committed to the bit.

"I understand that, Carn, and I'm sorry. He promises to make it quick. Right, Mr Phillips?"

"That's right, Ms Derringer. Thank you."

She stepped away so that Carnegie could talk without shrinking from her gaze.

"Phillips? The gumshoe?"

"That's me."

"They're saying you were with him when he died."

"He was outside my cafe."

"You saw it happen?"

"I did."

He rolled away from me, buried his head.

"I should have been there. He shouldn't have gone out on his own."

He was convincing, or perhaps laying it on too thick. Hard to tell.

"Apparently you were unwell."

"Shove your fucking *apparently* up your ass! My guts have been twisted up all night."

"Eat anything strange in the last twenty-four hours?"

"Fucking staff meal at the printing press that did it. Should have known better. If I'd just waited to get myself some real food, the boss never would have gone without me."

The bucket beside his bed served as evidence of his story, but he wouldn't have been the first person to make himself vomit on purpose.

"If you'd gone out with him, both of you might have met the same fate. Seems like that fancy new vehicle wasn't as perfect as it looked."

He rolled back to face me, his eyes wet and red.

"You think that's what happened? Something wrong with the car?"

"I don't know. It blew a hole in my cafe and damaged the buildings on both sides of the street. Seems a hell of a manufacturers' fault, if that's all it was. Could anyone have got to it? Maybe put something inside?"

"What like an explosive? I suppose someone could have snuck onto the grounds. Stuck something in the car. Maybe under it? Oh, I wish I'd caught them if they had." He looked me up and down, trying to work me out. Good luck. I barely knew my angle myself. "Who you working for?"

"I was brought in by Volta, but Ms Derringer has given me her blessing and I've decided to hand over any information to her first. If Isaac was murdered, there's always a chance it was someone close to him. Maybe a business associate. I'm not ruling out someone from the *Star*."

Carnegie gave a grunt, but I couldn't parse its meaning. Maybe I'd made a mistake by suggesting that someone at his favorite newspaper might not be trustworthy.

"First, we need to determine whether this was intentional," I continued. "So any information on the vehicle would be a huge help."

He only thought it over for a moment. His loyalty to the Derringers appeared to be iron-clad, and though it clearly caused him pain, he got out of bed and shuffled to a cabinet in the corner of the room, keeping one hand on his abdomen for comfort.

He rummaged around and came out with a thick manual on glossy paper. As soon as he handed it over, he made for the bed and curled himself up again, breathing deep to crush the nausea.

"Thanks, Carnegie. I hope you feel better soon."

He groaned into his pillow.

"If someone did this on purpose," he said, "you find that fucker and you let me know. I can do more with a tire-iron than change a spare."

Despite his tender state, I had no doubt that his actions would match his words if I came back with answers.

"Will do, Carnegie. And you let Ms Derringer know if you think of anything else that might help."

I stepped back into the light and was thankful for the perfumed air of the Derringers' dense garden.

"Any luck?" asked Trixie, waiting at the entrance to the main house, as unreadable as ever.

I held up the brochure, before remembering that it wouldn't get the point across.

"I've got the manual to the car, which seems like a good start."

Before I left, she leaned in and hugged me, and I tried not to shudder when the snakes fell over my bare arm.

"Everyone thought they knew Isaac, but nobody knew him like I did. If his story's going to be told, then I want to make sure those words are worthy of the life he lived."

I nodded, unsure if she was ready for what I might bring back. Guys like Derringer don't get to the top by doing good deeds, and secrets are harder to keep when you're not around to staple everyone's lips shut.

On my way out, I passed a delivery truck parked on the street. No driver inside. Perhaps Carnegie did paper runs when he wasn't waiting on his master. Is that what he'd revert to now Isaac was gone? What about Trixie?

In that house, you might as well have turned the world on its head. For the rest of us, nothing would really change. Derringer was dead but his job had already been filled. The *Star* would keep spewing its lies, and it looked like life would go on as usual.

But looks can be deceiving, and Whisper's next move was already in motion.

13

The officials had moved on to more pressing matters, and I finally had the stomach to cross the police tape and look inside the cafe. The dining room was neither better nor worse than what I'd witnessed the night before: every window shattered, half the tables in an unusable state and the blinds ripped and ruined. I tried to focus on the bright spots. Some of the metal chairs were sturdy enough to survive the explosion, and the damage to the walls wasn't much worse than what had been there before.

The register had been skewered by a piece of metal – maybe a door handle – and I doubted it could be repaired. Fine. That wasn't essential to running the place. It was the kitchen that worried me most.

That fucking service window.

I'd been so proud of putting it in there. I could keep an eye on the dining room while I was busy cooking, pile orders on the countertop, and pour coffees right into my customers' hands. Who could have anticipated that it would also give easy access to airborne pieces of exploding motorcar?

A brick, ripped from the curb, had collided with the ice box at impossible speed. It was still sitting there, perched on the paper-wrapped bacon. The summer heat had already given the rashers a slimy coating, and the smell of curdled milk filled the air.

A set of shelves had been knocked over but only a few of the containers had broken. I got it back up and stacked the unbroken boxes, throwing everything unusable in a big pile to be dealt with later. Beneath a split bag of lentils, a slab of brass caught my eye. I dusted it off, read the words etched into the front, and – despite the state of everything around me – cracked a smile.

Fetch Phillips: Man for Hire
Bringing the magic back!
Enquire at Georgio's Cafe

When Georgio and I had first screwed the sign into the wall, we never would have imagined a future where I'd be the one in the kitchen while he was out on a quest, searching for remnants of magical power.

I wondered if he'd found anything. If the voices – the ones that started speaking to him after a Genie jump-started his Shamanic senses – had led him anywhere enlightening. I had to assume that he wouldn't get stuck at that same mental crossroad where I'd spent so many years: never sure if I was wasting my time on a fruitless fantasy or if the secret to fixing the Coda was just one more leap of faith away.

Wherever he was, I hoped he had no regrets. That whatever he found – or didn't find – he never wished that he was still here, frying eggs instead of searching for a miracle. It was one of the reasons I felt compelled to keep the hotplates warm. Not knowing the extent of his finely tuned intuition – or if those mysterious voices were keeping him abreast of my efforts – I wanted him to know that his customers weren't going hungry without him. I doubted the great Gorgoramus Ottallus would let a little thing like a deadly explosion get him down, so I wouldn't let it hold me back either. If he was out there, looking for a way to stick the broken world back together, then I could handle whipping up a couple of meals around my murder investigation.

The fryer had been strong enough to withstand the blast, but the metal vent above it was dented and dangling from the roof. If I tried to cook anything without fixing that first, I'd smoke the place out and have firefighters at my door in no time. So, I turned on the radio and started banging the vent back into shape.

It didn't take long to hammer out the largest dent, then I drilled some new supports into the wall and tested the fan. In a rare bit of luck, the exhaust still worked, so I'd be able to cook a meal or two without suffocating. I ordered an express delivery of essential ingredients and, with the prospect of serving a few meals reinstated, finally opened the manual I'd got from Carnegie.

It was mostly impenetrable to my simple mind: a detailed handbook that described the various components of a uniquely engineered car, written mainly as a maintenance guide if anything ever went wrong. I knew next to nothing about cars, so I couldn't tell which components made this one different to the others in the company's arsenal. Was the car itself the cause of the explosion? Or was there something else inside, either carried by Derringer intentionally or secreted away by someone else? If I could answer that, I would at least have a line of inquiry. As it was, there were too many possibilities, all outside my realm of expertise.

Leaning over the counter, looking out at the decimated dining room, I remembered Derringer's face right before it was engulfed in flames. He was already panicking, like he knew something was wrong. Before I could see any spark, any smoke, Derringer had his hands pressed to the car window, mouthing the question that now burned in my mind.

Why?

Before I could get anywhere close to an answer, I heard a familiar voice.

"Good evening, inquirers. This is Tabatha Ratchet for Lamplighter Radio's investigation hour, and I'm sure you already know what tonight's topic is going to be. Though I hate to give any more airtime to the integrity-deprived political puppets over at the *Sunder Star*, this little mystery is too juicy to pass up. And no, I'm not speaking about the death of the paper's founder, Mr Isaac Derringer, because I'm sure there is many a person in the city who is celebrating the fact that his voice and his name are out of our ears once and for all. No, I'm speaking of the appearance of another newsletter from the mysterious provocateur known as Mister Whisper. This time, impossibly, within the pages of the *Star* itself.

Let me read you the piece from this morning's edition, and don't worry if you can't recognize the hidden meaning at first, this little puzzle was not made to be read out over the air."

One of the city inspectors had left a copy of the paper among the dining-room detritus, so I brought it back to the counter.

"This isn't an article, but an advertisement for vegetable seeds, of all things. Well, planters. It doesn't really matter. I'm not sure who first noticed the hidden message, or what tipped them off, because anyone who has ever read the *Star* knows confusing grammar isn't an uncommon sight within their pages. We only got word of it this afternoon, and the title of the advertisement is 'Miracle Soil Will Make Your Garden Grow!'"

I found the advertisement on the second-to-last page, crammed into the bottom-left corner. No wonder it took more than a day to identify it. I read along with Tabatha.

Dead garden getting you down? Worried your crops can't cop the heat? Do your lilies wilt no matter how much you attended to them? Then it's time for you to try our super secret formula. Dr Lynne Ryan has devised a glorious meeting of science and nature, combining rich fertilizer with ingenious modern chemical compounds from top Sunder scientists. Dr Lynne Ryan is one of the industry leaders in post-Coda horticulture.

This miracle cure can be yours! Just send us the attached paper coupon and Dr Lynne Ryan and her expert team will send you a starter pack for half price! Customers will not be disappointed!

Tell your friends!

You could have the greenest garden on your street within the month, and if you decide that we have not told the truth, you'll get your money back!

I have used this product many times. I'm sure that you will love it too.

MARVELOUS VEGETABLES!

RADIANT FLOWERS!

WATCH YOUR GARDEN GROW!

"Those last three lines are all in capitals, but the first letters are in bold, if that helps you at all. As I said, it would be near impossible to crack this over the airwaves, but looking at it, you'll clearly see that the first words of each line spell out a message that is beyond coincidence."

Goddamn. She was right. A simple trick, but I could have read the paper a hundred times and never caught it.

"Dead cop attended secret meeting with Sunder leaders. This paper will not tell you the truth. I will. And then three letters: M R W, which, without a doubt, are a reference to our mysterious underground writer Mister Whisper. But what are we to glean from this? Whisper seems to have some hidden insight into the goings-on of these so-called 'Sunder leaders'. There was reference to them in a previous message, decrying the *Star* as being propaganda, and spreading 'Niles-designed tales' and 'unsafe falsities', but Whisper's last message was more – what's the word – active? A call to action. So, what does he hope to achieve by sharing this information? Does he merely wish to taint the memory of a recently deceased police officer? Or does Whisper happen to know the details of this young man's death? If that's the case – which Whisper is at least alluding to – perhaps this could be, in fact, a warning. A warning to others who might partake in these so-called 'secret meetings'. I'm only speculating, mind you. But considering what happened to Isaac Derringer just hours before this message was published, we must ask ourselves whether these incidents are not connected." She adjusted her tone from conspiratorial investigator to bright and bubbly friend of the listener. "So, what do you think? Do you believe that Sunder's leaders are truly conspiring against us? Or is that just politics the way it's always been? And what about this Mister Whisper character? Maybe one of you has some insights into their identity. The line is open, and Lamplighter Radio would love to hear from you."

Oh God. Talkback. I turned it down low. If I wanted to hear an uninformed idiot speculate on things beyond his understanding, I could just tune into the thoughts in my own head.

Tabatha did her best to humor them, but it was clear that this wasn't her favorite part of the job. Once the show ended, I called up the hotline and told Tabatha about my case. I must have said something to pique her interest because she invited me to the station the next morning.

Then my delivery arrived and, with my obligations to the investigation suitably fulfilled for one day, I got back to the work I wanted to be doing.

Slice the onions. Heat the hotplates. Spread the oil.

Inero must have caught the smell because he came down a few minutes later and poked his head through the busted door.

"Ah, shit," I said, having forgotten that the young man existed. "I'm sorry. I was supposed to go shopping."

The poor guy was still wearing his Druid's uniform, and who knew how long it had been since he'd washed it.

"It's fine."

"No, I'm sorry. Let's get this stuff sold and then use the profits to sort you out. Would you do us a favor and put a couple of tables out on the sidewalk? We're pivoting to street food for the time being."

While he was outside, I picked up the phone and asked the operator to put me through to the museum.

"Do you mean The Niles Company's House of Tomorrow?"

I almost took a bite out of the receiver.

"Yes, I suppose I do."

After a couple of rings, it was answered by a voice like roiling magma.

"House of Tomorrow, this is Baxter Thatch."

"Hey, Baxter. It's me. Do you know anything about the Sect of Frondescence?"

"I've encountered some members of their fellowship before. Peaceful Druids of the Togul. Why?"

"Got a young man here who came from out that way. He's a bit cagey, but I'm trying to help him out. Thought you might be up for meeting him."

Now, you might not expect an ancient Demon to be the best choice for bringing a wayward youth out of his shell, but aside from curating the museum (I refused to address it by its new title) Baxter was also the Minister of Education and History. That meant that they had more experience than I did in dealing with the needs of Sunder's younger population. We'd come to each other's aid more times than we'd been at each other's throats, so I counted them as one of my few allies.

I explained how Inero had come into my care and how he was being less than forthcoming, but that I wasn't experienced enough in the behavior of teenage boys to know if that was something to be suspicious about or whether it was run-of-the-mill adolescent moodiness.

"I'll see if I can come by the cafe tomorrow. I've been so busy I haven't even got my head around this Derringer incident. I assume you heard about it?"

"*Heard* about it? I've still got pieces of the guy on my ceiling. He exploded right outside."

Baxter took a moment to process that information, likely swallowing their disbelief that the hapless gumshoe was somehow ahead of the curve on Sunder's latest development.

"You're there now?" they asked.

"Yep. We'll be serving sausages out front for the next hour or so."

"I'll see you there."

The street-side set-up was as sloppy as my customers had come to expect from this establishment, but we were soon standing behind a tray full of bangers, buttered rolls and barbecued onions, selling them at a price that had me barely breaking even. But it felt right. All I had to do was swap money for food, keep the meat hot and wave the flies away. It was nice to focus on something simple after my day of too many open-ended questions. Even Ophelia and Ashton stopped by to make it feel like nothing had changed.

They were an odd pair. Ashton's straight, blond hair looked like he went to the barber every morning, while Ophelia's mass of dark curls gave Trixie Derringer's snake pit a run for its money.

They expressed their commiserations about the state of the place, but the excitement of the event soon overrode their sympathy. They must also have listened to the Lamplighter, because they were each carrying a cut-out copy of the hidden message and sat on the curb to compare notes.

"Whisper got this message out quickly," said Ashton, leaning over Ophelia's piece of paper as if he didn't have his own (even a blind gargoyle on the next street could see he was crushing harder than a trash compacter). "The cop only died two nights ago."

"Yeah, but maybe that's because Whisper knew what was going to happen before it happened?"

"What do you mean?"

"Whisper knew the cop was going to die because he already planned to kill him."

Ashton reacted like it was a twist in a radio serial instead of a real-life murder.

"Oh, shiiiit. That makes sense. Nobody saw anyone at the cop's apartment, right?"

"If they did, they're too scared to say anything. I wouldn't want to be the one to report on a group of killers who aren't afraid to execute a cop in his own home."

"So, Whisper must lead a gang then, eh? And he's so confident that he sends out the obituary even before he kills the guy? Fuck yeah."

He was talking too loud, oblivious to the customers who were casting side-eyes. I stepped over to their little powwow.

"Keep it down, will ya? Your voices carry out here. We don't need anyone trying to shut us down."

Ashton scoffed. "Oh, that's right. You're friends with the cops, aren't you? Must be angry that Whisper is fighting back against your boys."

My boys? Almost all my interactions with the police had involved threats and beatings. That said, Bath had always been more of an annoyance than an adversary. He was an overly polite, uninspiring sort of guy. The kind of cop who ran his life from the rule book while never bothering to ask who wrote it. He was no hero, that's for sure. But no real villain either.

Right?

Whisper's first newsletter had accused the cops of helping criminal organizations. Could Bath have been the first casualty in whatever reckoning Whisper was preparing for? Is that why Simms was so spooked? Because she was afraid she might be next?

"Fuck him," said Ophelia, as casually as if she was talking about someone missing their train. "His fault for signing up to the Sunder PD."

That only irked me a little. These kids might have lived through the Coda, but they were still green. The world at large was mostly an idea to them. It was easy to talk about what you would do if you never had to put those plans into action, never faced up to the consequences of following through with all your talk. But their day would come. When it did, I hoped their wake-up call would be less dramatic than mine.

"Yeah," agreed Ashton. "One less prick locking up anyone who doesn't fall into line."

"You know you met him," I said. Their expressions revealed

that they did not, in fact, know that. "He was on your tail the first time you came here."

The cocky expression fell from Ophelia's face. It was nice to see that she wasn't completely heartless, it just took a beat to get her head out of her ideals and into reality.

"Oh," she said sadly. "Not much older than us, right? He was kind of sweet."

Ashton had a harder time changing tone.

"Sweet? You work for the cops, you work for Niles. The constable deserved exactly what he got."

He helped himself to another sausage and bun.

"Fair enough." I stepped back behind the serving table. "But where do you draw the line?"

Ashton sneered. "What?"

He was waiting on his onions. I had them in my tongs, hovering over the banger in his outstretched hand. "In your view, what constitutes allegiance? Do you have to be paid directly by Niles, or should anyone who benefits from his corruption be marched into the firing line? Should we not walk on new streets if the company constructed them? Not eat food that was carried on their trucks?"

"Don't be stupid. We can't control that."

"Doesn't it just take a little more effort? Some extra diligence on your part?"

Only after I said it did I realize who I sounded like. This was just the kind of thing Hendricks used to ask me; my old mentor's words coming out of my mouth.

"Those things are different."

"How? Aren't you also benefitting from Niles's crimes?"

"Whatever benefits I'm getting, I'm using them to fight back."

"Oh, right. I see the difference." I gave him his onions. His reward. "It's all about whose side you're on."

He didn't approve of the simplification.

"It's about your *actions*," he stressed. "It's about what you *do*."

"And what have you done, exactly?" I was embarrassing him in front of Ophelia and the simmering resentment was as obvious as an Ogre tap-dancing on the roof. "You've made some interesting signs. Slashed the tires of trucks too, right? Real revolutionary stuff."

"I've risked my own safety to slow their operations. We've sent a message to Niles and everyone else that this city won't take his occupation lying down."

"That makes things better, does it? Is there anyone out there whose life has improved because you slowed down some deliveries? Or have you just made a few people's lives harder without bothering Niles at all?"

The argument came easy. I'd made it with myself most nights when I was playing the role of magical investigator, trying to ignore my own guilt by kicking other people in the shins.

"At least I'm doing something," grumbled Ashton.

"You're making yourself feel good, kid. The jury's out on anything beyond that."

He got to his feet.

"You think you're helping anyone here, Fetch Phillips? You're hiding out. Scared to do anything that matters in case you fuck things up. You're the last person who should be questioning us."

He grabbed his bag and waited to see if Ophelia would join him. When she made no sign of moving, he put his meal back on the table and left. We watched him go, and I went back to serving sausages. Inero pointed to the one Ashton had left behind, and I nodded to let him know he could adopt it. Ophelia didn't say anything until a few minutes later when she got up to grab a napkin.

"You should go easier on him."

"Ashton? Come on. I'm just asking some questions. You lot do it to each other all day."

"It's different coming from you."

I scoffed at that. "If he's hoping to make a difference in this city, he needs to be able to hear some feedback without losing his shit. Especially if he's going to criticize someone who just died.

Bath was a misguided simpleton who couldn't think for himself, but he wasn't a real son of a bitch like Derringer."

A Kobold customer was just about to buy a sausage, but she froze halfway to handing me her coins.

"Isaac Derringer was a brave defender of the truth," she said. "How dare you speak ill of him so soon after his death?"

I turned to Ophelia.

"See, she gets it." I turned back. "Personally, I found the old prick's reporting to be biased and manipulative – and the city is a brighter place without him – but maybe that's just me. Onions?"

She dropped the sausage on the ground and walked away. Inero's eyes fell on it.

"Don't even think about it, kid. I'll make you a fresh one."

I put together another freebie for Inero. After he took it, he kept standing there with a puzzled look on his face.

"What is it?"

The words took a while to find their way to his lips.

"Are you saying he deserved to die?"

Inero – as far as I could tell – meant the question in earnest, but his piercing gaze gave me pause.

"Well . . . I don't know if anyone *deserves* to die, but I don't know what we're supposed to do with folks who wake up every morning and ruin other people's lives just to fill their pockets. Derringer knew how easy it was to turn people against each other, and he sold that feeling for two bronze a pop. I'm not saying I woulda killed him myself, but I can see that Whisper – or whoever did it – had a point. Why do you ask?"

He shrugged . . . then froze. He looked terrified. I thought he was staring at me, as if he was so appalled by my answer that he'd become overwhelmed with disgust, until I realized his gaze was going past my shoulder.

Baxter Thatch had arrived: three hundred pounds of marbled muscle tucked into a tailored black suit. Their eyes were glowing embers, and the lamplight from overhead shimmered off their obsidian skin.

"Ah," they said, voice a vat of boiling oil, "this must be the Druid in question."

They dipped their ram-horned head, but Inero backed away in disbelief. It seemed there weren't many Demons out in the Togul. In fact, to the best of my knowledge, Baxter was the only one of their kind in existence.

"Inero, kid, it's all right. Baxter's a friend. They know this city backwards, so I asked them to help you find your feet."

He composed himself with admirable speed.

"Oh, thank you."

Baxter didn't flinch. It was far from the first time they'd been introduced to a gawping, bewildered guest.

"I'd love to hear more of your story," said Baxter. "Shall we step inside?"

"Ignore the police tape," I told them. "It's just ornamental."

Baxter and Inero crossed the threshold of broken glass, and I went back to my serving station. I was looking forward to sinking back into the simple task, but Ophelia had finished her dinner and I could practically hear the thoughts trying to kick their way out of her head.

"You really think Derringer deserved it?"

I sighed. "Pheels, I don't know. I don't think anyone deserves anything. Not objectively."

"You mean you don't believe in an innate rule of right and wrong?"

"Ah, shit. I . . . I don't *think* so. Things change, don't they? There's context."

"In that case, didn't Derringer just do the same thing as everyone else, only more successfully? I mean, what does everyone always say? It's *business*."

"Just because everyone says it, doesn't mean it's right."

"But guys like Niles and Derringer aren't doing anything that different, are they? It's the same racket only on a bigger scale."

"I suppose. But the more powerful you are, the more chance you have to control things. To create real change. The worker who's struggling to feed his family doesn't have as much influence as the boss on the hill."

"Maybe. Or maybe it's harder to see the other options when you're right in the center of it all. Maybe it's only those on the outside who can even imagine how to break things. Maybe it's up to us to show everyone else other ways of being."

"Maybe. But hang on, I thought you hated Derringer most of all."

"I did, but . . . well, where do you draw the line?"

She smiled. *Gotcha*.

"All right, Pheels. Point taken. I don't know if you can divide Bath and Derringer's crimes, and I can't say for sure that either of them deserved it. But I'm not the one who killed them, am I? Maybe Whisper knows something we don't."

"Yeah, maybe." She furrowed her brow. There was some trouble brewing in there, but I wasn't sure what kind. I suppose seeing your dreams of violent revolution play out in real life – even if you're not the one to do it – can take the wind out of your sails. Or maybe she *did* do it. Maybe I was the dumb fool everyone thought I was, and I couldn't see the killer right in front of my face. It had happened before. The thought made my head hurt, so I focused on serving the last of the sausages.

Soon, the trays were empty, and the sun set on the stall. We didn't make much money, but enough to do it again tomorrow while sparing a few coins to buy Inero a more appropriate wardrobe.

I was piling up the utensils when Baxter came back out. The Demon stood on the curb and looked around, as if they were confused.

"Bax . . . you all right?"

They briefly looked at me then looked away again, as if searching for something.

"Ah, yes. Sorry. It's just strange being back here, I suppose. This cafe. It already feels like something from a different time."

Interesting. I often thought of Baxter as being part of the

establishment. Just as committed to "progress" as Niles and Piston. Maybe they were starting to have second thoughts.

"So, how's the kid?" I asked.

"He's no Druid," they said. "Someone gifted him the clothes while he was out on the road."

"Then what is he?"

"Oh, you mean species? I don't know. Mixed background, I think. You know: half Elf, quarter Angel, quarter Human? Something like that. The point is, he's not much to worry about. Just a lost kid looking for somewhere safe."

"He got a spook when he saw you."

Baxter chuckled: a fresh log on a roaring fire.

"Not the first time."

Baxter finally looked at me. Something was off. It took me a few moments to work out what it was.

"Baxter. Your eyes."

"What's wrong with them?"

"They're . . . empty."

There was no other way to say it. Those two roaring fires had gone out.

"Oh, that happens from time to time."

Does it? I'd never seen it before. Every time I'd seen Baxter, their eyes had been two mesmerizing orbs of burning light. Now it was like staring into a twin abyss. If they were that way when Baxter had arrived, I hadn't noticed. Had being back here really affected them that much?

They turned and looked back at the cafe.

"I heard from Georgio."

That shocked me as much as their eyes being snuffed out.

"What? When?"

"A few days ago."

"Really? What did he say? Did he find something?"

"Maybe. I'm going to go find him."

They turned to leave.

"What? You're going *now*?"

"I'm starting to think I've already waited too long."

"But . . . Baxter, wait! What do I do with the kid?"

They laughed. I felt like it was supposed to put me at ease, but it did the exact opposite.

"The kid's got some memory issues. Whatever he's been through, the trauma has messed with his senses. Go easy on him, and he'll come good. I'm sure."

"I thought you'd know where to take him. Isn't there some kind of . . . I don't know . . . *place* for new arrivals if they need assistance? Helping them find work and stuff like that?"

Baxter gestured to the trashed cafe.

"I'd say there's plenty of work to be done here."

They turned, south, and strolled away.

"Baxter! What did Georgio say?!"

They waved without looking back.

What the fuck? First Georgio leaves without telling me where he's going, now Baxter follows? Another old friend off to track down the magic without me?

Though most of me wanted nothing to do with another unsubstantiated rumor of returning magic, I was tempted to run after them. Some part of me would have loved nothing more than to head off on an adventure instead of sliding back into a life of cheap meals and unpaid babysitting. But I only needed to think about the last time I made that mistake to know that I should stay where I was.

I called out to my new ward.

"Hey, Inero. Come here!"

He slunk up beside me.

"What the hell happened in there?"

"Nothing. They asked me some questions and I told them what I could. My memory ain't so great."

I sized him up: nervous, bashful. Not that different to most teenage boys who haven't found their place.

"They say anything helpful?"

"Sure."

The kid must have had a quota on words per day. He doled them out sparingly, like the last chocolates in the box.

"Care to enlighten me?" I asked. "Or . . . woah. Kid, you've sprung a leak."

The kid's nose was bleeding. Dripping down his face onto his ragged robes.

"Oh, I'm fine," he assured me, wiping it with his sleeve. "It does that sometimes."

"Well can it do it somewhere else? Here." I handed him a wad of napkins and his share of the take. "Ophelia, show him where the night market is. Get him a change of clothes, a towel and a blanket. Anything else will have to wait until tomorrow." Ophelia scrunched up her face. "Either that or help me with the dishes. I didn't see you throwing anything in the till."

She stood up, begrudgingly, and looked Inero over. She'd all but ignored his presence so far, perhaps not liking this uninitiated member being welcomed into her domain.

"He does need a wash. All right then. Let's go."

Inero looked back to me, his eyes almost pleading, as if he didn't trust that this wild-haired firecracker would get him back in one piece.

"It's all right. She'll look after you. If she doesn't, she'll have to start paying for her meals."

"Yeah, yeah. Let's go, Inero. And let me do the talking; the vendors will see your naïve little face coming a mile away."

Quiet. Finally. I packed up the tables and scrubbed up the kitchen as best I could. It was still a bomb site, but I'd been able to complete a service. That was something. Satisfying enough to take myself to bed early and get a good night's sleep, in preparation of my date with the irrepressible Tabatha Ratchet.

14

Lamplighter Radio was broadcast from the top-floor apartment of one of the Trilogy Towers. The pillars had once been smokestacks for some short-lived underground mines, but after it became easier to import resources from the north than mine beneath Sunder's foundations – so dangerously close to the subterranean fire pits – the three chimneys were converted into a unique set of apartment blocks. The inner west wasn't the safest part of town to live in, but every room in the circular building came with a view.

I arrived early and loitered outside, staying in the shade until Tabatha made her appearance. After our brief but friendly phone call the night before, I'd been expecting a warm welcome. Tabatha had clearly spent the night rethinking my potential motives, and greeted me with all the cynical suspicion her job required.

"It was Simms who sent you here, right?" she snapped. "Or someone above her? If this is going to be some kind of warning to make me drop the Whisper story, don't bother, because I won't."

She was used to speaking into a microphone that didn't answer back: asking question after question without leaving room for a response.

"Last time we met, *I* asked *you* about Whisper, remember? I'm after answers too."

"But for who? You were buddying up to the detective like you were old pals, so what happens to Whisper if you find out who he is? You're Human, right? You're probably with Niles. You going to track down whoever's talking shit about your boss so you can drag him into a dark room and beat some respect into him?"

"Can you let me answer one goddamn question before asking me three more?" I soon realized it was an effective tactic, because

I coughed up the truth just to stop her speculating. "Derringer tried to hire me to find Whisper but I refused. Now that he's dead, his old employees are threatening to blame the murder on me and some friends of mine."

"*Did* you kill him?"

"No. And I'm pretty sure my friends didn't either. They're just teenagers. Troublesome, but not in the killing business. The *Star* is going to pin Derringer's death on them if I don't come up with a better story, and I have a feeling Whisper is the key."

"Oh, great. So you're going to sell Whisper out to save your skin?"

"I hope it won't come to that. For now, I just need to talk to him. Find out what he's after. I'm sure Whisper won't want a crew of idealistic young rebels getting arrested for his handiwork. That's if he's even responsible. For all we know, he might have done nothing more than write a few paragraphs of inflammatory prose."

"You don't think he killed Derringer and the cop?"

"If he did, I'm hoping he'll make that clear, and possibly reveal his identity at the same time. Then I won't have to do anything. Shit, maybe he's already told us who he is, but it's jumbled up in some other secret message you haven't stumbled on yet."

Tabatha tilted her head one way and then the other, like I was wearing a mask and she was trying to see the man behind it.

"You're not reporting all this back to Simms?"

"No. All I want to do is clear the kids, then I'll walk away."

That seemed to satisfy her. She turned to the door of the cylindrical building and got her keys out of her overalls.

"All right. There's not another announcer here for at least an hour. Barry will have finished the dawn shift and set a record playing for the mid-morning slump. We can hash this out until I take the air." She stopped, looked at me, and raised an eyebrow.

"Fun night, Mr Phillips?"

"Uh . . . what?"

"You've still got lipstick on ya."

My hand shot up to the side of my neck, though I knew there was no wiping away the kiss-shaped burn. It was a memento left by Khay, the wayward Genie, while we were out on the road. Her touch was only supposed to affect magical creatures, and we'd never figured out why her lips marked my Human skin.

"It's not lipstick, it's . . . Never mind."

The spiral staircase in the center of the tower was a claustrophobic nightmare, turning so tightly that my knees were aching halfway up. The spectacle at the top was worth it, though: a whole floor with windows on every side, offerings views over Main Street, Swestum, down to Amber Hill, all the way up to Cecil, and even to those truly terrifying neighborhoods further west.

I was struck by how much the skyline had changed over the last two years. Because I looked out my own Angel door every day, the shift had been gradual, and seemed less dramatic. From here, with the whole cityscape surrounding me, the Niles-effect was plain to see: streets of small cottages replaced by sheet-metal storehouses, widened streets and large billboards, and a variety of automobiles zooming in all directions like caffeinated ants.

The perfect place to watch over a city, questioning the motives of those in charge.

"Nice digs."

The interior was one large space with a small room portioned off by glass. Inside, there was a desk covered in audio equipment including a spinning record player. The muted sounds of a jazz trio – so relaxed they were borderline comatose – bled through to the untidy communal space full of couches, desks and a kitchenette.

"We got it for its height – helps with the range – but the view is one hell of a bonus." She opened her backpack and took out a pile of newspapers and magazines, dumping them on top of an already healthy collection. "I was up all night, reading through every paper put out in the last week, looking to see if I'd missed any messages from Mister Whisper. Now everything looks like a hidden code and I'm finding words that nobody put there. It's run my brain through a blender and I'd love a better plan, if you've got one."

I sat on a low, firm seat. All the options were uncomfortable, but if it was my job to carry the furniture up those stairs, we'd both be sitting on cardboard boxes.

"I don't. But I have a bunch of questions that might lead us somewhere, if you have the patience to answer them."

"Try me."

"All right. How would you get an ad like that in the paper?"

"Didn't you say you were working with the *Star*? Why don't you ask them?"

"Maybe I don't want to give them any ideas before I know where it will lead them."

She liked that. It wasn't going to be an easy process, but I could begin to see a world where she believed we were on the same side.

"Anyone can submit an advertisement to the paper. Just pay a fee and send over the copy."

She picked up a magazine and flipped through it as we talked. She clearly found my line of questioning so pedestrian that she could look for secret messages at the same time.

"The *Star* will have a record of who paid for it?"

"They will. Though I doubt it will help you. Whisper wouldn't have made it that easy for them."

"Probably not." I pulled the copy of the advertisement out of my trouser pocket. The hardest thing about summer was losing all the carrying space that came with a jacket and coat. I smoothed out the clipping and reread the hidden message.

Dead cop attended secret meeting with Sunder leaders.

That had been posted in yesterday's paper, but Bath died two nights before. "Do you have a phone?"

She pointed to it, eyes not leaving her magazine.

"Operator, put me through to the advertising department of the *Sunder Star*."

A few buzzes and clicks, then a long pause before someone said, "*Sunder Star* sales. How can I help you?"

Probably unnecessary, but I made my voice higher and more nasal in case any of my current employers recognized my voice.

"I'd like to place an advertisement please."

"Of course. How many words?" I estimated the word count of the advert in my hand and went with that. "Any images?"

Using Whisper's message as my template, I answered her questions, and watched with satisfaction as Tabatha stopped flipping pages and focused on my side of the conversation.

"Yes, that sounds perfect. Thank you. And could I have that in tomorrow's paper? The morning edition . . . Yes . . . Oh, really? How about the day after? . . . Oh, I had no idea . . . Yes, I suppose that makes sense. How soon could you . . . Oh, that long, huh? . . . Yes, I understand. Well, let me talk to my colleagues and call you back. Thanks for your time."

I hung up, smiling to see that Tabatha had already put it together.

"Whisper didn't get the ad in the paper through usual means."

"Unless he could see the future," I said, looking over the message again. "A dead cop. A secret meeting that may or may not have happened. Is it possible he got lucky?"

"No. I don't think so. Those details are too precise to line up weeks in advance. That means Whisper, or someone connected to him, must have inserted the piece into the paper themselves." She got up and started pacing around the room. "When you first came up to me, outside the dead cop's apartment, you asked me if I thought Whisper was a journalist. I didn't think they needed to be – not to print a newsletter – but now I think he *must* be in the business. More than that, I wonder if Whisper might work for the *Star*."

It seemed likely but raised further questions.

"If he does, and we figured this out, there's a good chance Volta did too. Would Whisper really take such a risk if he does work at the printing press?"

"It *would* make it dreadfully obvious. So, if not someone from the *Star* itself, then perhaps a person who works at another paper; Whisper clearly has a good understanding of how the pieces are put together."

Our eyes returned to the pile between us.

"All right," I said. "Let's make a list of every other periodical currently in print."

"Let's include those that have recently closed, too. Especially if they were pushed out of the market by the growing success of the *Star*."

"Good point. Let's start there, and if nothing fits, I'll turn my attention to the writers inside the *Star* itself."

I seemed to have proved myself for the moment, and Tabatha ordered some take-out so we could keep up our energy while we went about our search.

We worked on both tasks at once: listing writers and editors named on the articles, while scouring recent editions for more secret messages. It was brain-melting stuff, both monotonous and confounding. Soon, I was seeing hidden words in every sentence – all of my own making – reading lines backwards and upside-down, and going cross-eyed in the process. Every M and W in close vicinity had me hoping it was his signature, scrambling for a nearby message, desperate to connect the dots.

Two giant double-ues in the headline "Wedded to Wealth" kept me on a page long enough to notice the photograph. It was Ms Beatrix "Trixie" Derringer stepping out of the huge front doors of her house, cocktail in her hand, to greet two well-dressed guests. The photo was attributed to Owen Ward.

"Ward," I mumbled. "I met that guy."

"At Derringer's? Yeah, that makes sense. His entire job has boiled down to stalking Isaac and Trixie for pictures. I suppose he'll have to survive on half his wage going forward. Though in truth, Isaac was rarely his target."

She went back through a pile of previously examined magazines, pulled a glossy one from the pack, found a colorful double-page spread, and dropped it in front of me. This must have been the same set of photos that Carnegie had been in an uproar about when I'd first visited the estate: Ms Derringer in her private garden, reclining on a sunlounger, her reptilian hair cascading over her shoulders, wearing the bottom half of a bikini and nothing else.

"Stare a little harder, Phillips; there must be a hidden message in there somewhere."

I closed the magazine.

"So, this Ward guy has a fixation on the Derringers?"

"To put it mildly."

I remembered that shorter-than-usual Cyclops with his horrible brown suit. The way he laughed when Carnegie threatened him, like he believed he was untouchable.

"Seems strange that Derringer would let a guy like that keep breathing, especially after what he shared with the world."

Tabatha looked me over, assessing me once more.

"Not as dumb as you look, are you? I've wondered that myself, but you never know what arrangement they've got going on. Maybe that's how rich folk like the Derringers get their kicks."

"I don't know about that. From the way the driver was talking to Ward, the photographs didn't seem consensual."

"Well then, he must be protected somehow. Isaac wasn't one to let anyone walk over him, but Owen is always there, snapping away, selling his pervy pictures to Derringer's competitors." She checked her watch. "I'm needing to get on the air. Feel free to keep reading if you like because this is only a short slot. I'll be done in an hour, and you can show me what you've found. You can bet Urik Volta will be making a list of his own potential Whispers, and anybody on it will be better off if we get to them first."

I stopped her halfway to the booth.

"You journalist types have a funny way of talking, don't you?"

"I have a unique command of language," she corrected. "Which is not a trait shared by as many of my colleagues as they'd like to claim."

"But Whisper's newsletter had a strange style too, right? Does it remind you of anyone?"

"You mean the bad grammar and stunted flow? That's why I first assumed he wasn't from our world. Though I'd be lying if I denied the fact that many a passionate hack has forged a career with a lackluster vocabulary and weak sense of style. Derringer himself was a longways from being a wordsmith, after all. But I like where you're headed. Keep your keen eye out for common phrases and similar mistakes. If he's written before, there might even be the exact same wording in one of those papers somewhere."

She handed me a copy of the original newsletter and sealed herself away behind the glass, leaving me with one more ill-defined link to look for. Was it really worth going through all the same magazines again? I wasn't sure my eyes could handle it.

As Tabatha sat herself behind the desk, and I plonked myself down in front of a week's worth of press, I became even more frustrated with what Derringer and his accomplices had done to this city and its relationship to the news. There were real journalists in this city. People who worked tirelessly to speak the truth and give us the facts we needed to make informed decisions. Writers who had faith that an educated population would steer themselves in the right direction.

How easily their efforts were undermined by cheap headlines that played to our basest instincts. Either you believed the lies the *Star* spread or you tuned out completely, becoming cynical of anything you saw in print. Whichever way you went, the bastards won; the more uninformed and ignorant we were, the easier it was to shape our world without resistance.

They make it so easy to tune out. So frustrating to plug back in. They provoked guilt, anger, fear. Painted a world so complicated that engaging in it felt futile. *Just look away*, they said. *Shut off. It's too confusing. Too exhausting. Even the experts can't handle it. This world is so rough that just getting through the day is an achievement. So get through your day. Look after your own. Look away.*

But for once, I couldn't look away. There was an answer in here somewhere. A way of saving my friends, myself, and helping one of the few good journalists this city had managed to hold on to.

I started by refreshing myself with the original newsletter.

Friends, Rebels and Youngsters,
    Brave Actors, True Hearts,
    I see an afflicted city.
    Doesn't everyone remember reading information not gossip?

You're fucking kidding.

After a whole morning of seeking out hidden words, the message jumped out like it was lit up in lights.

Brave Actors, True Hearts.

Bath.

Not the first word of every line this time, but the first *letter* of every word. A hidden message, right there in Whisper's opening statement. I scrambled for a pen and wrote out the pieces. Some words were clear, while others appeared to be pure nonsense, or not part of the puzzle at all. By the end of the newsletter, my page read:

FRAY
BATH
ISAAC DERRINGER
REDONNADEMOOR
HENRY PISTON
AND THURSTON NILES
HAVE LET SUNDER SUFFER BY CHOICE
THESE TRAITORS MUST DIE

I rapped against the booth and Tabatha looked ready to put a hoof through my chest. To quell the Satyr's anger, I held the newsletter and the message up to the glass.

Her curiosity trumped her temper, and she carried the microphone with her as she came to inspect what I'd done. She was so stumped, her mouth stopped moving mid-sentence: a rare break in the reporter's flow.

I was a kid showing off his homework, thrilled to see that I'd won her approval. She wrapped up the spot, put the record back on, and opened the door.

"Holy shit, Phillips. That was there *from the start*. Six names, two of them already dead. But who or what is Fray?"

"I don't know. And I don't know what these other letters mean either."

"Which ones?"

"Between Derringer and Henry Piston. R, E, D . . ."

"Redonna Demoor?"

"Yeah, those."

"Redonna Demoor."

"*Yes*. It could just be a mistake, or—"

"The Lattician Priestess."

"The what?"

"Redonna Demoor runs the Church of the Lattice."

"Tabatha, I have no idea what you're talking about."

"Blow me down, I'm working with a nincompoop."

"Hey, this nincompoop cracked the code."

"Indeed you did. But if this is Whisper's true plan, and Demoor is next on the list, then you'd better educate yourself if you want to stay ahead of the game."

"You're not coming with?"

"I'm working! And I'll be happy if you stop interrupting my show. Good work, Phillips, but you've got some catching up to do."

She was already pulling the door shut.

"Okay," I blurted, "but how?"

"I think it's time you took yourself to church."

15

Religion has always been other people's business.

As a child, they tried to teach me about Weatherly's vengeful God, but he was wrapped up in a story that was impossible for me to invest in. I'd spent my first couple of years outside the walls and – though I was only an infant – it was enough to know that the stories they told us in Weatherly didn't make sense. There was no room in their Human-centric religion for flying creatures with scaled wings or men with hooves and hairy legs. So, knowing that one of their beliefs was a lie, I assumed the others were too, distrusting their lessons from the start. I adopted some of their *goddamn* vernacular, and internalized plenty of their problematic ideas, but my time inside the walls cemented the idea that faith and I were a bad fit.

After leaving Weatherly and seeing the real world in all its glory, no part of me yearned for a greater sense of meaning. I needed no more answers and my world needed no more magic. After all, I'd spent my whole life dreaming of a more meaningful existence than the one I'd been trapped in, and then I'd escaped into that dream. What else was there to search for? What need of further investigation? The various myths and rituals of Archetellos were wondrous celebrations that I was grateful to witness, but not systems I would dare buy into myself. I was a late arrival to the party and wasn't about to squeeze my way onto the dance floor uninvited. Besides, I lived in Sunder: a godless land that dampened even the most devout believers.

Here, money had long ago taken morality out the back and put a bullet in it. The day-to-day dealings of business trumped any warnings of eternal damnation or rewards after death. We were realists. We were practical. We did what we did to make a buck and weren't supposed to judge anyone who did the same.

So why would anybody pay attention to a Priestess arriving on these dirty streets? And why was she on Whisper's list?

I'm sure Niles, Piston and Derringer had talked together hundreds of times – drinking expensive whiskey and planning how to bend Sunder to their will – but Bath? He was a low-level cop who only took orders. How was he thrown in with these captains of industry? And what did Whisper hope to gain by outing them all?

These traitors must die.

Was Whisper writing these messages to justify his murders? Or was he just hoping to incite the violence while watching it play out from the shadows?

Bath had been killed the same night as the first letter dropped. Coincidence? Surely nobody could have found the secret message and acted on it so quickly. Maybe it all happened at once: Whisper went out into the night, dropped his box of newsletters, and stopped by Bath's apartment to fill him full of lead. One night later, he takes care of Derringer. But what did *Fray* mean? Another name? If the list was in some kind of order, then their name was before Bath's. Did that mean they'd been killed already?

And if it *was* in order, then Redonna Demoor was next.

As I went down Fourth then Grove, I wasn't overly excited about spending my morning crammed into some tiny church, listening to a self-important leader read ancient texts, but as I crossed Riley onto Third – and saw the congregation waiting to enter Credence Textiles Mill – my prospects for an entertaining day greatly increased.

The derelict factory had been transformed into The House of Lattice, and – judging by the size of the crowd – hope and solace were selling like hotcakes.

Back in my Opus days, I'd met spiritual supporters from all across the continent, and witnessed religious services that ranged from the restrained to the barbaric: cities of silent monks, stoically faithful warrior clans and flailing rites of sacrifice. These Lattician constituents were notable only for their apparent normality. Individually, none of them would have stood out on any Sunder street. They wore no obvious iconography or outfits. Nothing to help you pick one out in a crowd. Only crammed together like this, in a united congregation, might you notice the common traits that bound them together.

They all looked like they were off to a job interview: their suits and skirts fresh and tailored, the men clean-shaved, and the women's hair tied back in buns or ponies without a lock out of place. Their make-up wasn't subtle but it was a far cry from the painted faces of the Rose Quarter. Their dark eyes and dulled lips made them look severe and serious, and they stood with a confidence that made me uneasy, like I'd stumbled upon an army that was ready to embark on a war they knew they would win. These weren't the pious worshipers I'd expected to find at Sunder's burgeoning new church. These were just more young professionals cut from the same cloth as the rest of the city's growing middle class. They'd just given themselves a bit of extra polish.

The sound of a gong emanated from within the old mill, and the crowd moved forward, funneling through a sparkling wooden archway that had replaced the old roller door. I moved with them, my tattered shirt and three-day growth standing out against the rest of the pressed-and-laundered pack. They moved with patience and politeness, congenially making room for each other, all wearing calm and welcoming smiles.

We traded the morning heat for the cool of the church, and my mouth fell open in awe.

The last time I'd been there, it was a cobweb-ridden relic, rusted and rotting after being abandoned for years. Now, my brain struggled to believe that I was standing in the same place. Eight marble pillars, threaded with gold, had been erected inside the building. They held up a domed roof of undeniable beauty, painted with a spectacular fresco that filled every inch. It was brightly colored and immaculately detailed, depicting a battle between a godlike feminine being and the colossal creatures of history: Dragons, Giants, Gryphons and Trolls, with Wizards and Lycum filling in the background.

The crowd moved around me, filing onto benches on either side. I found myself a seat, trying to fit this grand monument into my memories of the old mill. Where once there were looms, there were now pews and parishioners. The reams of wool and cotton that had hung from the ceiling were now glowing candelabras. The busted-up foreman's office had been replaced by a mighty stage that held a golden gong, and an ivory stand that cradled a blood-red, three-wick candle. Around the gong, a dozen people in cream-colored suits stood silently, their faces hidden behind white veils. I'd almost forgotten about the white-robed disciples that had been disrupting traffic when Carnegie had first taken me to the Derringers' place, but these were surely the same people just without the bedsheets.

When one of the white suits struck the gong again, an immediate hush filled the room. I sat back on the bench and a creak echoed through the whole place. I felt like I'd already blown my cover as an outsider but, thankfully, the noise was soon overshadowed by the chanting of the people on stage.

It was unintelligible at first, and I wasn't sure if they were speaking in a language I didn't know or if it was a meaningless set of sounds intended to evoke emotion rather than make sense. Nobody in the audience moved, and nobody spoke, until the words coming from the stage became comprehensible and familiar; a stanza from an ancient poem called "The Wayfarers", attributed to Sir William Kingsley.

"The spark will breed the fire, and the fire take the track."

I nearly shot out of my seat as the crowd roared a response, completing the verse in passionate, synchronized enthusiasm.

"We move forward through the mire but we can't go back!"

Silence fell again. There was anticipation in the air. The chanting resumed, low and wordless, and when the chanters parted, a striking figure in white emerged from between them.

The Priestess was a work of art. Her gown consisted of the same cream cloth as those chanting behind her, but it fell from her shoulders in cascading folds, each layer detailed with subtle patterns, sparkling jewels and delicate feathers. She towered over us all, her already impressive height enhanced by platform heels of pale animal hide. Her hair was pulled back in the same severe manner as her followers but crowned with a thin tiara of fine diamonds. Around her neck she wore a thick silver necklace set with a mighty blue stone that matched her eyes.

She moved as if time would wait on her, staring out at the crowd with a frozen look on her face. Not empty, but seeming to contain the deadly pressure of a pot of water that had reached boiling point with all its energy held in by surface tension, ready to explode at the slightest touch.

She waited, and waited. Every follower leaned forward, their faces beaming with adoration and the desire to be seen. The cynic roared inside me, desperate to laugh or scoff or destroy the moment, but I would be lying if I said that I didn't feel I was in the presence of something sacred. Not the Priestess necessarily, nor the beautifully reworked space, but the faith itself. The hope. The wonder. After seven years of staring into the eyes of folks who'd accepted that their best days were behind them, seeing people believe in something good was a miracle in itself.

The Priestess leaned her head over the three-wick candle – her long, straight hair tied safely back – and outstretched her arms. Two of the chanters moved in close, stood either side, and each tossed a handful of something that looked like dried leaves into the flame.

The fire erupted, expanded and lit up the room. We all gasped. The Priestess's head lifted and she took a lungful of the pluming green smoke. She held her breath and we all held ours along with her. Finally, she tilted her face towards the lattice-covered window and exhaled like a Dragon on the attack.

Arms outstretched, her body shook in tremulous spasms, making the smoke dance in the sunbeams. Then she screamed: a wail – halfway between ecstasy and the crescendo of a song – that bounced off the walls of the old factory. This outburst broke the trance that had so perfectly enraptured the audience, and when her body relaxed, so did ours. Her shoulders slackened. Her expression, no longer statuesque, was now warm and welcoming, with a benevolent smile that sat easy on her pale face.

"I see you," she said, and someone beside me whimpered in glee. "I feel you. Beneath and above me, over and through. We grow strong, together, and the future grows strong along with us. Do you see me?"

"We do," said the obedient crowd.

The wafting smoke danced through the diamond-shaped beams of light, making golden shafts above our heads.

"I feel you," she continued. "Unburdened. Buoyed by your belief. Held up by each other. Moving hand in hand towards a life of abundance. Do you feel me?"

"We do."

She stepped to the front of the stage, the light hitting her back and flowing between her fingers as she raised them out towards us.

"I know you. I know your pain and your hope. Your shame and your desire. I know you are here because you are tired of living in the shadows. The shadows of old ideas and old ways. You are tired of living your life at the bottom of a valley, staring up at mountains all around you. Mountains waiting to be scaled." The woman sitting in front of me was nodding. They all were. "You are tired of being told that your life is nothing but the death rattle of a brighter age."

The crowd was vocalizing their agreement now. Sporadic affirmations of "Yes!" and "We are!"

"Tired of your future being painted in darkness. Of your life's meaning being tied to an event in the past. I have relinquished the past. I have freed myself from the legends and the stories that bound me to the old world, and my life has never been more meaningful."

There were jubilant cheers at that one. The man next to me wiped his eyes.

"I have never been happier," she said, smiling. Some of the crowd got to their feet.

"Yes!"

"I have never been more beautiful." There was a wry smile in that one, but not enough to undermine its sincerity.

"Yes!"

"I have never been richer!"

"Yes!"

"I have never been more alive!" Cheers and applause. "Do you know me?"

"WE DO!"

And the crowd was on their feet. Somehow, I found myself on mine, clapping along with the rest of them. I always was susceptible to the will of the mob.

The Priestess called for us to be seated, and the chanting stopped.

"I look around and I see so many success stories. Some already reaching divine luminescence. Others only beginning to flourish." With each sentence, she picked a parishioner out of the crowd and nodded at them, acknowledging their presence. "I recognize many whose journey is only just beginning, the spark inside them waiting to be fanned into a glorious fire."

She continued speaking to her adoring flock, bathed in fingers of golden sunlight. The chanters remained behind her, hidden by their white veils, their bodies perfectly straight.

Except for one.

While the others were facing the Priestess, this one had their head turned towards the audience, facing the exact part of the crowd that I was sitting in. It was impossible to be sure – and I told myself I was being paranoid – but it felt like they were looking right at *me*.

"What does a world want with suffering? Those that feel safe in the shadows will tell you that suffering is noble. That you should go without. That you should abandon hope. Free yourself from desire and be happy in the dark. But what can a poor soul offer that a rich soul cannot? Nothing. What can a rich soul give? They can give shelter. They can give nourishment. They can give hope. They can build a future for those they love!"

As the audience applauded, the chanter who had been looking in my direction stepped out of line. They approached the Priestess and put their mouth to her ear. I held my breath. The interruption was obviously unplanned and felt somehow dangerous.

The Priestess nodded and the chanter returned to their spot, but their head remained cocked to the side, keeping watch. I looked along the pew, but it was full in both directions. There was no way of leaving the church without scrambling over everyone's heads.

But surely – I told myself – whatever was happening had nothing to do with me.

The Priestess continued.

"How many of you here were gifted your first communion by another member of the church? Given your blessing by one whose life had already been raised into the light?" Proud and grateful cheers swelled in response. "And who is ready to pass on that favor? Who among you is willing to reflect that light down on some poor soul still waiting in the dark?"

Less cheers at that one, but still a few. A man in the third row got to his feet. The Priestess recognized him immediately.

"Calamir," she said, the tone of her voice warm and wondrous, "how has your life been illuminated?"

Calamir, whose species was unclear to me, beamed as his leader addressed him. When he spoke, it was with a country twang, at odds with his fresh new suit.

"I sold my failing business and invested with my brother-in-law.

Moved from blacksmithing to building street signs. The ones you might have seen on buildings tops, all lit up and flashing like. We can barely keep up with the work, and I made more money this month than all last year."

More applause. This time, I heard the rabid desperation in some of it: folks eager for this divine stroke of luck to find its way onto them.

The Priestess approached Calamir.

"And you would like to share your success with someone in need? To pay the communion of a soul in waiting?"

"I would."

The Priestess gazed upon him like he was the most generous man who'd ever lived.

"Thank you, Calamir. The light shines within you."

The crowd echoed her words.

"The light shines within you."

Though it had a powerful effect on a new attendee like myself, it wouldn't take many rehearsals to get the performance down. One of those simple rituals that can quickly turn an outsider into one of the flock.

Calamir held up a purse. From the size of it, this communion fee was quite the sum. The Priestess stayed where she was, on the stage, as another of the veiled singers stepped forward to retrieve it from the man in the crowd.

"I know there are many of you who have come seeking communion," continued the Priestess, as the rest of the chanters moved from their positions on stage into the center aisle. "And you will soon get your chance to approach the Mirrors and make your offerings of flesh and gold." She gestured to the chanters – or *Mirrors*, I suppose – as they took their places at the end of each pew, like a barricade against any overeager followers who might decide to leave their seats. The formation was out of step with what I'd seen so far. Such a militarized procedure that I could only imagine one reason for it: they were there to protect her.

Was there really such a risk of an attacker in the crowd? Or had Demoor also cracked the message in Whisper's newsletter and decided to take precautions?

"There are some present here, still in the shadows, who do not yet crave the light. They have become comfortable in the darkness. They feel at home there. Safe. Do you all remember what that was like?" Laughter washed over her as she glided down the aisle. "You once believed that you deserved that life, didn't you? That the light was meant for other, *better* souls. You kept to the dark corners. The alleys. Kept your curtains drawn against the sun. We all understand what that's like, don't we?"

"We do!"

"We don't blame you, do we?"

"We don't!"

She stopped at the end of my pew.

"We want to see you shine, don't we?"

"We do!"

The Lattician Priestess found my eyes before I could look away.

She extended her hand, and every head in the church turned in my direction.

"Stand, you darkened soul, and let us lead you into the light."

16

I've faced horrors unknown to most men. I've committed acts of unfathomable cruelty that will disturb my sleep till my final days. I watched the world end, and witnessed the decrepit monsters that came after.

I should be beyond fear. It should take nothing less than a sledgehammer to weaken my knees. But looking around at all those staring faces, willing me to take the stage, I wanted to wet my pants and run crying home to Mommy.

"Your name?" asked the Priestess.

"Martin," I said, unsure why I'd reverted to my original title. I'd left that name behind in Weatherly but perhaps I was already anticipating the fallout from what the *Star* planned to do to Fetch Phillips. Maybe I was just hoping that whatever was about to happen – and how embarrassing it would be – I could later pretend that it happened to someone else.

"Martin?" she repeated, with a knowing smile that made me shudder. "Come."

What could I do? I wanted to walk out of there. Throw some little quip over my shoulder and let their kooky party go on without me. But I dare you to try it. Have a few hundred eyes on you, all expecting one thing, and see how easy it is to do the opposite. If I'd been able to do that a few years earlier, I might have saved this whole world a lot of trouble. What chance did I have of breaking that habit now?

Besides, could communion really be that bad?

I stood, and the audience cheered. The Priestess led the way back to the stage, and the crowd pushed me towards her with their applause. I took the stairs carefully – I couldn't imagine a worse time to trip – and did my best not to shrink under the gaze of those veiled Mirrors, marching close behind me to prevent a quick escape.

"I can see the light already upon you, Martin. Calamir's gift is guiding your path. Do you feel it?"

The crowd waited.

"Sure," I said.

Some laughter. A few disapproving groans. The Priestess turned to our audience.

"Be patient with our new member. The light may shine upon him, but it takes time, and will, to let it in."

More nods and sounds of agreement. I didn't like being made an example of, but there was nothing left to do but go along with the act until it was over.

"Martin, we were all burdened with the weight of the past. Held down by old horrors, begging us to drag them into a future where they don't belong. They cling to our bodies, to our hearts, hoping that we won't realize they have nothing left to offer. Our future is hobbled while we hold on to relics of history that refuse to be released." She placed a hand on my shoulder. So soft. So full of care. "Communion requires two offerings. Calamir has paid your offering of gold. Now you must make the offering of flesh."

I looked from the Priestess to the Mirrors, to the crowd, and my clunky old heart cranked up a gear.

"What the hell?"

I sensed some frustration from those in the pews. Calamir was surely questioning his investment, but the Priestess was the queen of keeping her cool.

"We are all weighed down by the broken promises of our blood: wings that scrape along the ground instead of cutting through clouds; teeth made to drain what no longer nourishes; scales that harm the flesh they were born to protect. What part of the old world clings to you, Martin? What part of your body keeps you bound to the shadows?"

No fucking way.

That's why the audience looked so strange. Why I couldn't pick the species of so many of them. They were different kinds of magical creatures who had all gone under the knife. They'd cut the wings from their backs and the tips of their ears. Lopped off limbs and extra senses. Sanded down teeth and nails to better fit their once-magic forms into nice new suits.

This wasn't exactly original. Ever since Niles arrived, folks had been working to assimilate into his industrial world. I'd never liked the sound of it, but I'd never expected it to turn into this.

The crowd of streamlined faces waited for my reply.

"I don't have anything like that. I'm . . . I'm Human."

There was silence for a while. Then the Priestess laughed, so everyone else laughed too.

"You think Humans can walk into the future without baggage? That you carry nothing from the past along with you? Are you free from shame, Martin? Are you unburdened by guilt?"

My line was so clear, I might as well have been reading from a script.

"No."

"NO!" she repeated with glee. "Of course not. The question is, where do you keep this shame?"

Oh, fuckety fuck.

Demoor had been leading every step so far, but this time the crowd went first. The audience's eyes all moved to my arm. Some even pointed. The Priestess followed their gaze.

"Ah, it appears you've made it easy for us."

I'd stopped hiding the tattoos a few months ago. Decided to let people wonder, and brushed off their questions with a few rehearsed lines. I'd felt safe. Got careless. But showing off my marks in the back of a kitchen was a long way from explaining them in front of an enraptured crowd.

"What meaning do these relics carry, Martin? What burden does your arm refuse to release from its grip?"

Fucking, fuckety fucksticks.

Publicly picking apart the four rings of ink could be as bad for me as letting Volta put my story in his paper. They told my whole life, from being a Weatherly shut-in to an Opus Shepherd to a Human soldier and a Sheertop prisoner. Mix that with a few known rumors and a bit of common sense, and the tale of my misdeeds would be teased out in no time. I desperately needed to turn the audience's attention anywhere else.

"Here!" I said, and used the offending arm to direct everyone's eyes to the red mark on my neck. Away from my tattoos and towards the burn left by Khay and her unstable Genie powers.

"Martin," chided the Priestess, reading my obvious attempt at deflection, "when pain becomes familiar, we forget that there can be a life without it. It tricks us into seeing it as essential, when in fact . . ." She stopped. She giggled. "Well now, this *is* interesting." She giggled again. All thoughts of my tattooed wrist were forgotten as the crowd became fixated on whatever had so delighted their leader. "I'm not sure if you all can see this . . ."

She guided my body around, and I obeyed, presenting the audience with the lip-shaped burn on the side of my neck. They echoed her giggles, though anyone behind the first two rows would have no idea what they were looking at.

The Priestess rubbed her thumb against it, checking to see if it came off. When it didn't, she giggled again.

"An eternal kiss? When did you have this done?"

I tried to shut up and play dumb, but the urge to explain ourselves is strong, even when we know it will only get us into trouble.

"Didn't happen by choice."

"Oooh. Her lips did this?"

"Yeah."

"A lost love?"

"A friend."

The Priestess cackled and her congregation mimicked her, their laughter ricocheting off the walls and hitting me on all sides.

"Of course! All my friends leave permanent lip-marks on my

neck, too." Let them laugh. Anything to get through this without having my arm amputated and put on display. "So this was an accident, was it? Part of her power?"

"Yes."

"And where is she now?"

"She's . . ."

"She's gone, isn't she?"

"Yes."

"You feel shame, don't you?"

"I do."

"You feel guilt."

"Yes."

"I see it. I see your past dragging you down. Down into the darkness. You know it to be true, don't you?"

"I do."

"Then let me free you, Martin."

A blade appeared. Long and lean, like the kind used to fillet fish. I pulled away, but her hand had the back of my hair and, as soon as I attempted to move, more hands came in to hold me.

The Mirrors.

"It's time to let go, Martin. It's time to let yourself heal. It's time to be happy."

I looked out at all those smiling faces, rapt in manic joy at the sight of my struggle. The knife glinted in the sunlight as it neared my neck.

"Nooo." I tried to escape but the hands held me tight, and a voice, familiar, whispered in my ear. It was one of the Mirrors.

"It's just a little nick. For show. Play along, and this will all be over."

Before I could put a finger on the voice, the Priestess shouted again.

"Martin, I welcome you into the light. Do you hear me?"

God fucking damn.

"I do."

"Do you see me?"

"I do."

The cold metal kissed my sweating skin.

"Do you feel me?"

"I do."

She wrenched my head back and raised the knife above her.

"The spark will breed the fire, and the fire take the track."

The crowd erupted, louder and more passionately than ever before.

"We move forward through the mire but WE CAN'T GO BACK!"

The blade was just about to fall when—

"LIAR!!!!!"

The blade stopped.

The Priestess, for the first time, had an actual expression on her face: that serene mask of omniscience momentarily lost. This was not some rehearsed part of her show, and all the crowd knew it, turning in their seats to see a tall, long-haired, shirtless man on crutches standing in the aisle.

"Lying butcher! Useless tool! Traitor!" A kilt covered the man's hairy, hooved legs. He was the tallest Satyr I'd ever seen. And where were his horns? Why was he having trouble standing? Satyrs had their problems but as far as I knew, the Coda had caused no issues with their legs. "Don't listen to her! She does not believe what she preaches. She breaks your body for her masters. For glory. For gold!"

Demoor hissed at the Mirrors who were holding me tight.

"Take this one out back and get the heathen out of here."

She worked quickly, attempting to take back the room as if the shift in mood had never happened.

"One moment, my child. This poor soul must complete his journey."

Before I knew what was happening, the blade slashed through my skin, flicking blood onto the polished stage. It was only a surface wound – not long or deep – but try telling that to your brain when cold steel passes across your throat. My clammy hands reached for the cut as the Mirrors jumped into action and dragged me towards the back of the stage.

"The light is upon you, Martin! Feel the weight of the old world drip from your veins! And let us welcome our lost soul back from his unfortunate return to the dark. A lesson to all of us that our work is never over."

"You lying bitch! Give me back my legs!"

Legs? But he has legs.

Oh, shit.

The man in the aisle was a fucking Centaur. Cut in half to better fit Sunder's new shape. My heart ached for the Elves who'd trimmed the points off their ears, but this was on a whole other level. No wonder the guy was pissed.

"Ryan, my lost child. I see your pain. The temptation of the darkness has once again taken hold."

The Centaur screamed back, but he was met by a wall of Mirrors, moving him with the same soft, strong hands that pulled me in the opposite direction, through a set of black curtains into the dim backstage. He shouted louder but Demoor spoke over him, reframing his words as the tragic passion of a misguided soul who had merely lost his way. I couldn't see them any more, but the diminishing volume of the Centaur's voice told me the Mirrors had been successful in forcing him out the way he'd come.

I put my fingers to my bleeding neck. Nothing a small bandage couldn't fix.

"Now that that's over, is there a back exit I can slip out of?"

That familiar voice returned to my ear, and put another blade to my already bleeding throat.

"Sorry, Fetch. You're not going anywhere until you talk to the Priestess."

The other Mirrors pulled my arms behind my back and wrapped a rope around my wrists, then I was shoved into a back room where my blood was far from the first to paint the floor.

17

Redonna Demoor, the Lattician Priestess, slapped me awake. She appeared to be as confused as I was.

"Did you knock him out?" she asked the Mirror beside her.

"Nope," he responded (not the one with the familiar voice). "After a while he just fell asleep."

"I'm a good napper."

This crowd was far less responsive than the one I'd had earlier. Despite their bloodlust, some part of me missed the attentive audience.

I was tied to a tall iron chair – wrists, waist, ankles and bloody neck held tight – in a small area that was akin to an actor's dressing room. There was a vanity with a padded leather chair placed in front of it, a coatrack, hat stand and an ice box. The priestess removed her outer-most robe and the Mirror received it with reverence.

I bit down on all the obvious questions I could have asked. *What's this all about? Who do you think you are? Why are you doing this?* Sometimes it's best to shut up and let the person in the driver's seat begin the journey.

"I'm told you're an investigator," she said, removing her gloves.

"Former."

"So why are you here?"

"I'm investigating." I swear, with an audience that would have killed. "Which one of your minions recognized me?"

"She's performing a communion right now, but she'll join us when she's done. Did he have any weapons?" The Mirror shook his head. "Nothing that could be . . . you know?"

I didn't know what she meant but the Mirror had no problem understanding.

"Can't know for sure," he said. "But I don't think so."

"All right." She removed her tiara and her platforms. She was still striking – jet black hair, flawless pale skin, high cheek-bones and a painted cupids bow of a mouth – but she'd shed her dramatic majesty and looked more like someone you could pass on the street without walking into oncoming traffic. "How did you plan to do it?"

"Do what?"

She slapped me. One of those real mean ones that cuts your cheek on your teeth and makes your ears ring. The good mood my nap had given me vanished without a trace.

"How were you going to do it?"

I grunted. I knew this game but I preferred it when the roles were reversed.

"Whatever I say, you're gonna hit me anyway, so just go ahead and—"

She slapped me again, on the other side. At least my eardrums had harmonized.

"We saw your little warning."

"What warning?"

"The newsletter."

"Oh, yeah. That's why I'm here. I make obvious death threats then walk in the front door. Criminal genius, I am. Haven't you got one more slap for me? Rule of threes."

She did. Despite the pain, I felt better for completing the cycle. She pulled out the curved knife that still had my blood on the blade.

"A hidden anarchist threatens to kill me." She ran the tip of the knife along my tattooed forearm. "Then a Human soldier with a criminal history enters my doors, clearly not interested in what we have to offer."

"I'm not Whisper."

"Of course not. I'm told you're more of a follower anyway. That you like taking orders from powerful men. Maybe that's why you've decided to do Whisper's dirty work. But you have no weapons, so were you just here to scout? Observe a sermon and report back like an obedient little puppy."

"Lady, I'm looking for Whisper."

"I am Redonna Demoor, the Lattician Priestess. Do not call me *lady*."

"I thought the show was over."

"Just because we celebrate our faith with ritual and vibrancy, do not dismiss our church as lacking in substance. I commune with the spirit of Veshra, the third Riverweaver, and together we will free the creatures of today from the burdens of history."

Oh, great. I was more relaxed when I thought I was speaking to a charlatan, not a woman who got high on her own lies.

"No need to repeat yourself," I said. "I heard your sermon." She gave me another slap. "Great. Now you've started the routine all over again. Twice more or I won't be able to sleep tonight."

It was satisfying to watch her struggle with the desire to slap me but not wanting to do what I'd asked. She was forced to move past it and return to her ridiculous line of questioning.

"I'm told you're a believer in the Ravvivando."

"Listen, your lordship, I don't know where you get your info but I barely believe in myself, let alone . . . whatever the hell you just said."

"The Ravvivando is the false belief that the great river can be revived, returning us all to the glory of the past."

She'd finally landed on something I could reasonably be accused of.

"Sure, I took a few shots at turning back the clock."

I didn't tell her that since my attempts to bring the magic back, a few unfortunate experiences had damaged my optimism. Like visiting the Wizard City of Incava where the sacred river itself was being mined for its power. It was common knowledge that the river froze up because Humans infiltrated it with their machinery. Interrupted the flow and attempted to steal its power. If that first intrusion was enough to freeze the soul of the world, then the fact that Wizards had been hacking it into pieces – and using those pieces to power their clay servants – was all the evidence I needed that we were never going back. The magical age was over, and we were all walking hand-in-hand into the dark.

But sure, lady. Whatever you say.

She put a palm on my cheek.

"You still believe it would be the best option, don't you? You still hope?"

She was setting me up, sure, but maybe some easy answers would move this along.

"Who wouldn't?"

She closed the trap with one of her all-knowing smiles. When somebody really wants to tell you something, sometimes the best thing you can do is serve them the open door they're looking for.

"You're a Human."

"Guilty as charged."

"You're from Sunder."

She was on a roll. No need to slow her down with silly things like facts.

"Sure."

"You think you've seen magic, but all you witnessed was the pre-packaged version of what magic once was. The domesticated descendant of true divine power. By the time you put your feet on this planet, the age of magic was already over."

"I remember life before the Coda."

"The Coda was the last beat of a song that had been winding down for eons. By design, of course." She leaned forward as she said that. Waiting.

"You want me to say 'designed by who', don't you?" She gritted her teeth. "Sorry, I know you're used to telling this story to your gaggle of groupies, so I'll do my best to play the part." I adopted an overly awed tone of voice. "Designed by *who*?" She went to slap me, then stopped. The routine had finally got old and she looked properly frustrated now: even more put out than when that severed

Centaur had kicked up a stink during her stage show. She searched for solace in a familiar story.

"There has always been a sentient force inside the river. The first was the creator. The second was Eshree, the dreamer: youthful, indulgent and idealistic. Her influence created the Age of Almighty, which gave birth to the most glorious of the magical beasts. For a thousand years, the world was overrun by those creations, as majestic as they were destructive." I thought of the domed fresco on the church ceiling: Unicorns, Dragons and Trolls being pushed back by a godlike figure.

"Some individual mind inside the sacred river?" I scoffed. "Telling it what to do and how to bestow power? Who the hell deserves to wield that kind of influence?"

"Perhaps nobody. Not for long, anyway. Even the designs of pure-hearted Eshree caused chaos. So, it was *Vethra* who usurped Eshree's position and brought about a calmer age. An age where the smaller creatures of Archetellos were safe to claim their stake in this world. The Riverweavers who came after Vethra have learned from her example, tempering the power of the great river so that those of us on the surface are not overwhelmed by its majesty. Some say, over time, the Riverweavers went too far."

"You think that's what caused the Coda? Magical forces turning the power down a few notches? I know some Human soldiers who'd be soothed by that story and the opportunity to shift the blame."

She moved the knife under my chin and used it to pull my face in line with hers.

"I'm sure you do. I, like Vethra, understand the importance of balance. Of celebrating the bounty that the great river gives us without being seduced by its potential. The decision to temper that power was made by a far greater being than I."

"A being you talk to, right? Anyone else corroborating your little chats?"

She ignored the question, too busy getting off on her own bullshit.

"The Riverweavers decided to end the age of magic for good. Now, I have been called upon to make their message clear. To alleviate the pain of any magical creature in Sunder who is stuck mourning for what was lost. Seduced by you, and others like you, who remain invested in the dream of Ravvivando. I am here to teach them how to move on. How to be free."

"By cutting the magical elements off their bodies? Bit of a drastic way to show their faith, don't you think?"

Redonna Demoor moved behind me, out of sight, running her blade across my tattooed forearm.

"Surely you understand how even symbolic gestures have a tangible effect on our lives. Look how desperately you hold on to mementos of the past that are only skin deep. Though they carry no weight, do they not still cause pain? I offer an opportunity to ease that pain. Communion is the pact my followers must make to themselves before they can begin looking forward."

I wasn't convinced – for a lot of reasons – but pressing her with an opposing point of view wouldn't work out well for me, so I pretended that I was ready to play ball.

"I get it. Kind of. You're right that I don't know what they're going through. I never will. That's why I decided to keep myself out of it. Why I quit sticking my nose into places it wasn't welcome."

"Then why are you here? Why are you chasing Whisper, and why did you come to my church?"

Look tired, Fetch. Make her think there's no fight left in you and that you've got nothing to offer up but the truth. Use the real truth but make it the kind she wants to hear.

"I'm being blackmailed. Because of those old magic-hunting days you're talking about. I just want to work in my cafe, make my orders and keep my head down, but if I don't find Mister Whisper then the *Sunder Star* is going to ruin the last bit of life I have left."

She sat back in her seat. My answer seemed to have softened her, a little.

"You're working for the *Star*?" she said, finally interested in something I had to say.

"Against my will."

She nodded to herself. "Derringer was named in the letters too."

"Yeah. You cracked the code, right?" She scoffed at that, as if it had been no great feat to find the names in Whisper's newsletter. That disappointed me, as I was still feeling proud of my achievement.

"There were several names on that list," she said, cagey. "I have no idea what they're supposed to mean."

My brain knew not to say anything further, but it didn't get the message to my mouth in time.

"So, were you and Derringer in cahoots?"

There was that mask again. The frozen visage of divine wisdom.

"I commune with eternal spirits, Mr Phillips. The secrets of small men hold no interest." I nodded, as if that made any kind of fucking sense at all.

"Then how about you let this small man get back to work? I'll make sure I don't disturb you again."

A strange look came over her face. A shift from the all-knowing superiority to something more inquisitive. She closed her eyes, like she was listening for something.

"*Human*," she said, as if the word itself was confusing her.

She moved to the vanity and plucked up a small three-wicked candle: a handheld version of the one she'd used on stage. Her long fingers flicked open the lid of a tiny, decorative tin, and plucked a pinch of some kind of herb from it. This was just like the ritual she'd performed in front of the crowd, but less flamboyant. She dropped the herbs onto the flame and, as they flared with light and smoke, she closed her eyes. Even without an audience, she imbued the act with the same holy reverence.

The Priestess breathed in deep, sucking the fumes out of the air. The subsequent shuddering was more contained and less performative than it had been on stage, but all the more unsettling for its intimacy. She exhaled the smoke out of her nose and stared into me with giant pupils.

"Are you so sure about yourself?" she asked, as she placed a hand around my throat, rubbing the bloody mark she'd made with her knife. "I feel . . . something."

I don't go to doctors unless I'm about to die, but back in my soldiering days they used to force full-body examinations on us. I'd always hated it. This felt the same, but somehow more invasive. She moved the flesh of my face around, pulling down my cheeks to inspect the whites of my eyes, and smearing blood over my chin and lips as her doped-up senses searched for something other than standard Human elements within my sub-standard Human body.

"What's wrong with you?" she asked.

"You know, for the amount of times I've been asked that question, you'd think I'd have a good answer. But I can't tell you, lady. Maybe a sniff of your magic dust would help me out. Looks like a hoot."

There was a knock at the door.

"Enter," called the Priestess, removing her hand and her equally suffocating stare. The Mirror who entered had blood splattered on her gown and gloves. "You've completed your communions?"

"For the day." It was the one with that familiar voice. I almost had it: feminine, tough, with a hint of an out-of-town accent.

"I think I've learned everything I can from your friend," replied the Priestess, turning back to me. "No need to take things further."

"Good." The Mirror pulled off her veil with bloody fingers. "Because I'm exhausted."

"Dr Exina." I sounded excited to see her, but I was just glad to put a voice to the name. "Well, this finally makes some fucking sense."

The doctor was one half of Sunder City's famous duo of Succubae surgeons. Exina had put a couple of my friends under the knife, back when she worked at an underground augmentation service that specialized in body modifications. When they moved their business above ground, I was disappointed to see them specialize in jobs like this: tapering ex-magical bodies to fit them into this less-magical world. The church was an unexpected change of scenery. Exina's skills would be priceless to Demoor's operation, but her old surgery had been in such high demand that I wasn't sure why she would have left it behind. "Dr Loq under one of those veils too?"

Exina didn't flinch, but even that was telling.

"No. Loq is not part of the priesthood."

Ah. I'd uncovered a weak spot, but until the rope around my body had been untied, it would be best to avoid pressing on it. I bit my tongue and let the Priestess speak next.

"I will let you leave, Mr Phillips, on the condition that you deliver any information on Whisper back to me before it ends up in the *Star*."

I nodded, and the joy of being set free made me speak without thinking.

"Apparently I get paid in blackmail these days. What are you going to offer?"

No laughs from the stone-faced ladies.

"If you find Whisper and don't come to me first," said Redonna, "I'll turn your body into replacement pieces for my new followers. Deal?"

I was ready to agree to anything as long as it got me out of there. Even promising yet another person that I'd give them Whisper first.

"Deal."

Exina pushed me out the back door with nothing for my troubles but five rings of rope burn, and a plaster on my neck, dumping a blood-soaked cloth bag in the trash beside me.

"What the hell's in there?" I asked, before she could close the door.

"Remnants."

"You mean the offcuts? Ears and tails and shit? You're just throwing that away?"

Back at the surgery, Exina and Loq used to save every scrap. They'd take something off one client and keep it on ice to add to the next. Every toenail, tooth and patch of fur was treasured. I couldn't believe it.

Exina rolled her eyes.

"Did you not hear a word in there, Fetch? That's the whole point of this place. Learning how to let go."

The door slammed shut.

What a roaring success that had been. I now had three unwanted clients pressuring me to solve the Whisper case, all expecting me to bring them the news first. Would it even matter who I told? They were probably talking to each other anyway – Trixie Derringer, Urik Volta and Redonna Demoor – and if I managed to hand over Whisper's identity to any of them, there was a good chance that we'd both take a trip into oblivion before either of us could spread any more inconvenient stories.

I hoped to stall them until Whisper made his next move, but how much longer could I get away with that? And what was the ideal outcome? Volta printing his article or Whisper's being thrown to the wolves? I couldn't assess that until I knew what he had planned.

Redonna had cracked Whisper's message. She was expecting him. Scared of him. Were Piston and Niles preparing themselves the same way? Paranoid of being taken out like Bath and Derringer?

Bath and Derringer. You couldn't have found two men more opposite. Whisper had targeted a lowly constable and the most powerful media mogul on the continent. If this was all about sending a message, then what kind of message was that?

I turned from Fourth onto Main Street, grabbed a bag of ice from the corner store – hot coffee would be too much to take in the midday heat – and went back to the cafe to find Inero gripping a stale bread roll like it was a king's ransom. He froze when he saw me, except for his jaw that kept on chewing, perhaps worried that I was going to scold him before he swallowed.

"At least let me put something on it," I said. "My kitchen may be shot to shit, but the place still has standards." I set a pot of coffee boiling and searched through the mess for a jar of unspoiled preserve. "Nice outfit, but aren't you hot?"

He was out of his secondhand Druid suit, but his new attire was just as unseasonal: dark trousers, long-sleeved black sweater, black boots, and even some black woolen gloves.

"I'm fine."

I went to argue but thought better of it. The kid could feel the temperature. If he was comfortable, who was I to tell him he wasn't?

"How's your room working out?"

He nodded. "Fine."

"Not much of a talker, are ya?"

"No."

"Fine by me. Too many chatterboxes come by as it is."

He nodded again.

"The floor's a bit hard."

"Yeah. Shit. Sorry. We'll use some of tonight's profits to—"

Footsteps came fast across the street.

"Fetch!" Ophelia's sweaty face came through the broken window. "Fetch! They found us fucking with a billboard and chased us out west."

"Who did?"

"Niles's guys, but they're not the problem now. We tried to lose the suits down some winding streets and we thought we'd got away but then . . . then Ashton disappeared."

I got that cold feeling down my spine.

"Winding streets out west?"

"Yeah."

"Not the ones with coal-black cobbles, so narrow you can't extend both arms all the way out?"

"That's them. Why?"

I turned off the heat, grabbed a tenderizer and my largest kitchen knife, and went straight through the dining room and onto the street.

"For fuck's sake, Ophelia. Didn't anyone ever tell you not to go near The Snatch?"

18

I stopped on West Fourth and used the phone booth to call Richie. Told him where we were going.

"Are you fucking mad?"

"I'd call the cops, but—"

"Even cops don't go down The Snatch."

"Exactly. You have any insights? Any tips?"

"Yeah. DON'T!"

"Not an option. One of the kids got lost in there."

"One of the mad ones from the cafe? Shit. Well, just wait. We'll get a group together, go in with at least a dozen of us or—"

"No time. It's already been half an hour."

"Fetch! Just—"

I hung up.

"Pheels, follow me out west and show me exactly where he went missing. And—" Inero was standing behind her, looking just as nervous as always. "What do you want, kid?"

"I . . . is someone in trouble? Do you need help?"

I didn't know what we were getting ourselves into so I couldn't flat out reject an offer of assistance.

"All right, both of you stay close. I'm cutting through the city and I'm not looking back, so keep up."

Every turn we took was one I wouldn't recommend. West, through the back alleys of the Rose Quarter, across the Kirra, and – to avoid pushing through pedestrians – down a risky shortcut between April Ave, Ebony and Vine. I could still hear the kids close on my heels, so we followed Seventh until it got murdered by Wistwill Street, then took a path best avoided beside the old city walls, through Brandy to Bard, over the

Fearling Bridge, where Ophelia and Ashton's work was waiting in all its glory.

Derringer Deserved It. Do You?

"Real fucking subtle, Ophelia."

It was one of the *Star*'s own billboards, bolted to the top of a liquor store. The message was scrawled in black paint, the remainder of which had fallen from the rooftop and exploded on the sidewalk. Judging from the empty footprints in the splatter, it looked like someone had been standing right beneath them when the pot was dropped.

Stupid, unthinking idiots. With my ramshackle heart kicking its way up my throat, it was so tempting to just stop. To let the little bastard meet his fate on his own. Either learn a lesson or cease being a problem. All I had to do was stop running.

But I couldn't. For all his infuriating, juvenile belief in his own bullshit, the kid didn't deserve to be diced into bite-size pieces. Besides, I knew I was too harsh on the fucker. The poor kid had the misfortune of reminding me of myself, and there was no face I like swatting better than my own.

"Fetch!" came Ophelia's harsh whisper. She pointed to the neighboring street where the police were still gathered. They hadn't seen us yet, so we resumed our run, taking an irresponsible right turn from Wyvern to the wrong end of Ryland, where we ended up at the near-suicidal intersection of Teeter and Ike. Finally, we were standing at one of several entrances to Sunder's most fiendish neighborhood.

"Do you remember the path you went down?" I asked Ophelia. "Was this it?"

"I . . . I don't know. They all look the same."

It was one of the oldest parts of town, built to house workers in the first boom. When the city expanded, it was converted into cheap apartments, and quickly became a place where shady dealings were done out of sight. It was already a dangerous area back then, but after the Coda, even the most hardened crooks learned to stay away.

It really was the perfect set of streets to get snatched in. A maze of identical-looking laneways so narrow that you were always in reach of one of the countless black doors, with no room to back away if one of them unexpectedly opened.

I'd heard that warning but nothing else. No sense of what lay down the spiraling snickets other than rumors of black-market slavers and organ harvesters. There was a chance it was all spin – many corners of the world preserved their secrecy by spreading terrifying stories – but if the rumors were false, then why had Ashton gone missing?

"Stay here," I said. Ophelia wasn't having it.

"I'm coming."

I turned, brandishing my utensils more menacingly than I'd intended. Inero was a few paces behind, happy to heed my warning, but Ophelia attempted to step past. I grabbed her collar.

"I'm not losing you to this place too. Wait here. I'll call out if it's safe."

I stepped into the claustrophobic alley without giving her a chance to argue. Richie was right: we needed a dozen armed fighters and a coordinated plan of attack to do this safely. But if Ashton had been taken, I couldn't just wait to see if his body washed up in the Kirra minus a few key organs.

The narrow alley caught the summer breeze and intensified it, forcing a Dragon's breath of hot air against my back. The houses were only two stories high, but they loomed overhead, threatening to close in completely and swallow me whole.

I approached the first door like it was a jack-in-the-box wound to popping point. There was no way to keep my distance: for every door on the left, there was an identical door on the right, and each pair was barely an arm's length apart. Once you passed the first duo, you were in snatching range until you got out the other side.

Surely this was only a story. An urban legend, made up by kids who wanted to scare their friends. Right?

I tucked the tenderizer into my belt and pulled on the wooden frame of the first door. It wouldn't budge. I couldn't even see the hinges. A false door, maybe? Or just boarded up from the inside and abandoned?

Keeping my footsteps quiet, I examined the door opposite. They both looked the same. I moved along and examined the next pair, wondering which one – if any – might be able to open. No hinges, no knockers, no knobs, no locks. I approached the curve in the alley and peered around.

Had the street become even narrower? Or was I already getting paranoid?

Knock, knock, knock.

I spun.

Ophelia was a few doors behind me.

"I told you to wait!"

"I can't. We need to find him."

I didn't want to waste time arguing – and I did feel safer for the company – but I wasn't going to be responsible for her getting lost down here too.

"Go back. And stop making noise."

She was pale, shaking her head.

"That wasn't me."

What?

"You didn't knock?"

"No. They were doing that before. When I lost Ashton."

I'd be lying if I said I didn't seriously consider running for my life. Ashton had been a thorn in my side since we'd met, and I had no idea what kind of mess I was trying to pull him out of. I needed more allies. I needed more information. I needed better weapons and younger bones and a smarter brain in my skull, but every second we waited only increased the chance that we'd never see him again.

Knock, knock.

I was standing between two more doors, directly opposite each other. There was still no sign of how they would open, but there were scuffs on the cobbles at my feet, suggesting that there might be a way inside if you only knew the secret. I took the tenderizer out of my belt and tapped twice against the door on the left. No response. It was like playing hide-and-seek but instead of a gleeful toddler smothering their giggles, I was likely searching for a stone-cold assailant who wanted to stick a knife in my guts.

Ophelia stepped towards me, just as a sound rang out from the door on the right.

Knock, knock!

I turned towards the sound, raised the knife, and pushed Ophelia behind me to protect her . . . only to immediately feel her body lose contact with mine.

When I looked back, the door on the left was not only open, but full of dirty hands that had already swallowed Ophelia up. I dropped my weapons and reached out to grab her, but her feet flew from my grasp, over the threshold, and disappeared behind wriggling fingers. The door, which had opened inwards, slammed back onto my hands with brutal force, sending shockwaves up my arms. Beneath my screams of frustration and pain, I heard a mechanism fall into place.

All sense left me. I shouldered the panel and kicked it repeatedly, but the lock wasn't going to give in for anything less than a battering ram.

Fine.

I got my fingers behind the top lip of the doorframe and pulled. There was a tiny bit of movement. Not much, but compared to the rock-solid wall I felt when I pushed against it, this was practically an open invitation.

I held on tight, lifted my legs from the floor to the wall, and leveraged all my weight against the wooden panel. There was the grating sound of wood sliding against metal, and the door shifted half an inch. That was more encouragement than I could have asked for, so I dug in deep, pushed with every muscle I had, and pried the doorframe back until it snapped away and dropped me onto the ground.

It was open! I stumbled to my feet – unsteady but triumphant – before an avalanche of sand hit me square in the face.

I fell back, onto the ground, beneath a suffocating waterfall that never seemed to end. Of course the door was booby-trapped: ready for any overeager visitor who attempted to enter uninvited. I tried to stand but my legs were stuck, and the pile grew heavier on my flattened body. When I rolled to the side, the sand moved with me, and my face was forced down into the darkness. Without air – and my senses fleeing with my wits – every movement made me more unstable. Lost in the expanding pit, I screamed a mouthful of dirt, knowing it would do nothing.

Then I felt a hand on mine.

It was too weak to yank me free, but strong enough to tell me where to go and which way to push. I scooped the sand away with my other arm, kicking with my feet against the occasional gift of solid ground. Finally, in a burst of sunlight and beautiful clean air, Inero appeared before me.

I coughed and spat and groaned, feeling grit beneath my eyelids and all down my throat, hacking up mud pies and snorting out sandstorms.

"Thanks," I managed, eventually, struggling to get off of all fours. My redheaded ward stayed silent, looking warily at the next set of doors that surrounded us. "It's all right. They probably don't all—"

Knock, knock.

We looked at the door on the left. Inero instinctively jumped back from it, straight into the pair of arms that protruded from the door on the right. The doors slammed shut before I got to my feet.

I was alone. Again.

Shit, shit, shit.

My heart was rattling like sleigh bells in a blender. I went deeper into The Snatch, not knowing what would be worse: getting taken at the next doorway or finding no other way to follow them.

It was too silent now. No knocking. The kidnappers had got what they'd wanted and shut up shop. Kitchen closed. I kept going – anything other than standing still – and the street cork-screwed around on itself. The slash of blue sky above was whittled down to nothing, the roofs leaning in like diners who'd just been served their next course. The only sounds were my footsteps and my breath.

I longed for something to happen. Prayed that nothing would. Then—

Knock, knock!

Finally. The sound came from my right and, for the first time ever, I'd learned a lesson fast enough to act on it. I turned to my left and swung the kitchen knife towards the opening door.

I had no time to aim but my attacker had no time to react. They launched forward with such force that their momentum was more responsible for the success of my attack than I was.

The blade went through their shoulder. They screamed and spasmed. I lost control of the knife but grabbed a handful of the creature's hair, determined not to let the snatcher go back into the doorway without me.

The bastard stunk. I had no idea what species it was: humanoid in shape but gray-skinned, short and feral. The hair in my fist was matted and caked with dirt, and a foaming mouth full of broken teeth snapped at my arm.

The doors had opened inward, down the middle, and they started slamming open and closed on the creature's abdomen, surely causing it just as much pain as the knife. Whoever was controlling the mechanism was less concerned with their friend's safety than doing whatever they could to keep me out.

The next time they opened all the way, I pushed the squealing creature inside and continued on with him. The wood slammed on my shoulders but it was too late. We fell forward, through the closing gap, and when the doors finally snapped all the way shut, I was on my knees inside the dusty hideout.

It reeked. Not just the usual festering decay of an inner-city squat – though that was there too – but a burnt metal smell more akin to a Dwarven forge or the gunpowder room in Niles's weapon factory. The way I'd entered was now sealed tight, but enough light shone through holes overhead that I could find my footing around the detritus.

It had been an apartment block, once. Most of the interior walls, floors and ceilings had been knocked down, turning the whole neighborhood into a single collective nightmare. The supporting beams remained, indicating where the divisions had once been, but anything related to healthy, domestic living was long gone.

Despite the heat, everything was wet and stinking like a swamp. Muggy, as if the rain got in a decade ago and it hadn't been dry since. I squinted into the shadows and saw a pile of rags that looked like they'd been shaped into some kind of nest. There were the scattered remains of rusted weapons, rigging above the doors – surely the triggers for the troublesome sand traps – and plenty more of those snarling, mangled creatures.

The one with my knife in his shoulder was too distracted by his injuries to cause any more trouble, but the one who'd been controlling the mechanism made his move. He was small but fast, and scampered up my body before I could get away. His claws dug into my shoulder and back, irregular teeth snapping at my neck and arms. The claws hurt more than the bites did, but it was a close-run race. I flailed with the tenderizer, smacking its body, but anything that could exist in that kind of squalor wouldn't be worried by a couple of bruises. Only when I managed to get a good hit on the back of its head did the biting finally end, and the creature collapsed with an unsettling stillness.

The shadows howled. More monsters, but also something else. "FETCH!"

I turned towards Ophelia's scream. There was movement, down

in the darkness. The inside of the building seemed to have no correlation to the streets beyond. With no interior walls to guide me, it was one single horrific void with no escape. I focused on her voice and let it lead the way.

The darkness came alive. Two more creatures sprang at me, fierce and fast but thankfully not strong. They were only three feet tall, and their limbs were as thin as broomsticks. I kicked the first one in the chest to keep him away but the other one sunk his teeth into my side. I came down hard with the tenderizer and heard the crunch of broken bone. The first one didn't stop to acknowledge his fallen friend, just came at me again, teeth and claws vying for a piece of my flesh.

My swing was sloppy, and I hit his head with my forearm instead of my weapon. When I reached again and missed, the bastard scurried up my back and sunk his teeth into the top of my ear.

It was my turn to howl. The biter shook his head like a dog trying to win a game of tug-of-war. His teeth were too blunt to take a piece out of me, but I could hear my cartilage being crushed between his jaws.

I dropped the tenderizer and grabbed him with both hands, sinking my fingers into any vulnerable places I could find. I found something that was either an eye or an existing wound, gouged the tender flesh until the teeth let go, then pummeled his face until the body beneath it went limp.

Remorse would come later if it came at all. I found my iron mallet and marched off in Ophelia's direction. More little bastards came at me but there was no coordination to their attack, and when one made a solo effort, I had no problem discouraging it with a blow to the head.

What the fuck are these things? I wondered, when a shadow jumped from the darkness, hit me with all its weight, and pinned me to the floor. The figure had the same gray skin, same deranged and vacant eyes and same busted teeth as the little critters, but it was so much bigger.

It gnashed at my face and neck. I couldn't get any good punches in, so I grabbed two handfuls of rotten cloth from around its chest and shoved upwards, pushing the snarling face into a dusty beam of light.

Bloodshot green eyes stared back. Full of hatred, devoid of sense. Pointed ears poked out from its filth-filled hair, and there was something familiar about the shape of the beast, like an old neighbor was trapped beneath the creature's peeling skin.

Then a realization that couldn't be true.

Fae.

Impossible. No Fae had survived the Coda. Every sub-species was like a living extension of the sacred river. Too full of magic. Too pure. In the first days of the aftermath, every Fae creature became a petrified piece of wood or stone. Since then, none of them, anywhere, had returned.

Except somehow, this one had. This Fae had survived, and it really wanted to kill me.

I got my legs to his stomach and kicked him away. It did nothing to deter the anger or hunger that was driving him, but my desire to treat his head like a slab of cheap steak had been greatly reduced. How could I hurt him? This was a miracle. But – like every miracle I'd seen in the last seven years – this one had brought a boatload of curses along with it.

He launched at me again, but I was ready for him. I took hold of his tattered jacket, pivoted, and let his momentum carry him forward. There was a ripping sound as he fell away from me, stumbled into the next room, and tripped over one of the smaller, fallen creatures I'd already dispatched.

I was left holding a piece of his clothing. Rough in my fingers, it didn't feel like fabric. I rolled the material around and felt the many links. Chainmail? But such fine metalwork. So fragile. I held the material up to a dusty strip of sunlight: beneath the rust and dirt was some kind of dark metal with the faintest glint of shimmering green.

Adamantine.

The Fae-made alloy had been created as a response to the Human race's iron weapons. The iron-proof armor had been worn by many Faerie warriors throughout history, but in the era just before the Coda – when every species was attempting to put the days of bloody battlefields behind us – the material had become firmly associated with one specific collection of Fae. Not a sub-species, but a Fae military group dedicated to fighting back against Human invaders.

Gremlins.

That's why these Fae were still alive. Gremlins were Faeries who had used magic to protect themselves from the debilitating effects of iron. By subjecting themselves to a ritual that dulled their magical connection, these warriors gained resilience against Human-made weapons.

Gremlins were any Fae – Sprites, Boggarts, Imps, whatever – who had dedicated their lives to fighting Humans. Their operations were often covert and focused on turning our own weapons of war against us. Though there had been no public war between Humans and Fae in my lifetime, the animosity was always bubbling underneath, so I wasn't surprised to discover that there had been Gremlins in the shadows of Sunder, keeping tabs on the fire city for their leaders in the Farra Glades.

The ritual had spared these Gremlins a death sentence, but at what cost? They'd spent seven whole years in the dark, too scared to show themselves, and doing . . . what?

Sabotage.

Gumption and Reeves had claimed that the new firefighters were hired to fight back against people who were messing with the means of production. I'd thought it might just be young rebels like Ophelia and Ashton, but it turns out those kids weren't the only ones loosening the screws on Niles's plans for the city.

The dark Fae warrior got to his feet. One of his arms had become dislocated in the fall and it swung useless at his side, though the injury had done nothing to quell his fury.

"Please," I said. "I don't want to hurt you. I just want to find my friends."

Though he heard the words – perhaps even understood their meaning – nothing changed on his vacant face. As he took a slow step towards me, I realized that this creature had once been a Boggart: one of the thin, Human-sized, bat-eared Faeries who called the Farra Glades their home. Ruthless protectors of nature, a Boggart Gremlin would have always been a formidable foe for any Human, but this thing was beyond reason, and its empty eyes discouraged any attempt to negotiate a way out.

Behind the Boggart, more of those smaller, mutated creatures emerged from the rubble. *Imps*: once beautiful, literal forces of nature, now more akin to feral dogs.

I turned and ran.

"Ophelia!"

She didn't call back, but I heard a muffled scream somewhere ahead.

Another Boggart jumped at me. I fell, rolled, kicked him to the side and continued in the direction of the cries.

An Imp came next. I put my knee to his face, barely losing stride. There was a mass of moving bodies in the next room, and the muffled screams grew louder as I approached.

There were two more Boggarts and another shorter, rounder Fae holding Ophelia down. One Boggart saw me coming and turned its head, so I put my weight into my shoulder and shoved it to the wall. His bones cracked like kindling beneath my weight. The other tried to grab me, but he let go of Ophelia's legs to do it, allowing the little firecracker to fight back.

Her wild kicks distracted the Boggart so he couldn't see my haymaker coming. It knocked him off her and left his head hanging at a terrifying angle as he toppled into the wall. With both Boggarts out the way, I focused on the round beast that still had hold of Ophelia's arm and wasn't letting go.

I attacked, but it was like punching a sack of cement and didn't bother him one bit. Before I could think of my next idea, one of the busted-up Boggarts returned and wrapped his arms around me. Imps gripped my legs. Pointed fingers tore my shirt and scratched my skin. Not deep – not yet – but enough to draw blood. Ophelia was screaming. Her hand was still locked in the monster's grip, and he'd managed to grab a fistful of her hair.

I tried to push off the floor, kick off the wall, but the Boggart had me tight, and another came and joined him. More would be on the way. All those creatures I'd avoided were about to catch up, and even if their teeth were blunt and their brains were mush, they'd pull us to pieces eventually.

Blunt teeth chewed my fingers. Attempting to pull them free only made them hurt more. A jagged fingernail worked its way into the cut on my neck. Ophelia's screams added tears to their chorus. A Boggart moved his face right over mine, ready to chomp down on my nose.

Then the head of the Boggart was knocked violently to the side.

Another was yanked back, releasing the pain in my neck. There was still one biting my finger, but with the rest of my limbs set free, I was able to shove it against the wall and knee it in the guts until it let go.

I turned to help Ophelia, but she was already curled up on the ground, struggling to control her tears. I wrapped her in my arms.

"It's all right. It's okay. We have help."

She looked over my shoulder at Richie Kites – huge Half-Ogre and former police sergeant – as he lifted the round, snarling beast over his head and hurled it across the room.

"I fucking told you to wait for me! Is this the kid?"

"There's two more. One came in with us, but another has been here a lot longer."

Richie grunted through his tusks, and his breath made the floorboards rumble.

"Then find something heavy and let's fuck these cunts up."

19

"They can't be Fae," said Richie, taking a practice swing with a piece of copper pipe. "There ain't no Fae left."

As we walked further into the dark, I told him about the Adamantine armor and what I thought it meant.

"Gremlins? Poor fuckers. They look like they've gone mad."

"You reckon?" muttered Ophelia. She seemed to have recovered quickly, but I knew well enough that the ability to make jokes doesn't reveal anything about what's going on underneath. "What's that?"

She pointed to a pile of shadows that looked like a rat's nest and sounded about the same. Then I recognized Inero's body beneath the mass of deformed Imps.

"That the first one?" asked Richie, readying his makeshift weapon.

"Nah, he came with us."

"Fucking hell, Fetch. I thought this was a rescue mission, not a way to feed these bastards more kids."

Now that he knew what the things were, Richie did his best to use non-lethal attacks. He flung the first Imp across the room, did the same with the next, but once they turned on him, pulling punches became too dangerous and he started swinging with all his strength.

The crunching sound of pipe against skull might have made me throw up if adrenaline and fear hadn't put my bodily functions on hold. The whimpering moan that followed each kill was worse, but there was no appealing to these wild creatures. Even when half their face was caved in or a limb was broken, they kept coming — unaware or uncaring of their injuries — with a desperate bloodlust that, once ignited, couldn't be put out.

Ophelia used a chair leg to guard herself, choosing to defend rather than attack. You couldn't blame her. Her wounds were bleeding heavily, including a large cut over her left eye that must have been messing with her vision. Besides, Richie appeared to have a handle on things. I dragged the last Imp from Inero's prone body, and Richie sucker-punched it while it was still in my arms.

The kid kept laying there, the whites of his eyes shining in the murky dark. There was a long silence – too long – before he gasped a desperate breath.

"You all right?" asked Ophelia, surely aware that none of us would be anywhere near all right until we'd found Ashton and fought our way out of this freak show.

Inero nodded and I helped him to his feet.

"I'm so sorry," I said. "Can you walk?" He nodded again. "We need to find Ashton, then we get the fuck out of here."

Richie led the way, his copper pipe painfully effective against the few Imps who bothered us. We'd become a more imposing group, and the remaining Fae were inclined to keep their distance.

I had a moment to take in the horrific dwelling in greater detail. The ceiling of our level had been the floor of the apartments above, but the wood was so rotten, and there were so many holes, that anything heavier than an Imp needed to stay on the ground floor. Tattered ropes dangled down from above – perhaps used to traverse the two levels – and looking up through one of the larger gaps revealed occasional glimpses of the summer sky.

The floor was sticky beneath my feet, and I kicked through pieces of metal and bone: the remnants of the Gremlins' previous victims. They must have survived down here in the only way left to them, snatching those foolish enough to wander through the alleys and . . . consuming them? *Hell.* What a fate for the world's most sacred species.

Could their crimes be excused by the suffering that had been inflicted upon their own bodies? Did the unfairness of their fate demand lenience, or – despite what they'd endured and how damaged their minds had become – were their actions irredeemable, and the capital punishment we'd delivered in the past few minutes morally justified?

My questions were cut off when I saw more faces above: Imps peering down from that decrepit upper floor.

Ophelia was smart enough to sense that the break in action wasn't necessarily good news.

"What if they're waiting to attack us all at once?"

"Don't give them any ideas," said Richie from the side of his mouth.

"You really think they can understand us?"

"Oh," said a voice beyond the gathering Gremlins, "we understand you just fine."

The hoard of corrupted Fae parted to reveal a woman made of stone, sitting in an ornate armchair. Ashton sat at her side, bloody faced. There was a rope wrapped around his neck, the other end held in the woman's fist. Her dark skin was patterned like the frozen waves of set volcanic lava, and before anyone else could say anything, I surprised myself by blurting out, "Amari."

Richie, Inero and Ophelia all turned to look at me. The stone woman was clearly *not* Amari – the Faerie ambassador who stole my heart before the Coda stole her magic and her life – but in my defense, this woman was, without a doubt, a Sprite. While Amari was a child of the trees, this Gremlin leader must have born from fire. Pre-Coda, she would have burned with eternal embers, but now she looked more like a statue made from rock and volcanic ash. Unlike the Boggarts, her Adamantine armor retained an echo of its former glory. Though many links were missing, it was less rusty than the others, and an attempt had been made to polish it back to its former glory. Her face was in much the same state: still intact, but cracking away, like the front of a derelict building. When she spoke, her voice was the hull of a boat being dragged up a pebble beach.

"Amari? Now that is an old name, and certainly not mine." She leaned forward, maybe straining to see with short-sighted eyes. "A silly girl, as I remember. Foolish and irresponsible. Trusted those who we knew should not be trusted. We were sent here to watch over her, but it was already too late."

Gremlins growled around us.

"Give us the boy," said Richie, "and we'll leave without anyone else getting hurt."

The Sprite pulled on the rope, making Ashton wince.

"But my warriors are hungry for Human meat. It satiates their need for both nourishment and vengeance."

Ophelia couldn't stomach that one.

"Get your hands off him, you rank bit of rubble."

The Sprite looked amused as she ran her chalky fingers through Ashton's hair while her other hand kept the tension on the rope.

Richie piped in, his voice disarmingly casual considering the circumstances.

"You called these lumps your warriors, eh? Well, you might have noticed that you already lost a few good soldiers because of this madness. I understand you want your revenge – for the things done today, and the things done in the past – but I don't think it's worth the price you'll have to pay to get it." The Fire Sprite turned her head each way, perhaps examining her remaining soldiers. The sneer on her clay-colored lips suggested that she was well aware of how many were missing from her ranks.

"You are still outnumbered."

"Maybe," said Richie, matching her coldness. "But we don't go down easy, and I'm sorry to say that your soldiers do. I know you were something to be feared way back when. I respect that. But you won't be able to stop us before we take out a whole ton of you. That's a fact. I'm offering you the opportunity, as their leader, to ensure no more precious lives are lost today."

She snarled.

"You expect us to believe that our lives are precious to you?"

"Course they are. I haven't seen a Fae in seven fucking years.

You're the closest thing to a miracle I've ever laid eyes on. I feel bad for what's been done today, but that don't mean I won't do more if you don't let go of that boy."

She stared him down, but good luck to her if she was trying to read him. I'd known the guy most of my life and even I couldn't tell if he was bluffing.

"You'll just come back," she said. "With others."

It was my turn to interject.

"Not the way you think. There are people who can help you. All kinds of alchemists and doctors who are trying to put things back."

She laughed: a pickaxe cracking a boulder.

"There is no way back from this."

"Not the whole way back. Maybe just a way to ease the pain. To adapt. We can send someone down here to talk to you. They can bring medicine or . . . or something. We have friends."

I really wasn't selling it. Her expression said as much. That's why I was lucky, once again, to have Richie at my side.

"Or we start swinging until you beg us to stop," he said. "Personally, I prefer his idea."

The eyes of the Imps and Boggarts all turned to their leader. She tightened her fist on the rope, ran her dry lips over each other for a moment, then finally let go.

"Ashton!" Ophelia ran forward and put her arms around him. He flinched.

"Ow!"

"Sorry. You all right?"

He nodded, and she slipped the noose from over his neck.

"When you return," said the leader, "knock on the first left door twice, the next right door once, the next right door five times, and wait."

"You got that, Fetch?" asked Rich. "My memory's never been reliable."

"Left twice. Right once. Next right five. Shake your partner side to side."

"But if you *don't* come," continued the Fire Sprite, "with your doctors and your medicine, then we will come for you and finish what was started."

Once Ophelia had brought Ashton back to our side, she felt safe to start spitting attitude again.

"Yeah, right. You don't look like you've left this place since the Coda. How d'you think you're gonna come for us?"

The stone woman smiled – a crevice in a cliff face – and folded her hands in her lap.

"The Gremlin have been spying on this city since our arrival nine years ago. We feed on its shadows. We drink its secrets. Defy us, and even your own bed will not be safe."

With that, Ophelia was quiet. We backed away, barely breathing, until The Snatch was far behind us, and we could all turn our faces to the light.

20

We were silent until we reached the cafe. Then, I was anything but.

"All that to squiggle on a billboard? Seem worth it to you, Ashton?"

Richie put a hand on my shoulder.

"Fetch, go easy."

I shrugged it off. "Rich, you saw what was happening to Ophelia when you arrived. If you hadn't saved us . . ." I turned back to Ashton, and the cuts on his face did nothing to cool my temper. "What are you trying to achieve with your little displays of disobedience? I've spent countless hours in that kitchen listening to you go on and on about making a difference, but the truth is, you're not doing a thing for anyone else. This is all for you, kid. I was fine with you lying to yourself, but you'd better wise up before you get someone killed."

Ashton glared back. Despite my torrent of insults, he met my eyes and took the abuse, unblinking. Then, unexpectedly, he said, "I know."

Ophelia pushed me away.

"Shut the fuck up, Fetch. It was my idea too." She put her arms around Ashton and pulled him away. Then she thanked Richie and hugged Inero.

"You didn't have to come," she said. "It was good of you."

He just nodded, and I couldn't tell if he was still in shock or just continuing to define himself as a man of few words.

Ophelia and Ashton hobbled out together, leaving the three loners to tend to our wounds.

"All right, Inero, where were we? A hot meal?" He shrugged.

This silent treatment might wear thin sooner than I expected. "What about you, Rich? You eaten today?"

"Of course I've—"

"Something that didn't come from a can?"

He looked in on the busted cafe: broken police tape wafting in the breeze.

"Does it still work?"

"Can't do a full service, but I can manage something for the three of us. Come on."

Later, we sat on the curb with greasy sandwiches and strong coffees, trying to decide if we had the stomach to eat any of it. I had so many thoughts trying to squeeze into my head that they kept getting jammed before reaching my mouth. Richie must have been feeling the same thing, because he was as silent as my newest, quietest neighbor. It was a good few minutes before I sputtered out something to break the ice.

"They knew Amari."

Richie nodded. "Course they did. She was the only other Fae in Sunder."

Before the Coda, she and Hendricks were my only friends (but if two friends is all you have, you can do worse than a Faerie Ambassador and The High Chancellor of the Opus).

Richie finally took a bite. Encouraged, Inero started eating too. I joined in, but my mouthful didn't stop me talking.

"They didn't seem too impressed by her."

Richie chuckled at that, spitting a piece of lettuce onto the street.

"Of course they didn't. She was Amarita Quay: Faerie rebel. Most of her kind didn't understand her, let alone the ones who wore armor."

I stopped chewing.

"I knew she was kinda different to the others."

"Kinda different?" He choked on his sandwich and had to take a break while he washed it down with coffee. "She was a nightmare for them. None of her kind understood what she was trying to do or why she was trying to do it. She was the original misfit Faerie. Why do you think she liked *you* so much?" He was laughing as he spoke, but my expression gave him pause. "Oh, hell. What's wrong now?"

I felt foolish, but I had to ask.

"You think she really liked me?"

I thought he was going to spit his coffee.

"Did you see you two together? You were like a couple of kids. I tell you, Amarita was never like that when you weren't around. I sat in on meetings with her a few times, and she could be . . . well, she was fucking terrifying." My turn to laugh. I'd seen that side of her often enough. Caught myself on the receiving end once or twice, and did everything I could to avoid it happening again. "Why would you even ask that?"

"I . . . uh . . . I always thought she just tolerated me."

"What? You even thought that back then?"

It was difficult to say. The further I am from something, the more time I've had to rewrite the memory over and over again (and the editor in my head is a real piece of shit).

"Kind of. I dunno. At the time, I felt so strongly about her that I had to assume I meant something to her too, but you never know what's going on for someone else, do you? I'd feel it when we were together, but as soon as she'd leave, I'd started to wonder if she was just being nice."

"Fuck off. Amari was a lot of things but she was never nice. Nobody would dare get her to do something she didn't want to do unless they weren't too fond of their front teeth. If she was spending time with you – which she was, a lot – it was because you gave her something no one else did. From where I was, it looked like you were the only two people who understood each other."

That surprised me but, also, it didn't. That's what it had felt like at the time. *Some* of the time, anyway. When she wasn't around – even some of the times she was – I found it hard to believe that someone as intelligent and beautiful as her could see something of value in a clumsy kid like me. If I saw her as the ingenious ambassador that was trying to bridge the divide between the Humans and the Fae, there was no sense to it. But the misfit Faerie and the Weatherly outcast? Yeah, they would be friends, wouldn't they?

"I'm not going to deny the fact that you fucked things up," continued Richie. "But maybe it's time you stopped asking for forgiveness for what the boy did to the world, and ask yourself if you're ready to forgive the world for what it did to the boy."

"What the hell are you on about?"

"Fetch, you hate yourself so hard, it's spilling over onto how you see everyone else. You're too rough on anyone that might make the same mistakes you made. Like that kid. Sure, he fucked up. But I don't think he's the one you're really mad at."

Ooh, I didn't like this conversation one bit. It was one thing to rail at the version of me that lived in the past – in fact, it was one of my favorite hobbies – but analyzing my recent actions always made me squirm.

I looked around for a distraction and was given one in the form of a shirtless man with long, auburn hair and huge shoulders hunched over a set of wooden crutches.

He was lumbering his way from the south, taking up the sidewalk and forcing other pedestrians to move onto the street to avoid him. I became slightly afraid when he crossed the road and moved in my direction, and *very* afraid once I recognized him.

"You. Phillips?" grunted the Centaur.

"Yeah."

"Saw you at church."

"Saw you too. You weren't exactly playing the wallflower."

I took a bite of my dinner. Better to get it in quick in case the guy was here to break my jaw.

"You join 'em?" he asked, voice rumbling through his hairy, barrel of a chest.

"Turned out the light wasn't for me. Maybe I've got sensitive eyes."

He stood there, staring, with a lazy sneer on his sunbaked face. He had a beard but no mustache, bulging hooded eyes, and was hunched over his remaining pair of equine legs, his hindquarters sacrificed to Demoor's back-room butchery.

"You refuse them?" he asked, clearly needing me to spell it out.

"Yeah. I refused."

"Good. I want to talk to you about making church pay."

Richie took his meal to-go, and I left Inero on the curb while I invited the Centaur inside. He refused both coffee and food but gratefully accepted water and a chair – turning it around to sit on it backwards – and laid the crutches in front of him on the last unbroken table.

I sat opposite, trying not to be intimidated by the grunting brute.

"The Priestess called you Ryan?"

"My name Hyperion." He was new to the city, and his speech was simple and direct. "The church tried to steal my name, along with my body. I have reclaimed one if not other."

"Well, if you've come to ask me to find your hindquarters, I'm sorry to say that would be beyond my skills."

He didn't care for that crack. To be honest, neither did I. Something about the tragedy of the man made me nervous, as if I were somehow responsible.

I couldn't help but wonder about the work that would have been required to turn him from a quadruped to a biped. Organs would have been shifted. Decisions made about what to sacrifice. No wonder the Priestess had recruited Exina, she was one of the few people in the city with anything close to the qualifications.

"Why you there?" he asked. "At church? You wanted salvation?"

"If I did, I wouldn't request it from hooded crackpots who like cutting people up on center stage." He blinked but didn't change his expression. I supposed that meant he wanted me to continue. "One of the Mirrors recognized me: thought they'd make an example."

"Example?"

"You know, drag me up in front of everyone and embarrass me."

He leaned forward, and I was worried his chair was going to give out.

"Not embarrass. Make story. People see you there. You validate their cause."

I had to laugh.

"You really are new here, aren't you? Having me join a group is a long way from recommending it to anyone."

He huffed. "Now everyone knows Human goes to church. More desperate souls will follow. More people will get trapped. You made things worse."

I tried to huff him back, but it wasn't anywhere near as effective.

"They seemed to be doing just fine before I showed up. You clearly jumped on board the crazy train without my encouragement." He slammed his sledgehammer of a fist. "Please, be careful. This is the last table I have left."

"Have you ever been lost?"

"Plenty of times. I keep meaning to buy a compass."

"Not on map. Lost in your soul?"

He might not have been a man of many words, but I got his meaning with the few he chose.

"I sure have."

"Then you know the pain of it. The pain and the . . . euphoria that comes when you believe you have been found. The relief of not being alone. The fear of putting your trust in someone, and sweet heartbreak when it is not broken. You know this? This feeling of finding home?"

"Yeah. Yeah, I know it."

"*This* is what they gave me. And you may say, 'What saints they must be! What generous souls!' But they do this only so they can ask for something in return. They say, 'You know that feeling you feel right now? That ecstasy? That connectedness with all things? That is not yours to enjoy. No. You must *pay* for such things. Pay to our gods. Pay to *us*.' They ask not for payment when you are low, but when you are higher than you ever believed possible."

"Sounds like their religion really worked for you."

He slammed the table again and I heard something crack.

"What I felt was not theirs to claim! That feeling you have when someone cares for you. When you know the love of your brothers and sisters." He beat his chest with one fist, even harder than he'd smacked the table. "That feeling is *here*. Always. They put a price on what they do not own."

If the church's plan was to run a con on vulnerable residents of Sunder, they had guts to make Hyperion one of their marks. I wouldn't risk giving him incorrect change.

"So, you think they're taking advantage of people?"

"They are stealing the thing that makes life worth living," he reiterated. "Telling us that our brightest, most beautiful moments require a toll to their almighty. They do not create the joy in my heart, all they do is put a price on it."

Once I'd got what he was getting at, I felt just as disgusted as he did.

"So, they welcomed you in, made you feel like you had a family, and that's when they asked you to take communion?"

He seemed satisfied with my line of questioning, and I was glad to see him relax a little.

"*That* is when they strike. When you first make the leap of faith. When you feel so much better than you did the day before and you pray that this feeling will last. That is when they ask you to sacrifice."

"But why? What do they get out of encouraging their followers to cut up their bodies?"

"They get your soul!" He raged again, and the tabletop finally gave out, snapping in half and scattering the crutches. He breathed hard a few times, trying to control himself. The veins on his neck and arms bulged out from his skin. "I'm sorry."

"It's fine. Now it fits in with the rest of the place. What do you mean, they get your soul?"

"The more you give, the more . . . reason you must believe. The more afraid you are to be wrong."

I nodded. "Yeah. Safer to keep investing in the lie than risk admitting that you've made a mistake."

"Yes." He was calming. I committed myself to following his train of thought as closely as possible. The next misunderstanding might condemn me to the same fate as the tabletop. "Once you give communion," he said, "you are their soldier. Except me. In the end, I saw them for who they are. Admitted that I had been fooled."

"You're a stronger man than most, Hyperion."

"Yes. That is why we must stop them."

I chose my words very carefully, opting for questions over any kind of rebuttal.

"How will we do that?"

"I am nobody. Not in this city. Here, I am *Magum*. No newspaper cares. No minister."

"Most ministers are magical folk. I could introduce you to—"

"NO! They are not!" He gripped his hands tight to his kilt, forcing himself to strangle the cloth instead of my neck. "They have forgotten what they were. They have given up. They are tools."

I couldn't argue with that. The Centaur's simple truth was a nice break from the amateur philosophy of the rebel kids or anyone else I'd talked to. Sunder might have once been a multi-species metropolis that pretended to cater for everyone, but Niles's occupation had beaten all those disparate rhythms into formation until they marched under a single tune.

Still, what was I supposed to do about it?

"You are a Human," he stated. "You understand what they are doing, and you must warn others not to follow."

Oh, shit.

"Hyperion, I hear everything you're saying," already he was scrunching up his face, preparing for another outburst, "and I believe in your cause. I really do. I'm just not the guy you're looking for. I can find you someone to talk to. Lamplighter Radio are—"

"No! You! You are Human. Your voice will be heard."

"I'm nobody! I'm the biggest nobody there is. Trust me, my voice does more damage to your cause than you can imagine. Right now, there are multiple articles at the *Sunder Star* ready to go to print if I do anything they don't like. If I step into the spotlight, it will be a public execution. Figuratively and very likely literally. I am not the guy you want."

He stood up quickly. I slid back and raised by arms to defend myself, but he just grabbed his crutches and kicked the chair away.

"I saw you on the stage. I hear what people are already saying. Human who knows Niles, knows police, is now friends with church. You make them stronger if you say nothing."

"Look, I don't know anything about that."

"You know they're liars. *I* know they are liars. Now we tell everyone they are liars!"

"Nobody will listen!" Now that his hands were busy with the crutches, I felt more comfortable arguing with the guy. "Nobody ever listens to me. Nevertheless, I will help you find someone who can tell your story, I promise. There are people better suited to this than I am."

But his head was down, shaking slowly. He'd only wanted one thing, and now that he wasn't getting it, there was nothing else he wanted to hear.

"No. The church's story is too big. Too many voices telling it already. They have all the words. If you will not help me, I must stop them some other way."

I watched the grumbling half-Centaur shuffle away. I wished that I could say I was desperately thinking of some other way to help him, but there was no room for that among all the relief.

Inero was looking in at me through the broken wall.

"You tired?" I called out. He nodded. "Then let's clean up and call it a day."

I tried to sleep. Couldn't. Felt guilty about too many things. Guilty that I hadn't bought Inero his mattress like I promised, and guilty that I hadn't offered him the bed. Guilty that I'd been no use to the Centaur. That I'd killed a bunch of Imps and hurt the feelings of the kids I'd tried to save. I tried to tell myself it would all be better tomorrow. I'd do a load of washing and find my new neighbor something more comfortable to sleep on than the few spare pillows. I'd work out a way to help the Gremlins, then I'd track down Whisper before Volta lost patience and made Ophelia front-page news. That would be enough, right? A worthy to-do list of impossible tasks? No need to prove anything by teaming up with the Centaur to take on the Church of the Lattice?

I tried to tell myself it was enough. That I was allowed to keep myself out of at least one of Sunder's new wars.

But just because you look away from a battle, it doesn't mean it's not happening. It just means you won't see the cannonball when it comes flying at your head.

I let insomnia claim its victory, got out of bed, and headed off to see an old friend.

21

Sometimes you gotta treat yourself.

Having mostly kicked the hooch, and my days filled mainly with cooking and scrubbing, I had few indulgences outside the kitchen. I didn't make enough money to regularly frequent the Rose Quarter or gamble down the Sickle, so when I wanted to take some time for myself, I had to settle for a thermos of coffee and a walk uptown to climb a tree.

"Evening, Amari. How's the world looking from up here?"

I stepped over the crumbled bricks of the jailhouse once known as the Gullet and hoisted myself into the comfortable intersection of Amari's two thickest branches, wedging my thermos into a well-used nook. In winter, I could usually see the whole city from up here – all the way down to the south end of Main Street, out west to the smokestacks, and over to the burned-up library on the rise out east – but her foliage was thick and green from spring to summer, obscuring most of the view. That suited me fine. It meant that I was obscured too. I could nap in her shade and fill her in on my life without feeling like I was on show.

Amari had frozen up when the Coda hit. Turned into a wooden statue in the old Governor's mansion. I'd done my best to protect her, but Hendricks had set her free – if you could call it that – and turned her into this. I'd been furious, at first, but now I chose to believe she was better off.

Not that I'd been able to completely break my old habits. I'd tried a few experiments – adding Unicorn horn to her bark and roots, or watering her with alchemical concoctions – but nothing had any effect. Maybe for the best. Most of the struggles I saw in this city came from those who were trapped between two worlds.

If I got her talking, or moving her branches intentionally, what then? Is it really what she'd want? Based on the calming aura I felt whenever I was in her presence, I had to believe that her current existence was more peaceful than what the other ex-magical creatures of the city were going through. Certainly more than the Gremlins. More than Hyperion with his missing hind legs. She was still so full of life – so undeniably beautiful – that I told myself to just let her be. It wasn't easy. Even if she was at peace in this natural state – only occasionally bothered by my tedious accounts of life in the cafe – I couldn't help hoping for a day when she would answer me back.

"I met some Fae. I know, I know. I thought they were gone too. But they're Gremlins. Real creepy bastards. I think they were here for you, actually. To begin with. Make sure you didn't embarrass the Faerie community by cozying up too hard to the fire city and all us unnatural heathens. I'm going to go visit Portemus today, see if he has any ideas on how to help them. Linda might be useful too. She's been doing more traveling than I have."

That was an understatement. The Werecat had gone from black-market dealer to private investigator to founding member of The Bridge (a self-important group of optimists searching for remnants of remaining magic). We'd teamed up a few times but it always ended with her getting her claws into me.

"Hell, I've barely seen the sun since I took the cafe over. Oh yeah, it got blown up. Before you say anything, it wasn't my fault. This news guy was blackmailing me and . . . I won't bore you with the whole story but I'm still being blackmailed and if I don't find a smart way to deflect the attention, I might have to leave town. Which means you'll finally get some peace and quiet. I'm fighting it, though. Can't leave you here on your own without anyone to look after you. Look what happened last time?"

Talking like this stopped feeling silly a while back. Some days it made me feel good, other days just lonely, but I'd stopped worrying whether she could hear me or not. Sometimes you just have faith and forget about looking like a fool.

"I was talking to Richie, about you, and he said some stuff I found interesting. Reframed a few things for me. Maybe he got it wrong but, either way, I just wanted to say I'm sorry. I was so caught up with worrying what you thought of me – putting you on a pedestal and waiting for you to shower me with affection – that I was always . . . distracted. Stopped me from seeing you. Seeing all of you. I just . . . I think I could have been a better friend if I'd listened to you, you know? Does that make sense? If I'd been able to get over myself sooner, then maybe none of this bullshit would have happened. Then maybe . . . Hey, does the sky look weird to you?"

Through a gap in her canopy, thin wisps of white clouds were being drawn in from all directions as if every remnant of moisture in the warm summer sky was coming together for a dance. It collected overhead, slightly to the south. I'd only seen clouds move that fast when the wind took them, but rarely does the wind blow in from every way at once, converging on a single spot. I watched them form a spiral, spinning in place, growing darker by the second.

"You seen anything like this before?" I went further up Amari's trunk to get a clearer view. The oppressive heat that had been sitting over the city for the past week suddenly lifted, and the air was perfectly still. Silent. Brimming with anticipation. "I'm sure you did back in the old days, but not recently, right? This is like—"

The sky exploded.

Twin beams of lightning – one descending from the clouds, the other rising from the southern end of the city, met in midair and cracked each other apart, splintering off in all directions and filling the sky with blinding tendrils of light.

I closed my eyes until they stopped glowing red, and by the time I opened them, the clouds were dispersing back the way they'd come: slower and less dramatic, like wounded soldiers stumbling home after a battle. The summer heat slid back over my shoulders and the night sky shifted to a dormant glow, the light of the streetlamps bouncing off the city's smog.

Amari's leaves fluttered as a southerly breeze carried a faint burning smell from the direction of the anomaly.

There was no way I wasn't going to check it out.

"You coming with?" I put a gentle hand on Amari's smooth bark. "Sorry. Bad joke. I'll let you know what it's all about next time I visit."

I poured the rest of my coffee on her roots – she used to love the stuff – and shuffled south. At the bottom of Main Street, I let the screams and sirens lead me west.

A crowd had formed around Third. Rather than push through, I jumped onto the nearest fire escape and – when I couldn't see anything from there – went up on to the roof. I crossed to the other side of the building and looked down.

There was already a scene around the Church of the Lattice. Mirrors were coming out, screaming, ripping the veils from their heads and breaking down in tears. Police officers and firefighters approached with trepidation, spooked by the unknown source of the explosion, the strange burning smell still in the air, and the growing panic.

I don't know what they could see from the ground, but it couldn't have been more spectacular than the sight I was staring down at. The church was a mess. Half the roof had been blown to pieces and the edges of the circular hole still smoldered, dropping glowing cinders on the motionless bodies inside.

From this distance, I couldn't hear much, but one heartbroken cry sailed up above the crowd and arrived clearly in my ears.

"The Priestess! The Priestess! Redonna Demoor is dead!"

22

Fray. Bath. Isaac Derringer. Redonna Demoor. Henry Piston. Thurston Niles.

Three dead. Maybe more, depending on what "Fray" meant. Depending on how quickly Whisper was moving through his list. Surely, after the impact of Demoor's heavenly assassination, leaders like Piston and Niles would be keeping themselves safe. So, what then? What was Whisper's next step if his targets barricaded themselves away inside their expensive fortresses?

I had no suspects, no murder weapon, no motive, and the only thing that linked the three victims together was a cryptic allusion to a secret meeting that nobody seemed to know anything about. I was a long way from putting it all together, but when folks start dropping dead, there's one guy in Sunder who's always ready to catch them.

Some lights once burned so bright that you never get used to seeing them dimmed, always waiting for the day when they'll flare back up to their former selves. I'd seen Portemus a few times since his half-undead ward, Mora, passed away, and it always came as a shock. He wasn't the man he'd been a year ago, and the longer it went on, the more I had to accept that I wasn't looking at him under the shadow of grief – something that, in time, would pass – but witnessing a permanently altered version of my old friend. He was still warm with a welcome, both his attire and smile as sharp as a set of steak knives, and as dedicated as ever to his clients. He was still Portemus. Still the best damn mortician a city could ask for. He'd just finally learned that death, even for a Necromancer, can only be toyed with for so long.

"Fetch, my friend. Come in."

We used to do a little dance before he'd open the door. The morgue was technically a government building so Portemus had to answer to the police department, the Mayor and – most recently – Niles and his associates. As I was often on the naughty list of one or all of these organizations, my presence threatened his standing with his superiors. I'd usually have to butter him up to gain entry by promising an inside scoop on some new magical mystery. Not any more. Maybe, like the rest of us, he was sick of simpering to Sunder's charcoal-suited overlords and relished any opportunity to flex his independence.

"More serum?" he asked. "I have plenty of collagen but not much of the rest, I'm afraid."

"No, not that. But thank you. I was wondering if you'd received any significant guests over the last few hours? Maybe someone from the clergy?"

Portemus's cheeky old smile threatened to return, a ghost of its former self.

"And why would a humble fry cook want to see the body of a recently deceased Priestess? Have you taken up your old mantle, Mr Man for Hire?"

"Not officially, not for long, and not by choice. I just need to find out if Demoor was killed on purpose, and if someone named Mister Whisper might have been behind it. Otherwise, some friends of mine could be forced to take the fall for her murder."

He raised his eyebrows, so perfectly plucked that every expression was as clear as a cartoon caricature.

"For the sake of others again, is it? Fetch Phillips, always putting himself in the firing line for his friends, even if he only just met them." His tone was jovial, but the joke was poking fun at how easily I'd followed Khay, the fallen Genie, to the detriment of dozens of other people who'd crossed her path. One of the victims was Mora, so the gag had barbs on it. Thankfully, he moved on before they could get lodged. "Come with me."

The walk between the slabs never failed to disturb me. No matter how many times I'd been down there, I always felt like I was trespassing. As if I'd interrupted some conversation between Portemus and his expired friends, and they were forced to play dumb until I took my leave.

The morgue was as full as ever: a body on every slab and a few waiting on trolleys for their turn in the spotlight. The cadavers represented every species of Archetellos. Almost. No Centaurs that I could see, unless they'd all followed Hyperion to the church's chop shop and were blending in with the bipeds. The corrupted Imps and Boggarts hadn't found their way there either, and I shuddered to imagine how the Gremlins might dispose of their own.

Of course, not all in attendance could be identified. A group of bodies lying next to each other were conspicuously similar. Not in size or height, but in the mottled black texture that covered their naked, featureless bodies.

"More burn victims than usual," I said. "They all from the same place?"

"One cottage uptown, and a couple from the Rose Quarter."

The Rose Quarter? Maybe it was the same fire that Ophelia and Ashton almost got the blame for.

"Wasn't that a week ago?"

"Yes, but new arrivals keep jumping the line. Have you met the Priestess before?"

"Only once. Yesterday."

Portemus served me a side-eye that was sharper than his scalpel.

"Hmm. Same with Derringer, yes? He was visiting you when he met his demise?"

"He was outside my place, yeah."

"Oh, Mr Phillips, I fear you will once again find yourself a suspect in your own case."

"Occupational hazard, I'm afraid."

"Yes, yes. The closer you are to the killer's trail, the more likely you are to find yourself at the location of his next crime. I feel your job was not as risky when you were not so good at it. But don't worry too much; I doubt that they can pin this one on you."

"Why's that?"

"Because even a man as resourceful as yourself would have a hard time doing this."

Redonna Demoor lay before us, dressed from head to toe in the immaculate gowns of the Lattician Priestess. Tiara still on her head, rings on her fingers, bracelets on her wrists, and platform shoes sticking over the edge of the slab.

Her sternum was a blackened cavity, reminiscent of the hole that was blown through the church roof. Black scars like lightning bolts spread out from the wound, charring her pale skin and the soft material of her robes.

I stepped closer and saw that the wound itself was deep. The ends of her ribs stuck out from burned flesh, and – though I couldn't be sure in the low light – it looked like it might go all the way through to the other side.

"May I?" I asked, reaching my fingers towards a loose piece of charred material covering her collarbone.

"If you're careful."

I pulled back some of the cloth and saw that there were more than scars on her chest. Two lines of overlapping red circles linked the tops of her shoulders to the cavernous black wound: a perfect shadow of the heavy necklace she'd been wearing at the church.

"The necklace. Do you have it?"

"Either destroyed in the blast or somebody got to it first. Homicide encourages sticky fingers."

"That could be a problem. From the position of the burn, there's a good chance it was the murder weapon."

Portemus nodded.

"No more impossible than my other theories."

When I'd talked to the Priestess, there was a large blue stone set into the necklace. What the hell could it have been? Some kind of bomb set by Whisper to take out his next target? Perhaps the same kind of explosive he'd put in that car?

"You have Derringer here too?"

"Pfft. There is no Derringer. Some bits of blood, skin, hair. Nothing that tells a story. I do have the other one, though."

"The other one?"

"The other mentioned in the hidden message. The policeman. You want to see him?"

Bath.

He kept slipping my mind. Crushed under the weight of titans like Derringer and Demoor. Simms had been trying to get me to investigate Bath's death from the moment it happened, but she'd had the decency not to blackmail me into action like the others had.

I supposed I was overdue in inviting Constable Bath to the party.

"Can't hurt to take a look."

How wrong I was.

Anyone other than Portemus would have given me warning before pulling back the sheet, but an ancient Necromancer is the last person you should trust to anticipate your squeamishness.

"Goddamn it, Porty. What the hell happened to him?"

"That's what I'm trying to determine."

His body had been mostly stripped, and there were wounds covering his flesh: little black holes where the bullets went in and a couple of chunky purple craters where they'd come out. His abdomen was such a mess that his guts had spilled out onto the slab. Sunder's most polite police officer had been turned into a bag of meat with a pale head balanced on top. For all the mess, I expected him to smell worse. Instead, some sweet aroma emanated from the body.

"What is that? Peppermint?"

"Yes. I'm not sure why. He came in smelling like that. It was all over his clothes."

"Simms said eight bullets."

"Eight in, two out."

"Anything else?"

"Attacks were point-blank range. The bullets were the Niles-made, mass-produced type, so that tells us nothing. Several shots in close succession, centered around two places on his body."

"They say it was some kind of hit. A gang."

"*They* say a lot of things, but the theory does align with the number and proximity of the wounds."

"Why would someone do this?"

"The wounds have no opinion on that."

What game was Whisper playing? Send a group of armed men to execute a cop, blow up a car, and call lightning from the sky. If it wasn't for his letters, there wouldn't be anything to link these deaths together. They would just be three separate, unexplainable incidents.

Dead cop attended secret meeting with Sunder leaders.

These traitors must die.

Was Whisper really doing this himself, or was it some kind of call to action? Secret messages telling others what to do? Was that why each of these victims had been killed by different means? Whisper might have devout followers all around Sunder, ready to follow his orders. Maybe they'd seen messages the rest of us hadn't. Maybe this had been going on longer than we knew.

"You know him?" I asked. "Bath?"

"He came by once or twice. Dropped off patients. Picked up forms."

"He seem the kind of guy who would be having secret meetings with men like Isaac Derringer?"

"He seemed the kind of boy who would put his shoes on the wrong feet if his boss gave the order."

"Yeah."

Whatever Derringer and Demoor were guilty of, I'm sure they had a greater hand in it than Constable Bath, but maybe that didn't matter to Whisper. Maybe to him, following orders was just the same as making them. Besides, Bath would have been an easier mark. He lived alone. No gates and no devout followers. Whisper could just call in a hit and have the kid riddled by midnight.

Still, something smelled wrong about the whole thing, and not just the aroma of peppermint and pickled flesh.

"If that's all," said Portemus. "Let me get you the ingredients to make up some more of your cream."

"Best leave it for now. My kitchen's not at capacity, and city officials could drop by at any time. When I've got this thing worked out, I'll let you know."

Portemus raised one of his beautified eyebrows.

"Don't let this nonsense drag you away from your real work, Fetch. These folks are dead. You should prioritize the ones who are still alive."

Interesting advice coming from him. I'd thought we warm-blooded creatures mostly bored him. He really had changed.

"Now that you mention it, I have some new friends who are technically 'living', though I use the term loosely. I hoped you might be able to help them out."

I filled him in on the Gremlins and their Fire Sprite leader. It was nice to see some of the old enthusiasm tickle his mind.

"A secret society of military Fae lurking in the shadows, dedicated to disrupting Sunder's mortal rule? Are you sure you want to help them? Perhaps they are the very assassins you intend on bringing to justice."

"I never said anything about bringing Whisper to justice. Not yet, anyway. And I'd put saving the last of the Faeries higher on my list of priorities than catching Derringer's killer."

"So, you don't feel obligated to rush to Simms with every secret you uncover?"

"Come on, Porty. You know I'm trying to get out of this without giving anything useful to Simms, Piston, Volta or anyone else threatening to string me up. Let's help the Gremlins and worry about the lies we tell the cops later."

Portemus smiled: that diamond-sharp grin that rarely saw the light since Mora lost her second life.

"Come with me."

At the end of the hallway, across from the back room where Mora spent her final days, there was a metal rack fixed to the wall: a steel grid full of hooks, holding an assortment of diabolical-looking tools that you hoped would only be used on you when you weren't alive to feel them, and maybe not even then.

"Stand back," said Portemus, and reached for a metal spike that jutted out from behind the collection.

He yanked on the spike, levering the grid away from the wall. It was attached to a false panel that hid a secret alcove.

"Porty, you snake."

"Mention anything about this, and your next sleep will be on one of my slabs."

I shivered.

"I've been threatened countless times this week, but that was the only one that's instilled real fear. My lips are sealed."

Once the panel was moved out of the way, the briny aroma of preserving agents wafted from the hidden room like a freshly opened jar of olives.

Portemus went inside first, lighting a series of oil lamps around the small space. I stepped inside and attempted to play it cool.

"Wow. This is . . . nice."

It was a fucking nightmare.

Three walls were lined with benches. One was full of chopping blocks and utensils. The other held a complicated chemistry set with bottles and beakers of liquid in various stages of fermentation. The other, stacked with shelves, was where he kept his ingredients.

How to even begin?

I'll warm you up with the eyeballs: off-white orbs that floated in oily liquid like strange fish, trailing pink tendrils and staring at each other with unblinking attention. The full gamut of magical and non-magical creatures were accounted for: pure white Wizards, the pinprick pupils of the Elves, and the stone spheres of the Gorgons. One mammoth Cyclopean orb lolled around at the bottom of the jar, dwarfing the others. It seemed to look in my direction, expectantly, as if begging me to free it from some tiresome gathering of small-minded colleagues.

Speaking of minds, I couldn't tell you the species, race or gender of any of the brains on display, but they were at various stages of dissection, some with pieces removed, each given the prestigious honor of their own stone plinth.

As disturbing as I found these organic knick-knacks, I preferred them to the housings from which they'd been removed. The top shelf of the display was reserved for decapitated heads in all their horrific glory. Some were suspended in liquid-filled canisters, while others were mounted on spikes, their features molded into open-mouthed expressions like obedient patients who'd been told to open wide and say "ahh".

I always suspected that Portemus took mementos from his favorite guests before sending them to the cemetery, but I'd never desired to see the proof. This was surely where the secret ingredient of my skin cream was made, along with many other experimental concoctions. The end may justify the means, but I would have preferred to keep these means hidden behind the mortician's secret door and wrapped up in ignorance.

Having lit all the lamps, Portemus spun on his heels, awaiting my approval.

"Impressive, yes?"

I took a deep breath through my mouth, smothering the desire to be sick.

"I never expected anything less."

"Ha! Now, let me see what I can do for your Gremlin friends."

Portemus asked me a series of questions about the corrupted

Fae, and I answered as best I could. He collected potential components from the stacked containers, muttering to himself as he spread them out on the second bench.

"Goblin ointment for pigment protection, perhaps with some Shapeshifter skin. Amalgam blood for stability, and Kobold fat to keep it malleable. Hmm, I should make an Angel-down brush for gentle application. Fetch, this will take some time. Can you come back in a few hours?"

"Not a problem. I'd best keep on Whisper's trail while it's hot."

"Ah, so you know where to go next?"

Bath's death confused me, and I didn't like the idea of admitting to Simms that I was finally interested in the case she'd been encouraging me to investigate from the start. Besides, his death was already days old. Demoor, on the other hand, was as fresh as a daisy, and I was desperate to know how someone had managed to conjure a bolt of lightning out of the Sunder sky.

"I hate to say it, Porty, but I'm going back to church."

23

I really didn't like standing out.

I'd wanted to sneak in, unnoticed, to the back row of the sermon, wait for it to finish, then slip out the back to ask Dr Exina some questions.

That plan hit its first hurdle when I arrived at the Church of the Lattice as the only person not dressed in black. As my least-stained outfit had been damaged when Derringer's car exploded, and the next in line was covered in Gremlin blood, I was down to one of Georgio's baby-blue work shirts – too big if I didn't roll the sleeves – and some unseasonable woolen trousers that had shrunk in the wash.

The rubble had already been cleared, along with the pews, and the place was packed with congregants who were all on their knees, heads bowed, listening to the Mirrors chant unintelligible songs of mourning. The new skylight made the place brighter, hotter and more structurally unstable than it had been the day before, and only the smallest remnants of the fresco were still visible around the edges of the open ceiling. Whatever messages Redonna Demoor had been receiving from the spirits of the river, they certainly hadn't seen this one coming.

Just like the parishioners, the Mirrors had traded their white robes for black. Today, there were no triumphant cheers, but I had a feeling that even more purses full of coin would change hands. Enough to fix the ceiling and paint it with an even sillier portrait of their imaginary god in the river.

Had they really only been here six months?

I stood in the doorway, hunkering in the shadows, and considered the scope of this operation for the first time. A building this big, renovated with such extravagance? Sure, the followers of the church were being conned into handing over their savings, but it couldn't have been like that on day one. Redonna Demoor must have arrived in Sunder with a carriage-load of cash to set herself up. But from where? Was the Church of the Lattice already thriving across Archetellos? If so, should we expect any retribution for one of their leaders being killed on Sunder ground?

The service dragged on, with Mirrors alternating between rehearsed chants and recounting previous lessons told to them by the Priestess. After an agonizingly tedious hour, it dawned on me that this was less of a sermon and more of a day of mourning. Worried that the speeches may never end, I went out the way I'd come in and walked around to the back door that I'd been kicked out of last time. It was latched, but nothing a shoulder and a flick of a finger couldn't overcome.

Inside, it was even more of a nightmare than I remembered. There were rooms like the one I'd been tied up in – dripping in expensive cloth and smelling of incense – alongside small surgeries that attempted to uphold the same aesthetic but couldn't overcome the sobering sight of steel shelves full of medical instruments, and tiled floors with blood-caked drains. These were the sacred spaces where followers of the church received their communion, severing themselves from the parts of their body that had once made them special.

I found Demoor's old room. Another of her grand outfits was hanging on a hook, and the vanity was still covered in make-up and a discarded set of silk gloves. There was a gilded jewelry box on a bench beside it, but when I opened the lid, it was empty.

"Come to rob a dead Priestess?" I dropped the box in shock. Exina had snuck in behind me and was removing her black veil to reveal a tear-stained glare of disgust. "I'd say that this is some new low, but really, it's quite in keeping with what I'd expect."

There was a time when we were on the same side. Exina, her partner Loq, Hendricks and myself, all teaming up to find out what Niles was up to. I could understand why that whole adventure had left a bad taste in her mouth; every time I thought of it, I had to fight the urge to sock myself in the jaw.

"Sorry about your leader," I offered, unconvincingly.

"Oh, thank you, Fetch. I know how fond you were of each other."

I gestured to the empty jewelry box.

"I suppose someone is taking a look at the rest of her collection? Making sure she doesn't own a set of earrings that will summon a tidal wave?"

Exina stepped closer but gave nothing away. She could hug me or put a knife in my guts and I wouldn't have a moment's warning. The fact that she hadn't killed me already was my only encouragement.

"The police are studying them. Making sure no others are rigged to blow."

Just enough attitude in her voice to reveal some skepticism.

"But you aren't holding out much hope for an answer, are you?" She shook her head. "Why? Because you know the necklace was special?"

She shrugged.

"The gem was a stormstone. Imported from Ember and gifted to her long before the Coda. Even back then, it wasn't dangerous. The inert power could be harnessed by Mages and Wizards – drawing it out using ditarum – but otherwise they were harmless ornaments. Whatever happened to Redonna was . . . impossible."

"It's a big week for impossible things."

She rolled her eyes.

"Why are you here?"

"Same as before. If Whisper is responsible, I'm working to uncover him."

"Knowing you, you'll team up with the murderer, go underground, and create twice as much trouble as you were hired to stop."

"Look who's talking. When we first met, you and Loq *were* the underground." A sneer told me I was on thin ice but I kept on tap dancing. "Where is Dr Loq, anyway?"

"In the past." Exina took a long breath and I finally understood what a dick I was being. Her boss had taken a lightning bolt to the breast only a day before, and I was looking for sore spots to stick my finger into. "Go talk to her if you want to dig around in the old days. I have people to help."

So, the two Succubae really had split. I was surprised, but perhaps I shouldn't have been. Sunder's relentless "progress" meant that even the most reliable arrangements could change overnight.

Exina moved to go.

"Surely you want Whisper found," I said. "Help me understand what went on here and I'll have a better chance of bringing him in." If she was weighing it up, none of the thoughts reached her face. "Please, just tell me what happened. I only saw the aftermath."

When she spoke, I don't think it was to help me. I think she just took the opportunity to give voice to the confusion that was filling her head.

"The service was the same as always. Just like the one you saw, up until the first communion."

"Who was she working on? Anyone suspicious?"

She shook her head. "We looked into it immediately. If they were involved, it wasn't intentional."

"Could they have set off the stone without knowing?"

"It was one theory, but I don't think it holds much weight. Whisper's threat was clear, and it came to fruition so soon. I don't know how he did it, but using a randomly selected member of our flock leaves too much to chance."

That tracked, but it still didn't explain how a dormant piece of stone could be triggered into unleashing a bolt of lightning.

"Anything else you can think of?" I asked, and it broke through her last layer of patience.

"You came to me, Fetch, not the other way around. Get out,

and don't show your face without something worthwhile to offer us. Otherwise, we'll be the ones who decide what we take."

I was never sure if Exina's threats were the idle kind, so I got out of there before she could reach for her scalpel.

None of it fitted, no matter how much we wanted it to. Without Whisper stitching these murders together, they would have been three separate tragedies, each worthy of their own investigation.

Maybe Whisper was simply a shit-stirrer trying to make a point, just like the kids at the cafe. Then a cop gets killed – not a rare occurrence – and the editor of the *Star* kicks the bucket, so he builds a narrative and turns those random deaths into a plot. Not a bad way to send a warning to the elites of the city without having to actually do anything dangerous.

No. The letters were written in advance, right before the deaths. If Whisper hadn't killed them himself, then he'd incited them. Ordered them. I kept searching for alternatives, but there was no version of this story that didn't put Demoor's blood on Whisper's hands, either directly or by association.

But why? What had she done to deserve this? What did Whisper know?

I'd used up all the patience that Exina would give me, but she wasn't the only Succubae surgeon in town.

And I had a feeling the other one might not hold the Priestess in such high esteem.

24

"What a twat."

I'd started smiling as soon as I entered Loq's new establishment, and her response to me mentioning the Lattician Priestess only made me smile wider.

Her new parlor was smaller than the place we'd first met, but it was back below street level, far from the fancy clinic that she and Exina had moved into when they started gaining mainstream success. This was just one large room with black walls, and the furniture all looked like street-side pickups: a short but well-stocked wooden bar, a couple of low benches, some wall mirrors of various sizes and quality, and a few lamps with heavy shades to keep the light warm and low. The exception to her makeshift style was the expensive surgeon's chair in the center of the room: a remnant of her luxurious days above ground. Though the upholstery sported a few scratches, you couldn't hide the fact that it was a specialist piece of expensive machinery.

Loq had done away with her surgeon's gear and sat topless on a crate beside the chair, showing off the Cyclops eye that was grafted to her sternum in the space where her breasts had presumably once been. Her hair had gone from red to pink, and she was still as cool as a southerly breeze in a heatwave.

"You weren't tempted to join the congregation?" I asked.

Loq's forked tongue still gave her that trademark lisp.

"Oh, fuck off. What they're doing is disgusting."

She was, at that moment, removing the fingernail from a large Human's index finger so that she could insert a Werewolf claw in its place.

"Disgusting? I thought Exina was doing the same operations as you, just for a different establishment."

"Are you fucking stupid?"

The man squealed.

"I told you I didn't mind you talking while she worked," he said, wincing. "But could you try not to agitate her too much?"

"Sorry, Kyle," said Loq. "I'll be gentle."

Apparently Kyle's new wife was a Werewolf and he'd decided to take the first step in joining her pack. Back before the Coda, he could have gone to Perimoor, applied to the Lycum leaders for acceptance, and completed the ritual on Mount Kar. These days, Loq's den of body mods was his best bet.

"Exina and I were dedicated to revealing someone's true nature in their physical form," said Loq, with a passion that made Kyle understandably nervous. "We brought willing participants to actu-alization. When she wanted to move to the above-ground surgery, I wasn't a fan of the idea, but I let her convince me. I played the pretty businesswoman because I wanted to make her happy. When she decided to serve the Lattician Priestess, that was too much."

She put so much stank on that name, I knew I wouldn't have to dig hard to get to the dirt.

"Do you know where she came from?"

"Redonna? From the edge of greatness, apparently. She used to be a Muse."

"A real one?" blurted Kyle, before howling in pain. Loq had inserted the first claw into one of the red wounds where his Human nails had been.

I thought my days of asking the obvious questions were behind me, so I was a bit embarrassed as I said, "What's a Muse?"

Lucky for Kyle – who was bleeding profusely around his new appendage – Loq could multitask.

"According to self-proclaimed mystics like Ms Demoor, a Muse is a conduit for the river's power. Not only do Muses live a charmed life, but those close to the Muse become beneficiaries of their blessing."

"How can you tell?"

"That's the thing. There's no way to prove the power of a Muse. They all self-identify, and the proof is circumstantial. Many doubt their existence at all."

"Redonna clearly believed in her powers."

"Oh, yes. She claimed to have made kings and queens. Risen soldiers up the ranks and turned destitute scribes into famous poets."

"Sounds like quite the life."

"It was, until the Coda." When the Succubae were a team, Loq had been the strong and silent type, so it was nice to finally hear her string more than a couple of words together. "After the river froze, her luck dried up with it. She fell on hard times and in desperation, went back to the ones whose lives she had helped create."

"Let me guess. They weren't as grateful as she hoped?"

"Without her powers, she had nothing to offer these already powerful people, and they rejected her, one after the other. That's how she ended up in Sunder with a score to settle. Not necessarily against those who had wronged her, but against the world at large. A person hungry for validation can find many ways to feed themselves in a city like this."

That's what Sunder relied on: people who felt they'd got the short end of the stick and were entitled to do whatever they could to claim what they deserved. If you wanted to call yourself an underdog, then Sunder would gladly sell you a muzzle, leash and collar.

"But how did Demoor go from rejected Muse to leader of a church? That building must have cost a fortune, even before the renovations. Then there are the Mirrors and all those outfits. She can't have created it all on charm alone."

"Of course not. She was just a useful tool, ready to play whatever part was asked of her."

"So who was asking?" grunted Kyle. "Who would want her to pretend to be a Priestess?"

"Quiet, Kyle," said Loq. "Focus on the pain and forget everything you hear." She pushed the next claw in to emphasize her point. "Fetch, you've seen evidence that magic isn't as extinct as we once thought it was, right?"

"In a sense."

"And who in this city would lose the most if the river ever flowed again?"

That was easy.

"Niles."

"And if you were worried about the magic coming back – and what the magical creatures might do to you if it did – wouldn't you want to pull the wings from the backs of as many Angels as possible? Sand down fangs and claws in case the day of reckoning ever came?" Kyle squealed. "Sorry, I got a bit excited."

Her theory made sense, but only if you were willing to assume the worst in people. Had Demoor really been abusing her followers like that? Was Niles truly so awful as to spend a fortune convincing ex-magical creatures to mutilate themselves?

He was ruthless and he was an asshole, but that seemed like a step too far, even for him.

Didn't it?

I suppose my best bet was to ask him myself.

"Thanks, Loq. I appreciate it. Anything I can do for you in return?"

"Not with that boring body, Fetch. But stop by when you're finally ready to get freaky."

If only she knew that I was heading back to the morgue to pick up Portemus's latest brew. I should introduce them sometime. They could compare notes on how best to extract Elven marrow or pluck out an Ogre's eye.

"Thanks, Loq, but I've been cut up enough for one summer. Good luck with the rest of your journey, Kyle. I'll look out for you next full moon."

25

I returned to the morgue to pick up Portemus's new concoction, but I wasn't about to risk a trip back to The Snatch on my own. My plan was to enlist Linda Rosemary's assistance. She was a fierce fighter in possession of a tactical mind, so she'd serve as useful protection when I went back to the Gremlins' lair. And as one of the self-important do-gooders in the organization known as The Bridge – she could be my best chance of helping out the Gremlin long term.

Portemus instructed me to keep the jar on ice, so I rushed back to the cafe as quickly as I could. As I stepped over the curb, a cloud of brick-dust gusted out of the broken window.

"Woah. Sorry, Fetch. Didn't see you."

The cloud had come from the end of Ophelia's broom.

"What are you doing?"

"I know we've been running up a tab on coffees and chips. Thought it was time we tried to pay you back."

There were a dozen kids in the cafe, wielding dustpans, dish-cloths and tools, including Inero who was starting to blend in with the rest of the unruly gang. He was still overdressed, but not any more awkward than the others. Two of the older ones – who appeared to have some actual skills – were fixing the busted tables: reinforcing the broken tops with planks and screws and bracing the legs with metal rods. The kitchen was damn near spotless, and there was even a new icebox standing beside the old one with the hole in it.

"My parents had a spare," said that blue-haired kid with the nose piercing. "They just got the new model so they won't miss it."

"Thanks." I put the jar inside and saw that it was already packed with a fresh stack of bacon and a stick of butter. "Well, then. Who's up for a bacon butty?"

Enthusiastic sounds of agreement rang out from the workers, so I gathered the necessary ingredients beside the stove. While it was heating up, I called the headquarters of The Bridge. Linda Rosemary wasn't there, but I left a message with one of her colleagues, asking her to call me back.

I made enough butties to feed the kids, and a few extras to sell out front. I decided not to tell the workers that their efforts might all be in vain. That the city could seize the cafe any day now if I didn't convince them to leave it in my care. Securing the title would have been higher on my list of priorities if people could stop getting themselves murdered for two minutes.

"Grub's up!" I called, placing the plate on the counter. The kids dropped their tools and snapped up rolls with unwashed hands. All except for the two who were standing outside.

Ashton hadn't been part of the cleaning crew. He'd arrived while I was cooking and dragged Ophelia into a close and low conversation. After watching the heated discussion for a minute, I was back on edge. It wasn't quite an argument, but it looked like she was pleading with him.

I got a bad feeling. The kids were on thin ice as it was, and if Ashton made more trouble, it could be a disaster for all of them. Ophelia appeared to be trying to talk some sense into him, and I wondered if she might need my help.

When I stepped outside, the kids got real quiet.

"Got some food ready, if you're hungry."

Ashton just stared. Ophelia nodded.

"Thanks. I'll be in in a minute."

"Not hungry, Ashton?"

He ignored me. Turned all his attention to her.

"I'll see you after."

"Ash . . ."

She grabbed at his sleeve, but he walked up the street without looking back.

"What was that all about?"

Ophelia kept her head down as she passed me, heading inside. "You'll see."

Shit. Trouble for sure. Before I could enquire further, a *Sunder Star* delivery boy came out of the teahouse and headed for the next door along.

"Hey, kid! Bring one of them over here!"

The boy froze. Looked at me like I was a tripwire catching the light.

"Mister, you told me if I ever brought this rag anywhere near your place you'd shove it down my throat until I farted confetti."

"I'm giving you a special exemption. Bring it here."

He did what he was told, but when handing it over, he stood back and extended his arm as far as he could, like I might try to bite his fingers off. When I held out the bronze, he took his payment the same way.

"I thought they stopped doing the afternoon edition."

"Not when there's big news like this," he replied, and scampered out of my reach before I could read the headline.

Smart kid. It only took a few words before I felt like throttling someone.

WHISPER FOUND?
CENTAUR MADE THREATS TO PRIESTESS
HOURS BEFORE HER DEATH.

There was a picture of Hyperion on the front page, along with the accounts of Lattician worshipers. They told the story of how he'd interrupted her service but nothing more substantial than that. No concrete facts, just a page full of intentionally reckless hearsay.

I stormed inside – accidentally scattering a pile of swept-up rubble – and went for the phone.

"This is Sunder PD."

"Is Detective Simms there?"

"One moment."

The kids were all staring at me, and the mood changed quickly. According to Ophelia, they were already nervous about me being on the other side of the law, so making a direct call to a police detective must have sounded like a confirmation of all their fears. They just watched, waiting to see what I was doing, and I was surprised at how threatening it felt.

They just stared. Silent. They were kids, sure, but not babies. All of them far fitter than I was. Probably stronger. A strange thought burrowed into my brain . . .

Do I really know any of them?

Sure, Ophelia and I were friendly, but I was struck by the fact that my cafe was full of strangers. Though I'd been putting my life on the line to protect them, I had no idea who any of them really were, or what they might be capable of. Maybe Derringer had been right, and one of them was Whisper. Maybe they all were. Maybe they'd been taking me for a fool, like I'd been taken many times before.

"Hello?"

"Simms, you seen the paper?"

"Yeah, and I'm a bit busy right now."

"That guy visited me last night, right before the accident. I'm not saying he couldn't have done it, but he's not the fastest mover and—"

Her voice became fraught and excited.

"Fetch, are you saying you can vouch for him?"

"Not for the exact moment it happened. About half an hour before the lightning strike, he was in my cafe. I watched him hobble off in the other direction."

"That's a good enough start. I'm heading down to Backlash now. Wait on Main Street. I'll pick you up on the way."

"What's going on?"

"The *Star* have spread their story and now everyone's out for blood. We need to get you on record, now, before there's nobody left to alibi."

She hung up. So did I. The kids kept looking at me.

"You called the police?" asked the blue-haired one, unreadable.

"Just making sure someone doesn't get punished for something they didn't do."

The answer seemed to satisfy some of them, but the blue-haired kid kept staring. Only when Ophelia came over to clear his plates and told him to "quit it", did he let me be.

I wondered whether I was being foolish, letting them have the run of the place. I was trying to keep them out of trouble, but what if trouble was what they wanted? And what would they do if they decided that I was in their way?

I was pulled out of my thoughts by the sound of a backfiring engine, so I went out to meet the incoming black sedan.

Simms took off before both feet had left the cobbles.

"Simms, watch it!"

"What did you and the Centaur talk about?"

I managed to wrench the door shut before it swung into a lamppost.

"He wanted help getting revenge on the church."

"Shit. Did anyone else hear him talk about that?"

"Richie was there. Some of the kids. A couple of customers who were hanging about before I took the conversation inside."

"Fucking hell."

"But he didn't want revenge like *that*. He wanted it in words. He wanted me to denounce them. Make it clear I didn't approve of their methods just because I let them drag me up on stage."

"When did you—"

"Don't worry about it. Anyway, if Hyperion could summon a tiny storm to zap Demoor from the heavens, he would have had no reason to come to me for help." Despite her reckless speed, Simms took her eyes off the road to look at me.

"Maybe he just wanted your opinion before he did anything rash."

"Come on, Simms. You know nobody comes to me for my opinion. He believed I'd made an unwilling endorsement of their methods and wanted me to take it back." She held the stare even longer. "What?"

"Nothing." She put her eyes back where they needed to be, just in time to swerve around a wayward beggar. "He was on crutches, right?"

"Yeah, but he's still a tough bastard."

"If he'd wanted to kill Demoor himself, and he'd had a way to do it, you think he could have moved that fast? Left the cafe and pulled off the hit in time?"

It was hard to think while Simms seemed ready to drive us into a wall.

"Possibly, but it assumes too many things: a quick shift from correcting misinformation to committing murder, immediate access to a miraculous weapon and a way to deploy it without being seen."

"You're right. It doesn't add up."

"I'm glad you're convinced."

"Now we just have to convince everyone else."

The sedan went over the bridge, swung right, and was forced to stop behind a screaming mob that was growing around Backlash. The grieving Lattician followers were there, shoulder to shoulder with street cops and civilians of all races, some who'd come straight from the pub without bothering to put down their pint glasses.

We got out, and Simms cut a path through the throng, shoving the rabble left and right. I followed in her wake, making use of the gap before it closed behind her. Anyone who was initially frustrated by the jolt quelled their fury when they saw the determined lizard responsible for the slight.

Any cop who was present — whether they were on or off duty — was ordered to disperse the crowd instead of adding to it.

"But boss, Bath—"

"Bath would have obeyed my order without question. Do the same and consider it done in his honor."

"Yes, Detective."

We broke through the mass to see a dozen firefighters standing around one bowed and bleeding Centaur prisoner.

One of them – my old subordinate Private Reeves – had the prisoner's hair in one hand and a copy of the latest *Sunder Star* in the second. He pushed Hyperion to his knees and raised his voice over the crowd.

"Thank you, local citizens, for bringing this killer to justice! I've never witnessed a more loyal, self-sufficient population in all my years. For the memory of Redonna Demoor, Isaac Derringer and Constable Timothy Bath," cheers from the audience at each of these names, "we take this killer into custody."

I watched Simms pull down her scarf and chew for a moment, deciding on her plan of attack. She forced herself to swallow a gut full of fury and stepped towards Reeves with a businesslike nonchalance.

"Thank you, young man. I've got it from here."

Reeves was taken aback. He was still getting to know Sunder's Reptilian detective and wasn't willing to give up his prisoner (and his spotlight) without an argument.

"Miss, this is—"

"Address me as Detective, young man."

Reeves considered both paths and decided against outright hostility.

"Detective, this prisoner has killed several innocent citizens and—"

"*Allegedly.* I happen to have more information on the murders in question – thankfully not yet released to the public – including an alibi for Mr Hyperion here. I'll be taking him to the station for further questioning before any sentencing can be made."

Reeves's eyes fell on me, and some of his anger faded in favor of a shit-eating grin.

"Well, well. Captain Fetch to the rescue, is it? Detective, you sure you want to trust the word of a man with such a . . . dubious record?"

It was eerie how quickly the crowd had quieted down, hushing each other to hear our exchange.

Simms approached Hyperion.

"We're considering all evidence before jumping to conclusions."

She offered the Centaur a hand, but – when he attempted to get to his hooves – Reeves pushed down on his shoulder.

"Detective, this prisoner was handed over to the firefighters."

"Lucky he's not on fire. On your feet, sir. We'll continue your questioning at the station."

Reeves's smile cracked like a dropped dinner plate.

"Mayor Piston has entrusted the firefighters to keep the peace."

"Well, the Mayor isn't here, is he? Neither is Thurston Niles. As Senior Police Detective of the Sunder PD, my word is law. Unhand the suspect or I will place you under arrest."

"Now, ma'am—"

Simms took her pistol from her holster.

"I won't warn you again, citizen." Every firefighter stood to attention, but Reeves's sidekick, Gumption – who had been uncharacteristically quiet until this point – was the only firefighter to reach for his gun. Simms clocked it without having to turn her head. "Touch that weapon, young man, and I'll be forced to shoot first."

Gumption sneered but obeyed, his hand hovering at his side. Simms was playing a dangerous game, but her self-assured, weary tone of authority had trumped the eager youth of the firefighters. For now. They all looked to Reeves for guidance, as he pondered whether his new position was bulletproof enough to get away with shooting a city detective.

Simms didn't wait for him to come to a conclusion.

"Stand up, Mr Hyperion. You're coming with me." The Centaur raised an eyebrow at Simms, not as confident in her authority as she was. "Now." Still holding her pistol, she reached out her other hand and, this time, Hyperion took it. "Where are his crutches?"

Reeves didn't move. I don't think he even blinked.

"He was delivered without them."

"Fetch, give him a hand."

I stepped in so Hyperion could use my shoulder for support. He smelt like sweat and blood.

"You all right?" I asked. He just grunted. Good enough. We took two steps back towards the crowd when Gumption spoke up.

"This is bullshit."

I didn't see him go for his gun, but he must have. Otherwise, Simms wouldn't have shot him.

The crack made everyone jump, and I had to catch Hyperion as he lost his footing. Gumption screamed and clutched his leg. There was a splatter of blood on the ground beneath him.

Suddenly, there were guns everywhere, aimed at Simms and me, shaking in every excited firefighter's nervous fingers.

"I warned you!" called Simms, moving her body between me and the pointed guns. "The prisoner is coming in for questioning. Any attempt to subvert the course of justice will be regarded as a criminal act."

Reeves — the only burgundy-suited warrior who hadn't taken out his pistol — was smiling again. He seemed to genuinely be enjoying the turn of events.

"The Mayor will have something to say about this."

"When he's willing to come out of hiding, I'll be happy to hear it. In the meantime, we follow the law." She turned her head towards me and whispered, "Fucking move. Now."

I kept hold of Hyperion and pushed into the crowd. They were reluctant to get out the way, but not so determined that they wanted to risk Simms shooting them for obstruction.

"She fucking shot me!" called Gumption, a passionate declaration of the obvious.

"I know, buddy," said Reeves, not taking his eyes off us. "But don't you worry. We've got plenty of witnesses to what happened, don't we?" We pushed through the blockade, every face nodding in agreement. They'd come for blood – for vengeance – and we were dragging away their toy before they'd finished playing with it. "We've learned our lesson, Detective. From now on, we'll do everything by the book. And I can't wait to see what the law has to say about this."

I helped Hyperion into the back seat of the sedan. The crowd gave us no room. In fact, they closed in, constricting our movement as we slid into our seats and closed the doors. They didn't even back away when Simms started the engine.

"Lena, what do we do?"

"They'll move."

She revved the engine, lurched forward and, sure enough, even the most stony-faced members of the crowd jumped back. Once the car was moving, none of them risked jumping in front of it, and we slunk up the street under the onslaught of narrowed eyes.

As soon as we hit Main Street, she put her foot all the way down, and I grabbed the seat to stop myself being bounced around.

"They'll be right behind us," said Simms, checking her mirrors. "Centaur, have you got somewhere safe to stay?"

"There's a share house on Riley I've been sleeping at."

"No. Someone will turn you in, hoping for a bounty. I'll find you somewhere quiet."

"Where?" I asked.

"Don't you worry. I'll be dropping you off first."

The cafe went past us in a blur.

"Uh, Simms, we just—"

"Not there. I need you to slow down the firefighters."

"Why the hell would they listen to me?"

She dodged around a delivery van, then kept moving north.

"They won't. But maybe their boss will."

26

The sedan barely stopped at the gates to let me out.

"Simms, I don't think I can do anything."

"Bullshit him. Flatter him. Do whatever it takes to get him to call off his dogs. If you can't, then just buy us some time."

She pulled my door closed and drove further west, leaving me alone at the entrance to Thurston Niles's compound. It had been weeks, maybe months, since I'd been this far uptown. A fry cook had little need to hike up to the streets that housed Sunder's unelected elite, but somehow the Man for Hire always found himself being dragged in a northerly direction.

There were two of those indistinguishable men in charcoal suits standing guard on the gate, speaking to Thurston's favorite henchlady.

"Hello, Yael. Nice to see your face. It was too dark last time we caught up."

She seemed confused, as if sneaking into my place to shove a gun between my lips was an easily forgettable experience.

"Here to see the boss?"

"If he's free."

Yael's green eyes glinted.

"Come on, he always has a minute for an old foe."

The guards opened the gate, and I followed Yael up the drive, wondering if there had been a single day since this house was built where it wasn't under construction. They'd moved on from the main house to the garage, and even though that wasn't finished, they'd also started on the framework of a second building off to the side. What indulgent extravagance was he making for himself now? Perhaps his own theatre, where he could force desperate citizens to dance for his amusement.

There was a truck halfway up the driveway, dripping with water and sparkling in the sun: one of those burgundy numbers the firefighters rode around. Thurston wasn't even attempting to hide his connection to Sunder's newest collection of armed thugs.

One of the creeps in question had the driver's side door open and was sitting on the edge of the frame, smoking a thin cigar.

"We heading out yet?" he asked, with a lack of respect that should have had Yael sharpening her knives.

"Soon. Stay ready."

"Yeah, yeah."

When we were out of earshot, I dared to ask, "What's he preparing for?"

"Got some intel on a target who's been causing trouble. Just confirming the location and getting enough men together before we roll out.

Shit. I hoped Simms knew how to make herself scarce.

Cyran – Niles's number-one heavy – was waiting at the door of the main house.

"Tell the boss his little punching bag is here," said Yael, and the Ogre went inside.

Two more firefighters came through the gates and joined the one who was smoking. They tightened their boot laces and stretched their bodies like players getting ready for a game.

Cyran came out in less than a minute.

"Yeah, he'll see you."

When I went to step past him, a frying-pan-sized hand pressed against my chest.

"Pat down."

"Come on, Cyran. Aren't we past this?"

"Different times."

The Ogre knocked me about as he searched my pockets, ankles and under my shirt for any hidden weapons. I would have complained, but this, for him, was gentle; he could have held me by my ankles and shaken me out if he'd wanted to. When he was sure I had no guns, blades or brass knuckles, he stuck his fingers into my pocket and pulled out a coffee-stained napkin.

Cyran held it out towards Yael, seeking her opinion.

"You really worried about that?" I asked.

He ignored me. Waited for Yael to finish her inspection.

"Get rid of it. He's fine."

Cyran dropped the napkin in the trash, picked up a spray bottle and small towel, and used them to wipe down his hands.

"Come on, Cyran. I swear I showered this week."

Yael sprayed a second towel and turned to me.

"Hold out your hands."

I did as I was told – always a smart move when Cyran was close by – and Yael wiped the front and backs of my hands, and even my wrists.

"All good," she said, and cleared the entrance, pointing to a door on the right. "Through there."

"He's not in his parlor?"

"He takes meetings downstairs now."

I went where I was directed and stepped into a room that was half the length of the house (or about five times the size of my apartment). There was a small table just in front of me, and a much larger desk all the way down the other end.

Thurston Niles was standing in front of the desk wearing a white shirt over linen trousers. He was flanked by two young men in firefighter attire who each wore standard-issue six-shooters and expressions of extreme seriousness. Thurston, as always, was grinning like he'd guessed the punchline to my next joke and was waiting for me to set him up.

"If it isn't Sunder City's original Man for Hire, back on the case. It's good to see you again, Fetch."

"Yeah, I—"

The firefighters reached for their guns.

All I'd done was take a step towards Niles, barely moving

beyond the front of the tiny table. Apparently, that was enough to put his bodyguards on alert.

"Woah. Steady on, boys," said Niles, holding out his hands. "He's not familiar with the new rules. Sorry, Fetch. Different times. You might want to stay behind that table there. These fellas have been shooting nothing but sandbags for weeks and they're itching to try their aim on something more mobile."

Taking his advice, I sat down on the wooden chair positioned on the safe side of the small table.

"Those Whisper letters got you spooked?" I asked.

"The what?" Niles raised an eyebrow. "Oh, yes. I heard about that. No, no. Just taking extra precautions in these uncertain times. You never can be too careful."

Oh, great. Niles had many faces, and this was my least favorite. When he and I were alone, I was sometimes shown the one that – compared to his usual demeanor – had an ounce of sincerity in it. I clearly wouldn't be getting that today. Not with his obedient bodyguards sitting on his shoulders and Yael and Cyran by the door. This was Niles at his most impenetrable: the bulletproof politician who would lie to your face and make you feel bad for ever doubting him. Having a real conversation would be next to impossible, but for Simms's sake, I had to try.

"There's a commotion happening down at Backlash."

"Oh, yes. I heard about that. Apparently you and that detective stirred up some trouble."

"Tried to stop some trouble, actually. It was the article in the *Star* that got everyone's blood up."

Thurston sat on the edge of his desk and scratched one fingernail against another.

"That's why you're here? I'm sorry, but I have nothing to do with the news."

"We both know that's not true, but it doesn't matter. You do have a say in how men in charcoal and boys in burgundy react to the news. That Centaur is innocent."

"Surely that's a matter for the courts."

"Exactly. Detective Simms wants to know she can interview him without being accosted."

Thurston waved a dismissive hand and wandered around his end of the room.

"Sure. Whatever. We have no time for that anyway. Bigger fish to fry, right boys?" The bodyguards obediently nodded, sharing his playful grin.

What did that mean? Wasn't there a hit squad in the driveway ready to hunt Hyperion down?

"I'm surprised you're delivering the detective's message," mused Thurston. "I thought you and the police had parted ways."

"On this occasion, Simms and I want the same thing. That's all."

"You both want to catch Mister Whisper, right?"

"So, you *are* paying attention?"

"And you *are* helping Simms with her investigation."

He wrote something on a piece of paper and handed it to one of the bodyguards. The boy exited out the back door.

Niles wasn't going to change his mind because of anything I said. He had no reason to. But maybe, like Simms had suggested, I could keep him busy long enough for her to get Hyperion into hiding.

"Whisper's been writing some interesting things about you," I said. "You, Isaac Derringer, Redonna Demoor, the Mayor and poor Constable Bath. What have you all been cooking up together?"

Niles's grin only got wider.

"That's what he's saying, is he? Well, I used to meet with Isaac — rest in peace — every couple of weeks, and the Mayor and I are fond friends, of course. But I never spoke to the Priestess or . . . who was the other one?"

"Bath. A police officer."

"Never heard of him. But we do have so many promising young men joining the forces these days. Between constables, firefighters, company employees and conscientious citizens, we all need to work together to keep the city safe, don't you think? Look at what happened to that poor Priestess. I am glad we found the culprit before anyone else could get hurt."

He let the hook dangle, enjoying the fact that I couldn't resist taking the bait.

"I told you, he's innocent."

The satisfaction on his face made me want to leap across the room, twitchy gunslingers be damned.

"A poor, mad Centaur who lost his faith, right? So sad. Some people just can't be saved. Always want to blame someone else for their mistakes."

I knew my poker face was failing.

"How the hell would a Centaur on crutches blow up the Priestess like that?"

Thurston shrugged, as if it was the least interesting question that had ever been asked.

"I'm sure the investigation will uncover the truth in due course. Unfortunately, I can't oversee every little problem this city produces. Look at me. I'm stressed enough as it is." He spread his arms wide and gave the most relaxed shrug ever given.

There was a knock on the far door.

"Come in." It was the firefighter who had left with the note. "See, always something that needs my attention. What's the word, son? Are we ready?"

"Yes, sir. Men and vehicles are prepared and ready to deploy."
Shit.

"Thurston, I've got some questions about—"

"Sorry to cut the reunion short, Fetch, but we have a little fire to attend to."

"I thought you said you'd let Simms conduct her investigation in peace."

"Oh, I will. My boys are off to deal with something far more pressing. Apparently, some spies have been hiding out in The

Snatch and attacking innocent people for years. Luckily for us, these criminals have finally been brought to our attention."

Surely fucking not.

"Niles, wait."

"Sorry, Fetch. Business calls. Thanks for stopping by, though. I've missed you."

He left before I had the wits to say anything else, and I was suddenly aware of the sirens coming from the east. I went out the way I'd come, with Yael and Cyran flanking me all the way. We went through the front doors and back onto the porch to see a parade of burgundy vehicles zooming along Sixteenth Street: small square cars, and large red trucks with ladders on top, all with their lights flashing and sirens blaring. The truck in the driveway sped off to join the motorcade, firefighters perched on the running boards, hooting and hollering along with the alarms.

More firefighters emerged from the compound, running past me, out the gates and onto the road. They jumped into back seats or onto the sides of the overflowing trucks. Some were already brandishing their pistols, waving them in the air, while others laughed and cheered them on.

I walked down the driveway, watching them pass, and noticed one boy among the throng who wasn't dressed in red. His face was all scratched up: bruised and bloody from his battering at the hands of the Gremlins the previous day. While the others screamed in celebration of the upcoming violence, Ashton just looked at me from the passenger seat with cold and resolute eyes.

The procession moved on. An army, off to wipe the last of an endangered people off the planet, and there was nothing I could do to stop them.

I turned around, looked up, and saw Thurston Niles leaning over his balcony, his grin as wide as the city he held under his thumb.

He was beyond my reach. Unbeatable. And boy did he know it.

27

I grumbled to myself the whole way home, listening to the sirens as they faded out west. Old frustrations floated to the surface, along with latent, juvenile temptations. I wanted to go around kicking things just to prove a point. Make some senseless trouble, the way I used to when the world didn't turn the way I wanted.

I'd had notions of pushing back against Niles ever since he showed his face, but after a year of tackling the system – and my only reward being fists to the face – I decided that there were smarter, stronger, more dedicated people who could carry the mantle. Keeping those noble souls full of caffeine and calories was a greater contribution than gumming up the works with my personal brand of chaos.

Those kids had made it seem so clear: the next generation, ready to take over. When I was their age, I was still in Weatherly, trapped in a fabricated reality that denied the existence of magic and pulled the horizon to within arm's reach. These pint-sized rebels already had a greater chance of making real change than I ever did. As a bonus, they had each other. Strength in numbers and all that. I'd hoped they'd be able to keep each other in check. Hold themselves accountable.

Well, I was a fool once again. Doomed to witness someone else repeat my mistakes.

I can still remember believing that my cause was righteous. That it was my inarguable duty to slaughter the monster who'd hurt the people I loved. It had only taken a few encouraging voices to make the horrific sound reasonable. The unconscionable acceptable. The selfish selfless. The true power of men like Niles is how they make their own agenda sound like the rational solution.

General Taryn was the same: a charming military man who sat me down and told me how heroic it would be if I joined up with the Human Army to murder the Chimera that killed my family. That proposal was – as I'd recently found out – the beginning of a year-long ruse to make me feel so exceptional that I'd be inclined to cough up Opus secrets. It was a long time ago, but I'd say Taryn was even better at manipulation than Niles: a comforting father figure who could make mass-murder sound like the only sensible option.

I was considering giving up on my new position as babysitter of Sunder's rebel youth, when I arrived back at the cafe. To my surprise, I found Ophelia battling a hot plate full of hamburger patties, and Inero up on a stool, wiping dust – and maybe a little Derringer – from the light shade.

Maybe there was still hope.

"Thanks, Pheels."

She looked up from the impressive spread of sizzling beef.

"About time we pulled our weight."

I hated to spoil the mood, but her subdued demeanor told me that she was already aware of what her friend was up to.

"You hear those sirens?"

"Yep."

"You know what's going on?"

"Yep."

"You didn't want to try and stop it?"

Anger flashed across her face. At my dumb question or Ashton's stupid actions? Both would have been justified.

"He's doing what he thinks is right."

She went back to flipping burgers. I was about to offer to take over, when a voice purred in my ear.

"All right, Phillips. What's this special case you need my help with?"

Linda Rosemary – northern Werecat, and leader of the magical taskforce known as The Bridge – stood behind me in a long-sleeved linen shirt and green trousers. The silver badge of The Bridge was pinned to her breast pocket, polished and bright. "It had better be good, because we're still a long way from being on the same side."

"I'm sorry, Linda, but it's too late."

She scratched the countertop with the tip of her claw.

"You solved your mystery already?"

"Nope. The people I wanted you to help are all getting massacred by Niles's juvenile hit squad as we speak."

She gave a growl of disgust and her claws gouged four gulleys in the furniture.

"Tell me everything."

28

Ophelia and Inero took the extra burgers outside while I told Linda about Ashton and our expedition to The Snatch, then about the firefighters and what they were off to do.

"You should have called me straight away," she said. "We could have done something."

"How many Bridge members do you have in Sunder? Enough for open war with Niles?"

Her growl was an incoming thundercloud, and I understood her frustration. I'd been wrestling with the idea of fighting them myself, but the truth was – once the order was given – there was nothing that could be done. Even if we'd got the word out in time, who could we have counted on to fight the armed forces of the city, in service of a pack of psychotic, decrepit Fae?

"It's not right," she hissed, dropping her burger back on her plate.

"I know. But it's done."

She sighed at that, still weighing it up. I wouldn't have been surprised if she'd bolted out the door, off to take on Niles's goons single-handed.

"Fucking Niles," she growled. "There's no negotiating with him. I've been trying, but he's untouchable. Now more than ever."

"Is he taking your meetings from the other side of the room too?"

"Yeah. And they wipe me down with floor cleaner before I go in. What's that all about?"

"I have no idea, but he's spooked. After Bath, Derringer and Demoor, the Mayor and Niles are next on Whisper's list."

"What list?"

I took Whisper's messages off the noticeboard and laid them out on the table: the newsletter and the advert with their hidden messages spelled out beneath them.

"What happens if you find Whisper?" asked Linda. "You're really going to let the *Star* reveal his identity?"

"I don't know yet. First, I need to get him to tell me his plan."

"Let's hope he's forthcoming."

"I need to know if he's planning to reveal himself, or if he's even the one who committed the murders. Because if I don't find someone to offer up to Volta, those kids out there will take the fall."

"Like the one who's leading the troops on a Gremlin genocide? Maybe that's not the worst outcome."

It wasn't that simple, of course, but she did spark an interesting thought. Maybe Ashton could use his new-found leverage with Niles to convince the *Star* to drop their agenda against his friends. I could ask him, but that would involve talking to the little shit, and I wasn't sure if I could do that without knocking his lights out.

Linda picked up the first newsletter.

"You know who this guy sounds like?"

"Who?"

"*You.* Well, not you now, but a while back. When you were looking for any excuse to kick the shins of someone in power. I get that you're chasing this guy, but I don't understand why you're doing it for the other side."

What could I tell her? That the *Star* didn't just have the kids over a barrel, but that they were threatening to unmask me, too? That if I didn't give them someone to blame for Derringer's death, they'd post a front-page story that would drive me out of town?

Anyway, Whisper and I weren't anything alike.

"Linda, I'm not saying I got many things right, but at least I was willing to put my body on the line when I thought someone was a problem. As far as I can tell, Whisper's stirring up shit from the safety of a typewriter. That, or he's committing cold-blooded murder and letting others take the rap. I might have done a lot of things, but I never killed someone because I didn't like their politics."

"Well, maybe you should have." She smiled, but I don't think she was joking. "Because this place is getting sketchier by the day, and I don't think we know half of what they're up to."

"You agree with what Whisper's doing?"

She sighed. "I don't know yet. You don't have *any* idea who he is? Paper said it was some Centaur."

"They're just using him as free ink because they don't think he matters. Killing time until they track down the real culprit. At least, I think so. I suppose he *could* be Whisper. Or someone following Whisper's orders. Who the hell knows?"

"So, after all this, you have no ideas?"

"Nobody who fits. It could be one of the kids, but I doubt it. If the Centaur's to blame, he's going about it a strange way. Why would he draw all this attention on himself if he's trying to work from the shadows? No. I got nothing."

"Then maybe you should stop trying to work out who Whisper is and start listening to what he's saying."

"He's not saying anything new, is he? Just whining about corruption and alluding to some secret meeting."

"Exactly. This meeting must be what it's all about. Look at what Niles does in the open, and imagine how despicable something would have to be for him to try and keep it secret."

That *was* interesting, now that she mentioned it.

Niles prided himself in speaking plain. Whenever we were alone, he liked to brag that even his most cut-throat decisions were all for the good of the people, and that he was only giving us what we wanted. The worst part was, time had proven him right. We went along with anything he did as long as it kept the lights on and the paychecks coming.

But he had been extra cagey about that meeting, hadn't he?

Even pretended not to have met two of the people Whisper claimed were there. So, either Whisper is flat-out lying or Niles really didn't want me to know the truth.

"But who do we talk to?" I asked. "Three people from the meeting are dead and we have no chance of questioning Niles or the Mayor."

"Let's go back to the start. How did you first hear about all this? The newsletter?"

"The kids brought the newsletter in the morning it came out, then some guy from the *Star* took me up to Derringer's to ... . no, wait. Shit. Right before that, Simms came in. She wanted me to go to Bath's apartment with her. Investigate the crime scene."

Linda picked up the patty in her claws and took a proper bite.

"And what was it like?"

"I don't know. I didn't go."

"Fetch!"

"I thought she just wanted help avenging a dead cop. Sorry if I wanted to keep serving coffees instead of running off to help the police again."

"I get it. I would have done the same thing." She licked her claws and got to her feet. "But if Whisper's trying to tell us something, we need to work out what it is before this whole city is caught in the crossfire."

"Where are you going?"

"*We're* going where you should have gone a long time ago: to find out what happened to Constable Bath."

29

I led Linda back to the apartment block. The one where I'd seen Simms the morning after Bath's murder. With no cop cars or police tape outside, there was nothing to let you know that anything out of the ordinary had happened within.

"What number?" asked Linda.

"I don't know."

"What floor?"

"No idea."

She sighed.

"All right, we walk in with confidence and climb until we find a clue."

She made a move to enter the building, but I held a hand up in front of her.

"Wait."

"What?"

"You actually call them *clues?*"

"Shut up."

She marched in like she owned the place and I stayed on her heels, doing my best to look just as self-assured. The lobby was empty, and the stairs to the next level were at the back of the room.

"No clues here," I whispered, and Linda ascended without responding.

The only occupant out of their room was an old Satyr who was busy filling his pipe, and we got to the fourth floor before we saw a door with "Crime Scene, Do Not Enter" stuck onto it.

Linda pulled a set of lockpicks from a pouch on her belt, and we were inside in seconds. We closed the door behind us and both took a whiff of an unexpected smell.

"Peppermint," said Linda.

"Yeah. Bath's body smelt like it too."

"Strange. He was shot, right?"

"Eight times."

"Excessive. That sounds like more than just a murder. Someone was making a statement."

"Before they advanced to exploding cars and summoning light-ning bolts?"

"Perhaps."

The apartment hadn't been cleared, though I'm sure the landlord was already eager to scrub it down and find the next tenant. It was what you'd expect from a young man at the beginning of his career: a single room (shared bathroom down the hall) with cheap posters, a desk covered in unread books, an unmade bed with dark blue sheets, and no furniture that wasn't strictly functional. There were stains on the carpet. Mostly red. Then green.

Linda put her nose so close to the stain that her whiskers kissed the floor.

"That's the peppermint smell. Something spilt here." She looked around the room. "How many times did you say he was shot?"

"Portemus said there were eight entrance wounds, two exit wounds. Why?"

"Look." She pointed straight up. There was a hole in the ceiling. "That must be one that went right through him. Let's find the other."

It didn't take long; there was a hole in a print of a famous painting of Fintack Ro (one of Sunder's founders), and the wall behind it held a bullet. According to Portemus, that should have been it, but Linda was already digging another hunk of lead out of the carpet. There was another in the wooden leg of the bed and one more in the mattress. We spent a half-hour, fastidiously searching every square inch of the place. By the end, we'd found another three.

"Six bullets," said Linda. "That's two that went through Bath, and four that missed him completely."

We both looked around again, struggling to paint a logical picture. What kind of situation could have caused a shooter – or several shooters – to miss so many times in such a small space? And why would they fire in such a wide array of angles? The one that went straight up into the ceiling made the least sense. Were they lying on the ground, facing straight up, while Bath jumped over them?

"This is nonsense," said Linda, pushing around the objects on Bath's desk. "Whatever happened here, it was more than a simple execution."

"You mean the cops and the *Star* haven't shared the full story? Unbelievable."

"Looks like you're not the only one who was reading that rag." Linda opened up a wooden box full of scraps of paper. "Bath was collecting his favorite articles."

We rifled through the stories, but there was nothing that immediately linked them together. Headings like: "Are the Pipes Beneath the City Safe?"; "Building Up – Who Owns the Air Over Sunder?"; "The Legacy of Fintack Ro – Examining a Flawed Founder"; and a few others, covering a wide range of disparate topics.

"These must be connected to the case," I grumbled. "I just don't know how."

"You really call it a case? That's worse than clues."

I looked around one last time. More random facts, but nothing that shed any light on what Whisper was up to.

"Linda, at this stage I'll take any clues you've got. I can't make sense of this. Not the spread of shots or the smell or the meaning behind these newspaper clippings."

"Forget the papers for now. These, and the ones you've been reading. We need to talk to someone who saw this whole thing when it was fresh. Where do you stand with Simms?"

"After refusing to help her out with this, not great. But I did back her up during a showdown today so maybe she'll give us some insight if we ask her nicely."

"You'd better go on your own. Last time I saw Lena, I think I got under her scales."

"Really? When?"

"Let's talk outside. We've pushed our luck in here as it is."

We walked a couple of blocks from the crime scene and found a quiet alley where we could take a lean.

"Simms came to The Bridge headquarters a few days ago," said Linda. "Not a big surprise. We're used to cops pestering us. They come around a couple of times a week to let us know we're not wanted. We're past worrying, but it makes folks scared to be seen with us. There are people in need, but they're becoming too intimidated to seek help. I gave her the usual cold shoulder without enough attitude to warrant an escalation, but she kept hanging about. She was asking questions about some Witch. Wanted to know if we'd heard about anyone who'd been messing with magical medicines."

"She wanted you to rat someone out?"

"Yeah. I think she was trying to butter me up, but that tone doesn't come easy to a career copper with a forked tongue, so I sent her packing."

"Seems we both turned her down in the last few days."

"Yes, but sounds like you were more polite about it than I was. I still don't understand this whole *police* thing."

"What do you mean? No cops where you come from?"

"Fuck no."

"So how do you keep order?"

"Respect. Honor. Better provisions for the vulnerable."

"And if someone breaks that honor there's no punishment?" I asked.

"Of course there's punishment. You don't think society can't discipline someone without needing to hire a goon squad answerable to those in power?"

"Like physical discipline? Civilians cracking each other over the head when they don't like what someone does?"

"That's the same as what happens here. You just give some civilians a uniform that lets them crack without accountability. Does that really sound like a smart way to discourage violence?"

"Uh . . ."

It didn't take strong feline senses to pick up on my uncertainty.

"Our ways might be considered barbaric in this city, but where I come from, the violence is visible. Every person in Sunder is complicit in the same kind of violence, but by keeping the mechanisms hidden – by giving you all a bit of distance and the illusion of ignorance – you believe you are absolved from the responsibility."

"Come on, Linda. Most people here are struggling to make ends meet."

"You comfort yourselves by believing you are powerless: a convenient lie that lets you pretend you're not accountable. But you enable it. You desire it, even. Cunts like Simms crack skulls so you don't have to. So you can pretend you're just another victim of a broken system, when you could all fix it tomorrow if it was what you truly wanted."

She said it so matter-of-factly that I didn't dare argue. Besides, I knew I wasn't smart enough to make a decent case if I tried.

"You're right," I said. "If you're going to talk like that around Simms, I really should see her on my own."

She smiled, letting me off the hook.

"Let me know what she says. I'm also interested in tracking this Whisper guy down, but not so Simms can put him behind bars. Maybe we can help him fight back against this city before it kicks us out for good."

I made a noncommittal grunt. The Bridge were an unscrupulous organization that was still working through its teething problems. I might have tried to keep my distance from the police force, but that didn't mean I wanted to tie my fate to Linda and her collection of high-and-mighty altruists.

Not that I needed to tell her that.

"Sure thing, Linda. If I find any clues, you'll be the first to know." I went to walk away, then stopped. "Hey, did you go back?"

"Back where?"

"You know. The castle."

The castle of Incava. Where she and her comrades massacred the mad Wizards who were mining the river. Where we barely escaped their clay constructs, and saw the soul of the planet being carved up and pushed around in mine carts.

"Not me," she said. "But a band headed back there last week to see what they could find. We don't know if there are any Wizards left, or what state the place is in, but they should send word soon. When they do, do you want me to tell y—"

"No." I said it firmer than I'd intended. She nodded. She understood. The Bridge could deal with that mess. They could spend their days digging up the past, trying to find a way to fill the future. When they were worrying about what to do with a castle full of dead bodies and an army of clay constructs, I planned to be back in my kitchen with no bigger concern than an undercooked omelet. "Thanks, but no thanks. I'm confident you can handle that without me."

I approached Simms's place solo, hoping she was back from stashing Hyperion somewhere safe.

She might hear me out, but the challenge would be convincing her to give me information without me agreeing to help her catch Whisper. I needed to get her on side without creating an alliance I'd be forced to break.

I used the doorbell and applied my most apologetic face, but it turned to surprise when Eileen Tide pulled the door open.

"Fetch?"

Eileen was usually found at her library, though on several occasions she'd joined me on a case. It was on one of my cases that she'd first met Simms. I knew that they'd been spending more time together but I still hadn't expected to find her here.

"Hi, Eileen. Uh . . . is Simms home?"

She had that look. The look I've seen too many times before, when reality has been trying to blow down your house of cards all day, then I show up to kick the table.

"Oh, Fetch. It's awful. I don't know what to do."

"What is it? What happened?"

"It's Lena. I can't believe it." She wiped her tears and took a deep breath to stop her voice from breaking. "She's been arrested."

30

It was the first time I'd been inside Simms's home. I'm not sure what I expected, but I wouldn't have guessed it would be so . . . cute.

I knew that this was some kind of violation. For Simms, pulling the scarf from her mouth was an act of vulnerability. Now her whole domestic life was spread out in front of me, and it felt wrong to be gazing on it without her approval.

The couch, covered in cushions, was sat before an open brick fireplace. There was a small table on either side of it, each holding a half-read book with matching bookmarks sticking out the ends. I assumed that Eileen was reading the cozy romance with the roadside inn on the cover, while Simms was reading the handbook on Centaur battle tactics, but I was quickly learning that any assumptions I made about either of these women would likely miss the mark.

Structurally, the place was mostly concrete. Few buildings in Sunder had wooden exteriors (because unlike Niles, not everyone could afford their own fire department), but the living room was lined with wood panels that made you forget you were tucked into the city's most densely populated suburb. There were photos of the two of them above the mantelpiece. Simms was even smiling in one of them. If I was here under any other circumstances, it would have made me laugh. Instead, I started to get very, very worried.

"When did you talk to her?" I asked.

"She didn't come home tonight. I called the station and they said that she'd been locked up in Backlash. I went down there but they wouldn't let me in. They told me she should be given a phone call so I've been standing by but . . . nothing yet."

She looked at the phone on the wall, willing it to come to life, like a novice Necromancer gazing upon an uncooperative corpse.

"Looks like you've properly moved in," I said, hoping to distract her.

"Yes, I gave up my apartment a few weeks ago."

I'd seen Eileen in all kinds of situations — running from a deformed Vampire who wanted to suck the marrow from her bones, chasing a shapeshifter through the markets, and held at arrow-point on the side of the highway — but this was a whole, deeper level of panic. Her long hair was out of its braid and there were fingerprints on her spectacles.

"It'll be all right," I said. "It was just a misunderstanding."

"Really? Wait, were you there?"

Shit. Why did I have to be the one to tell her that her girlfriend had shot someone in public?

"Yes, but . . . I think I need a drink. Do you want a drink?"

"Fuck yeah. What do you want? I have everything. Sam closed The Roost and sent me all the remaining stock. It's in Lena's study, through here."

Before I could tell her that any old plonk would do, she was off through the neat little kitchenette and into the next room. I followed, doing my best to resist pushing my nose too far into Simms and Eileen's private life.

There was a two-step drop down into the study: a round, dark room below street level that was also partly beneath the unit next door (you could hear one of the neighbors creaking the floorboards as they crossed the room).

On the street-side wall, there was a small, frosted window only a couple of inches high. Blurred outlines of feet occasionally passed on the sidewalk. A large, cluttered desk took up most of the space, and an alcove cut into the wall had become Eileen's overflowing bar.

"I really do have everything," said Eileen, grabbing at random bottles. "Every liquor and mixer imaginable. I hate the sweet stuff, but it's all here if you want it. Maybe whiskey? Yes, I'll have something southern. If you want a cocktail, I could—"

"Whiskey's fine. Thanks."

She grabbed a light-colored bottle from the floor.

"I'll get some glasses."

While she was gone, I went over to the desk. The bar might have been Eileen's, but this mess was all Simms: chewed-on pencils, stacks of photos and plenty of papers stamped with the mark of the Sunder PD.

A notepad was lying open, and someone had scribbled "Meeting. Who? Fray???"

Fray.

It seemed Simms had cracked Whisper's hidden message too. Unfortunately, it seemed she also had no idea what that first floating word was supposed to mean.

Eileen returned with two glasses, generously filled them, and sat in Simms's desk chair.

"All right, Cowboy. What the hell happened to Lena?"

I did my best to recount the events of the morning in the most tedious way possible, though it's not easy to tell someone that their partner shot an armed man in the middle of a crowd and make it sound uneventful.

She was shaking her head, willing the story to change, when the phone rang.

Eileen moved like lightning, up the step and back into the living room, lifting the receiver before it had completed its second ring. I went to follow but heard the tone of her voice and thought better of it. It was evidently Simms, and I'd already intruded enough without eavesdropping on their conversation.

I took the seat at the desk and moved some papers around. There was a glob of red wax on the corner of the wood that had dripped down towards the floor but frozen during its journey. I couldn't see where the stuff had come from. Perhaps that was how the cops sealed their documents: wax seals to keep their correspondence safe.

Some drops had fallen on a manilla folder so I flicked it open to see a set of black-and-white photographs.

Bath.

Splayed out on his apartment floor, dressed in his uniform while his blood soaked the carpet beside the peppermint stain. The official police report was in there too, along with some of Simms's handwritten notes. Before I could read them properly, Eileen was in the doorway, her cheeks glistening and her eyes red.

"They've locked her up for assisting that murderer. The Centaur."

"He didn't kill anyone."

"I know that. Lena knows that too. But she can't prove it while she's inside."

Ah, shit.

"Eileen, I'm trying to work this out. If I can find out who killed these people, I'll let you know, but—"

"I told her you were here. She was glad. She told me to ask you if you'd worked out why Derringer and Demoor were dead."

"I told you, I don't think it was the Centaur but my list of alternative suspects isn't substantial."

"She didn't ask who, Fetch. She asked *why.*"

I sipped my whiskey. What was Simms getting at? Probably just some police trick. Some old detective saying, like "The *why* will lead you to the *who*", or whatever. Still, I was in no position to turn down established wisdom.

"Fetch, you need to help her."

"I—" Excuses lined up on my tongue: the strangeness of the killings and the case, the fruitless hours I'd already spent on it, the many people I'd promised to bring information to first, and my reservations about handing anything to the police even if it meant freeing my occasional accomplice. I left those excuses where they belonged and just said, "I'll try."

"Thank you."

I lifted up the manilla folder.

"She talk to you much about her work?"

"Not really. She tries to leave it at the door, but a bit always sneaks in. That young officer getting killed really shook her up."

"Bath."

"Yeah. You knew him?"

"Only a little. Remember when we raided that maskmaker's shop? He was there with us."

"Was he? Oh, I didn't realize." She came back to the desk and halved her drink with one sip. "I tried to talk to Lena about it but she . . . I don't know. I guess it's hard for her."

"Were you with her when she found out?"

She nodded her head.

"The night it happened, I'd stayed late at the library, stocking a new delivery. When I got back, I expected her to already be in bed, but she was in here. She seemed stressed. Quiet. She gets like that sometimes, after a big day. So, I went to sleep without her. When I woke, the phone was ringing. She answered and it must have been the station – it's always the station – because she just left. The next day, when she came back, she told me about Bath."

I held up the wax-stained folder.

"Could I take these notes?"

"Oh, Fetch. I don't know."

"I promise it's only so I can help set her free. It looks like Whisper killed Bath, Derringer and Demoor, and knowing Simms, she will have already put things together that I missed." Eileen was still reluctant. "If she finds out, I'll say I swiped it without you knowing."

Eileen tried smiling but it didn't take. She nodded instead.

Underneath the folder, there were some curly, brown strands of fiber. I took a pinch and put it to my nose. Tobacco.

"Does Simms smoke?"

Eileen shook her head.

"No way. I'd have smelt it on her."

"Any recent visitors?"

"Hardly ever. Well . . . maybe."

"Maybe?"

"The night Bath died. Before that, when I came back from the library, there were two glasses in the sink. I suppose Lena could have used both of them, but it did seem strange. Well, not strange, just . . . I don't know. She doesn't usually drink alone."

"You didn't ask her about it?"

"No. She was already out of sorts. Then Bath died. Since then, she's barely been here."

I leaned back in the chair and looked up. There were more photos stuck to the wall. Most of them recent. Clearly Eileen had brought the camera into their lives, as all the older photos had been professionally taken: Simms's initiation into the Sunder PD and a couple clipped out of newspapers.

Fucking newspapers. There was a picture of Simms with Trixie Derringer, Isaac absent this time. A little reminder of who I was dealing with. Eileen may be a hard-drinking librarian, but Detective Simms was a finely tuned tool of the city, and – though her actions that day had gone admirably against the grain – I had to remember that her desire to find Whisper wasn't coming from the same place as mine.

"Thanks, Eileen." I stood up and finished the whiskey. "First thing tomorrow, I'll do everything I can to clear her and Hyperion's names. I promise."

She hugged me.

"Do you have to go?"

"Uh . . . no."

"Then please stay. I don't like being here at night without her."

"Of course. Of course, I'll stay."

We stayed up talking until Eileen was exhausted enough to quiet her anxieties. I curled up on the surprisingly comfortable couch and must have slept heavily because when I awoke, the sun was coming through the window and Eileen was dressed for work.

"What time is it?" I asked.

"Eight."

"Shit. I haven't slept this late in months."

"You looked like you needed it. Keep going if you want. I'm off to the library, but you can let yourself out."

"No, no. I'd better get to it." I picked up my wallet, keys and the manilla folder containing the Bath case. "I'll call you if anything comes up."

"Thank you, Fetch. Really. I feel a lot better knowing you're looking out for her."

Usually, I would have made some disparaging remark about my history of ineptitude, but I chose to keep my doubts to myself. If Eileen Tide wanted to put her faith in me – even after everything she'd seen – then that was her business.

It was my business not to let her down.

31

When I got back to 108, I was surprised to find the cafe alive with excitement. Ophelia and Inero were in the kitchen, and whatever experiment they were attempting had caused black smoke to waft into the dining room. To my horror, one of Niles's firefighters was leaning over the counter, talking at them as they worked.

Shit. Maybe they were here to tell us that, without Georgio, we weren't legally allowed to operate. Surely finding a bunch of unpaid adolescents in the kitchen wasn't helping my case.

I got myself puffed up for an argument, and didn't change my tune when I saw who it was.

Ashton. All spruced up in his brand-spanking burgundy jacket, showing off his new Niles Company toys. He had his gun and ammunition spread out on the counter with no regard for anyone's safety.

"They give you the uniform straight up," he said. "Tailored and everything. Plus a brand-new six-shooter, fully loaded, and another six bullets in reserve. I get a knife too, but they said they're making mine special so I'll have to wait."

Ophelia had spotted me, and the look on her face drew Ashton's attention. When he turned, there was only a fleeting glimmer of sheepish embarrassment before he covered it up with indignant pride. We stared at each other, waiting to see who would make the first move.

Ophelia cut the tension.

"Sorry about the smoke. I tried to show the new guy how to do a full breakfast, but it turns out he really is just a pretty face."

I kept my eyes on Ashton.

"You've made some new friends."

He kept his eyes on me.

"Yeah."

How was he not dying from guilt? I wanted to cut my own throat for the part I played in taking out the Gremlins, and I wasn't the one who joined up with the firefighters just so I could wipe them from existence. All his ideals and principals thrown away just because of a little kidnapping. I wanted to grab him by his collar, drag him out onto the street, and leave him in the gutter, but what would that accomplish? First, I needed to see if his newfound position could solve a problem or too. If not, there was still plenty of time to throw him in a sack and dump the little shit in the Kirra where he belonged.

"Remember what I told you about the *Star*?" I said. "How they're thinking of making you kids the scapegoats of all these murders."

"I thought they already named the Centaur."

"The Centaur's innocent."

"Sure."

I gripped my trouser leg to try to stop myself from slapping him.

"When they realize that – and decide to put your friends back in the firing line – are you going to be a big enough man to step in and save them? Profess their innocence to your new buddies?"

"It's my first fucking day, Fetch. Screw this."

He stood up straight, packing away his deadly little trinkets.

"You don't think you should talk to Niles about your old friends? Make sure your gang doesn't get caught in the crossfire of his war with Whisper?"

He sneered. I wasn't sure why. It seemed like something we'd both want.

"Niles doesn't get close to new recruits," he said, like this was common knowledge. "Only the top soldiers get anywhere near him. Well, them and you, right? You're old pals. Maybe you should be the one asking him for a favor."

He slotted his pistol back into his holster and the ammo into his pocket.

"I'm not the one wearing his threads, kid."

"Nah, you're just trying to stay comfortable in this city he built for you. Same as everyone else." He drained his cup and spun on the heels of his new boots. "I'll see what I can do. Thanks for the coffee, Ophelia. Best one I've ever had."

Ophelia watched him leave.

"Fetch, he thinks he's doing the right thing. Give him a chance to—"

I looked past her to the sizzling stovetop.

"You need to use more oil. Clear off the burnt bits before you cook anything else or you'll smoke out all of Main Street. I'll be back down in an hour."

I left them to their attempted breakfast and went upstairs. The room was dark and muggy, but I didn't open the Angel door or windows just yet. I wanted to work through a couple of problems first.

I opened the manilla folder and spread the papers across my desk. There were Simms's personal notes, a form from Portemus, the official police report and black-and-white photographs of the crime scene including multiple angles on Bath.

I'd seen him down the morgue, stripped and laid out on the slab, but here he was fully clothed, in uniform, lying in a crumpled heap on the stained carpet.

The police report was dense, full of acronyms and jargon I couldn't understand, so I turned my attention to Simms's notes.

Door locked and bolted from the inside (officers forced to break in).
NO FINGERPRINTS on exterior door handle.
Window small. No signs of entry or exit.
Twelve shots fired. ALL ANGLES.
Bottle shattered (by bullet?). Contents spilled into carpet.
Pistol???

I felt some pride at the fact that Simms and I had hit on similar questions regarding the case: the strange angle of the shots, the stain, how the killers escaped. Unfortunately, she hadn't offered up many answers.

Bottle shattered? I flicked through the pictures and found one that showed a bunch of broken glass around the puddle. The shards were clear, with no apparent label. That must have been where the peppermint smell had come from. From the way it covered his body and leaked into the carpet where he fell, it must have been on his person. Perhaps in a pocket. But why would Bath be lugging around a bottle of peppermint essence? It wasn't the kind of thing you'd wear as cologne, and though peppermint was used in some cocktails, only a madman would drink it neat. Besides, any peppermint liqueur I'd seen came with some green-glassed, ornate bottle, not a small unlabeled flask. Had Simms noted it down because she'd worked out why it was relevant? Or was she as lost as I was?

I tried to imagine the shape of Bath's apartment superimposed over mine. The size was about the same. His front door was more or less where mine was – *locked and bolted from the inside* – but he had no Angel door or fire escape to give the killers an alternative entrance or exit, just that tiny window, about the size of a shoebox.

So how had they got in, and how the hell had they got out?

I moved the hat stand to the center of the room – standing it on the spot where Bath's body had been found – then took a pack of gum from my desk and started chewing.

I never had much money, but since taking over the cafe, there was always change about the place. I dropped a coin on the floor, at the spot where Linda had pulled the bullet from the carpet. Then I tore a bit of gum from the wad in my mouth and stuck five more coins around the room: all the places where the stray bullets had embedded themselves. I even got up on the desk and stuck one to the roof.

Then I stepped back.

It was madness. The bullets had hit all four walls, the floor and the ceiling. If there were four shooters firing at once, they'd risked shooting each other, either when they'd missed Bath – which had happened four times – or with one of the secondhand bullets that had gone right through their target and out the other side.

But how had they missed him so many times? Bath's room was even smaller than mine.

The window?

I opened the Angel door into a gust of hot wind, then turned around and looked back into the room.

Not a chance.

If someone had dangled themselves outside and fired twelve shots through that tiny window, the bullets would have roughly ended up in the same place.

Could they have stuck an arm in?

I reached in, and tried to see what range I had access to, but when I pointed in all the directions the shooter (or shooters) would have had to fire in, I felt like I was going to dislocate my arm. The kickback caused by firing a gun at all those odd angles would have fucked up your wrist and elbow for sure, and what would have been the point? Unless Bath was flying around the room like a trapped sparrow.

That meant at least one shooter must have been inside. Linda and I had searched for any other way to escape and found none, but that didn't mean it was impossible. We could always go back, rip up the carpet and search for a trapdoor. Or perhaps the killer had remained hidden until the door was unlocked, then found a way to sneak out. That was possible but illogical. Why keep yourself locked inside the murder scene when you could just open the door and flee? And even if the killer *was* inside, the directions of the bullets still didn't make sense.

Simms's note – *Pistol???* – confused me. Of course it was a pistol. No other weapon can fire Niles Company bullets. Even if it did, some new kind of gun wouldn't solve the major issues with the mystery.

I looked through the rest of the notes and found something in the police report that I could actually understand: a list of Bath's belongings taken as evidence.

ON PERSON:
  Wallet
  Keys
  Knife
  Holster
  Burgundy Uniform

Burgundy?

I flipped back through the pages to the photo of Bath lying on the floor. Without color, I hadn't noticed that the uniform he was wearing wasn't from the Sunder PD.

Bath was dressed as a firefighter.

I don't know why that changed things, but it did. Bath wasn't just a cop doing his job like any other; he'd left the force to join Niles's private squad of gun-toting yahoos. He must have been one of the first. Maybe the one you'd single out if you wanted to deter others from putting on the same suit.

But why had Bath done it?

Working for the Sunder PD was already a dubious decision, but there was room to imagine he'd entered that profession with good intentions. For all their violence and corruption, the police were seen — at least by some — as part of the community. Even I could acknowledge that they were occasionally helpful. But to give the same grace to a Niles firefighter would be too generous. They were a privately funded army created to keep people in line. Anyone with brains could see that. Couldn't they? Was I giving Bath too much credit, or too little?

I looked at that list of evidence again.

Uniform. Knife. Holster.

Just like Ashton had been showing off. Except . . .

No pistol.

Where had it gone? And not only that . . .

No Ammo.

Ashton had spelled it all out, hadn't he?

Six shooter. Fully loaded, and another six bullets in reserve.

Twelve Bullets. Six in Bath's body. Six embedded around the room.

Bath had brought all the bullets in with him, then . . . what? Fired them himself?

No. There was no way in hell any man would fire into his own guts, then reload the weapon and shoot himself again. Even under some kind of magical mind control, that would be a hard one to pull off.

So, if he hadn't fired the gun, then . . . *the bullets had gone off on their own.*

But how? It was hot, but not so hot as to ignite dormant powder inside the shell. If that was possible, half the city would have shot themselves by now, not to mention what would have happened to the factories uptown where they store the explosive Desert Dust that's used in the ammunition.

All twelve bullets must have gone off one after the other, the six in the chamber along with the extra ammo in his pocket. But that would require . . . I don't know what, but more than a warmer-than-average evening.

And where the hell was the pistol? Surely the mangled hunk of metal would have told that story, but it had apparently vanished from the crime scene. Another unexplainable phenomenon, or just a corrupt cop hiding evidence before it was logged?

I'd had some experience with miracles, but I'd had plenty more experience with unscrupulous officers, and chose to put my money on the latter. So not only had something impossible happened, but someone on the force was covering it up.

Based on these notes, the culprit wasn't Simms. She had been seriously trying to work out how Bath had died, and I wished I'd offered to help her when I had the chance. Not because I thought the police department were on the right side of anything – or that Bath didn't deserve what he got for switching to an even worse arm of the law – but because she asked me, and she was a friend. At the very least, I would have been someone for her to talk to when she was trying to make sense of why a person she cared about was gone.

I was about to end my little reenactment when I noticed something else on her notes.

NO FINGERPRINTS *on exterior door handle.*

There was a circle around the "NO" for some reason. Why the emphasis? Was Simms just frustrated that she couldn't identify the killer as easily as she hoped?

NO FINGERPRINTS.

I flipped back to the photo of Bath on the floor in a pile of blood and his brand-new firefighter uniform. The same as Ashton's: steel-capped boots, suspenders, and a three-quarter-length jacket.

But no gloves. No firefighters wore them. Simms did, to protect the scales on her hands, and women like Trixie Derringer who wouldn't let the weather get in the way of her elegant style, but they were anomalies this time of year.

NO FINGERPRINTS *on exterior door handle.*

Simms didn't just mean that there were no helpful leads from the fingerprints they found, she meant that there were *no fingerprints at all*. Not even from Bath, who had just let himself in.

That means . . . What the hell does it mean???

It could mean that somebody wiped down the doorknob after Bath entered. It *could*. But why? If nobody exited the room after Bath went in there, why would anyone need to wipe down the door handle?

I hit myself on the head a few times, trying to knock it into a higher gear. I was out of practice on this kind of thinking. Hell, I'd never been *in* practice.

If someone had gone into Bath's apartment and left any kind of trap – some device that could have set off his ammunition – they would have wiped the doorknob clean as they left, but Bath's own fingerprints would have marked the handle after. So why wait until Bath got home? Why risk it?

Did they forget? After Bath was killed, did one of the killers realize their mistake and return to the scene to wipe away the last shred of evidence? Or was it the same corrupt cop who removed the mangled pistol . . . if that had even been a thing.

Maybe. But a piece was missing. There was some other reason for the missing fingerprints, and Simms had picked up on it.

Would the guards at Backlash let me in to talk to her? Would they idly stand by as we swapped ideas about Whisper's identity, when Simms was already in trouble for setting their favorite suspect free?

With questions about Bath's death only multiplying, I went downstairs and made myself a coffee. The kids had cleared out and the sink was full of dirty, soaking dishes. The only sound came from the radio where the Lamplighter station played a melancholy piano tune.

I waited for the pot to boil, musing over my next move, when the music came to an abrupt halt. The piano was replaced by the voice of Tabatha Ratchet, seemingly out of breath. Her tone was less confident than her usual measured, broadcaster voice.

"Excuse the interruption, but we have just been issued with a government order to broadcast this message immediately. 'In light of recent events, Mayor Piston's scheduled announcement from Five Shadows Square has been moved forward from tomorrow to sunset tonight. Citizens are still invited to attend but asked to keep their vantage from beyond the square itself. This request will be enforced and unruly attendees with not be tolerated. The city firefighters will be on guard to ensure everyone's safety' – *lucky us* – 'and for those who cannot attend, be ready to receive the Mayor's new orders at a later date, as they will affect every person in Sunder.'

"So there we have it, folks. Rest assured that Lamplighter will be on the scene, ready to relay these new developments back to the station, so stay by your radio for the next few hours and do not change your dial. This is Tabatha Ratchet, bringing the stories of Sunder right to your ears."

The piano number picked up where it had left off.

So, Piston was changing his schedule and using his goons to force everyone to keep their distance. Niles was conducting conversations from a half-mile away, and Demoor had been trying to use her Mirrors as bodyguards so that nobody could approach her without being selected.

Was this caution all because they'd been named by Whisper? Had they also cracked the secret message and decided to take the threats seriously?

Secret message.

I pulled out the wad of newspaper clippings from my pocket: crumpled and squashed because I'd slept on them. Why had Bath been collecting these? Nothing in the content of the articles seemed related to the case, except for the fact they all danced around the edges of investigative journalism. Linda had assumed they were from the *Star*, but this kind of informative, thought-provoking copy wasn't the tabloid's usual repertoire.

Was there another secret message contained in these pieces? Something everyone else had missed?

I scanned the first words of each line, but it wasn't a repeat of the soil advertisement. I looked at the first letters in each line, and the last, but couldn't even make a word. What I *did* notice, after far too long, was that the same initials were written in bold at the bottom of every story.

J.M.

I called the radio station.

"Tabatha Ratchet for Lamplighter Radio. Do you have a question you want to ask on air?"

"Hey, it's Fetch. I have a question, but off air would be preferable."

"Make it quick. Less than two minutes left on this song."

"Do you know a journalist at the *Star* with the initials J.M.?"

"Uh . . . I don't think so. There's a J.T."

"I have some clippings here, all signed J.M."

"You sure it's the *Star*? That could be Jackson."

"Who?"

"Jackson Murray. He publishes a magazine about lost magical artefacts. Well, that's supposed to be the subject but, in truth, it's just a platform for him to peddle his complaints about how the city is being run. He spent a few years freelancing for the *Star*, way back when, writing opinion pieces and such, but when they stopped publishing him, he started his own magazine."

"You're telling me there's another journalist in Sunder City with an interest in magic, strong opinions on Sunder governance and a vendetta against the *Star*?"

I heard her mentally kick herself.

"Well, you smart-ass bleedin' bastard, I suppose that is what I'm saying. Though I feel daft for not saying it some days ago."

"Where is he?"

"Murray? I finish my show in half an hour. Meet me here and I'll take you to his place. If he really is Whisper, then I want the scoop."

I wasn't sure I liked that idea, but now that I'd tipped her off, she'd be heading to Jackson Murray's place with or without me.

"All right, but let's talk this through before you announce anything."

Tabatha avoided agreeing to those terms, ending the conversation quickly.

"Song's wrapping up. Gotta go. I'll see you outside in thirty."

She hung up, and her voice moved from the phone to the radio, cheerfully recounting the name of the composer and composition.

If Jackson Murray was Whisper, what would happen when we confronted him? Would I really throw him under the bus to save the kids, the Centaur and Simms? Would I hand him to the *Star* to save myself?

Ophelia and Inero hadn't done a bad job cleaning the place up. Sure, they'd immediately made another mess with their attempt at breakfast, but I could start to believe that the place could get back on its feet. Turning in Whisper could give me some clout with those in power. Perhaps enough to convince someone to get those pesky pencil-pushers off my back. Maybe even officially put the cafe into my care. Then everything would go back to normal, and I could keep cooking until Georgio returned.

Jackson Murray would have to be one hell of an underground hero for me to choose his safety over this cafe and the future of Ophelia and her friends, but I was willing to give him a chance to convince me, and I hoped that Tabatha would do the same.

I had a hundred questions for Mister Whisper, and it looked like I was finally going to get my answers.

32

Tabatha stood in the middle of the street, her mouth hanging open in shock.

"What the hell?"

Jackson Murray's house was a mess of black bricks, burnt wood and ash. A worker's cottage reduced to rubble. The houses on either side were singed but still standing, so the fire clearly came from inside Murray's home.

"You didn't know about this?" I asked.

"Oh, of course I did. We wandered all the way across the city in the summer heat just so I could enjoy the feeling of sweat sliding through my fur." She put a hand on what remained of the stone doorway and closed her eyes, taking a moment to absorb the news. "Shit on a biscuit. Give me a minute, I'll call some contacts."

While Tabatha went to find a phone booth, I stepped into the wreckage. This had been more than a candle catching the curtains. Judging by the decimated furniture and skeletal walls, the heat must have been extreme. I kicked out the last few inches of a lone, free-standing table leg, and pushed my boot through a pile of soot to reveal nothing but more soot. I scrounged around and found a few steel pens that were warped and useless but still reminiscent of their old shape. I dug out some silver buttons, a door handle, a pair of cufflinks, a light fixture and a bunch of twisted wiring, but that was about it. The walls had come to pieces, exposing the pipes. As hot as this fire must have been, it was no match for the ones beneath the city, so the nickel tubes that had been responsible for bringing the house its power were still intact. They were warm to the touch, too. If this accident had been caused by a burst tube, the main supply would have needed to be shut off or the fire would still be going.

No, this mess had been caused by something else.

On my way out, I kicked another pile of charred debris, and cursed at the pain that shot through my foot.

A hunk of black iron was buried beneath it, as heavy as an anvil. After I'd stopped swearing and wiping my eyes, I blew the muck away from the hidden object and tried to work out what the hell it was.

Metal squares. A lever. Letters?

A printing machine.

An older model, similar to the one I'd seen at Derringer's. There was a plate where the paper would go and a square of stamps set opposite. It was the size of a magazine, and must have been the tool Murray used for publishing his investigations into unknown artefacts. A convenient contraption to have on hand when you wanted to create an underground alter ego like Whisper.

I took a closer look at the side that held the letters – a grid that contained tiny stamps, each with a symbol on the end – and realized that Murray's last story was still sitting in the machine.

I couldn't parse it easily – the whole thing was backwards and covered in soot – but some words stood out: killed, fire, Demoor.

This was another Whisper newsletter: unseen, perhaps, by anyone but him.

No paper had survived the fire, of course, but I'd managed to keep my hands fairly clean. So, I pressed them onto the stamps, side by side, and when I took them off, the story was printed – almost perfectly – across my palms and fingers. A few letters were lost at the edges and in the space between my hands, but otherwise it was a perfect print.

It appeared to be the second page of an article about – ironically enough – a fire.

Sources tell us that Angela   s no mere factory
worker. Her skill as a maker   f both poison and medi
known long before the Niles   pany came to town. We h
ave reason to believe tha   fire, which caused
considerable damage to prope   the Rose Quarter was
not only deliberate, but tha   a Fray was the target.
Killed, to keep her quiet a   destroy her research.
Angela's discovery was reve   d to only a few people,
the night before the fire: ry Piston, Isaac Derrin
Thurston Niles, Redonna Dem   nd Constable Timothy
Bath. One of these people,   their associates, must b
responsible for her death. B   the question remains...
WHO KILLED ANGELA FRAY?

Fray! The first name on Whisper's list: Angela Fray! Even without the full article – and some words and letters missing – it was enough to sell me on one thing: *Murray was the man we were looking for.*

Tabatha returned from the phone booth.

"This is him!" I exclaimed. "Jackson Murray has got to be Whisper. That's why someone burned his house down. We should—"

"Jackson's dead. Killed in the fire. A week ago."

"A week?" That made no sense. Whisper had barely got the ball rolling by then. "That's impossible. Unless he wrote all his stories beforehand. Had some system for distributing them after he died."

Tabatha shook her head.

"They were too up-to-date. Too specific."

"But . . . but look!"

I held up my hands. Tabatha read the article and inspected the press, but it did little to lift her spirits.

"Murray was too dead to be Whisper," she said, "but the story might still have started here."

"What about Angela Fray. You heard of her? Or anything about her death?"

"I don't think so." Tabatha looked around the decimated room. "Somehow, Jackson knew about this secret meeting. Not only that, it seemed he'd already connected it to another fire, down the Rose Quarter, a night or two before."

The Rose?

"When would that have been?"

"Not sure exactly, but more than a week ago if Murray was writing about it."

I couldn't be sure, but it might have been the same fire that Ophelia and Ashton were running from the first time we met.

"So," said Tabatha, heading back out onto the street. "Murray believed that Angela Fray's house was burned down to destroy her secrets. Then before he can get his story out, Murray is killed in a fire too."

"And Bath – who Murray was about to name as one of the conspirators behind Angela's death – was in possession of a bunch of articles that Murray had written."

"Maybe everyone at this meeting had worked out that Murray was onto them. Wanted to squash the story before it got out."

If the dates lined up, then on the day of Angela Fray's death, Bath had chased down Ophelia and Ashton. Chased them down *and let them go.*

I thought he'd given up because his polite demeanor and lack of confidence was no match for our improvised performance, but what if it wasn't that at all? What if he let the kids go because he knew they were innocent? Knew they were innocent because he knew damn well that someone else was responsible for burning Angela Fray's house to the ground.

Somehow, news of this meeting had gotten out, and everyone who'd attended wanted their rendezvous kept secret. Had Bath – Niles's new lapdog – been tasked with tracking down the story before it leaked? Was he there when Angela Fray went up in flames? He'd collected a bunch of articles that led him to Murray, but was he really the one who'd lit the fuse?

I told Tabatha the story of Bath and the kids at the cafe, and suggested how it all might line up.

"It's a theory," she said, "but in a stroke of bad luck for Constable Bath, Murray had already passed the news on to someone else. Whisper – whoever he is – must have received Murray's secret, and now he's telling the story his colleague wasn't able to finish himself."

"You really think that's what happened?"

"As I said, it's just a theory at this stage. We need more evidence. There's no Murray to talk to. No Bath to interrogate."

"But we do have a place to go back to."

"We certainly do. The heinous first act that started it all, and the question that Murray was asking the day he died."

Who Killed Angela Fray?

We stepped out of the charred cottage and went south, towards the part of town that no case could seem to avoid.

The sun was baking, it hadn't rained in weeks, but in Sunder, the Rose was always in bloom.

33

I don't know how the Rose Quarter first got its name, but it surely wasn't because of the aroma that wafted out of its narrow alleys during the summer months. The canal was down to a trickle, emitting a stale funk made worse because each establishment attempted to cover it up by spraying perfume or burning fragrant oil. From a block away, it smelt like someone had been boiling a bouquet of flowers in a swampy stew.

It was too early for most workers to be out on their balconies, and too hot for the few that were to promote themselves with any enthusiasm. A couple of Satyr boys sat in a doorway sharing a bottle, lazily offering themselves to anyone who walked by. Their eyes passed over me before landing on Tabatha with fascination.

"Well, well. A *lady* Satyr?" purred the first, running his fingers through the fur on his chest. "I hope you're not planning on working down here, darling. An act like that could put us boys out of business."

"Let's be making this quick," said Tabatha. "I hate this part of town."

We made our way along the main drag, beside the steaming canal, breathing through our mouths and keeping our heads low. We passed the Baroness and the Tincture before turning up the alley that took us to the Heroine: the only establishment in the area where they knew me by name.

"Hello, stranger." Gabrielle – the sardonic Siren – was leaning against the doorframe, wafting a fan with one slender hand and smoking a tiny cigar with the other. Tabatha put her mouth close to my ear.

"One of this lass's regulars, are you?" There was a hint of judgment in her voice, so I was happy to disabuse her of that notion.

"Gabrielle has helped me out on the occasional case. As long as I promise to tread carefully, she's my top source of Rose Quarter intel."

Tabatha gave me an approving nod, before a slender Half-Elf in a sheer robe bumped into us on her way inside.

"Fetch! You're here early. Let me rinse off then I'm all yours." She disappeared down the hall before I could tell her that I was only here on business. Tabatha's look became less approving, and I gave a sheepish shrug.

"I am one of *her* regulars, though."

Gabrielle picked up on Tabatha's discomfort.

"Fetch, you better not be bringing jilted wives down here. That kind of business will be bad for both of us."

"Nothing like that. Tabatha is working on a story that crosses over with my latest case. We want to know about the fire that happened here last week. Killed a woman named Angela Fray."

"You mean that poor Witch and her brother?"

"I guess. All we have is a name. Don't know anything about a brother."

"Fire got both of them. Real shame. There's nothing much left, but I can show you where it happened."

I gratefully accepted the offer and Gabrielle led us through the backstreets, away from the canal. These lanes were easy to get lost in if you didn't know your way, and easy to get killed in if you didn't keep your wits. I might have Sunder stuck under my finger-nails and filling every pore, but there were still neighborhoods where even I wasn't local enough to venture unattended. The people who lived and worked around here got a pass – probably bought with a monthly fee or a bartered friendship – but anyone else was considered an enemy or a mark. I stuck close to Gabrielle, and Tabatha stuck close to me, her eyes searching every open window or cracked door.

The noises that bounced down these streets were an insight into people's desires that I could have done without. There were enough wild offerings in the canal-facing establishments that you'd have to be after something particularly niche to go searching for your kicks down here. Not that all the activity sounded consensual. When a john didn't pay up – or got caught with counterfeit cash or an undeclared infection – they'd likely be invited to take a stroll into the backstreets, and there was a good chance they wouldn't be strolling back out. A gurgled scream caused Tabatha to jump, and made me grateful that when I'd first crossed Gabrielle's temper, I'd been dumped under a bridge rather than dragged into an alley. Tabatha trotted gingerly around the more worrying puddles, trying to keep her hooves out of the muck. Heads poked around corners but quickly lost interest when they saw that Gabrielle was our guide.

"It's not the biggest surprise that it caught fire," she said. "With all the fumes that came out of that place, it was only a matter of time before one of her experiments went wrong. Such a shame, though. Just when her brother was getting better."

Tabatha's ears twitched at that.

"Was he sick?"

"Sick like the rest of us, just unluckier. He was a brewhound back in the day. Not sure if it was by choice or if his sister just liked using him as a test subject."

"You mean, he experimented with potions?" I asked.

"Yeah. He was born Human, so the Witch tried to give him powers artificially. The usual tricks: tough-skin tonics, quickstep, silverspeech, nighteye."

Tabatha looked to me.

"You ever tried them yourself?"

"Only once. Took a swig of a Hardyhearing potion when I was young. Thought I'd lost my mind for a few hours, then had a splitting headache for a week. Decided to call it quits after that."

Despite that first experiment, I had always been tempted to try again. Even with the side effects, the chance to ride a magical wave, however briefly, felt worth the risk. Until I met Hendricks and Amari. Their opinions on Humans who meddled with potions was clear, and as much as I wanted to see in the dark or walk on water, I was far more interested in gaining their approval. That desire to impress them might have saved me, because I soon learned that few Humans could dabble in potions without turning it into a habit.

To effectively use potions, you had to build up a tolerance to the side effects. The catch was, by the time that happened, your body was already starting to rely on their power, and the withdrawals became torturous.

After a day of being artificially armored, when your skin returned to normal it would itch like mad and break out in sores. Strengthened senses would be warped and unreliable when they dwindled back to their mundane Human levels. That was why some – the addicts known as brewhounds – attempted to keep the high going indefinitely. Every hound had their own technique to extend the energy without burning out, claiming to use the perfect ratio of diluted potions and days between doses to fend off the itches and the sweats, but few had found a reliable way to make it work. Certainly not in the city. On the battlefield or in the wilderness, you could ride an elixir for as long as you wanted without caring how hard the crash would be when it finally came, and back before the Coda, plenty of warriors made potion abuse part of their brand. Unfortunately, once you went long enough, there was no giving it up. Brewhounds often became chained to the Witches and Warlocks who mixed up their doses, or whichever rich benefactor could afford to keep them in constant supply. When the magic fell out of the world and the elixirs lost their power, then the brewhounds suffered the same punishment as the magical creatures they'd attempted to emulate, with an extra dose of painful potion withdrawal thrown into the mix.

"Brewhounds don't get better," said Tabatha, speaking with the certainty of personal experience.

"This one did. The Witch had been caring for him full time

for years. Then she got some shiny new job with Niles. They say money can't buy happiness, but it did for those two. First time I'd seen him out of his wheelchair since the Coda."

Tabatha and I looked at each other. I didn't need to ask her if she'd heard any stories about miraculous healing like that, because of course she hadn't. For two years, I'd been the city's most prominent investigator of magic-related mysteries. I'd heard every hopeful tale out there, and this was a new one even for me. After all my encounters with the inexplicable, I felt lucky if I was able to offer up a tiny, temporary solution like Simms's skin cream. I couldn't fathom the kind of cure that would help a struggling brewhound walk again, even if his sister had a nice new paycheck to burn.

There was something else going on here.

"This way," said Gabrielle, and opened a door into a small, two-level apartment block. It was a strange experience because – due to the huge hole in the other side of the building – there was more light inside the apartment than out in the alley. "Luckily, no other residents were home when it happened."

The fire had been on the bottom floor, but took out the ceiling and the apartment above. It was Jackson Murray's place all over again: furniture reduced to soot, no roof and not much wall. Because there were two apartments' worth of furniture that fed the fire, there was twice as much debris, but the intense heat had turned it all to charcoal with only tiny remnants of fabric or uncharred wood to hint at what had once been.

Scavengers had made use of the hole in the wall and picked through the remains for valuables, decreasing our chances of tripping over a helpful piece of the puzzle. The humid air had turned the soot to slush, and shoveling through the mulch looked dangerous and futile.

Tabatha kicked a pile of damp ash.

"Jackson Murray believed that Angela was at the meeting, right?"

I checked the smudged letters on my hands. They weren't as legible as they had been, but helped jog my memory anyway.

"Not exactly. He said that information about her research was revealed to the people who were there. If she was working for Niles, he might have been the one to pass it on to the others."

"Then, not long after, someone up and torches her place." Tabatha turned to Gabrielle. "Tell me about the brother."

"I only saw him in passing but he was often gossiped about. At first, the girls lamented the life of the poor Witch who spent the better part of her life taking care of him. Then, after they heard his screams and saw new, raw injuries on his body, we sent our security guys to check that he wasn't being abused."

Tabatha had her notebook out.

"When was this?"

"Last year, sometime. He assured everyone that he suffered the injuries willingly, allowing his sister to test out potential remedies on him. We left them to their own devices after that. They were in the right neighborhood for confusing moans and strange aromas, so we stopped paying attention until a couple of weeks ago. Word had got around that the brother paid the boys at The Muskrat a visit. Walked there on his own, apparently."

Tabatha scoffed.

"Seven years in a wheelchair, and as soon as he can walk on two feet, the first place he goes is out for a fuck?"

Gabrielle was less surprised.

"It was only a few doors down, and he probably didn't want to push his luck by venturing any farther. He didn't have much coin – and the boys were wary of getting too close – so they only gave him the pauper's special." It took everything I had not to ask what the "pauper's special" was, but I didn't want to make Tabatha any more uncomfortable than she already was. "After that, word got around that the Witch and her brother were on to something. I don't know how far the message spread before someone took them out."

Tabatha and I stood quietly, mulling over how these reckless siblings might be connected to the string of murders. If the rumors had spread far enough and fast enough, then someone else could have got involved. Someone who had nothing to do with Bath, Niles or anyone at the alleged meeting.

We must have been quiet for a while, because Gabrielle grew impatient.

"Anything else I can do for you?"

"No. You've been a huge help. Thanks."

"You're welcome. It's more fun when you ask me to sing, though. Let me know if one of those jobs ever comes up again."

She moved towards the main door.

"Wait," I said. "Will we be safe?"

"Go back out the way you came. You'll be fine. If anything happens, just scream."

While I was watching her leave, Tabatha grabbed my hands and looked over the smeared news story.

"We keep assuming that this was intentional, but why not just an experiment gone wrong?"

I looked at the blackened plot of land, so similar to the one where Jackson Murray's home used to be.

"Doesn't that seem like too much of a coincidence? Two fires?"

"It would be a double bit of bad luck, but that has been known to happen."

"Well, it was Murray who believed that Angela's death was suspicious."

"Old Jackson Murray had a propensity for joining threads that had no business being tied together, so I want to turn his theory into fact before I commit to making his story mine."

I went to argue, but thinking back on my own jumps towards incorrect conclusions, an injection of journalistic integrity was probably what I needed. So, I tried to put it all together in a way that would satisfy her editorial standards.

"Murray had the Fray story, but we don't know where he got

it. It turns out everyone in the Rose Quarter suspected the siblings of stumbling on to some kind of cure, but nobody here would have linked that to Niles, or any meeting, or the names on Whisper's hit list."

"So how did word of this supposed meeting slip out? Who could have spilled the beans on this clandestine catch-up of upper-crust assholes?"

"I don't know. The so-called Sunder leaders – Niles, Derringer, Demoor and Piston – would all be practiced in protecting the inner circle."

"Someone close to them?"

"Drivers and henchmen would have known who was there. Or . . ." I pulled those newspaper clippings out of my pocket. The ones that Constable Bath had been collecting. "Bath was there, and he clearly knew who Murray was. Maybe it was him."

"Unless Bath was tracking Murray so he could shut him up," said Tabatha, deathly allergic to jumping to conclusions. "But you're right; the clippings link him to Murray in a way that feels significant. So, either Bath spilled the story or he tried to burn it up. You knew him, right? What seems more likely?"

"I have no idea. Bath was a follower. He was good at taking orders, not much else."

"Then we'd better find out who was calling the shots."

There was nothing else here. Nothing that wouldn't require three days and a large sieve to sort through.

"Let's get moving," said Tabatha. "I've had enough of the Rose for one day."

On her way to the door, she pulled a handkerchief out her pocket. When she turned the handle, she kept the cloth between the metal and her skin.

I jolted to a stop.

"Fuck me," I said.

"Nope. But plenty of people down here will do that for the right price."

"Tabatha, what are you doing?"

"What?"

"In your hand."

"You mean my handkerchief?"

"Yeah, what are you doing with it?"

"Nothing against the locals but I can't imagine the kind of residue that's on their fingers, and I certainly don't want to get any of it on mine."

"Exactly!" I shouted.

"What in the Mad Hatter's blasted gray matter are you on about?"

I walked slowly towards her, my head throbbing with a half-formed idea that I was struggling to make whole.

"The doorknob on Bath's front door. Outside his apartment. There were no fingerprints on it."

"So, the opposite of a clue then."

"*No* fingerprints. Somebody had wiped it clean."

"Surely something the killer would do, after they left."

"But Bath died alone. Door locked and bolted from the inside."

She was starting to get it.

"So, if Bath was the last person to enter, then his fingerprints should have been on the handle."

"Unless the killer wiped it *after* Bath went inside." I was getting excited now. A murky vision starting to take shape. "Not to wipe away evidence, but to wipe away . . . something. A substance – a kind of poison – that had been put there on purpose."

Tabatha caught my fever.

"We were wondering how the killer got out of the locked room, but what if the killer was never in the room to begin with?"

"Right! Bath goes home, touches his doorknob, gets the substance on his skin, lets himself inside, locks the door, then . . . he feels it."

"Feels what?"

"Panic."

A flash of Derringer's face in the grip of fear and confusion. Knowing something bad is happening but not knowing . . .

Why?

"This substance." I walked in circles. I didn't have all the pieces, but I could start to see the picture. "Whatever Angela Fray had discovered, it helped her brother, but what if it unlocks magic in other ways? What if – when it gets into someone's body – it reacts to magical things around them?"

"What magical things?"

"Like *something* in Derringer's bespoke car."

She nodded.

"I see. And maybe twelve cartridges full of exploding desert dust."

"Yes! That's why Niles is keeping his distance. Why his henchmen are searching pockets for old napkins before you can see him. Why Demoor tried to keep her followers out of reach. Why Piston wants everyone to stay back when—"

The sound of tiny bells tinkled from the watch on Tabatha's wrist. Her alarm, letting us know it was time to make our way to Five Shadows Square.

The Mayor of Sunder City was about to make a speech.

34

Tabatha and I weren't the only ones interested in hearing the Mayor's speech first-hand. A few hundred audience members had gathered at the square, along with food vendors, tea trolleys and men weighed down with waterskins and flagons of wine. One of Tabatha's colleagues was on the scene, commandeering the phone booth to report his commentary back to the station. The audience was spread out, unsure where the Mayor would be speaking from, and unsure what to expect from the announcement.

Before the Coda, Mayor Piston had made his living running an abattoir and delivery business. Because his company didn't rely on any magical animals or vehicles, he didn't miss a step when his magic-powered competitors went out of business. We made the guy who supplied our meat the Mayor, and he'd fulfilled his role with the somber practicality of his previous station, vowing to ensure we always had access to the essentials but making no great promises beyond that. His position as Mayor wasn't highly contested, even by other ministers, so he rarely bothered to remind us why we'd appointed him in the first place.

This city was built on business, so rather than being a full-time politician, Piston's slaughterhouse empire was his true point of pride. As Mayor, he'd been amiable and unobtrusive, until about a year ago. Shortly after Niles arrived, Piston declared certain magical practices illegal. All policy changes were made in the name of safety, but nobody believed that. The edicts were designed to increase the Niles Company's monopoly. Ever since Thurston arrived in town, it was a coin-flip as to whether a speech from the Mayor would be outlawing some sacred ritual or peddling a new flavor of sausage. With a pattern of high-profile murders, we were all expecting something more serious, but that hadn't stopped plenty of Sunder's hungrier residents making their way to the square in the hope of a free sample.

I was looking for a podium — or any information about where to stand — when I caught a large body moving through the mingling crowd, a head higher than the rest, muttering apologies to anyone that he accidentally shoved to the side. I moved in and made introductions.

"Richie, this is Tabatha. She's been looking into the Whisper case with me."

His heavy jaw fell open.

"Tabatha Ratchet? I listen to your show. Big fan!"

I'd never seen Richie beam a smile so big, and he grabbed her hand with boyish enthusiasm.

"Oh, thank you."

"Careful, Rich. She's not a can of paint."

"Sorry. Nice to meet you, Tabatha. You here to report on the Mayor's speech?"

"Depends what he says. But there's a chance that—"

Screams. A second later, the driver laid on his horn and sent an eardrum-shredding shriek through the waiting mob. People scattered, narrowly avoiding the firetruck that had arrived without warning, aggressively forcing the crowd to the edges of the square. A woman, knocked by the fleeing horde, stumbled into my back, and would have taken me down too if Richie hadn't reached out and braced us both, already shielding Tabatha with the rest of his sizable body.

"This way," he said, able to see above the swarm. Tabatha and I grabbed hold of his coat, and he dragged us along, shoving others aside as respectfully as he could manage and regularly bending down to lift fallen people from the floor. I couldn't see much beyond Richie's back and the sweaty faces of people stumbling beside us, but I heard a second truck arrive, prompting more screams. The crowd was pushed out to the edges of the square, cramming people up against the stores and into the alleys. Richie maneuvered us to comparative safety around the base of one of the lamps which gave Five Shadows its name.

"Move back! Now!" Firefighters jumped from the trucks, brandishing pistols, their childish grins betraying any sense of the authority they attempted to convey with their voices. The juvenile attitude didn't make them seem less dangerous, but only heightened the chaotic sense that we were on the precipice of a truly dangerous situation.

I'd long suspected that soldiers were recruited at a young age not solely for the strength of their bodies, but also for the softness of their minds. At a certain point in life, you can no longer be told to run in one direction with a pointy stick and poke anyone who comes the other way. You need a simple, youthful mind for that. A certain kind of corruptible innocence. The more you start thinking for yourself, the less useful you become. Unfortunately, for most of us, that independence of thought happens too late, and I was living proof that dressed-up delinquents in unearned positions of power could do ungodly amounts of damage to the world around them.

For a moment, I thought I saw myself in the crowd with the others, wearing a flash new suit and standard-issue boots and belt. Tense jaw. Eyes open yet unseeing. Mind out of the moment, busy writing my story before it had happened. Fear of failure and fear of embarrassment all crushed up against the strange new possibility of gaining outside approval. Desperate to believe that I'd found a place to call home and a group of people who'd accept me. Fighting not for a cause, but for validation.

That's how they get you. That's how the bastards convince you that their desires are worth your life.

But it wasn't me, there in the crowd, waving a shiny new firearm at civilians who were already cowering. It was Ashton, standing on the tips of his toes, snarling to cover his terror and his shame. His voice was an unrehearsed performance of an intimidating officer, but he was unable to hide his uncertainty.

"Back behind the lamps," he yelled. "Behind the line!"

Richie and Tabatha took the extra step required to obey the command, but I stood in place, leaning on the lamp with my legs still breaking the boundary. Ashton saw my feet, looked up, and opened his mouth to repeat his order. When he recognized me, nothing came out.

"Hey, Ashton," I said. "Enjoying your new job?"

I saw a satisfying flash of embarrassment, quickly replaced by an unconvincing mask of fearlessness.

"Step back, Fetch. Behind the line."

"Or what? You gonna shoot me?"

He gave me a look that said he just might. Wouldn't that be a way to go? Blasted by a teenager for not moving two inches. Then his face shifted, softened, and he spoke just loud enough for me to hear.

"Fetch. *Please*."

Richie piped in, leaning over my shoulder, an icy coldness to his voice.

"Kid, what is that? In your belt."

All eyes looked down, landing on the weapon that was tucked into a leather sheath on Ashton's hip. He'd finally received his city-issued knife, except the metal of this one – unlike his fellow firefighters – was made of dark metal that shimmered green when it caught the light.

Richie growled his words.

"Is that Adamantine?"

There was that embarrassed flash again. Only a moment, but enough to make the subsequent bluster even more pathetic.

"Yeah."

Richie was already a few steps ahead. Not only had he guessed the type of metal, but also where it was sourced from.

"Just like the Adamantine we saw on those Fae?"

"Yeah," confirmed Ashton, proudly. "It's my reward for leading Niles to the Gremlins. He melted down their armor and made me this."

Richie tensed, and I thought he might crush the kid's head in his fingers. I wouldn't be able to stop him if he did. Maybe then we'd both get shot for no reason.

"When you do a shameful thing," he growled, "you're not supposed to take a trophy."

Ashton only smiled.

"Good thing I'm not ashamed then."

We were all quiet for a moment, wondering who was going to escalate us into unnecessary violence, when Ashton's backup arrived.

"Well, look at this little stand-off!" Reeves stepped up beside his comrade, twirling his baton and grinning like the whole thing was a sporting match and his side was winning. "Come on, Captain. It's only the kid's second day on the job. Don't be so hard on him."

It was a small mercy not to see Gumption anywhere, likely still nursing his bullet wound and calling for Simms's blood. Besides, we were close enough to a shootout as it was.

I'd had my fun, and was ready to step back, but the sight of that Adamantine knife had shifted Richie into a mode I hadn't seen him in for a long time. I could hear his teeth grinding against each other, and the hot air shooting from his flared nostrils sounded like a steam engine going uphill.

"All right, Rich," I said, working to de-escalate the situation that I'd started. "No point starting a fight we can't win."

"I don't know about that," he grunted. "Some things are fun no matter what the outcome is."

Reeves reached for his pistol, but Tabatha stepped into the firing line and put a calming hand on Richie's shoulder.

"All right, big man. Let's be letting them have their little win and find somewhere to enjoy the show, all right?"

"But—" He started to argue, but the kind words and physical contact from his celebrity crush were quickly cooling his blood.

"Not saying they don't deserve it," she said, leaning in closer. "Just saying there are smarter ways to make your point than offering your body up for target practice. Now come on!"

He let himself be moved, and I followed. Ashton, to his credit, looked apologetic. Not that it mattered; Reeves had smugness to spare.

"Thank you for your obedience, good citizens!" yelled Reeves. "Your peaceful compliance is appreciated. Now wait patiently, the Mayor will be here soon."

The crowd had become an unruly, confused mess. Everyone was bumping into each other and searching for a place to stand that wasn't in everyone else's way. Richie – the adrenaline of the confrontation fading – now looked sheepish. Members of the crowd kept being shoved into him, and he had a hard time moving past without shoving them back.

"This is a nightmare," he groaned. "Why don't we forget the whole thing?"

"Works for me," agreed Tabatha. "Let's find a radio and a drink."

We grabbed hold of Richie's shirt and let him drag us on, against the crowd, past the first set of shops that faced the square. Stepping beyond the impacted mass, I felt like I could breathe again, and was all on board to leave the Mayor and his hooligans behind.

Then a voice dropped down from above.

"Hello, Phillips. I saved you a seat!"

We all looked up. On the roof above us, leaning over the gutter, was a set of feline eyes framed by long, dark locks. Of course. I'd almost forgotten that the building beside us had once been the office of Linda Rosemary: Magical Investigator.

"I remembered the code for the stairs from when I rented the place," she explained. "Come on. I'll show you the way up."

35

The flat rooftop, though covered in crow shit and clumps of ash, formed a comfortable viewing area for Linda, Tabatha, Richie and me to enjoy the show. There were four firetrucks now – one on each side of the square – and with the audience having been forcefully moved behind the perimeter, there was nothing left to do but wait for the guest of honor to arrive.

"Nip?" offered Linda, holding out a flask.

"No thanks. I bet Rich will take you up, though."

"He already has. Thought I'd give you a chance to steal some before he drains the lot."

Richie was leaning on the chimney, firing question after question at his favorite reporter, oblivious to anyone or anything else.

"I really appreciate your honest take on what's been happening to the police. You know, I was a copper myself until recently. I'm not blowing smoke when I tell you that it was one of your stories that gave me the clarity I needed to leave the force for good."

Linda threw the flask at his chest.

"Rest is yours, Richie. And careful with the chimney, it's only built of bricks and mortar."

The smitten Half-Ogre stood up straight, took a swig, then continued his barrage of compliments.

Down below, the firefighters were running the joint, but there were cops down there too. I could see two groups of them, standing back in the alleys, assessing the situation from a distance. It was strange not to see Simms there – part of the squad but separate – surveying the area with her narrow eyes. As frustrating as she'd always been, it was hard not to long for her overbearing brand of law enforcement in the face of these gung-ho gunslingers.

"This is some operation," observed Linda. "They sell pistols to every person in the city, then have to bolster their security in case one of us points the toys in their direction."

"I don't think it's the guns they're afraid of."

I gave her a rundown of what Tabatha and I had put together, and I saw the frustration in her furrowed brow as she struggled to fill the gaps in the facts.

"If you're right, then Piston must know all about this poison too. Whatever Whisper was planning, he won't be getting close to the Mayor today."

Another firetruck came down Twelfth, and behind it, a sleek, simple black sedan with tinted windows. Piston had been known to travel in more luxurious, bespoke automobiles, but Derringer's accident must have encouraged him to play it safe.

Rich and Tabatha hadn't noticed the new arrival.

"Come on, you two. Show's starting."

We lined up along the brick border of the roof and watched the car pull into the near end of the square, beside a small podium ringed by ready firefighters. One of them opened the car door, and the Mayor stepped out wearing a navy suit and orange tie. He gave us a wave, and most of the crowd applauded in response. The only movement on the roof was Richie upending the flask for its last drop.

Piston approached the podium and removed a piece of paper and a cigar from his inner jacket pocket. The paper, he placed in front of him. The cigar he lit and puffed, waiting for us to settle ourselves into a respectful silence.

When he was satisfied, he blew a plume up over his head, leaned forward, and spoke in that unassuming manner he'd cultivated to convince the common folk he was one of their own.

"Hello, Sunder." That got some hoots and hollers. "Thank you for coming out today. I wish I had better news. You are all likely aware of the unfortunate accidents that have befallen two of Sunder's most noble citizens in the past few days. Isaac Derringer and

Redonna Demoor were guiding lights who dedicated themselves to bettering our lives, gifting every member of this city with knowledge and hope." It was a good thing that Linda had distanced us from the rest of the crowd, because our chorus of scoffs wouldn't have gone over well with the more obedient members of the population. Some of them even had their hands on their hearts. "We have reason to believe that these tragic deaths were not accidental, but rather the work of some nefarious person – or persons – hidden in our midst. They chose to attack these mighty pillars of truth and faith because they wanted to send a message. A message to you, my dear Sunderites. These evil forces want you to be afraid. They want you to believe that if giants like Isaac Derringer aren't safe, then neither are you. They want you to believe that if the light of the Lattician Priestess can be dimmed, then so can yours. Do not believe them. We are a glorious city at the height of prosperity, and we have found our way here because of your hard work. Your faith. You have earned this. *We* have earned this. I promise you, if we band together, we need not be afraid of anything."

The crowd cheered. What chumps.

"You have built your own future, and I swear to each and every one of you that I will fight to protect it. Protect it from those who are jealous. From those who fear hard work and just rewards. From those who resent your sacrifices and your belief in better days. Better days that will only come if we stand up and build them!" He was all fired up now, his face red with passion. "To this end, I have given our firefighters greater responsibility over your protection, and stronger tools with which to enforce the law. Until the culprits behind these killings have been brought to justice, there is no greater threat to the stability of Sunder City. In this moment, they are the fire. The fire that . . . FIRE!"

It became clear that the red tinge to Piston's face was not caused by enthusiasm alone. His orange tie was burning from the bottom up, flames shooting towards his chin.

The cigar dropped from his mouth as he slapped at his chest.

The firefighters looked on, helpless, their knives and six-shooters unsuited to the task at hand.

They scrambled to the trucks, but seemed unfamiliar with how to even open them, and the tie burned quickly. People screamed. Piston knocked the podium over as he slapped at himself, wailing. Then, the driver emerged from the car, metal thermos in hand, and flung the contents at the Mayor's fiery front.

We'd all stopped breathing. There was a cloud of smoke around the Mayor's beetroot of a head, but it appeared that the fire had gone out. Piston panted. His sweat-and-coffee-covered face was unrecognizable, impassioned confidence replaced with sheer panic. We all stood silent, waiting to see what he'd do and what the hell would happen next.

From our vantage point, off to the side, we had a clear look at the expression he hid from everyone else. I could see the effort it took him to compose himself – resisting any urge to scream or cry – and reapply a version of his carefully considered, unflappable temperament. He accomplished this incredibly quickly, and stood up straight, dusting himself off.

Either out of habit or in defiance of the unexpected display of pyrotechnics, he picked up his cigar again, and took a puff.

The crowd went fucking wild. Even us cynics in the peanut gallery had to crack a smile.

"Mother fucker," said Linda, not bothering to hide that she was impressed.

He gestured to the podium, and two firefighters stepped forward and righted it. Piston adjusted the microphone to stop it squealing, tapped it a few times, and gifted the rapt audience with a winning smile.

"I—"

The rest of his tie ignited, including the strip of material that was beneath his collar, wrapped around his neck. His whole head went up like a bottle of moonshine dropped on a gas stove, and everyone started screaming.

36

Some of the audience fled in terror, perhaps fearing the Mayor's affliction was contagious (for those that lived through history's Wizard-induced plagues, their paranoia was understandable). Others cleared out shortly after, worried that they'd be retained for questioning once the cops had got over the shock. After a while, the initial crowd had been exchanged for another: rapt citizens replaced by cops, doctors and suits.

Richie, Tabatha and Linda wanted to get to a bar and claim a table before they all filled up, so I told them to go ahead.

I remained on the roof, wishing my Clayfields hadn't been stolen by the city and that the cost of replacing them hadn't become so prohibitive.

A few rubberneckers remained around the outskirts, keeping their distance and trying not to draw the ire of any policeman who might give them a hiding just to regain a sense of order. Across the square, one onlooker in a brown suit was hiding in a gap between stores, standing on cinderblocks and observing the crime scene through the lens of a large camera.

It was Owen Ward, the creepy shutterbug I'd seen outside the Derringer estate. The one who made a living selling compromising pictures of Trixie but had somehow escaped Isaac's retribution. I didn't understand how the greaseball was still walking. Even without the Sasquatch wringing his neck, what was the city coming to when a man could sell compromising pictures of a blind woman and not get his teeth kicked in?

A black hearse arrived on the scene, and there was a scramble as the cop cars and firetrucks tried to clear out of the way. Piston's sedan was driven away so that Portemus could collect the body with the least disturbance.

That was when I saw it: a small object, hidden behind the tires, and revealed as the sedan pulled away. It had so far gone unnoticed by everyone down below, who had all been too busy covering up the Mayor, ushering away dignitaries, and keeping both eyes on the crowd.

I went down the stairs, through the gate with the combination lock, and back out into the square. There were enough onlookers around the scene to approach safely, but I knew that my face – when separated from the crowd – would quickly draw attention. For anyone whose job was law and order, my mug signaled trouble like a thunderhead.

I kept my head down as I fumbled in my pocket for a crumpled napkin – thanks to my clumsy fingers, I always had one on hand – and headed for the place where Piston's car had been parked. My eyes scanned the cobbles, hoping that nobody else had yet seen what I had.

There.

Piston's cigar – what was left of it – was still untouched, and I was only a few steps away when one of the firefighters unknowingly kicked the damn thing in the opposite direction.

Believing I was still being overlooked, I stepped past the line of policemen, closed the distance, was about to bend down, and—

"I don't think you're supposed to be here."

Private Gumption.

Not wanting to miss out on the action, he must have dragged himself out of his hospital bed when he heard about Piston's inflammatory speech. He had his weight on his left leg, right calf bulging from the bandages wrapped around his recently received bullet wound.

"Just here to help," I said, not yet sure of what angle I was going to play.

"I think we've got all the hands we need. Shouldn't you be scraping some fat somewhere? Holding your sausage?"

There was a lovely little pause as Gumption, out of habit, looked around for Reeves's approval. With disappointment, he realized that Reeves was assisting Portemus in getting the stretcher under Piston's headless body.

Suddenly, I had my plan. I didn't like it, but I needed to get that cigar before anyone else.

"You know, Gumption, I wanted to thank you for what you told me, back at the cafe. Things are a lot clearer now."

"You mean it finally clicked that we all knew you was a chump from the start?"

There was that snicker again. Like a rat trapped in a wine bottle.

"Exactly. I'd avoided thinking about that time too much, but it's nice to have a proper understanding of my past. Makes it easier to move on, you know?"

He stepped closer. Smacked his gum in my face.

"You really are dumber than dog turds. Never would have got it on your own, would you?"

"Well, did you?"

"What the fuck do you mean? I was in on the ruse from the start, genius. We all were."

I tried out a snicker myself (just a little dalliance, not something I'd turn into a habit).

"You really think they would've put their best and brightest on 'operation babysitter'? It was a two-birds-one-stone procedure, buddy. Keep the Opus rebel busy till he's ready to play ball, while also sticking the dumbest privates somewhere they couldn't get into trouble."

He scoffed unconvincingly.

"You were precious cargo, Captain. We got our orders from General Taryn himself."

"But that's only because your fathers were VIPs, right? I saw your record. If your parents didn't hold power, you would have been discharged within a week. Hell, your whole enlistment was a way to get you out of your dad's sight, right? I read the letter."

He showed his teeth.

"You shut your trap."

"What did it say? 'Take my son as far away from home for as long as possible, and return him as a man or not at all'? There was something about getting too close to the family dog, right? Did you kill it or fuck it, Gumption? I never could work that out."

"I'll gut you, you bastard."

"And did Daddy approve when you were finally sent back? Are you the man he wanted us to make you into? Or are you here because he still can't stand the sight of your pathetic—"

The punch finally came. I knew it would. I let it connect but rolled with it, twisted, and hit the deck.

Shouts and gasps and scraping boots. I staggered forward, on all fours, and – stumbling enough to cloak my intentions – put my hand over the cigar with the napkin protecting my skin (if my hunch was correct, I didn't want to risk my brain igniting like the Mayor's).

"Woah, Gumption, buddy." Reeves had arrived at his partner's side. "I think we've had enough excitement for one day."

It was the disapproving looks from the rest of the crowd – rather than Reeves's better nature – that made him come to my aid. Having retrieved my prize, I was happy to let him de-escalate.

I dropped the napkin-wrapped cigar into my pocket.

"Was just trying to help," I said, holding up my hands and staggering to standing. "Didn't mean to scare you, Gumption. I'll clear off."

There were other young firefighters, fresh from out of town, who assumed I was a local drunk or lunatic, but the cops and charcoal suits were more dubious. One of the older suits – whose face I might have punched once upon a time – stepped forward.

"What the hell are you up to, Phillips?"

His subordinates stood to attention, and I was in danger of being grabbed and patted down, when an excited voice rang out from beside the hearse.

"A little help!" Portemus was gripping one side of the stretcher that was carrying Piston. "We must keep the body perfectly flat or it will disturb the liquids in his system. More hands, please!"

Heads turned, and I slid away. Good old Porty. Whether it was his typical pedantic nature or an intentional lifeline, it was enough to get me away from the square and into the alley.

"Got a real nice snap of you copping that slug, Gumshoe." Owen Ward. Sweating through his brown suit and gripping his camera with greasy fingers. "Give me your address and I'll send it to you when it comes out."

"Why don't you burn it? Along with anything taken at the Derringer estate."

He smiled at that.

"I knew I'd seen you before. Friend of Trixie, right? I took your picture."

He had. When I was in the back of the big automobile on my first arrival.

"Don't need to be a friend to know that snapping secret pics of a blind woman is bad form. Maybe it's time you let that little revenue stream go."

"What about the deal?"

"What deal?"

"The pictures of you—" He caught himself. Realized he'd said too much. "Don't worry about it."

I shoved him up against the wall, grabbed the camera strap in both hands and pulled it tight around his neck.

"What pictures?"

"Ack!"

I loosened it enough to let him breathe.

"Talk, or I pull. Try to scream, I don't stop."

"You can't! Didn't she tell you?"

"Tell me what?"

"If I die, or I don't check in with my contact, all my photos go out. Trixie knows. She agrees."

Of course. That's why Derringer never scraped the Cyclops's face down his driveway. The little slime ball had leverage.

It was my turn to smile.

"Bad luck, buddy. I don't give two shits about any photos."

"But your girlfriend does! Think about it. What happens to Trixie if your affair comes out?"

Affair?

Ward had his wires crossed but I wasn't about to unwind them.

"You got pics of that?"

He saw a chance to get the upper hand. Clutched at it. Spilled more than he should have.

"Oh, yes. Prints and negatives. You, arriving at her place the night Isaac died. All rugged up, trying to stay hidden. Not careful enough, though. Anything happens to me, those pictures go out. She can no longer play the grieving widow then, can she?"

Trixie Derringer had a secret visitor? Not all that strange. The woman spent most of her life alone in that house, husband busy making papers. It was the least surprising revelation that had come out this week.

"You're bribing her so you can keep taking pictures of her with her top off?"

He shrugged. "It's just business, mate. Giving the readers what they want."

I let go of the straps, grabbed the long lens of the camera, and punched the glass.

"FUUUUUCK! You prick!"

I left him swearing and cleared out before he could draw too much attention. Hopefully every cop in town would have too much beef with the guy to follow up on his complaints anyway. He probably had the same racket going with every department in the city: a stash of secret photos that he thought made him untouchable. To a guy like me – whose public persona was barely above a bed bug – it only made the idea of knocking his lights out more tempting, because when Owen Ward finally disappeared, all kinds of interesting pictures would come floating to the surface.

For now, I was only concerned with the charred cigar in my pocket and finding out if it had anything to do with the Mayor's exploding skull.

When I was away from the square, I pulled out the stub, careful to keep the napkin against my fingers.

It was mostly intact. Some burnt spots on the side. Ashy at one end and charred on the other, but the label was still intact.

Boralo.

The same brand as Isaac Derringer. Exactly the same as the box on his desk, from memory. Did that mean anything? Or was it to be expected that two close friends and business associates would have similar tastes?

I put it under my nose and smelled something unexpected.

Peppermint. Just the faintest hint.

What did that mean?

I put the cigar back in my pocket and closed my eyes, trying to make sense of this latest murder and how it fitted in with the others. I was starting to feel like I had all the pieces, but no idea how to fit them together.

To do that, I'd need help from a few minds sharper than mine.

37

When you've been through enough good days and bad, you stop measuring things that way; you just remember the days when shit happened. The day the Mayor's head turned into a jack-o'-lantern full of fireworks was undoubtedly one of those days.

Every bar was bursting because nobody wanted to be home alone while everyone else was out together, processing the event over cold beer, and trading theories about what had happened, why, and who was behind it. Dunkley's was at capacity, but I spotted Richie, Tabatha and Linda down the road in the Ditch, commandeering a table beneath the dartboards.

I'd been avoiding the Ditch for a while now. Too full of memories. Some of those memories were mine, like the times spent drinking cocktails with Hendricks – my oldest friend and greatest mentor – both before and after he'd become the destructive force known as Mr Deamar.

Some of those memories belonged to others, like the local Dwarves who were unwilling to forgive the way I'd sold them out. A selfish move I'd made to preserve the plot of land where Amari's body had been waiting, back before Hendricks turned her into that tree up in the Gullet.

Luckily for me, there was no space left for the bad memories to fit. Every person in the city was playing the role of amateur detective or journalist, throwing theories from one table to the next.

"It's a curse! I've seen it before! I'd bet all my money that this is the work of a Witch."

"I'll take that bet, because Witches can't do shit these days. I could rig you up an igniting tie with a stopwatch, some copper wire and a box of matches. It's simple!"

"You're both fookin daft! That was ditarum, same as it was before. Smaller, but just the same. I told you! Someone worked it out! Someone's doing spells again!"

That sent everyone into hysterical debate, and Richie had to fight his way through the arguments to get another round of drinks. I intersected him.

"Fetch!" He was in good spirits, likely caused by the company as much as the alcohol. "What you drinking?"

Boris the bartender was so overwhelmed with customers that he didn't recognize me at first. Richie was halfway through his list of drinks before the Banshee clocked me. I expected to read his disappointment – fearing that my presence would spark violence on a day that was already threatening to combust – but Boris leaned over the bar and gave me the warmest hug he could manage with a wooden counter between us, and he was pouring ale before I found my words. There were three lagers, three whiskey chasers, and even though I didn't ask for it, one burnt milkwood.

"Thanks, Boris. It's good to see you."

He put his hand over his heart, pointed to one eye, then at me, and held up two fingers: *Good to see you too*. Then Richie lifted the drinks up over his head and used his belly as a battering ram to lead us back to the table.

Everyone tapped their drinks together and took a healthy sip. We were the quietest table in the whole place.

Linda broke the silence.

"It's got to be Whisper, right?"

Richie nodded. "Mayor was on his list."

"Let's not be jumping to conclusions too soon. Causation and correlation, and all that." Tabatha brought out her notepad and hunched over it as if she didn't want anyone to see the contents, though the scribblings that filled every page were unintelligible to anyone else anyway. "This may be someone responding to Whisper's accusations, not necessarily the man himself."

"Either way," Richie was making a valiant effort to not act giddy at finding himself trading notes with his favorite radio star, "there's only one person left on that list now."

Linda leaned back and smiled.

"If Whisper killing Niles is the end of this mess, then why should we do anything? Let's just stay here and drink until his mission's complete, then go out and take our city back."

"What if it doesn't end there?" I asked, but Linda waved away my reluctance.

"I know you've got a soft spot for Thurston, Fetch, but he's the one holding this whole mess together. I'm not going to miss Piston or Derringer's influence, but they'll be replaced by identical assholes within the week if Niles remains where he is. If Whisper's going to get rid of him, I'm not saying I'll fight at his side, but I don't know why anyone would want to stand in his way."

"Remember, Whisper might not be doing this," Tabatha re-iterated, ever the pragmatist.

I should have let the conversation move on, but I didn't like the idea that they all thought I was protecting Thurston.

"I don't care about Niles. I just don't know enough about what Whisper is up to, and where this whole thing might lead us."

"Why would you think this would go any further?" Linda was now matching the enthusiastic energy of the other tables. "The only name left on Whisper's list is Niles. Why not just wait for him to finish the job?"

"If Whisper completes his plan and vanishes without a trace, then the punishment for his crimes will fall on Simms, Hyperion and Ophelia." I didn't bother mentioning that Volta would also publish his article about my sordid history; no need to bring my personal agenda into this noble meeting of minds.

Richie leaned forward, exhibiting a tinge of uncharacteristic self-consciousness.

"I've got no love for Niles, Piston or most of the police, but Simms is . . . undeserving of the punishment she's been given. She stood up for the Centaur, and they'll both take the rap if we don't find out who's really doing this."

Tabatha nodded, and I thought Richie might faint.

"I don't need a reason to uncover the truth. This is the best story Sunder's seen in seven years."

Linda shrugged. "I still think there's more to this than just murdering cunts. I don't want to stop Whisper, but I agree that we should work out why he's doing it. Those secret messages weren't for nothing."

So, it was decided. Four investigators on the case, each for different reasons.

"All right, you rag-tag team of rascals and reprobates," said Tabatha, readying her pen over her notepad. "How did Whisper – or whoever – ignite the late Mayor's bleeding necktie?"

"Million ways to start a fire," said Richie.

"But doing it at a distance, on someone else's body?" Linda was leaning back in her chair, staring at the ceiling. "Some kind of new fire-blasting pistol?"

"Sounds like magic to me," muttered Richie.

"Don't be trying to win with easy answers like that, big fella," Tabatha said with a smile. "I want real, evidence-based answers that don't pretend the Coda never happened."

"But it went out when the driver splashed coffee on it, before firing back up outta nowhere. That's not normal."

"None of this is normal," I said, and told Richie about the experiment I'd played out in my office. That Simms had been trying to work out who killed Bath, how her notes had led me to question why there were no fingerprints on the doorknob, and my theory of the unknown substance that had ignited the bullets in Bath's gun.

"That's impossible," said Richie.

"Improbable," corrected Tabatha.

"Then, there's this." I placed the napkin-wrapped cigar stub on the table. "Bath's body smelt like peppermint after he died.

So does this." Richie went to pick it up. "I wouldn't do that, Rich. As far as we know, the elixir could be activated by touch alone."

"What do you mean? You get that peppermint stuff on you, then it sets off any magical elements in the vicinity?"

"That tracks with the other murders," said Linda, her eyes wide with excitement. "Wasn't Demoor wearing some kind of necklace?"

"A stormstone," I said. "But the power was supposed to be dormant. Not dangerous."

"Neither are bullets, unless you fire them," said Tabatha, coming to the party. "Could there have been some similar kind of artefact in Derringer's car?"

Goddamn it.

"Unicorn horn. There was a piece of it set into the steering wheel. Richie, you remember what happens when that stuff's unleashed." He nodded. We'd both been on the receiving end of my first experiment weaponizing the crystalized element. "But what could have—"

Tabatha was a step ahead.

"Phoenix feather. That's what Piston's tie was made of. One of his favorites; I've seen it up close during interviews."

We all sat back, processing the implications. Linda waved a hand in the air as she talked, conducting the facts as they fell into place.

"So, Whisper – or someone who believed fanatically in his stories – has hold of a secret weapon. A substance that – when absorbed by a living creature – can unlock hidden power in nearby magical artefacts. But where would he get something like that?"

Tabatha and I said it at the same time.

"Angela Fray."

She'd healed her brother, somehow. Right before her house got torched. Tabatha laid it all out, and Richie held his head as if all the new information was having trouble squeezing in.

"So what? She heals her brother with it? Someone kills her,

steals the recipe, and uses it to assassinate some folks? A lot of unnecessary steps when you could just shoot someone in the guts."

"To do that," I said, "you need to get close to your victim. For all we know, when these victims were dying, Whisper was sitting at home on the other end of the city, free from suspicion."

"And what if they wanted it to look like magic," said Linda, who'd been in the firing line of the smear campaign against magical practitioners. "This is just the kind of propaganda Niles and Piston need to justify their new laws."

I shook my head.

"But aren't the people trying to make magic look dangerous the ones getting killed? Anyone who'd want to sell that story would be an ally of Derringer, Piston and Demoor."

"Maybe they are," said Richie. "Niles could be cleaning house."

Linda nodded, liking that idea.

"He doesn't want to share the spotlight, so he takes out his colleagues in a way that reinforces his story about post-Coda magic being too dangerous to mess with."

Tabatha leaned forward.

"Then he puts his name on Whisper's list to avoid suspicion."

It was starting to make sense. I got my own notepad out.

"Not many people have the kind of access Thurston has. He'd have no problem getting close to Derringer or Piston. Nobody would question his goons walking around the printing press, so he could slip a story in the paper easy enough."

"Then he frames someone else," Richie was getting excited, "and can pretend that he survived the attacks because he stayed in his mansion and played it safe. Nobody will question it."

Just as we were ready to lock the pieces in place, Linda shook her head.

"I buy the killings, not the newsletters. What would Niles have to gain by having everyone think he was colluding with the others and keeping secrets from us? It doesn't make sense."

It didn't, and nobody offered up any explanation.

We all went quiet for a while. The excitement of putting a few pieces together had been smothered beneath an avalanche of multiplying questions. Like a jigsaw where you easily get the border done then have to face the abstract mess of what waits in-between.

Our table might have quieted down, but the rest of the raucous crowd was only getting louder. It was going to be a wild night: everyone deathly aware of their mortality and the unpredictable ways we could be wiped from existence at any moment. There was already a sense of abandon among the patrons, with unguarded displays of affection at several of the tables. The lads closest to us hadn't got that far yet, but were loudly partaking in the ritual of immediately deifying the deceased. They'd likely been complaining about the Mayor mere hours ago, but his death had turned him into an upstanding pillar of the community.

"You know, I had dinner with him once."

"Really?"

"Well, we were at a barbeque together. At my sister-in-law's place. They're second cousins or something."

"Wow."

"Yeah, he was real friendly. Not high and mighty or nothing. Just a regular guy with a whole lot of steak he was happy to share. So down to earth. And funny! Real jokester, you know?"

Richie had his ear cocked to the offending table.

"I hear people talk like that all the time," he said quietly. "Telling tales about the glory days – all the heroes of old they rubbed shoulders with – and I always think, *Old Fetch would put them to shame if he ever bothered to tell his story*."

Tabatha raised her eyebrows.

"Ooh, a hobnobber of high society, were you?"

He leaned in with glee. "You wouldn't believe it." Oh no. Richie was a little boy trying to impress a girl and I was the favorite toy he was hoping to show off. "Best friends with a High Chancellor. House guest of Governor Lark."

"Richie . . ."

"Lover of Faeries, soldier on both sides, and the only man I've met who set foot in the walled city of Weatherly. You could put every loud-mouthed braggart in this bar to shame, Fetch. Imagine if you told that asshole his barbecue buddy was standing over your bed a few nights ago. See how down to earth he sounds then."

Richie laughed at himself, and Tabatha smiled, but I could see her mind ticking behind her eyes and I didn't like the look of it. I still hadn't found a way to keep myself out of the *Star*, and the last thing I needed was Lamplighter Radio doing an exposé on my terrible past.

I tried to turn everyone's attention back to the case.

"Let's go over the facts. Assume, for the moment, that Whisper is the sole killer, and he needed to get this substance onto the body of each of his victims. He put it on Bath's doorknob, then wiped it clean."

"Unless there was an eyewitness account of someone in the building," said Tabatha, making a list in her notebook, "I can't see any leads on that one."

"Then Derringer explodes inside his car."

"Someone must have got onto the estate," said Richie. "Put it on the steering wheel or something. With that one, there was no need to clean it off because the explosion destroyed the evidence."

"That limits the possible suspects," pondered Linda. "Or maybe not. Their hedges are high but not impenetrable. Wouldn't be hard to sneak onto the grounds, lay the trap, then leave."

I moved to the next name on my list.

"Demoor died in the middle of performing her ritual. She keeps her distance from the crowd, so unless one of her Mirrors betrayed her, the trap must have been laid in advance."

"And then somebody snuck the elixir into Piston's cigar," said Richie, before Tabatha took us back a step.

"What's Demoor's ritual entail?"

"Drugs and dancing. She puts her head over a candle, throws

some herbs in it, gets high and starts slicing body parts off her followers."

"Could have easily put something in the herbs," said Linda. "Then she inhaled it, just like Piston and his cigar."

"Or contaminated the candle," added Tabatha. "And if Niles isn't the one committing the murders, he's probably got loyal employees testing his food and . . ."

I'd stopped listening.

The candle.

Yes, Whisper could have replaced that red, three-wicked candle before her ritual. If I'd managed to sneak backstage, I'm sure someone else could. But some people get into those places easier than others. Just like some people would raise fewer alarm bells if they gifted Piston an expensive cigar.

Shit.

"Going to the payphone," I announced as I drained my drink and weaved between the tables to the other end of the bar.

I put a coin in the slot, asked for the new Sunder library, and waited. I knew it might take a while. Eileen was often up a ladder or giving a guest her full attention. At the table next to the phones, a young Werewolf returned to his friends with a tray of shots.

"Three whiskey, three mouthwash," he announced, receiving cheers from his pair of companions. I found it hard not to judge. Why bother with whiskey if you were just going to slam it down and immediately kill the taste with a chaser? Mouthwash was an aniseed-flavored digestive combined with peppermint liqueur that would overpower anything else that had passed your lips. It was mostly used by husbands who wanted to destroy evidence on their breath before heading home, so every bar in Sunder kept bottles of both ingredients on hand.

As soon as the shots were placed on the table, the peppermint aroma overtook the area.

It was the same as Bath's apartment. As his body in the morgue. But why would Bath have been carrying a bottle of that shit around? He lived alone. No need to hide what was on his breath. Unless he'd started drinking on the job? No. It was far from unheard of among police, but not him. Not polite young Constable Bath. Where would he have got it from anyway? Nobody kept that stuff at home. It was only in bars.

Only in bars.

Or, only at a home that was full of bottles, taken from a bar that had just closed down.

Fuck.

"Sunder Library, this is Eileen."

"It's Fetch. Close up and get home. I'll meet you there."

"You found a way to free Lena?"

"Not exactly. Meet me at her place and I'll explain everything."

38

I got there first, but not by much. Eileen arrived red and sweating a minute later.

"What is it?"

"Let's go inside."

The place was just as we'd left it, only more potent: the trespass feeling even more profound. I moved through the living room and down the stairs like I expected every floorboard to be booby-trapped. As if the walls were watching. Like the whole apartment was wearing a disguise that could be ripped away at any moment.

We went down into the study, and I stopped at the bottom of the steps.

"What is it, Fetch? What do you know?"

Eileen was smart. Too smart to lie to.

"Look, I'm not sure about any of this. Still putting it together."

"Putting what together? Is Lena in trouble?"

I went to the desk first. Moved the papers around. Revealed that dried puddle of red wax.

"Redonna Demoor died performing a ritual. That ritual involved breathing in the fumes from a red candle."

Eileen took only a small step towards it, as if she were afraid of what the desk might do if she got too close.

"She could have just been sealing letters."

"I thought the same thing at first. But . . ." I flipped through the notebooks and rediscovered those loose pieces of tobacco stuck between the pages. "The Mayor's head caught on fire while he was smoking one of his trademark cigars."

She scrunched up her face.

"What are you saying? They were poisoned?"

"In a way. I believe that someone has created a substance that, when it makes contact with the body, unlocks the magical potential of nearby artefacts, unleashing the dormant energy."

"A poison that unlocks magical power? That's impossible."

"Until recently, I would have agreed. But the same thing happened with the Unicorn horn in Derringer's new car. Same thing happened to the bullets in Bath's gun."

"Wasn't Bath some kind of execution?"

"Yes, but done with a smear of poison on his doorknob, not a gang of armed goons."

Eileen looked from the wax to the shreds of tobacco. I waited, silently, as she grasped the extent of the accusation I was making.

"Fetch. No."

"I know it's . . . tough to consider."

"It's ridiculous! Why would she do that?"

"I'm not sure. Yet. But she's able to go places others can't. She's one of the few people in this city who could have got close enough to all of them. Left a candle in the church, a cigar in Piston's collection."

"She's been locked up since yesterday!"

"It doesn't matter. She would have left the poisoned objects in their possession and been long gone before they were used."

Eileen shook her head, rapidly, hoping to fling the thoughts loose.

"You've got it wrong, Fetch. Lena loved Bath. After he died, she was in here for days, trying to make sense of it."

"Could have been dealing with her guilt."

"No!" Desperate, she searched the papers and the notebooks, shoving them around, looking for the proof that would invalidate my theory. "You saw her notes, remember? She was trying to solve the case. She had no idea how it happened."

That stopped me. The list Simms had made at the crime scene, the notes and questions, they weren't the kind of thing you'd create if you were the killer. Unless she was just covering her tracks.

Playing the detective for her partner and anyone else who came looking.

Eileen locked her wet, red eyes on mine.

"She asked you for help, remember? Why would she ask you to solve a case if she was the one who did it?"

"Distraction? Maybe. Her faith in my abilities was never that high. She must have hoped I'd make a mess of it. Obscure the truth."

The dark look she showed me was one I hoped to never see again.

"She begged you to help her because she was in pain. She was alone, and she wanted answers." A spark of comprehension shifted her tone. "What if that's what all this was? What if she'd worked out the same things you had? The candle and all that. She could have been doing experiments, trying to discern how Whisper made the poison work."

"The tobacco was here before Piston—"

"Someone could have filled their pipe here! You weren't the only one she asked for help, Fetch. I told you someone else was here, remember? Anyone could have dropped that tobacco. She didn't commit these murders; she was trying to solve them!"

Eileen made a compelling argument, and I might have believed it if there wasn't one last piece of evidence in the room.

"Eileen, I don't understand it all, but—"

"NO!" Then her voice got real low, and she spoke with an assurance that would have stopped a stampede. "The others, *maybe*. Maybe I could believe that. But not Bath. No. Fetch, you've got this all wrong."

I sighed. She had a point. A good one.

The thought of her killing Derringer, Demoor and Piston: it was weird – it was unlikely – but I could imagine it. I could conceive of a motive that drove her to go that far. But Bath?

Bath.

Yes!

My hands jumped up from my sides, hovered in the air like I was trying to grab the thought before it flew away.

"Eileen, you're right! She didn't kill Bath!"

"I told you! But . . . Fetch, what are you doing?"

I moved over to her makeshift bar and searched through the dozens of bottles tucked into the alcove.

"Bath started this whole thing!"

"Yes, he died first."

"No! Before that!"

"I don't follow."

I turned back to her, then closed my eyes. I could barely follow my own thoughts, but it was *almost* clear. Some of it. I still couldn't fit Whisper and his newsletters into the mix, but some of the story was starting to fall into place.

"If Whisper's letter is to be believed, then Bath was at a meeting with Niles, Piston, Derringer and Demoor. A meeting that must have been all about this new substance. There was a Witch there, too. She'd been working for Niles. Her name was Angela Fray. She died in a fire the following night."

"I knew Angela. You think she's connected to this?"

"She found a way to heal her brother, a brewhound. Maybe she used Niles Company materials to do it. Must have been experimenting with forces she was supposed to keep hidden."

"You think Niles found out about it?"

"Perhaps. He could have been the one to call them all together. Share what Angela had been able to do."

"And they killed her for it?"

"Yes! Her and her brother. To crush whatever miracle she'd stumbled onto."

Eileen sat in Simms's office chair.

"How do you know all this?"

I pulled the crumpled newspaper clippings out of my pocket.

"Because Bath was there. Niles had taken a liking to him. Was using him as personal security. So Bath overheard what they were doing and tried to get the word out. He went to a journalist named Jackson Murray to spill the story, but before they could get it off the printing press, Murray's house went the same way as the Fray's."

"You think Niles killed them both?"

"And Bath. The same night as Murray. But . . ." I turned back to the collection of bottles and continued my search. "But they lost track of him for a few hours. So, they set a trap: a smear of that substance on his doorknob for when he got home. Bath went inside and a dozen bullets full of desert dust exploded through his body. That would have been the end of it, if Bath hadn't already passed some of his story on to someone else."

Eileen's eyes were wider than I'd ever seen.

"The two glasses in the sink. Bath was here?"

"He was. And I think he left something behind."

I plucked the bright green bottle of Weevil's Peppermint Liqueur out of the collection and carefully held it at a distance.

"Bath left this study with his flask full of peppermint liqueur. His apartment and body reeked of it. I'm not sure why they didn't just pour it down the sink."

Eileen shook her head.

"That stuff's too potent. The pipes would have been coughing up minty bubbles for days."

"Right. They didn't want the aroma to give away the hiding place. Bath must have planned to dispose of it somewhere else."

"Then why use that bottle in the first place? Could have hidden it in any of them."

"Eileen, if you were here alone, what are the chances you'd pour yourself a glass of this?"

"Zero."

"Exactly. Too sweet and not your style. Simms knew that. She wanted to keep you safe."

The relief on Eileen's face damn near broke my heart.

"I told you! I told you she couldn't do it. She's not a killer."

I felt bad dissuading her of that belief, but I had my teeth on the truth now, and I wasn't going to let go until I'd torn off a piece.

"Not at first. Simms must have tucked the stuff away without any intention of using it. Just a piece of evidence to be stored for a later date. Something to be investigated further. It was only after Bath died that she decided to see what it could do."

"You don't know that."

"I do. Because now, the poison has been tainted by this bottle. This is the cigar that killed Henry Piston."

I took the napkin out of my pocket. Unwrapped it.

"Fetch, you've got it wrong. She——"

I held the cigar under her nose. She fell silent.

"Nobody else would have known it was here. Nobody else could have snuck it into a cigar and delivered it into the Mayor's hands."

She had no rebuttal now. Her mind was searching for arguments but she couldn't find anything that would hold up.

"But . . . she's a good person."

"Maybe that's what did it. Whoever killed Bath didn't know where he'd been. Didn't know who he'd given the substance to. But Simms was here with a bottle of poison and a clear idea of who was to blame. A list, given to her by Bath himself, detailing everyone at the meeting that had set this whole thing in motion."

Eileen's face softened. It was like she was begging me to change the facts. Tell her a different story.

Suddenly, sirens. Lots of them. Alarmingly close and closing, loud enough to snap Eileen out of her stupor.

"What's happening?"

The brakes squealed right above us and there was commotion outside the frosted window. Doors opened. Boots landed. Firefighters shouted at each other.

Had someone worked it out? Had Simms confessed?

"This is it, boys!" said one of the firefighters. You could hear the smile in his voice; the mock-serious declaration of a ham actor on opening night. "Somebody reported a fire blazing inside this apartment."

"Wow, you sure are good at this, Rex. I can't even tell." Laughter from the group. A whole bunch of them. "Oh, wait, I think I see it."

There was the sound of breaking glass in the room above. The whoosh of flame catching fuel.

"Oh, you're right! I think I see another one!"

A boot crashed through the frosted window, spraying glass over Eileen as she moved away from the wall.

I held the green bottle close to protect the evidence.

"Eileen, is there any other way out?" She shook her head. Damn. Then we had no choice but to run out the front door – right into the firefighters – and pray they didn't shoot us on sight.

Hoots and hollers drew our attention to the window, just as a flask stuffed with a burning rag came flying through. I covered Eileen with my body as the projectile hit the desk and turned it into a pyre. The firefighters on the street screamed in triumph. I lifted Eileen to her feet, determined to get out of there before the fire caught the bootleg moonshine in her booze collection.

"Come on!"

The living-room window had been smashed, and the couch where I'd slept the previous night was engulfed in flames. Cushions coughed burning feathers into the air, and black smoke ran around the roof.

The kitchen windows shattered, and another flask exploded, hitting the drapes and the pile of cookbooks on the counter. I grabbed Eileen's hand and made for the front door, only noticing the puddle when my boot hit the rug with a splash.

For a moment, I thought it was water: naively believing that the firefighters had flipped their script and were attempting to put out the blaze they'd just set burning.

Then the smell reached my nose.

"Get back!"

I fell on Eileen as the door ignited, engulfing the rug and my right boot along with it. I slapped at the flames but the fuel had soaked into the old soles. It was too hot to remove the boot with my fingers, so I tried to force it off with my other foot, toes roasting in the leather like I was cooking chipolatas.

Just as I started screaming, the flames burnt through the laces and the boot came loose. I kicked it off and coughed up smoke. Already, you knew there would be nothing left of the house. Fire had found its way onto everything. Eileen looked around in horror, her eyes red and weeping, watching her new life – only recently won – turn to ash.

The smoke above our heads was thick and black. Soon, there would be no air to breathe. The windows were broken but burning furniture barricaded our escape. The door – having been so heavily doused in accelerant – was warping enough to show daylight.

I wrapped my arms around Eileen, pointed my back at the door, and charged.

I hit it with all my might, yet the door remained intact. Because I'd dropped my whole weight onto it, I couldn't regain my footing as fast as I'd like. I could smell my hair burning and feel the heat on my neck and scalp. Then the frame must have burned through because the world spun around us as we fell into the sunlight.

Eileen toppled from my arms, and I twisted, landing on my face and chest and, also, on the green bottle that was still clutched in one hand.

It shattered beneath me, releasing a peppermint aroma and a pint of black liquid. I pulled back but the fluid was already on my skin. In cuts on my fingers.

My breath caught painfully in my chest.

The poison peeled back the edges of reality.

The world went mad.

39

I've been transported. I am somewhere else. Somewhere bright and shimmering. There's a ringing in my ears like my head is floating between the prongs of a tuning fork. Crystal. Everywhere. Around me and inside me, resonating with dormant power. Singing. A chorus of eternal voices hidden in the wings while I stand on stage, under the spotlight, unable to speak.

My eyes snap open and I force a strained breath into my burning lungs. Eileen thinks fast. Knows to scramble back. She's full of panic but her wits aren't completely lost. She stares at me, waiting, wondering what will happen.

A ring on her right hand is fizzing. Not from the heat. From the power emanating from my poison-filled body. I can feel it, pulsing in my blood, reaching out like my own magnetic field of magical energy. Searching hungrily for a dance partner. For a friend who wants to play.

Eileen slides the ring from her finger and it explodes when it hits the cobbles, turning into lightning bolts that make her hair stand up on end. She backs away. Her eyes are apologetic but she knows there's nothing to be done. I am full of the same toxin that killed the most powerful people in Sunder. It's a death sentence. Surely. But unlike them, I know what I'm dealing with. It's not the poison that killed them, but the dormant magic that it awoke around them. If I can get away. If I can steer clear of anything magical until the substance leaves my system. Maybe there's still a way to survive this.

A hand lands on my shoulder.

"Don't move—"

I don't turn to see him, but I know from the eardrum-shattering sound and the pain in my calf that his pistol just exploded and at least one of the bullets has gone straight into my leg. Even my own scream is muffled by the ringing in my ears.

When I spin around, the kid's face is pale, and blood is already trickling from his open mouth. He has no idea what happened, and he won't be around long enough to put the pieces together. The burgundy suit hides the rest of the blood, but there are at least five bullets yet to be accounted for, and I'd put money on at least one being somewhere in his guts.

His friends stand around us: stunned, for now, but I know it won't last. They might not understand the mechanism that killed their friend, but that won't stop them firing at the guy that's nearest to him. I move first and manage to get to my feet. Adrenaline is dulling the pain of the leg wound, and it will only get worse if I run on it, but I have no other option. I flee down the closest street, barely hearing the bullets that ricochet off the bricks beside me.

I have no idea where I'm going, and I can see two worlds at once: the grime-covered Sunder streets and that crystalline maze inside my mind. Are my ears still ringing, or is that their song? A choir from that other place, luring me away. Away from this broken, bleeding body. This walking time bomb.

"Watch it!"

I've stumbled into someone. A well-dressed Dwarf with a briefcase in his hand. I lurch back but it's too late. The briefcase explodes in a surge of green gas that knocks his legs out from under him. His head hits the curb and his eyes roll up and away. His body shakes in an uncontrollable fit. I can't help him. I can't help anyone. I run, forcing myself to ignore the crystal world that overlays my vision, and see the one that's truly in front of me. My watering eyes stay peeled for anyone else in my path. Can't let them touch me. Can't let them get hurt.

I stop to wipe my tears, leaning one hand against a pole. As soon as I touch it, I feel the power. The bubbling fury of the underground fires, locked inside the nickel pipes.

It's not a pole I'm touching, but a lamp. The energy surges inside it. The top blows off. A fireball as big as a building fills the sky.

The shockwave knocks my teeth together and puts me on my ass but I can't stay here. Everyone's coming out now, poking their heads from their windows and stepping onto the street to see what's happened. The top of the lamp is split like a peeled banana, and it continues to belch unfiltered flames straight from the pits below. I can't risk anyone offering me assistance. I need to keep moving.

I run. Well, I try. It's a limping, chaotic stumble away from the open streets. I blink and blink, trying to clear the hallucinations from my failing eyes. I want to step into the other place. Away from the pain in my leg and the fear of what I'll do to anyone who gets too close.

I find an alley and lurch into it, praying that there's a way out on the other side. I need to leave the city. I need to get far away from anyone and everyone. But how? I'm stuck in Sunder's heart and every road out of town will be full of people. Vehicles. Guns. Power. I can't—

A door opens out of nowhere. The back entrance to some bar. A green-skinned Kobold has seen me. He's reaching for something out of sight. Probably a weapon.

"Don't!" I scream in my underwater voice. "Please, just let me pass."

I think I've stopped him. I think he's safe. Then I feel the invisible arms of the magical field latch on.

No.

The poison shares its knowledge: a fake eye, made of some precious, sacred stone.

"Get back!"

The Kobold reads my plea as a threat. He lifts the baton, ready to swing. There are metal spikes at the striking end, rusted and deadly.

The poison bellows – glorious and triumphant – and the

Kobold's eye turns to liquid fire. A ball of frozen magma has been thawed inside his skull. His scream never makes it from his throat. The spoonful of molten rock expands his eye socket. Opens up his cheek, his sinuses, and all the way to his slack-jawed mouth where gums disintegrate and teeth fall to the floor.

I'm gone before his body knows it's dead. He's still standing when I reach the intersection of another main road. I know, because I look back and see the firefighter enter the other end of the alley, back the way I came.

He goes for his gun, so I move, out into the open. A delivery van slams the brakes just before it hits me. I stumble, my hands on the hood, and watch the driver yell at me behind the windshield.

This is a post-Coda car. Mortales manufacturing. No magic in this model. I'm safe.

I'm not.

The poison latches onto something in the back. *People?* No. Not quite.

Fuuuuuuuck.

I run across the road. Maybe with enough distance, I'll break the connection. Put them back to sleep. Another car swerves to avoid me. I keep going. Got to get away before the cargo comes to life.

Too late.

The back door of the van is kicked open by a clay leg. I can't help but turn and watch as three stone Constructs step out onto the street.

What the hell are those things doing here?

I fought those things out in Incava, where their Wizard creators brought them to life with pieces of the river itself. If they're here, that means someone has gone out to the Wizard City and brought them back. That means someone has seen the chasm that goes down into the crystal depths. Knows that the Wizards were mining pure, frozen magic.

Niles. It has to be.

Is that how this substance was made? A synthesized form of that pure power?

No time to ponder it now. The firefighter on my tail turns his attention to the first Construct. He unloads a few useless shots into the creature's clay chest, and doesn't back away in time. The giant grabs the boy's skull in his fist. I run. The horrified wail of the bystanders gives me all the information I need. More firetrucks pull up. The boys shoot their weapons from the windows. I could tell them not to bother — that only a point-blank shot to a Construct's crystal eye will do the trick — but I need to make use of the distraction.

Just as I'm about to run, a firetruck speeds down the street and collides with one of the stone statues, shattering it into rubble. Maybe there are more ways than one to take out a Construct when you're not trapped in the confines of an ancient castle.

At the next corner, I see Cecil Hill and finally get my bearings. I'm too far north to get home like this. Even if I made it, I wouldn't be safe for long. Too many rooms around mine. Too many unknowns. The road south is the only way out of the city that doesn't involve crossing bogs or swamp water, and if I try to take that route, I'll set off half the city.

Instead, I go east. Then a little more north. In these richer streets, I'm safe from generous onlookers offering me help. The streets are wide. Potential victims stay safe behind their gates and the bars on their windows.

Soon, I'm on a familiar path. I've walked this way before. Too many times.

Amari.

She takes me into her branches and cradles my aching body, catching my blood in the cracks of her bark. She holds me, safe beneath the cover of her leaves. I rest in her twisted limbs, waiting for the visions to fade and the crystalline singing to quiet.

I thank her for her sanctuary, but then I worry.

I worry because I know what it felt like when this poison found the magical energy in a ring, a false eye and a lump of clay. I can still feel the poison, reaching out around me. Grasping in every direction for a hint of magic to dance with. It searches the tips of the leaves. The trunk. The roots of this tree.

And finds nothing.

40

"Hey, kid."

The plan had sounded great in my head.

Thinking that she would appreciate a front-row seat to the parade, I'd arrived at the bar early and taken over a table that faced the street. I soon discovered that, on a day like this, the owner wasn't going to give over the spot for water alone, and told me I had to order a drink or get out. Then he revealed the "special" menu with the jacked-up holiday prices.

Fifteen minutes before the parade was supposed to start, I was toasting my dwindling savings with a fourth cocktail – if I didn't order one every half-hour, the owner threatened to hand my table to someone else – when the crowd swelled with latecomers. The tardy guests crammed themselves onto the sidewalk between me and the barricade, so by the time Amari finally squeezed her way into the beer garden, all I'd gifted her was a perfect view of a row of bobbing asses.

"Interesting spot. Don't you want to watch the parade?"

"I—"

She snatched up a menu.

"Fuck me. These prices! Let's find somewhere more our style." There must have been something comical about the way I got to my feet because she started giggling. *"Couldn't wait for me to start celebrating?"*

"Had to know what a three-bronze cocktail tastes like."

"And what did it taste like?"

"Like a two-copper cocktail with an umbrella in it."

"And a hangover you'll feel in two places, I imagine. Come on, money-bags, let's walk them off so I have some chance of catching up."

Amari looped her arm around mine to keep me upright and we squeezed our way through the packed sidewalk and onto a backstreet.

"You don't want to watch the parade?" I asked.

"I've seen the Sunder PD before. I prefer them asleep at the station to receiving applause." She must have seen the confusion cross my face. "Something wrong?"

"No."

"You weren't really set on watching the parade, were you?"

"No. I just . . . I just thought that's what we were supposed to do."

"As good a reason for not doing something as I've ever heard. You had cops in Weatherly, right?"

"Guards."

"Oh, yes. I forgot. That's how you made your escape." Amari pulled back my sleeve and traced her fingers over the single tattooed band marked on my forearm. "And were these guards well respected?"

"Unquestionably."

She cackled.

"I believe you've hit the nail on the head." Amari purchased two flagons of wine from the street-side vendor and pulled the cork out of one with her teeth. When I reached for the other, she slapped my fingers away. "Don't even think about it. You're on water until you can walk straight."

There was a half-constructed bell tower on the next block: locked up and abandoned while the workers observed the holiday. Wiping residual wine from her lips, Amari pulled a seed from her pocket and dropped it into the keyhole. Then I held her flagon while she placed her hands over the lock.

"Pretty sure those things are coated against magical—"

The lock snapped open, dropping leaves and bits of twig.

"Protected from alchemy and ditarum, perhaps, but the beauty of Sunder is they never expect a Fae." She spat onto the street. "Touching iron does leave a bad taste in my mouth, though."

It left a red mark on her palm as well, but she paid it no notice. Just kicked the gate open and began to climb.

Because the tower had not yet been fitted with its bell, you could sit on any side of the structure and see the city laid out in all directions. Amari kicked off her shoes and walked around the edges of the unfinished *platform, but my eyes were drawn to the police station. The marching band had emerged and was snaking out of Eleventh then south down Main to wild applause.*

Amari's hands landed on my shoulders, her skin cool against my neck.

"They're just people, Fetch. That should mean they're as equally well intentioned and fallible as anyone else. But then you've got to ask yourself what kind of people choose to go through life wielding a baton and a badge."

Amari was decades older and far more experienced that I was, but I'd learned not to let that stop me from speaking back. Better to let her teach me another lesson than risk her becoming bored.

"But aren't they the ones who put themselves in danger if we get into trouble? Don't they help people?"

"In theory. And, sometimes, in practice. A good person can become a police officer. They can use the powers of the position to do good things. But to access those powers, they need to pick a side. And once you've joined a team and you're wearing their colors, then everyone else becomes an ally or an opponent."

Like ink from a spilled bottle, the wave of blue flowed towards us. From up here, you could see no faces. Could not differentiate the species, race or gender of each officer. They were one unified force. One monstrous blue line of authority, pushing its way through the city like a wandering beast. Friendly when respected, but always ready to show its teeth.

"It's the same everywhere," she said. "Armies, factions, Shepherds, Guards. They only function if everyone wearing the uniform commits to marching in the same direction, no matter what lies down the road."

She was right. I thought about my brief time as an obedient defender of the Weatherly walls, and how it was the first time in my life I felt a sense of calm. All my questions had answers. My choices were limited to those outlined by my superiors. I was no longer an individual, I was part of a group of men who shared a common goal and common ideals.

At least, that was the idea. But it hadn't lasted long.

"I don't know how to do it," I said. "I can't stop questioning things. I sometimes think I'm incapable of just doing the job I've been assigned."

I'd meant to confess it as a shortcoming, but Amari kissed my cheek like she was bestowing me with a reward.

"That's why I like you." She sat down beside me and looped our arms again. "I suppose some people need rules. They want to feel a sense of order before they can move forward. We can't all be out here, cut loose from the rabble, trying to make sense of the nonsensical. Doubting our actions, making mistakes, repenting and reforming and trying again."

"It's nice of you to suggest that we're both like that, but I'm not on the outside by choice. I just haven't found a way in."

"I don't believe that, kid. You've had plenty of chances to join up, and I've enjoyed seeing you brush them aside. You're watching, listening, biding your time. Maybe one day you'll choose your colors. Pick a team. It happens to the best of us."

I thought about refuting that idea. Making a declaration of my own independence. Telling her that I'd always be like her — solitary and rebellious — but I didn't believe it. The days were too long on my own. When she wasn't in town, I spent too much time feeling ostracized and lonely. She was right. One day I would fold myself in with a company.

"How will I know how to pick the right side?"

She laughed and handed me the bottle.

"That's the thing, Fetch. There is no right side. As long as you remember that, you have half a chance of keeping your head."

The band changed tunes, playing some triumphant number with drums and horns. I took a swig of the wine and passed it back, thinking how much better it was to be on the outside when there was someone else there with me.

I wondered if I could stay out there, on the edge. If I had Amari to guide me, then I would avoid too many mistakes. We could brave a life beyond the simple rules and the well-worn paths. We could be happy. Alone, but together.

How quickly we forget.

41

As an aficionado of hangovers, I know a good one when I feel it, and the post-poison after-effects were up there with the worst. I can't even imagine how bad the headache would have been if I wasn't distracted by the gunshot wound and glass shards.

Amari had kept me hidden, but her trunk was on the solid side and the cleft created by her branches was far from ergonomic, so I woke around midnight knowing I had to move.

I blinked to wet my dry and aching eyes, and was confused to find the world inside my eyelids lighter than the world beyond them. That crystalline realm was still there. A fainter, less focused version than what I'd seen when the poison had me in its clutches. A piece of the dream world carried into waking life.

The humming, too. That chorus of unintelligible voices, coming in from some distant place.

What did that mean?

I forced my eyes open and tried to put both feet in the present. In the real world, where there was still so much to be done.

It was dark, and there were sirens echoing through the city. I was sore and bleeding and a wanted man, but at least I was no longer a walking weapon.

I reflected on my last awful thoughts before sleep had taken me. How the poison could sense no magic in the tree. Surely that didn't mean anything. The substance had only reacted to magic that was dormant – locked up and frozen from the Coda – and that definition didn't fit Amari any more. She'd been freed. She was alive. There was nothing more the poison could do for her, right? Just because I couldn't feel her, that didn't mean she wasn't still in there.

Maybe she could even hear me. Feel me in her arms. Who the fuck was I to say one way or the other? I'd been a one-man magical army for all of fifteen minutes and I thought I knew how to sense Fae spirits in foliage? Forget it, Fetch. You know nothing.

Well, not nothing.

You know that Simms killed Demoor and Piston. That's more than you knew yesterday. That's something, isn't it? Maybe you're good at this detective business after all.

But it took you long enough. Too long. She even spelled it out for you, back at the start. She came to you for help. Asked you what you'd do if you found Whisper's identity. Whether or not you'd turn him in. She was testing you.

Maybe she still is.

Lena Simms is Mister Whisper.

Right?

Not quite.

I rested my forehead on Amari's trunk, thanked her, and got moving.

It hurt to walk, but I was good at hurting. My body was bleeding, but that was more common than breakfast. I was tired and sore, but excited because the pieces were finally coming together.

And from here, I didn't have far to go.

42

It was only a few blocks to the Derringer estate, but every step was likely doing permanent damage to my leg. It was only a flesh wound, but in case you weren't aware, flesh makes up a whole lot of your body, and is where you keep important things like blood and nerves. I was just thinking about how unfair it all was, when fate delivered me a way to lift my spirits (or at least a way to vent my anger).

Owen Ward – the filthy shutterbug – was sitting by his hedge, camera in one hand and a bottle of beer in the other. He grinned when he saw me, and raised the viewfinder to his eyes.

"Well, if it isn't the man of the hour."

I broke his lens and his nose.

"You fucker!"

"Piss off, Ward. Your shift's over."

I went to stomp on his camera, but I couldn't work out how to do it without hurting my injured leg, so I picked it up and threw it on the street. The machine made a satisfying crunching sound as it exploded into shiny silver pieces.

"You've done it now! I'll publish everything I have."

"About the Derringers? Be my guest, dickhead. Tits and scandals and secret meetings. Get it all out there. I've had enough of everyone's secrets."

I put my thumb down on the Derringer doorbell for an obnoxiously long time. Ward kept swearing at me but was smart enough not to come inside swinging distance.

"Hello?" It was the lady of the house.

"I'm back."

"It's late, Mr Phillips."

"Too late for me to tell you who killed your husband?"

There was a long pause, then the gate slowly opened.

"*I* want to know," said Ward, suddenly polite.

"Then read tomorrow's paper."

The driveway was empty, and the door was unlocked. There were no lights on inside – Trixie Derringer didn't need them – but the door at the far end of the hall was open.

"Down here," called her voice from that direction. I ignored it. Instead, I turned left into the study and approached the Derringer desktop letterpress. Here was the machine that Isaac had used to build the foundations of his empire. It might even have saved his life if I'd looked a little closer on my first visit.

I placed a sheet of paper into the contraption and pulled the handle. The mechanism swung one plate onto the other, and there was enough residual ink for the type to leave its mark.

I brought the print with me, down the hall, to where Trixie Derringer was waiting.

As soon as I stepped out the back door into the glass atrium, I started sweating. The indoor garden could have been a house in its own right, though only for a dedicated exhibitionist. I lit a lamp, illuminating the many greens of the many leaves on the many plants that grew in well-tended rows along narrow aisles.

Ms Derringer was down to nothing but a slip, her veil and a set of gardening gloves. She continued her work – repotting a seedling from the base of a larger plant into its own vessel – as if I were a door-to-door salesman not the man who'd said he could reveal her husband's murderer. I removed my jacket and hung it over a garden chair.

"Goddamn," I said, pulling at my collar. "You could incubate a Dragon's egg in here."

"Nothing quite that interesting, I'm afraid, but we have a lot of plants you won't find anywhere else this side of the Farra. Isaac was the collector but neither he nor Carnegie have a talent for tending to them. It's taken a few years, but I've finally learned how to keep the plantlets alive until they're large enough to go outside."

I nodded, uselessly. Was she really not that interested in hearing my theory? Or was it because she had little faith that I might have stumbled on the truth.

"Impressive," I said. "But how do you deal with the pests?"

"Slugs?"

"Photographers. I found one in your hedge on the way up."

"Oh, him."

She placed the seedling on a shelf and wiped her brow with the back of her hand. I was a little unsure of where to look, but tried to entertain my eyes with exotic plants instead of the underdressed Gorgon who couldn't return my glare.

"Your husband was full of threats when I met him. That was after Carnegie gave me a whole routine about how he liked to turn people inside out."

"I hope you don't think that was just talk, Mr Phillips. Like all of Isaac's stories, there's at least a speck of truth in there somewhere."

"I believe it. That's why I was so surprised to find Owen Ward walking on his own unbroken legs and smiling with a full set of teeth after he posted such a . . . salacious set of pictures."

She took off one glove and ran her fingertips up the length of a fern, stopping when she came across a leaf that was going brown. After rubbing it between her fingertips, she used a set of shears to remove the weak stem with a pointed snip.

"Oh, Isaac dreamed of doing terrible things to that awful little shutterbug, but the Cyclops had him over a barrel. Months ago, Isaac received a detailed account of all the dirt that Ward had on him, along with a description of how it would be released if he received any retribution."

"Smart move, I suppose."

"Yes, a lack of scruples doesn't always mean a lack of intelligence. In fact, loose ethics and strong business sense often go hand in hand. Apparently, if Ward doesn't contact certain associates on a daily basis, then some of Isaac's sensitive material will be released to the public."

"Did something go wrong? Is that why Ward went ahead and released those pictures?"

She gave a good, full-bodied laugh, and the shears danced in her fingertips.

"You mean my tits? Come now, Mr Phillips. These are admittedly glorious, but they're of limited importance to my husband's media empire. Apparently they sell for good money, though, which is all Ward wanted: the freedom to pursue his filthy brand of photography without fear of Isaac's henchmen coming for his head."

So, whatever Ward had on Derringer, it was enough leverage to let him photograph his wife half naked and sell those pictures to the tabloids. I didn't know much about Derringer, but he must have been plenty scared of the real story coming out to let himself be manipulated like that.

"And that deal still stands, does it?" I asked.

"What do you mean?"

"You'll let Ward hide in your hedges if he agrees to keep your other stories secret?"

"I suppose I'll have to think about it. Now that it's not Isaac's reputation being protected, but his legacy."

"I was thinking of stories that have more to do with you."

She felt her way across a row of plants, moving in my direction. I stepped back to let her through, but the tip of the shears scraped against my thighs.

"Really? What kind of stories?"

"Oh, I don't know. Like the gentleman caller who paid you a visit a few nights ago? The same night your husband felt compelled to drive himself to my cafe to get himself blown up."

Snip.

"Seems you're putting together a story of your own, Mr Phillips. Hoping to break into the newspaper business, are you?"

"I heard there's a recent opening. Shall I run the piece by you? See if you can give me some pointers?"

"By all means."

"Great. At first, I was trying to kill too many birds with too few stones. Couldn't find a common thread. So, I've decided to simplify things."

"Always a smart move. Choose the most interesting angle and build out from there."

"Exactly. Forget about murders and secret meetings for the moment. Let's center the story around a powerful media mogul and his gorgeous wife, alone in their estate at the top of the city."

"That's not quite true, though. Remember, you can dance around the truth but never turn your back on it."

"Fair. They're not completely alone. A driver called Carnegie follows his boss everywhere. It would take a serious bout of illness to cause him to abandon his duties." I looked around the humid greenhouse. "We could hint at the possibility of some rare poison derived from an exotic plant, but I don't have the expertise to back that up."

"No need. It could just as easily have been done with some expired food or a hidden dose of the boss's digestive medication. Not as exotic, perhaps, but the outcome is the same."

"Point taken. But why poison the driver in the first place?"

"Skip the rhetorical questions, they're hackneyed and you don't need them. Stay on point."

"Fine. With the driver out of the way, the wife could execute her plan without harming a loyal friend in the process."

"You haven't even said what the plan is. You're getting muddled."

"Edit me later. There was a fight between the couple. He discovered something. Didn't like it. Lost his temper. How am I doing?"

"I'm following the thread so far. But you're lacking in evidence."

"I was hoping you could help me with that."

"How so?"

She turned her veiled faced toward me.

"You must be hot under there, Ms Derringer. Isn't it hard to breathe?"

She stroked the bottom of the veil with her gloved fingers.

"It's a sign of respect. For my dearly departed husband. One must keep up appearances."

"No cameras here, Trixie."

She took a beat then lifted the veil, revealing a bright purple bruise that painted her cheek. It was swollen to the point where one of her eyes was only a silver slit. A big guy like Derringer didn't need to swing hard to hurt a little thing like her, but it looked like he'd put all his weight behind that one.

"Yes," she said. "I'd say your story has substance so far."

I growled into my mouth.

"And perhaps a happy ending. Headline could read, 'Asshole Gets What He Deserves'."

"No opinions yet, Phillips. We must remain objective. What did he discover?"

She placed her veil on a shelf and went back to her pruning.

Snip.

"Owen Ward would say it was infidelity, and he has pictures of a gentleman caller to support his theory. So, the wife decides to kill her husband and she's just been handed the perfect way to disguise it: an imported luxury car. A one-of-a kind automobile so unique that the police would have no way of knowing if it had caused the explosion or not. No other vehicles to compare it to. No experts to declare that this could never happen, only some manufacturer in Mira who would do their best to bury the questions without giving any concrete answers. To the public, the accident would be accepted as an unlikely but believable consequence of Derringer's excessive displays of wealth."

"This sounds like a lot of hearsay, Mr Phillips. I don't want anyone suing this paper for libel."

"Good, because I think Ward's got it wrong."

She smiled, and it looked like it hurt her to do so.

"I'm glad. I'm not so petty as to murder my husband over some torrid affair."

"Then why *would* you murder him?"

Snip. She cut a stem by accident. The flower dropped to the floor, scattering petals.

"Oh dear." She bent down and retrieved the fallen bloom. "Did you know that I met Isaac when I first arrived in Sunder? I was pitching stories for the *Sunder Bulletin*."

"I didn't know you were a writer."

"I was *the* writer, darling. Isaac loves to praise his letterpress as the secret to his early career, but all it could do was put ink on paper. Without my words, he wouldn't have gotten anywhere." Trixie held the flower, stroking its petals in her fingertips. "Do you know why Isaac loved me?"

"You saved him a fortune on shampoo?"

"He loved me because he wanted to *be* me. His own writing lacked character. He worked at it. Desperately. But his mind was too simple. Sure, he understood the business side of things – he could talk the talk – but when it came to putting his voice on paper, he was sadly limited."

"You wrote for the *Star*?"

"In the beginning." Trixie slid the flower between the ringlets of her snakeskin hair, then went back to work. "We were partners, for a while. Until he was invited into the elite boys' club of big business and found new muses in the VIPs of government and commerce. It turned out simple writing was what the people truly wanted. For a while, he let me amuse myself creating the puzzles for the back cover, but eventually he felt it prudent to keep his business and home life separate."

Snip.

"Weather's a bit warm for gloves, isn't it? Come to think of it, I've never seen you without them."

"You've got a keen eye, Mr Phillips."

"A keen eye doesn't mean much when it's paired with a slow mind." I looked at my own hands. If the stain was still there, it was lost beneath the dried blood and grime. "I touched that press the first time I came here. Couldn't get the ink off my fingers all day."

Trixie Derringer lifted her hand to her mouth and bit the end of her glove. Slowly, she slid out her fingers. There were purple blots on all the tips.

"Occupational hazard, I'm afraid." She rubbed her fingertips together. "Hard to cover up evidence when you can't see it."

"I'd say you did a stellar job under the circumstances."

She dropped the glove and turned herself towards me. Her arms were slack at her sides, her body as languid as butter melting into soup, the only tension left was in the fingers that gripped those shining shears.

"Whisper's first letter," I said. "Did you and Simms write it together?"

She shook her head, making the ghostly snakes dance to an unheard charmer's tune.

"I don't see much, but I hear things in this house. I was here when Angela Fray told Isaac, Henry and Thurston what she'd found. Some kind of cure. A way to help."

"So Fray brought the substance to Niles?"

"Not exactly. Niles had come into a kind of poison. An unstable element that he hoped to weaponize. Fray was one of the people hired to build him that weapon, but she found a way to turn the poison into medicine instead. A way to help people. I could only listen from a distance so I didn't hear everything, but I heard their plans to keep the discovery a secret. To destroy the medicine and anyone who knew about it. It took me a few days to get the word out, and by that time Fray and Bath were already dead.

"When did Isaac figure it out?" I asked.

"After someone at the *Star* discovered the secret message. It was the same trick I used back when I was crafting puzzles for the back cover."

"Then he gave you the shiner, called off the investigation, and came over to visit me."

"Yes, whatever you said on the phone stirred something in him. Or he just wanted to get as far away from me as possible."

I nodded, but there were still too many gaps in the story.

"Isaac wasn't the first one to work it out, was he?"

Trixie's stony eyes glistened in the moonlight.

"I met Lena back when she was a beat cop. When I was writing real stories, rather than being confined to the funny pages. As soon as she read the newsletter, she put it together. Bath had just been killed and she was searching for a way to get her revenge without being the next victim on Niles's hit list."

"Was Bath the one who told Simms about this whole conspiracy?"

She nodded.

"Niles had taken the kid on as his personal security. He was here through the whole meeting."

"And then what? He got a guilty conscience and ran back to his old boss."

"Not exactly. But you should probably talk to Lena about that."

I nodded, forgetting she couldn't see me.

"Yeah, maybe I'll do that."

I was still holding the piece of paper I'd taken from the study, and when I moved, it ruffled through the air. Trixie cocked an ear. "What have you got there?"

"From the headline, I believe it's Mister Whisper's latest newsletter, hot off the press."

"I see. Would you read it to me?"

JUDGE THE JUDGMENT

It's time for the truth.

No more hidden messages. No hints. No allusions.

Let's speak plain.

The Niles Company is involved in many enterprises that seek to subjugate the people of this city for their own gain. To this end, they have been harvesting crystalized pieces of the sacred river and hiring workers to weaponize the substance. One worker, named Angela Fray, found a different use.

Fray used this base alchemical solution to synthesize a new

type of medicine. One that, in early tests, could stabilize the body of someone who was suffering debilitating post-Coda effects.

Angela's reward for such a discovery was murder at the hands of her employer.

Isaac Derringer, Redonna Demoor, Henry Piston and Thurston Niles chose to kill Angela Fray and her brother rather than let her medicine see the light of day.

They do not care for you.

They want Sunder to remain sick. Remain weak. Remain scared.

They want you in their palm and in their debt.

Corporal Bath approached a journalist named Jackson Murray to get this story out.

For daring to tell the truth, both men met the same fate.

That's why I killed Derringer, Demoor and Piston.

Niles must be next.

I don't know if I can do it.

But now the truth is exposed, perhaps one of you will.

Thank you for your readership, and sorry for all the drama.

I just needed to know that you'd listen.

Whisper

Trixie scrunched up her nose. "What do you think? A bit dry?"

"It gets the point across. But why not just print this in the first place? You could have ruined their reputations with your first edition."

She shook her head, and the snakes sprung up like they'd been spooked.

"Nobody would have cared. They'd have talked about it for a day or two. A journalist might have attempted to follow the thread before being silenced. No. This was the only way to stop them, and the only way for their crimes to be heard. Now everyone is listening." She sidled up to me, tapped the tip of the shears against my chest. "So, what happens next?"

Good goddamn question.

I had Whisper's identity, but was I really going to hand Trixie over to Volta? Turn her in to save my own skin? Would it even matter? What would happen to the city when the last newsletter went public?

"When are you posting this?" I asked.

"Carnegie's out there now. He's going to wait until everyone's awake then let the newsletters loose from the bell tower."

"Wait. He was in on it?"

"If there's one person in this city you should never trust, Mr Phillips, it's Carnegie. He dreamed of being a thespian before he fell into our employ, and he still delights in acting inscrutable. In all those years, even Isaac never realized how much Carnegie despised him."

I'd never suspected it, but of course it made sense; only a fool would spend an hour with the Derringers and favor the Sasquatch over the Gorgon.

Not that Trixie was all sunshine and roses: after all, she was half the brain behind a string of explosive murders.

"What about you?" asked Trixie, tapping the shears even harder. "Are you going to run to the *Star* or the Lamplighter and tell the rest of the story? Clear your friends from the suspect list? Pay Volta his ransom?"

Did I still need to? It all depended on the fallout. Most of the accused were already dead. Their punishment dealt. Only Niles remained. How much power would he hold after Whisper's last drop? What would the population of Sunder do when they finally learned the truth?

"I don't know what I'll do," I said, ignoring the metal scraping against my sternum. "Perhaps I should speak to your accomplice first."

The shears traced up and down my ribs. I thought she might be searching for an entry point, until they finally pulled away.

"About time, Phillips. If you'd listened to her in the first place, we might have had you on side from the start."

She went back to her work. So calm. She wasn't really worried about what I'd do. Her work was complete. Justice served. The truth had been spoken, and now it was up to the rest of us to decide what we'd do with it.

I patted myself down.

"You don't have a spare bronze, do you? If I want to make amends, I'd best not arrive empty-handed."

43

Backlash was built to house hundreds of inmates. At its prime, it would likely become a crowded, impenetrable fortress with police on every corner. As it was – with only a single prisoner being housed and a couple of guards keeping watch – I had no problem slipping inside unnoticed.

After all, Simms wasn't a real criminal, was she? They were only making an example of her. A political offering to the public until they could capture Whisper and hang him in the town square.

Did anyone else know that the killer had already been caught? Or was it just me, Trixie, Carnegie and Simms herself?

She was lying in the dark. Motionless on the steel bed.

"Hello, Lena."

They'd taken her scarf and her hat. No more hiding her face. No protection for the peeling scales and raw flesh. Her cracked lip was eternally curled in an expression of distrust, disgust and impatience.

"Hello, Fetch. You look like you've been on quite the adventure."

"I have. Sorry it took so long. But I've finally worked it out."

"Worked what out?"

"The question you wanted me to answer."

She sat up.

"Why did Whisper kill them? You think you know?"

"Well, some of it." I pulled out a fresh pack of Clayfields – purchased with Trixie Derringer's spare change – and flicked one through the bars. "It was because they killed Bath."

Simms bit down on the twig with her venom-stained fangs and used her forked tongue to spread the painkiller along her aching lips.

"He was a good man," she hissed. "At least, he tried to be.

Stupid enough to serve Thurston without question. Simple enough that Thurston took him for a loyal soldier. Brought him along to that meeting as protection. But when Bath heard what they were planning to do, he came to me. It was my idea for him to get closer. Become a firefighter and steal a sample. He couldn't get his hands on the medicine – they were careful to dispose of all of that – but managed to procure a bottle of the raw serum it was made from. A weaponized version of the sacred river."

"That you stowed away in a liquor bottle."

"Hidden in plain sight, I suppose. And I knew Eileen would never touch the stuff. I wasn't sure what I was going to do with it until Bath got killed, and then I read that newsletter."

"So you and Trixie didn't plan this together from the start?"

"No, but I knew her work as soon as I saw it. I used to proof-read her stories. Tried to solve her puzzles before she sent them to print. After you refused to help me, I went to visit her."

Simms was the gentleman caller that Owen Ward had spotted. Not covered up as a disguise, but just because that's how Simms liked to make her way through the world.

"You went to the Derringers' with your bottle of peppermint liqueur, and Trixie told you what she'd overheard?"

"And I told Trixie what Bath had told me."

I heard footsteps echo around the corner. Distant, for now. A door opened and closed, then it was silent again.

"Whose idea was it to take Derringer out?"

Simms stood up, came to the bars, and reached out a hand. I put another Clayfield in it.

"We discussed how to get the truth out there. Trixie knew that if we just printed the story, it would be too easy to discredit. Isaac could sweep it under a rug of contradictions and distractions. She said we needed to drip feed the pieces until everyone in the city was talking about it. I agreed with her, but I feared it wouldn't be enough. Then, Isaac came home. It seemed I wasn't the only one who recognized her writing style. As soon as someone told him about the hidden message, he knew who Whisper was. It was straight out of Trixie's playbook: puzzles within puzzles."

"You were there when he hit her?"

She nodded. "Out in the atrium. I hadn't brought my gun but I had that poison with me. I put a few drops inside the car and told Carnegie to stay clear."

"You trusted him not to tell Isaac?"

"Oh, he pretends to be Derringer's lapdog but his loyalty is all to the lady of the house. When he had a moment alone with her, he told her what I'd done. Let her make the decision."

"What decision?"

"To tell him to leave. To get in his car and get out. Which he did, right after calling you."

That's what Derringer had been so emotional about. He'd just discovered that his wife had betrayed him. Was tarnishing his name to the world. Revealing his secrets.

Do you think you're a good man, Mr Phillips?

You sure weren't, were you, Mr Derringer? You wife-beating, Witch-murdering bastard. It's almost funny that on that final night, he was still pondering his own heart. Hoping to convince himself there was some justifiable reason behind his actions.

How could he not see what a monster he was?

Or is that even possible? No matter what we've done, who we become, will we always refuse to see the truth? Will we always take our own side? Will we always be convincing ourselves, right until the end, that we're someone good?

"That explosion . . ." said Simms. "I'm so sorry. I wasn't even sure it would work. If there was going to be any reaction to the substance, I thought it would happen before he left the driveway. We didn't have much time to think. Bath was dead. Isaac had beaten Trixie. Niles and Piston were tying up loose ends. I needed to do *something*."

"And your first thought was to start blowing shit up?"

"I didn't know what it would do. It was just a way of dealing with Isaac from a distance. It wasn't supposed to be so . . ."

"Dramatic?" I offered.

"Yes. It wasn't what I wanted. Not at first. Just a way of taking care of business while I was far from the crime scene. But then . . . well, Trixie convinced me that if we wanted her story to be read by as many people as possible – to make the truth known – then a little extra attention only helped the cause. What happened at the church was . . . regrettable. We had no idea she was wearing a stormstone."

"You planted the candle?"

She was looking at the blank wall like there was something there. Perhaps playing out her crimes, over and over, weighing their worth.

"After Hyperion showed up at the church, they wanted to make a complaint, so I answered the call and went down myself. Before I left, I switched out her candle for one imbued with the poison. All seemed to go smoothly until they wanted to pin it on the Centaur. Couldn't let the poor fellow take the fall for my actions, so I ended up stuck in here."

"Trixie still managed to finish off Piston, though."

"That was already in motion. Carnegie delivered Isaac's cigar collection to the Mayor's office, along with our specially prepared present. I was worried that Henry might save them as some sort of memento, but lucky for us he isn't that sentimental."

She was so relaxed. So forthcoming. I'd seen more tension in her when she was reading out the coffee order to bring back to the station. I'd witnessed that before: the relief that comes with confession. The peace of no longer worrying about getting caught.

"Simms, how did you think you'd get away with this?"

She shrugged. "I'm not sure I did. But I couldn't be a part of this any more."

"A part of what?"

"This fucking city. The way it twists everything. I build one prison to house one dangerous criminal, it becomes this monstrosity. Beat cops become armed goons. Newspapers become propaganda. There are good people here, but when they are ruled by immoral leaders, all their work becomes tainted. That's why those leaders needed to go."

Did I detect some hesitation in her speech? Some doubt? She might have talked like this around Trixie, but how true did her reasoning ring now that she was saying it to someone who wasn't an accomplice?

"But what about the risk?" I asked. "Everything you could lose?"

"It doesn't matter."

"What do you mean? I've been in your apartment. With Eileen. You had a home. A partner. A life."

She spun, and then those eyes were full of fire again: golden, passionate, brightly shining slits of molten fury.

"Is that the price of obedience, Fetch? The cost of compliance? Don't you see what they've done to us? These bastards have convinced everyone that our happiness is not ours to own. That we must earn it with unquestioned loyalty and blind faith. They know they can get away with murder because we won't complain if we think it will cost us our comfortable little lives. We condone the actions of this regime because we think we owe them. But we don't! This city is ours, not theirs, and we must not allow them to convince us that evil deeds are the cost of progress, balance and peace."

I'd never seen her like this. Unmasked. Unfiltered. Unhinged? It didn't seem like it. In fact, I'd never seen her speak so confidently. Perhaps I'd never seen her at all before this moment.

Despite her passionate confessions, I still struggled to fit the actions of Whisper into the body of dutiful detective Lena Simms.

"I thought you believed in the law more than anyone."

"The law means nothing if a single person is above it! I believe in justice. I believe we must be held to account." She tried to sit on the bed to calm herself, but immediately got up again. "This city only works because we all play our part. You know that, don't you? You see it? You've finally become a proper piece of it. The title of policeman, mayor, minister, boss is only another role. None more important than any other. When we remember that, this city is a miracle. When we forget it . . ." She trailed off. Lost her train of thought or perhaps was just fighting with her conviction. "They chose to let us suffer just so they could retain power. Keep control. Make more profit. What kind of civilization allows that to happen? What kind of person knows the truth and does nothing? Who would dare keep silent just so they could keep their peaceful life for a little longer?"

I shrugged. "Most people."

Simms nodded, sadly.

"Yes. After they killed Bath, I knew what I had to do but I was scared to act. That's why I went to your cafe."

I chuckled. "You wanted a reliable Human shield to take the hit if things went sour? I'm sorry I blew you off."

Simms seemed frustrated by my response.

"I needed your help, Fetch. I was . . . unpracticed in making decisions that went against the grain. I don't think you appreciate what it's like for those of us that have never done it."

"Done what? The wrong thing?"

"Yes! It's terrifying. I've never done a thing in my life without some kind of backup. Some set of rules or guidelines to fall back on. To light the way. This . . . this is an entirely different way of being, and you were the only person I knew who had the . . . I don't know what . . . the stubborn, stupid, gall to live like this."

I was having trouble following her.

"Live like what?"

"By your own compass. By a set of rules that are unseen to the rest of us."

"Simms, I've fucked up more times than anyone in this city."

"Exactly!" She leaned forward and wrapped her dry, cracked-scale hands around the bars. "That's exactly the point, Fetch. You fail, but you try. You try to do better. By your own merits, for your own sake. Do you not know what that takes? How many other people just give up? Take a simple, easy set of rules and stop questioning? That's what men like Niles depend on. That's how they get away with it. I thought you of all people would have understood, but then . . ."

Then she came and saw me. In my kitchen, with all my customers. I turned her away to preserve my simpler, easier life. Just like everyone else.

"Simms, I'm sorry."

"Don't be. Please. I told you, I know what this kind of life costs. You, as much as anyone, are allowed to leave it behind. Afterwards, I read the newsletter, found Trixie, and with Carnegie's help, we did what we needed to do. Whatever happens next is out of my hands."

She exhaled, long and slow, like she'd been waiting to tell me that for a long time. Like she was satisfied, even though her job was unfinished.

"But Whisper's list isn't complete," I said. "Niles is still alive. Keeping himself safe. He's the one with all the power. He's already used these killings to expand his influence. Don't you worry that you might have made things worse?"

"Our lives were worth less than some prick's profit. How can it get worse?"

"The *violence*, Lena. You don't think these killings will provoke killings in return?"

Simms rolled her eyes.

"When there are men with guns keeping you in line, there is already violence on every corner. Just because you don't see it acted upon, it doesn't mean it isn't there. If it is the threat of violence that is keeping us in line, that stops us from acting out, then I introduced no violence into this situation. I just highlighted the violence that was already there." She went back over to the bed. "Trixie will put out the final newsletter, revealing to everyone what Niles and the others have done. How evil their actions, and how corrupt their souls. After that, it's out of our hands. If everyone out there hears of his crimes yet lets him live . . . then there was nothing worth fighting for in the first place."

She laid down and closed her eyes. Work completed. Job done.

While at the top of the city, a bell was ringing, and Sunder was about to wake to the truth.

44

Whisper's final scoop fell upon Sunder City.

Carnegie made the drop and made his escape. He went back to his master to wait for the response, safe behind the gates of the Derringer estate.

Detective Simms, in her temporary confinement, might have kept an ear cocked to the outside world, straining to listen for the outrage and indignation.

The summer wind got beneath the news and carried it to every corner. On my long walk back to the cafe, the paper was already in people's hands. I witnessed their disbelief and their displeasure. The way they spread the story with bitter amusement and an exasperated acceptance. It was just the kind of betrayal they'd come to expect.

Voices were raised in wild declarations of revenge or justice.

"They get away with murder in this city!"

"Who are they to change our fate like that?"

"I told you they were crooked!"

By the time I was two blocks from the cafe, there were copies marked with grubby fingerprints already discarded in the street.

I heard radios turned up loud. The talkback spewing bile.

The city was bubbling with a different kind of excitement. The story was out. The truth revealed.

And yet . . .

The people of Sunder talked about that truth as they walked to work, dressed in Niles Company uniforms, driving Mortales-made cars. Off to work their government jobs, or in one of Thurston's factories.

They were annoyed. Maybe even furious. Maybe they agreed

that, yes, those other leaders had to die, and the world would be better if someone finished the job.

Not them, though. Their rent was due. They had bellies to feed. Educations to complete so they could be better tomorrow than today. So they could make their own kind of difference, perhaps, in time.

They finished the newsletters then picked up the *Star*, and mixed Whisper's big reveal in with all the other dross that Volta and his employees had found to fill its pages. A little distraction was needed after such a shocking dose of reality. Hard to focus on your job with too much truth rattling around in your head. Need to settle it down with sports and gossip. See the bigger picture then make your life a little smaller. How else can you expect all the work to get done?

The world needs to turn, after all. Each little world, and the big one we've built together. Somebody would surely hold Niles accountable, right? Someone responsible. Someone who understands these things. Who are we to stick our uneducated noses into that kind of business? That's what we pay the police for, right? They do their job so we can do ours. That's the basis for this whole civilization. You find your way to contribute and trust that everyone else will find theirs. Look after yourself, and leave the big swings to someone else.

It will all sort itself out in time. Right? No need to stick your neck out.

Ophelia was the only person in the cafe. She was sitting at the counter – looking over Whisper's words – when I walked past her into the kitchen and started preparing a pot.

"You want one?" I asked.

She held up the cup in front of her.

"Please. I tried to make my own but it's shit." I emptied her mug into the sink and rinsed out the grounds. "You work out who he is?"

"Whisper?"

"Yeah."

"Yep," I said.

"You gonna tell Simms?"

Would have been a funny question if I wasn't too tired to laugh.

I checked the order board out of habit, and there was a piece of paper pinned to it. Instead of a request for coffee and eggs, this one read.

Baxter. The Ragged Roadhouse. Call back.

"What's this?" I asked.

Ophelia finally looked up.

"What the fuck happened to you?"

"Oh. Uh . . ."

"You get shot?"

"Among other things. What's this message?"

Apparently, Baxter had called when I was out. All they said was that I should call them back. But when the operator put me through to the roadhouse, the phone kept ringing until the coffee pot was boiling over.

I hung up, poured our drinks, grabbed the first-aid kit and pulled up a stool. It was finally time to look at that hole in my leg.

I was hurting, but Ophelia looked just as haggard as I did. No wonder. She knew what was out there: a city willing to let horrific crimes slide if it could keep hold of the comfort. People who prefer to believe they have no power than face up to the evil being done in their name. Folks happy to be dominated if they can go about their lives with as little disturbance as possible.

And was I any different?

All I wanted was this story to end. To get back in the kitchen and block out the world. These tough questions were giving me a headache. I wanted simple recipes that could be mastered with enough repeating. I wanted limited options and low stakes. There was a right way and a wrong way to fry an egg. But this mess? It was an unnamable shape that looked different every time you turned it around. A million little decisions that could have huge effects on real people's lives. It was exactly the kind of shit I didn't trust myself with any more. The kind of choices I should never have had to make.

And yet, Simms had come here when she needed help.

"Ophelia . . . what do you think of me?"

She let out a single hoot of laughter and almost fell off her stool.

"Fetch, I've met some self-centered pricks in my time, but that's a hell of a question to ask on a morning like this."

"I'm sorry. I know I'm a bit of a joke to you and your friends. I just—"

"A joke?"

"Yeah. I know this place is silly for how serious I take it. I'm a grump and a greaseball and I take too much pride in simple things. To be honest, I've just been happy to go a couple of months without fucking anything up. It might be a low bar, but if you knew the things I'd done, you'd understand. I know it doesn't look like much – *I* don't look like much – and I'm fine with that. I know I'm just one more chump taking up space in this city, but maybe that's okay. Right? Maybe it's a good thing that most people know they're supposed to keep their heads down. Maybe there's too many wannabe heroes messing things up as it is."

Those big eyes were staring at me like I'd grown snakes out of my head.

"Fetch . . ."

"I'm sorry, this isn't important. There's a lot going on. It's just been a crazy few days and—"

"Fetch, you're not a joke. Not to us. We know who you are. Not all of it, sure, but we're not stupid. Why do you think everyone wanted to hang out here? Sure, the coffee's good and you've almost learned how to season the meat—"

"Woah. What do you mean, almost?"

"But my friends come here because they can't believe you're real. Haven't you seen them staring at your tattoos? That shit's crazy, man! The things you've done are out of this fucking world. We didn't know whether to look up to you or burn your place down, but it sure as shit opened our fucking eyes. You're a living piece of history. You're proof that even some normal-looking galumph can change things. For good or bad. Do you know what that does? We all grew up being told we'd missed out. That we'd arrived too late and the party was over. That we should accept this rigid, dulled-down life they're offering us. Look out there! Look at what this city has become. It's fucking asleep! But you, you're a Human, and you *did shit*. Right? We see that. That's why we come here, not your bland bloody eggs."

I was too complimented and insulted to get my thoughts straight.

"Uh . . . what?"

"We're all trying to work out what we're supposed to do in this world. You don't know what a relief it is to see someone who's lived through it all but is still struggling with the same shit we are."

"But Pheels, I checked out too. I'm not fixing anything. I'm making breakfasts."

"Are you really? Because my belly is empty, and you've got a bullet hole in your leg."

"Yeah. I should probably call a doctor."

I went for another Clayfield – the pack was already half empty – and Ophelia helped herself to one too. I thought about stopping her, but who was I to play teacher when she was the one schooling me?

"Fetch, you're not a joke. We listen to you more than you think. Why do you reckon Ashton did what he did?"

"Cause he's a stubborn little shit? Please, Ophelia, don't put his stupid decision on my shoulders. I've got enough regrets of my own without adding his to the list." She shook her head. Lowered it. To my surprise, a tear fell onto her lap. "Shit. What is it?"

"Nothing."

"Did I say something wrong? I'm sorry, I'm not thinking straight. I've been chewing these up all morning and I think my tolerance is—"

"He *did* listen to you, Fetch. He really, really did."

"Come on. If he had, he wouldn't be where he is right now, and he wouldn't have done what he's done."

"I'm not defending it, all right? He thought those Fae were beyond saving. You know that people have gone missing out there, yeah? You know those Gremlins did terrible things."

"You think that justifies his petty revenge in wiping them out?"

"It wasn't . . . Forget it."

She was real torn up, and I was being an ass.

"I'm sorry, Ophelia. What am I missing?"

She wiped her cheeks and breathed out. She'd closed up. Whatever she'd wanted to share, it had been tucked away, out of reach.

"Don't worry, Fetch. You'll see."

"Ophelia, please. I'm sorry I wasn't listening. What is Ashton doing that I don't get?"

She chewed the Clayfield for a bit, weighing it up.

"I promised I wouldn't say."

A sudden memory of the two of them, out on the street, right before Ashton signed up with the firefighters.

"You were trying to talk him out of it, right? Joining up with them?"

"Yes, but not because . . . It's not what you think."

Her tears came again: really flowing this time.

"Ophelia, it's all right. As you said, I don't always know what to do. I don't always get things right. But share this with me, and we can discuss it together. It can't be that bad."

"Oh, it is. He knows what will happen but he doesn't care. I thought he might have changed his mind but now that this is out there," she smacked her fist against Whisper's last newsletter, "now he'll have to do it. I know he will."

"Do what?"

Those big eyes rolled over me, sympathetic but patronizing, wondering how I hadn't guessed it already. Wishing I was smart enough to put it together so she didn't have to break her promise.

"Fetch, you don't really think he wants to follow Niles, do you?"

"Why else would he join up with them? Why else would he hand them the Fae like that?"

She sighed.

"It was his only way of getting close."

I was out the door before my next breath.

45

"Well, looky here!" Snicker, snicker. "The revolution has arrived after all!"

Gumption. One of the many firefighters who was standing along the sidewalk, outside the grounds, ready to deter anyone who might have read Whisper's newsletter and decided to finish off the list.

To everybody's great disappointment, I was the only person who'd made an appearance. There was no protest. No revolution. Just a pale, bloody Man for Hire looking for his friend.

I scanned the line. Ashton wasn't there. Was he inside? Or off on some other hit job? Burning down another house?

I was about to turn away when Reeves stepped forward.

"Careful, fellas. He may not look like much, but this one's unpredictable." Though he hadn't been in Sunder long, Reeves had already secured a leadership position with the men. Some guys are just like that. People you listen to. I never thought that had been me, but maybe I was wrong. Maybe I should have been more careful what I said around someone like Ashton. Someone who'd been searching for ways to make a difference. Do some good.

There were more firefighters inside the grounds. Some were working on a truck. A couple of others were walking through the yard wearing boxing gloves, on their way to a sparring match in the backyard. Was Ashton one of them? Had he already read the newsletter, or was there still time to find him before things went sour?

"What's brought you up here, Captain? You been perusing the morning news?"

"Maybe."

"Ah, back to following orders, are you? Taking your cues from Mister Whisper?"

"Oh, I wouldn't say that. Just thought I'd see if there was any action. Maybe the city's sleeping in."

Snickers from the cheap seats.

"Call the boss," Reeves said to his men. I tried to intercept the order.

"Oh, that's all right. I was just passing through."

I tried to leave, but Reeves put his hand on his pistol. All his buddies got excited and followed suit.

"Stay there, Captain. I think Mr Niles will want to talk to the revolution's lone soldier."

Gumption peeled off from the pack and went over to the call box. I knew, with frustration, that Reeves was right. Thurston would want to see me. He had a plethora of things to gloat about and I was his favorite audience when he had a new triumph to flaunt in someone's face.

The gate buzzed open, and Reeves ordered his new subordinates to search me. I thought about refusing, but those prominently displayed revolvers made me think twice. The bastards swarmed like excited puppies, pulling me every which way and being as rough as they could justify without knocking me off my feet.

One kid pulled out my Clayfields, went to pocket them.

"Hey! They're mine."

"What are?" He had an even more punchable face than Gumption.

"At least give me two to chew on. I'm in pain."

"What the fuck?" One of the idiots pulled their hand back in shock. Held it up to show the others.

"Oh shit, Captain," said Reeves. "You bleeding?"

"Bullet wound. Not deep. Don't worry about it."

"Shiiiit. Maybe you're tougher than we thought. Give the poor fool his medicine." The kid with the Clayfields put two in my mouth while the others held my arms. "All right, Gumption, let's go!"

My two ex-privates escorted me up the driveway. Yael and Cyran must have been on other business – likely investigating the bell tower to find out who was behind the drop – because I was led straight into that large room I'd been in last time. Niles was there, waiting all the way up at the other end in linen shirt and slacks. Like before, he was keeping his distance. If someone did have a drop of that poison on them, they'd have to run a dozen paces before touching Niles, and that would be plenty of time for the trigger-happy firemen to unload their pistols.

There was a copy of the newsletter on the desk in front of Niles, sitting limp and harmless like a blunted knife.

There was a new addition to the room. Behind his desk, one of the clay constructs was posed like a scarecrow, a divot in its forehead where crystal had been removed.

"Nice art," I said.

"Oh, you like it? An import from Incava. We destroyed the others after inspecting them, but I chose to keep one around for posterity. It can be useful, when life gets tough, to be reminded of one's conquests."

Life was a long way from tough for Thurston Niles. And what conquests? He wasn't out there when Linda, Khay, Theo and I raided the Wizard City. But he'd clearly paid it a visit. Well, not him, but his minions. They'd dragged the Constructs back to Sunder, along with samples of the crystal river to make his deadly poison.

"You didn't want to put it to use?" I asked. "I thought stone servants would be an asset to your factories."

"Magically powered workers?" He adopted an expression of mock-disgust. "How awful. I'd never dare steal employment from the common man. Besides, power like that is unpredictable. Too easily manipulated. I prefer the more reliable nature of nuts and bolts." He looked to the firefighters. "You sure you searched him good? Fetch is one of the few men in Sunder stupid enough to read Whisper's story and try to do something about it."

"He's clean."

Thurston laughed.

"Well, I wouldn't go that far."

I took a seat, removed one of the Clayfields from my teeth and put it on the table; Thurston could speak for hours once he got going, so I might need to make them last.

"Where are your usual off-siders?" I asked. "Or is Yael too busy leaving death sentences on doorknobs?"

He didn't answer me, but his smile was all the confirmation I needed. Of course it was the roguish Half-Elf who had killed Bath. She'd left the toxic substance on his door handle, waited in the shadows for him to enter, then wiped it clean. A good detective might follow up that inquiry with questions about where she might have been when Angela Fray and Jackson Murray's homes were going up in flames, but there were no good detectives here. The only good detective was locked up in Backlash, and she'd moved way beyond asking questions.

"So, Fetch, what brings you to my side of town? Expecting a better turnout?" Niles leaned back and put his feet on the desk. "Sorry to disappoint you."

I shrugged. "I've got no idea what you mean."

"So, you haven't read the news?"

"You know I don't subscribe to the *Star*."

It was petty, but Niles had a whole city full of people who played into his hand, so I liked being the guy who would spit in it instead.

"I was speaking of something more independent." He picked up the newsletter by one corner and held it like a dead fish.

"Niles, I've got a bullet in my leg that I haven't dealt with. You think I've bothered to keep up on today's latest scandal? What's the big story? Some farmer's got Harpies in the henhouse?"

It was easy to frustrate him. Niles led a carefully curated life where everyone followed his lead. He had enough money and influence that his suggestions would become reality, reinforcing the idea that he was so savvy he could anticipate the future. It must be that way with all businessmen rich enough to sway the market: they tell people how things are going to turn out, and they hold so much wealth that their belief becomes a self-fulfilling prophecy. Then everyone remarks on how intelligent they are, and the asshole gets to believe that they're in their lofty position because they're just so much more insightful than anyone else.

Niles's whims had so often become reality, he saw himself as infallible. The fact that a little friction unsettled him so much was proof that I was the only person who ever disagreed with him.

"Have a read," he said, holding out the newsletter. It irked him, because he was sure that I *had* in fact read it, but he couldn't say the things he wanted to say unless I played my part. Reeves moved towards him – ready to retrieve the newsletter – but Niles held up a hand. "No, no, soldier. Best keep our friend under guard. You never know what that strange little mind is planning." He looked out the doorway to his right and beckoned someone I couldn't see. "Young man, come in here. Can you hand this to my guest?"

A second later, Ashton stepped into the room.

The scratches on his face had scabbed over, and he was already starting to look more at home in his burgundy coat. He walked differently. The weapons did that; you couldn't slouch with pistols and knives on your hips. He took the piece of paper and crossed the room.

I wondered how Niles couldn't see it. The anger in the kid. He was damn near vibrating. If you saw a piece of machinery quivering that way, you'd run to the next room and duck for cover because it was sure as shit about to explode.

I stared at Ashton, hoping to telepathically send a message.

Get the fuck out of here. Run. Whatever you think you've gotta do, it's not worth it.

Ashton dropped the paper in front of me. My attempts to connect bounced off his glazed-over eyes, but Niles recognized that something had shifted in me.

"Oh, that's right. You two know each other." Ashton headed for the door. "No, no, young man. Why don't you hang around? Let's see what Mr Phillips has to say about recent events."

Ashton nodded and took his place next to Niles's shoulder.

Shit.

"Take a read," prompted Niles, knowing that I had, of course, already read the damn thing.

I played along, pretending to run my eyes over it while I thought about what to do. How to get Ashton out of here.

"Interesting article," I said. "Unverifiable, of course."

"Of course."

"Supposedly, you're the last living witness to this alleged meeting."

"Supposedly."

"I imagine the authorities might want to question you about it."

"Well," he took his feet off the desk and leaned on it, "you did always have an active imagination."

I hoped I was the only one who noticed Ashton flinch.

"By now," I said, talking to Ashton but keeping my eyes on Niles, "I suppose Whisper has realized that it was all for nothing. The individuals in power don't really matter, right? Take them out, someone else will fill their place. Like Urik Volta, the new editor of the *Star*. I don't hold out much hope that he'll be any more upstanding than Isaac was. Didn't strike me as the conscientious type."

Niles narrowed his eyes. This line of conversation was unexpected, but the surprise seemed to interest him. He thought I'd finally come to play.

"Interesting. So how *do* you create change?"

"Well, you need to change the system, don't you? That takes time. People like things to stay the way they are, even if they know it's not working for them. If everyone's invested in a way of life and you destroy it, they see you as their enemy, not their savior."

"Oh, I agree. The secret to keeping power is to give people what they want rather than what they need. Aren't you and I both prime examples of a person's relentless tendency to reach for things that don't nourish them?" He turned to Ashton, oblivious to the boy's spring-loaded tension. "There's a bottle of whiskey on the sideboard in the hall. Could you bring it, please?"

There was a brief delay — a moment of indecision — before Ashton moved out. Niles clocked it. Watched him go. I couldn't let him ponder it for too long.

"Volta threatened me. He wants Whisper's identity or he tarnishes my name and the names of my friends."

"You mentioned that last time. Still haven't found a way to get him off your back? I'm surprised. You're usually more industrious. As I said before, I can't bail you out of this one. In fact, I'm invested in finding out Whisper's identity myself. You really expect me to believe you've made no progress?"

I raised my hands in a show of confessed helplessness.

"My days in the kitchen must have dulled my wits. I found out a few things, but then this newsletter shared all that and more so I'm back to square one."

Ashton re-entered, put the whiskey on the desk, and stood at attention.

Niles opened the desk drawer and removed two small glasses.

"I find that hard to believe, Fetch. After all, you felt the effects of the serum first-hand, didn't you? I'm not sure where you got it from, but my men reported all kinds of anomalies in your presence yesterday. That must have been one hell of a ride."

His words brought my attention to the humming that still echoed in my mind. It was so faint I could forget about it, but always there when I chose to listen. What was it? Would it ever go away?

Thurston filled both glasses, held one out to Ashton. "Pass this to him, please."

I raised a hand.

"You know I don't—"

"You said you were *mostly* sober, so I'm not taking no for an answer. I can wear all kinds of insults from you, Fetch, but forcing me to drink alone is where I draw the line."

Ashton was so stressed I'm surprised he was able to deliver the drink without shaking it all over himself. When he was close, I spoke quietly.

"Ashton, Ophelia's worried about you. You should go see her."

"What's that?" shouted Niles. "No secrets here, gentlemen. Please share with the rest of the class."

Ashton glared. Began walking back.

"The kid's got a girl who's sweet on him, back at the cafe. She's been a right mess since he stopped coming by. Any chance you can give him an early finish so he can go see her? The whining is driving me crazy."

Thurston had a good guffaw at that.

"Ah, young love. I don't see why not. But let's have our drink first. And I still need to know why you're here." He raised his glass. I raised mine. We both took a sip. "Are you sure you didn't come to kill me?"

How the hell to answer that? I couldn't confess that I was actually here to save his life.

"You know, Niles, as much as I want to, I know it won't make a damn lick of difference. You have your name on the uniforms and the trucks, but you don't matter as much as you think you do. I see what's coming in and out of this city, and you're nothing but a checkpoint along the road. If I take you out, there'll be some new asshole in your seat before the end of the week."

Did I believe it? I wasn't sure, but I hoped Ashton was listening.

Gumption and Reeves certainly were. All this talk of killing their boss was getting them antsy. They both had their jackets pulled back, the butts of their guns waiting and ready.

Niles only smiled.

"Fetch, you would be so disappointed if you knew how flattering

I found your attempts to insult me. The fact is, I agree with you. But I'd go one step further. I am not a checkpoint. I am a filter. Every day, I work as hard as I can for every person here. My job – well, one of them – is to shield you from the truth of what has happened to this world. I give you all the gift of ignorance. If everyone out there knew how lucky they had it, they would never have a moment's joy again. The guilt would crush them. Sink them into apathy and idleness."

I felt myself snarling. Was this Weatherly all over again? That place used walls to protect us from our own insignificance, while this place uses lies to protect us from our privilege.

I took a sip of whiskey without meaning to.

"You don't think so highly of us then?"

Niles was aghast.

"Fetch, I adore this place. If you only knew how deeply I care for every single person in this city, it would break your heart. I work tirelessly to let them live the fullest lives imaginable, free from the truth. A truth that would cripple most men. Render them useless. Hollow them out. I bear that burden so you can go about your lives believing in your own struggles and triumphs. That's why Whisper's goal is futile. Sure, he killed some people. That's easy. But he doesn't understand what *truth* really is."

"And what is it?"

"It's poison. I filter that fucking poison before it comes into this city. That's how much I care about you. Whisper and his like offer you nothing but pain."

He was more worked up than I'd ever seen him. He believed what he was saying, and he really wanted me to believe it too.

"The truth is," continued Niles, "we 'leaders' are the true followers. We enact the will of the people because we know if we don't, we will be rejected. The papers report what you already believe. The laws enforce the rules that make you feel safe. The church tells you the story you already wish to believe. We are your servants, not your masters."

"Go tell that to the Dwarves shoveling shit into the canal."

"But Fetch, why would I be so cruel? Don't you see? *That* is the gift. If they believe they have no power, they can rail against authority and complain about injustice. They can skirt around the laws that don't suit them while bemoaning the insufficient penalties bestowed on others. They can all be underdogs. A city full of them! Ridiculous, of course, but comforting. This way, they can have pride. They can have passion. They can have hope! Why would I rip that away? Why would you?" He finished his whiskey, filled his glass again, pointed a finger in my direction. "You are one of the few men who understand what I'm talking about. You tried to do it. You tried to make your own way through the maze. Judged your own actions. Attempted to be accountable. And where did that get you? What kind of man did that make you, Fetch? Were you able to offer anything of value to anyone? Or were you so weighed down with guilt and indecision that your life passed by without purpose? You couldn't do it. Most people can't. *I* can." He waved a hand at Ashton without looking at him. "Fill up his drink."

I hadn't noticed that I'd finished it.

Ashton approached, and it appeared that his resolution was wavering. Maybe I'd succeeded. Maybe this conversation had bought me the time I needed to speak to him, away from here, and convince him not to throw his life away.

He filled my glass halfway.

"Thanks," I said, speaking loud enough for the whole room to hear. "I'll finish this, then let's go see Ophelia. She'll be delighted to see you."

Ashton turned away. Walked back towards Thurston's shining grin.

"See, Fetch! That's what we leave room for when we keep the wolves from the door. The storm can rage in the distance, but we must shut the window, stoke the fire, and look after our own. If you only knew . . ." He trailed off. Was that actual remorse in the man's eyes? Real sadness? I wasn't sure I'd ever seen it there before. "But you don't know. You can't. Because I spare you. I spare you all." He gripped his glass tight, stared down at his desk. "I drink your poison."

He finished his glass and refilled it once more.

Things were quiet. Even Ashton's shoulders had slumped. Niles had no idea that his speech might have just saved his life. I'd get Ashton out of here. Have Ophelia talk some sense into him. Things were going to be all right.

I pushed the glass away, indicating my intention to leave. No need to surprise anyone into a shootout now that we were in the clear.

"Thanks for the chat, Niles. You've given me a lot to consider."

He wiped the remorse away. Back to his usual tone of invincible superiority.

"What's to consider? You know I'm right. If I wasn't, the people would have stormed my gates as soon as they learned the truth. But listen. That silence is your answer. There isn't a soul in this city who would dare condemn me if it risked disrupting their comfort. They are the masters, after all. Sunder has weighed its options, and I have been spared."

"Wrong."

It was Ashton. He was barely audible from this side of the room, but Niles – only inches away – heard him fine.

"What was that, young man?"

If you forge Adamantine correctly, it's the sharpest metal imaginable. Niles's factory must have done a fine job, because the dagger opened his throat like an envelope.

It was the last thing in the world that Gumption or Reeves expected, so I had a two-second head start. Gumption was on my right with his holster on his left hip. My hand found his pistol first.

It was him or Ashton, and I made my choice without thinking. I withdrew the gun, pointed the barrel straight up, and shot him under his jaw. The ceiling was high, but his brains still hit it. A bloody miasma floated down around us.

Reeves had his pistol pointed at Ashton when his buddy lost his head, and the shot confused his already struggling senses. He looked down at me, but was still assessing these two new threats, and the gun didn't move with his gaze. I fired twice into his chest. He fell backwards, body spasming with the panicked confusion of a short-circuiting machine. By the time he hit the floor, the question of whether he was dead or not was a matter of semantics. A few more seconds and the answer would be clear.

Ashton was frozen in place. Thurston Niles was on the ground in front of him, thrashing around in his own blood. His feet kicked out and knocked his chair over. His hand gripped his neck – uselessly trying to hold in his lifeforce – as he smeared himself across the polished floor.

It was probably enough, but with pricks like Niles you never know. The best doctors money can buy have saved many a rich man from a condition that would have killed someone with shallower pockets. If Angela Fray had invented her secret syrup in one of Thurston's factories, then who knows what other miraculous concoctions he had on hand. If I left him there, there'd be a small chance that he would be sitting up in bed in a week, planning his revenge.

My bullet cracked his forehead and blew out the back of his skull.

Ashton's eyes were wide open but empty.

"Kid, kid, look at me." I shook him. "Hey!" I slapped him. "ASHTON!"

He met my gaze, but I worried he was off in some dreamland, avoiding the nightmare at his feet.

"Ashton, nod so I know you're listening. *NOD, ASHTON!*" He did. "*I* did this, all right? I overpowered the other two, came at you. Shot you and took your knife. Got it?"

I needed some response, or I was worried he wouldn't be able to sell his side of the story.

"But . . . but you didn't."

Good enough.

"Yes, Ashton. I did."

I shot him through the shoulder. Away from the bone, but with enough flesh to make it convincing. He'd hurt, but with a bit of care, he'd live.

Ashton hit the wall and crumbled in a heap. He was shocked, then he was unconscious.

I took his knife and ran. If Cyran or Yael were there, they would have known to cut me off at the back exit, but the firefighters weren't familiar with that yet. Or, if they were, none of them thought fast enough to intercept me. I was out on the street and in the shadows before any of them arrived on the scene.

There was too much to do. No time to do it.

But I finally had a plan.

46

I was about to press the buzzer when Carnegie pulled up behind me in a black sedan.

"Cripes, Fetch. What the fuck happened to you?"

"Trixie home? Best I only have to explain it once."

"You ain't bringing trouble back here, are you?"

"Maybe. But the longer you leave me out here, the more I'll catch."

He grumbled and looked about for spying eyes.

"All right then. Hop in."

I scraped myself into the passenger seat and Carnegie did his best to keep the car on the driveway while his eyes kept drifting over to all the blood.

"Only some of it's mine," I said.

"Small consolation to my upholstery."

"So, tell me, Carn, did you really make yourself sick or was that all for show?"

He cracked a prideful grin.

"Two years of theatre school and a trash can full of old soup. Fooled you and the police. Maybe I should have stuck it out and got a career on the stage after all."

I had to laugh. If Simms had been the one investigating, I doubt the ruse would have got past her, but I suppose it's easy to get away with murder when the best detective in town is already on your side.

When we got out the car, Carnegie scanned the surrounding streets. Flashing lights were lighting up the horizon on all sides.

"Everyone's proper riled up," he said. "They looking for you?"

"Most likely. But nobody followed me here."

"You'd better hope not. I get a sniff of anyone on your tail, I shoot you and say you came here for revenge. Can't have you getting the lady nicked after she pulled off her plan without a problem."

Without a problem? A morgue full of bodies might disagree. Simms was still in prison, Hyperion on the run, Ophelia in the firing line and the cafe barely operational. Trixie might have kept her identity safe but from where I was bleeding, there were still plenty of problems.

The widow in question met us at the doorway.

"What's all the commotion?"

"Whisper's list is complete," I said. "But he still has one more story to tell."

I spoke my ideas out loud. Trixie edited on the fly as she fitted the type into the press. It was a wonder to watch her work: how quickly she could identify the letters by touch, and the speed at which she'd scan back over the story with a smooth stroke of her fingertips.

"That'll do," she said finally. "I'll make a couple changes then we can print off a copy and take a look. What are we thinking? A hundred copies?"

"As many as we can manage."

"Well, I should warn you, it's hard going on this old machine. Go get yourself cleaned up because once we go to print, you'll have hours of work ahead of you."

"Thanks, but I've got a couple of things to take care of. Can I borrow your phone?"

Ophelia arrived first. I told her what had happened with Niles and how I hoped she could help Ashton stay safe.

Would he have the wits to put all the blame on me? He'd expected to die in that room. Hadn't planned a moment past using his knife. I put my faith in the idea that self-preservation would have kicked back in once he woke up, and he'd currently be turning all his firefighter friends onto my scent instead of his own.

I brought Ophelia into the study and introduced her to Trixie, then she plucked the first of the newsletters off the press.

"Woah. You're really going to put this out there?"

I read it over her shoulder. Trixie had improved my pitch. Made it punchier and more to the point.

"Yeah. We'll drop it first thing tomorrow morning."

"You're fucking crazy, mate." She turned to Trixie. "Is there still time to add something?"

"What do you have in mind?"

"Just a few ideas we've been throwing around the cafe. Hard to pass up an opportunity to put them into print."

I left them to brainstorm as the buzzer rang again.

Eileen had gone to visit Simms who – I was relieved to hear – had not yet confessed.

"She's keeping silent for now. I told her you were working on something. She was dubious, but she agreed not to talk until she heard more. What are you planning?"

I brought her in to meet the others. Ophelia had blown out the word count and while Trixie was gently suggesting some edits, Eileen gave it a read.

After only a few moments, she looked up in shock.

"Are you sure about this?"

"I'm sure."

She chewed her lip.

"Fuck me, Fetch. This is wild." Eileen chewed a little longer, then looked to the ladies. "Do you mind if I make some suggestions?"

Richie arrived with Tabatha – either by coincidence or for reasons

I didn't have time to investigate – and they were kind enough to bring dinner. The sandwiches were laid out on Isaac's desk, then everyone got to shaking hands. Tabatha was overly formal with Trixie – keeping her guard up – until she saw the latest version of the newsletter coming off the press.

"Well, this piece of agitation is a long way from the *Star*, isn't it?"

"We hope so," said Trixie.

"Could do with a bit of trimming, don't you think? Get to the point, and all that?"

I'd already accepted that as the least literate person in the room, I shouldn't take their edits to heart. Trixie took the criticism graciously.

"Yes, perhaps these new additions could still do with some work," she conceded.

"May I?"

Dr Loq had reluctantly answered my call, and now seemed nervous upon arrival. She'd brought her tools with her, and it only took a few minutes for her to stitch up the hole in my leg. As soon as she was finished, I expected her to scamper, so I was happy to see Portemus poke his head through the door first.

"Porty, I'd like you to meet a friend of mine. I'm hoping you two might find an opportunity to collaborate."

"Oh, really? A pleasure to meet you, miss."

It took no time at all for Loq and Portemus to bond over the best ways to preserve amputated limbs and dissected appendages. I could already imagine her being invited into his secret room, planning exciting and unsettling ways to put his collection to use.

Hyperion and Linda arrived last and together.

"Took me some time to track him down," remarked the Werecat. "Found him hiding out on Stammer with some old friends."

"Thanks, Linda. Hyperion, help yourself to some sandwiches."

He grunted, suspicious of the fine estate, the midnight meeting and the rag-tag cast of characters I'd assembled.

Linda had spent the day looking into Whisper's claims. She had already organized a taskforce to commandeer some of the magical serum being transported out of Incava. From there, she was hoping to use it to replicate Angela Fray's work. Though the raw poison was dangerous, if the medicine that healed the brewhound could be recreated, it was worth some experimentation.

I folded Linda in with Loq and Portemus, and they fell easily into step, planning how they would hide their research and what they would do with the serum if they were successful.

"All right," called Trixie from the press. "What do we think of this one?"

Everyone in the group was handed a newsletter, and we all took seats in the study to silently read.

I couldn't help being distracted by the strange group I'd been able to assemble on such short notice. Trixie, Carnegie, Tabatha, Richie, Linda, Loq, Hyperion, Portemus, Ophelia and Eileen. Simms should have been there. Bath, too, I suppose. Ashton. Hell, in a perfect world, Hendricks and Amari would be leading the meeting and I'd be diligently following orders as usual.

I wished Georgio was back. And Baxter. Once this job was done, I'd try calling the Ragged Roadhouse again and see what they wanted. That would be too late for Baxter to help me with this mess, unfortunately. They had millennia of experience to count on, while I was barely scraping together a few dog-eared decades.

But they weren't here, and I was. So, we were going to have to make do.

The room was silent as everyone read the letter more than once. Then Ophelia leaned close to Hyperion and read to him aloud. He nodded along, letting the seriousness of the moment sink in.

It was a different beast to the one I'd first dictated. Better. It left no room for misunderstanding. No way to turn back. Nowhere to hide.

LET THE LIES BE DONE

My name is Whisper.

You might believe that I killed Isaac Derringer for his lies.

Killed Redonna Demoor for her exploitation.

Killed Henry Piston for his greed.

Killed Thurston Niles for his corruption.

I did not.

I killed them for you.

Because this city works only when we each play our part.

Every role contributes. Every person, essential.

We must trust that our leaders will play their role too. That they see themselves as equal parts of the whole.

It is so easy for a dealer to skim the pot.

For the town crier to create panic.

For the mentor to gain power over the protégé.

For the banker to manipulate the customer once they have their coin.

Without trust, we cease to function.

Without trust, we fall apart.

When that trust is betrayed, we must show no quarter.

If this city must have leaders, then they should share the integrity, values and dedication of the people.

I have shown what will happen to those in power who serve themselves before the common good. This same judgment will apply to any officer who attempts to subjugate us rather than protect us. To the bosses who seek to beat us into submission. To the companies who break us so we cannot survive without their business.

I believe in better days.

I believe in justice.

I believe in you.

My name is Whisper.

My name is Fetch Phillips.

My work is done.

Yours is just beginning.

Eileen spoke first.

"Fetch, are you really, really sure you want this out there? We don't need to put your name on it."

"Yes, we do. Otherwise Simms doesn't get cleared. Hyperion will still be a suspect. This will all remain a mystery in people's minds. We need to give them a name and a face so they can finish this story and start the next one."

Linda piped in. "But why you?"

"Because I'm already in the shit. I was there when Niles died, and if Ashton has any sense, he's pinning that murder on me as we speak. You all have work to do here, and that work will never be more important than it is right now."

Unexpectedly, I heard Niles's voice ringing in my head.

I drink your poison.

Portemus looked confused.

"Where will you go?"

"Doesn't matter. Now, does anyone want to make any more changes to the copy? Or are we happy to go to print?"

We spend a few minutes arguing over the position of a comma before Trixie made the executive decision to keep it where it was and lock the edit. Then we started printing.

Trixie was right: it was a laborious process. I made as many as I could before my arm started cramping, then Richie took over.

"Maybe I should come with you," he said. "It's not going to be safe out there for a Human. Especially one marked like you are."

I looked over his shoulder to where Tabatha was laughing with Eileen.

"Nah, Rich. Sunder's been hobbled and it'll need a few bright minds and strong bodies to keep it on its feet."

"Never been accused of being a bright mind."

"You're the strong body." I tilted my head towards Tabatha. "There's the bright mind. You two make quite the team."

"Oh, well . . . I—"

He was saved by Carnegie's interruption.

"What's the plan when they're done? The bell tower is a good drop spot, but they might be watching it after yesterday. I know a corner not far from here where the wind will catch them."

"No, I need to be seen sending these out myself. Don't want anyone questioning whether it's a frame job. I'll drop them from the fire escape of my building."

Things got quiet again. Linda raised a hand.

"Didn't you tell the kid to pin Niles's murder on you?"

I nodded. Eileen picked up her line of questioning.

"So won't your place be swarming with cops and goons?"

"Probably. But I want to get my stuff before I leave town – call me sentimental – and I don't think this story can be sold on words alone. We need eyewitnesses to see me, at my office, delivering the confession with my own hands."

Linda was still perplexed. "But the—"

"Yes, I'm sure there'll be some guards on watch." I turned to Ophelia. "Luckily, I have a few friends who are adept at giving police the runaround."

Ophelia smiled.

"I'll make some calls."

47

Everyone was confused about how to feel. Richie had voiced his half-hearted reticence but everyone else was focused on moving forward. The deaths of Derringer, Demoor and Piston had been big news, but nothing that shook the structure of the city. Thurston Niles, on the other hand, had become so infused with Sunder that it was impossible to imagine a world without him. Tomorrow, the city would wake to a new version of itself, and the people gathered in this room were determined to have a say in how this one would operate.

The exit of Sunder's self-proclaimed Man for Hire warranted little fanfare by comparison. Despite their initial arguments, putting the blame on me made sense. If Simms and Trixie could stay clear of this, they'd both be in a position to shape the way the city was reformed. Their influence could be crucial in keeping power out of the hands of the next megalomaniac. They had a responsibility to see their plan through to the next phase. But me? I had nothing but bad luck, bad press and a one-way ticket on the bad-luck express. Once everyone had thought about it for more than a minute, nobody had any good argument for making me stay.

Eileen was still conflicted, but that was only brought on by misappropriated guilt. My decision to take Whisper's name would hopefully allow Simms to get off scot-free, and I think she just felt weird about getting what she wanted while I took the rap.

"We need Simms back on the force," I reminded her. "To help clear Ashton's name. And to guide a Niles-free regime towards a better way of doing things."

"You really think so?"

"She'd fucking better. Tell Lena that if she thought she could take out a few assholes then lie down while the rest of us pick up the pieces, then she's just as naive as she thinks I am. Her work is only just starting, and I'm not staying around to finish it for her."

I only gave a passing thought to our acceptance of Simms's homicidal streak. Was it because I'd seen so much death already? Committed so much of it myself? Hell, I was still covered in the blood of two young men who had once followed my orders. Perhaps it was the nature of the murders themselves. They were such powerful figureheads that they weren't really people. Dehumanized by their own prominence. Less worthy of sympathy than the man on the street.

Did I really believe what Simms had said? That the violence was already inherent in the way we operated? Was her cause so righteous that we felt no need to question it?

Or were we just too afraid to start pulling at threads? Scared that if we looked too closely, our resolve would falter. It was just like Niles had said: the doubt and guilt would render us immobile right at a time when swift action was essential.

The forces on the other side of this fight would not be questioning themselves. Their operation relied on unrelenting movement towards their goal. They fostered an unwavering belief in their own genius and superiority, so in no time at all, they would fill the spaces, rein in the narrative, and rewrite the events of the last week to best serve their agenda.

No. Whatever change Simms, Trixie and Ashton had set in motion, there was no time to analyze the morality of their deeds. We needed to seize this opportunity with both hands. Eyes open. Minds awake. We needed to move forward before Sunder became lulled into submission by yet another self-serving set of leaders who would stoke fears and bury fresh ideas, turning the population into obedient little soldiers once again.

Our time was now.

No. *Their* time was now.

My time was over.

I was nearly knocked off my feet as Richie wrapped me in his arms.

"You're a bloody numbskull and a fool," he said. "So, make sure you find someone to watch your back. All right? Promise me."

"Uh, sure."

He sniffed. "I'll bloody miss you, mate."

I stumbled into another one of those awkward pauses. The ones that better friends would have been able to fill with hugs and tears and earnest words.

Better friends?

Some lessons you never learn, but the one I wish I'd been able to change was how I let people into my heart. I always felt like I was bothering them. Preferred to engage through work or service, sharing as little of myself as possible. Even with people I liked, I assumed they saw me as a colleague at best. My own fault. If you're too scared to reveal yourself to people, you can't be disappointed when they don't see beyond the mask.

Goodbyes always brought my mistake to light because it measured the distance between my true self and the person I appeared to be in someone else's eyes. Showed me just how aloof and cynical I'd been. How little I'd shared through so many years.

Other times – even more painfully – it called attention to the gap between my perception of how others saw me and the truth of their affection. In goodbyes, sometimes, their fondness was revealed. Their true friendship. Their love. But only when it was too late to turn back. To ask for another round. To try again, now grateful and aware. To play my part in the friendship that we'd apparently been having without my knowledge.

Always too late.

The best I could do was tell myself not to make the same mistake next time. To be better. Of course, I never did. I'd forget what I'd learned until my bags were packed, and the lesson would return, unlearned, once more.

A large hand fell on my shoulder, then spun me around. I was staring into Hyperion's soulful eyes.

"I told you." He poked me in the chest. "People will listen."

"Yeah, I guess I just needed help working out what to say."

The phone rang. Carnegie answered it.

"The kids are in position. You ready?"

Richie handed me the box of newsletters, and the smell of freshly pressed ink filled my nostrils.

"Yes," I said. "I'm ready."

With all of Sunder's most reliable leaders locked up or lying in the morgue, we had no idea what kind of response to expect. For all we knew, the firefighters could have been disbanded or – terrifyingly – taken to the streets to commit unhinged acts of revenge on anyone who crossed their path.

Either because a new leader was filling the gap or just out of habit and a lack of independent thought, things were far less dramatic.

We pulled into a parking spot and idled on Main Street. Carnegie spoke out of the corner of his mouth, not looking back to my position on the floor.

"One car. Two men, that I can see. Firefighters. I bet there'll be more inside, though."

There was a tap on the passenger window and Carnegie wound it down.

Ophelia poked her excited face inside.

"Got a dozen of us, ready to move on your signal."

I lifted myself up.

"Whenever you're ready, Pheels. But don't get anyone into trouble, all right? Just a bit of mischief. And make sure every single one of your friends gets away."

She scoffed, but there was gratitude and melancholy in those big, green eyes.

"You're the one who needs to be careful, old man. We'll keep them distracted as long as we can, but you better hustle. They'll surely send out more goons the moment we lead these ones away."

"Don't you worry. I'll be in and out."

She nodded, then looked down at her feet and back up at me.

"Don't forget about us. If we shake this place up the right way, it'll be safe for you to come back. Keep an ear to the ground, all right?"

"All right."

She nodded again. More thoughts that would remain unsaid. More regrets. Best to hope that a few gestures and an awkward smile would convey more than words ever could.

"Ah, fuck it," she said. "Let's go."

I dared to peek my head above the dash as she ran down the street and – without pausing – jumped up on the roof of a parked sedan. Then she put two fingers between her lips and let out a screeching, high-pitched whistle.

Carnegie huffed.

"Well, that's as subtle as a tiptoeing Troll, isn't it?"

Kids emerged from all corners, converging on number 108 and the suited men who stood guard. One of the firetrucks was parked across the road, and the blue-haired boy leapt onto the hood, ripped off a windscreen wiper, tumbled back onto the street, and immediately escaped to the south.

The firefighter in the driver's seat took the bait. He stepped out of the vehicle to make chase, oblivious to the Harpy who entered on the passenger side, reached across, and pulled the driver's door closed, locking him out. A Dwarven girl jumped in beside her and locked the other door, their two huge grins visible even from a distance.

They found the lights and sirens, and the commotion brought every armed guard out onto the street like the ice-cream man had pulled up at a schoolyard.

Then they turned over the engine.

Carnegie burst out laughing.

"Surely none of those kids knows how to drive."

The truck lurched into the phone booth, shattering all its glass walls at one.

"I think you're right."

The firefighters, police and charcoal-suited men were jumping up on the vehicle, trying to find a way in, but the girls soon discovered how to put it in reverse, and all the assailants went tumbling off.

The truck backed into the teahouse and knocked a few bricks from the front wall.

Carnegie hooted with joy and disbelief.

"Where did you find these fuckers?"

"They found me. Shit. I told Ophelia to play it safe."

"Well, they didn't bloody listen to ya."

The rest of the kids descended on the flailing mass of panicked young men. Ophelia managed to pickpocket the pistol from one of the firefighters — a redesign of the holster would surely be on the horizon — and fled down south, firing it into the air.

"Holy fuck," said Carnegie, his amusement turning to dawning terror. "You ready to go? There will be backup on its way, for sure."

"I'm ready."

The firetruck spun into the most chaotic U-turn ever committed, overtook Ophelia, and hooked down Fourth Street with all the guards on its tail.

"Let's go." Carnegie sped forward and pulled to a stop outside the cafe window. "I'll wait as long as I can, but any cops show up, I'm taking off too. Can't have them linking this to the lady."

"Understood."

I got out, grabbed the cardboard box from the back seat, and closed the door.

There was a sign on the broken cafe window.

NOTICE OF EVICTION. ILLEGAL PREMISES.
BUILDING SEIZED BY CITY.

So that was that then. I'd failed to keep the cafe safe. If Georgio returned, he'd surely be disappointed, so I was somewhat glad that I wouldn't be here to explain it to him. Being the rightful owner of the property, I hoped he'd be able to reclaim it without much issue. If he ever came back. Maybe he'd found something else out there. Maybe he'd forgotten all about his interlude as a cafe owner in the big smoke and had returned to a life of giving guidance to lost souls, blissfully unaware of our petty, urban struggles.

I stepped through the opening and was hit with that familiar smell of old grease, coffee grounds and good memories. Of course I hadn't been able to make the place mine. It was a nice dream for a few months, but a man with my history should know not to stand still for too long, because the past is always waiting to catch up.

I took out an old flour sack and put one of the coffee pots in it. I might be condemning myself to a life without warm showers, soft beds or close friends, but I'd be damned if I was going to move forward without a way to make a morning brew.

I went back outside and up the fire escape. I'd be visible, sure, but that was kind of the point. The world needed to see Fetch Phillips deliver his own confession or there would be too much doubt as to whether the words were really mine. I got to the top, placed the cardboard box on the doorstep of the Angel door, and prepared to remove the lid.

A noise. Inside.

More cops? *Damn.* Would one officer really have remained behind with all the madness on the street? Perhaps they weren't all as bone-headed as I'd predicted.

Then I remembered.

Inero. Shit.

I opened the door and called out to him.

"Kid, not much time to explain but—"

I froze.

"I told you I'd come."

The Fire Sprite – leader of the Gremlins – stood behind Inero with one hand over his mouth and a knife at his throat.

"You're alive?"

"No thanks to you, man of lies. You promised us assistance then sent assassins in your place."

Goddamn.

"I was looking for help. It was the kid. I had no idea what he was going to do."

"More lies," she hissed. "No matter. There is no recourse left but justice."

Inero sensed her rising bloodlust and risked an escape attempt, pushing himself to his feet and lurching towards me. The Sprite's clawed fingers slipped from his face, drawing blood, but she managed to grab hold of his shirt and swung the knife after him. The blade found its target, cutting his side, but it also compromised the material that was keeping her victim tethered. The shirt tore into pieces, and Inero broke free as I landed on top of the Fae.

The Sprite was a formidable warrior. Her back had barely touched the floorboards before she tucked her feet under my chest and kicked me against the desk. The knife came at my face, and I scrambled away, scattering stationery and old coffee cups. Claws scratched my neck, trying to grab hold. The knife came again, cutting the air, and I fell backwards through the threshold of the Angel door, struggling to get to my feet.

I thought about running – newsletter be damned – but Inero was still inside. Besides, the Sprite was barely a second behind me. She launched herself over the desk, knife raised above her head. I reached for her attacking arm, grabbed it, and took her weight. I fell against the doorframe. Pivoted. Pushed her away. She hit the railing and . . .

I'd forgotten about the Basilisk acid: the corrosive liquid that

I'd dropped onto the barricade to break it apart. The job was left half-finished – interrupted by Ophelia and Ashton on the first day we'd met – but the acid had weakened the barrier, and the Fae's weight was enough to knock it loose.

She tumbled backwards, into empty air.

I reached out, too late, only managing to kick the cardboard box after her.

Newsletters scattered to the wind. The Fae screamed – for only a moment – before her body smashed down on Carnegie's car.

The metal roof was crushed, along with the body of the world's last Fire Sprite.

Carnegie stepped out and shook the glass from his suit, then looked up in gaping surprise. I wished I'd been able to see his expression up close.

Everyone was out on the street now, screaming in shock and looking up at the pieces of paper that had obediently taken the wind.

Whisper couldn't have hoped for a more dramatic delivery of his final edition, but there was no time to witness the response from his readers.

"Inero, I'm leaving. Are you hurt or—"

The kid had always kept himself covered up even on the hottest days in the kitchen. Now I saw why.

The ripped shirt revealed a body that was only half flesh. The other side – half his chest, a bit of his neck and one entire arm – was made out of wood. Some of it bark, but also the paler, ringed timber of a tree's interior. There were cracks and knots, but it moved like muscle.

After years of investigating the remnants or possible return of magic powers, I knew how to recognize a miracle. Creatures like Trolls and Fae – who were pieces of the natural world animated by magical forces – all froze when the Coda happened. The closer you were to pure magic, the worse it was.

I'd seen the shadows of what had once been, and uncovered this city's faintest remnants of wonder. I'd pushed false hopes to their limit and tried to turn dreams – and nightmares – into reality. But this . . . this was something else. Something I hadn't seen in seven long years.

Half of Inero's body was a living plant, moving smoothly, beautifully, against the humanoid side. It was full of color. Full of life. Undeniably, full of *magic*.

"Inero, what the hell are you?"

He looked at me, embarrassed. Like he was afraid of how I might react.

"I . . . I don't know."

If Linda was with me, I might have palmed the kid off on her. Or Portemus, or Richie. But then I would have always been wondering: unsure of what he was and what this meant. Scared that he would be burned up and buried like Angela Fray and her brother. Silenced to preserve the modern, simple world that everyone else was willing to embrace.

So – as that wasn't an option – there was only one course of action left on the table.

"All right, kid. Get your things . . ."

I took my old Shepherd's jacket from the hook, slipped my arms through the sleeves, and placed my hat on my bruised and battered head.

". . . and let's go find out."

A Week Later

"All clear. Come on."

Inero was holding open the door of the Ragged Roadhouse, waving towards my hiding spot in the brush on the opposite side of the road. As I was a wanted man, it had been his job to buy supplies, ask for directions and try to reach Baxter by phone while I remained hidden.

He'd called this place every day but had never caught Baxter while they were in, so we'd kept on traveling. Away from Sunder and towards the old ally who might be our best chance of finding out what kind of creature Inero was. Sure, they hadn't been much help the first time, but they hadn't seen the mass of vines and bark that made up half of Inero's body.

After a wagon ride out of Sunder then five days on foot, we'd finally followed Baxter's trail all the way to its source. The parking lot was empty and there were no horses tied to the hitching post. I just had to hope that whoever worked here didn't bother taking note of the big stories coming out of Sunder because I was so in need of a comfortable bed and a break from the elements that I was ready to risk arrest for one night with a roof over my head.

"What do you mean they're not here?"

I'd been inside for thirty seconds and the tavern keeper was already giving me a look that told me I was on thin ice.

"The Demon left yesterday."

"Yesterday? But they knew we were coming."

The tavern keeper shrugged, as if she had plenty of theories about why my friend might not want to wait around for me but it wasn't going to be her business to share them.

"Your name Fetch?" she asked. I froze. Maybe she did get the

Star out here. Or maybe other travelers had already carried my deeds to these outskirts.

"Why?" I asked, confirming that I was indeed Fetch and that I had something to be nervous about.

"Wait here."

She left the counter and disappeared out back.

"I thought you left messages for Baxter," I said to Inero, a little too sharply. "They should have known we were coming."

"I did." He more regularly responded with words instead of nods, but still wasn't the greatest conversationalist. "I told her to write down just what you said."

The message had requested Baxter's help without going into detail, in case the person passing on the message might become curious. *Baxter. Inero's condition is more complicated that we thought. Perhaps the thing we've been searching for. Would love your insight so on our way to see you. F.*

I couldn't believe we'd traveled all this distance and had missed Baxter by only a day.

"The Demon left this." The tavern keeper returned and slapped a writing pad down on the counter. There was a message scrawled on the front page.

Fetch. I thought that might be the case. Sorry I couldn't stay.
Find Uldar Jerrick. He has your answers.

What the hell?

The tavern keeper was hovering, waiting to see how I'd respond.

"Ma'am, we're parched. Could we get two pints of whatever's coldest?"

As soon as she was out of earshot, Inero asked, "Who's Uldar Jerrick?"

"The first Necromancer. A character from history and fable. This doesn't make any sense."

"Where do we find him?"

"We don't. If Uldar Jerrick was alive, he'd be a thousand years old."

"Isn't Baxter a thousand years old?"

"Well, yeah but—" But that was different. Baxter might be a one-of-a-kind creature who had lived twice as long as any tea-totaling Elf, but Uldar Jerrick was a legend. A creature from horror stories. The first dark Wizard to raise the dead. To create the curse that brought Vampires into existence. He was a shadow from ancient history, not someone you went to for *advice*. "This must be some kind of . . . I don't know . . . puzzle or something. What if—"

I was cut off by the roaring of an engine, and a sleek black sedan pulling into the parking lot.

My blood went cold.

Two fizzing pints hit the counter.

"Four bronze."

I spun on her like I'd been slapped.

"Who did you call?"

"Nobody. What you on about?"

Car doors opened. Two men got out. Black suits. Pistols on their hips.

"You really didn't do this?" I pressed.

She shook her head.

"We're on the main road to Lanfield. Visitors like that come in all the time."

We could leave out the back way. Start running. But they had cars. They had guns. We'd never get away.

I slammed the bronze coins down on the counter.

"Thanks. Sorry. Didn't mean to scare you. It's been a rough few days."

She looked at the coins. Out to the approaching men. Back to me. Then raised an eyebrow.

The car doors closed.

I added two bronze bills to the coins.

"That's all I have."

She took them. Nodded.

"I recommend the private booth." She gestured to a dark table in the corner, mostly obscured behind a lattice. We picked up our drinks and stepped away from the counter. "Mr Fetch?" I turned as she tore the top page from the notepad. "You want this?"

"Thanks."

I snatched it and got behind the lattice just before the door swung open.

"Goddamn. It's good to be out of that heat."

"Get me a cold one. I'm using the facilities."

The gaps in the lattice were just large enough to see a rough image of the two men. The second peeled off down the hall while the first approached the counter.

"Two large waters with ice, and two pints of your best beer."

"Right you are, sir."

The man looked around while he waited, and his eyes floated past our hiding spot without registering us. Good. When he looked back the other way, I risked picking up my pint for a much-needed sip.

"Where you off to?" asked the tavern keeper as she delivered the waters.

"Sunder." He took a long gulp. "I'm part of the Mayor's personal security."

"I thought the Mayor died."

"Indeed he did. That's why they need a new one."

The whole place started to rumble. Glasses jingled. The windows rattled in their frames. The rats beneath the floorboards got spooked and started scurrying about.

More vehicles had arrived. I couldn't see them, but they must have been bigger than the sedan. Two or three of them. Multiple doors opened and closed. Jubilant voices joked and laughed.

The door swung open again, and a large shape entered.

"Speak of the devil," said the man at the bar. "Let me introduce you to Sunder's new leader. This is Mayor Patrick Taryn."

The big man stepped up to the counter with a confident, outstretched hand and a warm chuckle.

"It's going to take a long time to get used to that," he said. "Lovely to meet you, ma'am."

My hands were shaking. I was struggling to keep my breath silent, but there was a roaring bellow in my chest. Inero was staring at me, spooked by my reaction.

What? he mouthed.

What? Oh, nothin'. Just the fact that Sunder's new Mayor is the man who ruined my life. The man who plucked me out of despair and pretended to give me a purpose. Who enlisted me in the Human Army and manipulated me for an entire year. Who got me all twisted up in my allegiances until I handed over the location of the sacred river's weak spot.

This was the man who led soldiers to that very place. The man who attacked the heart of the world. The man who caused the Coda.

General Patrick Taryn.

The tavern keeper congratulated him on his new post, but Taryn laughed it off.

"Oh, this won't be ribbon cutting and canapés, I'm afraid. The city has recently fallen to rebels and reprobates. Good men have been murdered and we have a narrow window to save that city's soul. Sunder will be brought into line, but it's going to take a whole lot of muscle and blood to—"

My drink fell from my hand. It hit the table and tipped, spilling everywhere. I grabbed the glass before it hit the floor but the damage was done.

Taryn had stopped talking. All was silent.

Until . . .

"Who's back there?"

Acknowledgements

Thank you to Lochaz, Laura, and Estefania for once again being my beautiful beta readers and exceedingly generous sounding boards.

Thank you to my agent Alexander Cochran, and to Jenni Hill, Alyea Canada, Joanna Kramer, and everyone at Orbit for sending Fetch and me out on another adventure and so carefully lighting our way.

And thank you, readers, for coming back to Sunder. This city has been my second home for many years now, and though it feels strange to wander away from its narrow alleys, there's still plenty of this world to explore so I'm excited to get out there and stir up some trouble.

Hopefully you'll join us on the road.

extras

orbit-books.co.uk

about the author

Luke Arnold was born in Australia and has spent the last decade acting his way around the world, playing iconic roles such as Long John Silver in the Emmy-winning *Black Sails*, Martin Scarsden in *Scrublands* and his award-winning turn as Michael Hutchence in the INXS mini-series *Never Tear Us Apart*. He is co-writer of *Essentials*, a graphic novel, and also creates video games with brother George.

Find out more about Luke Arnold and other Orbit authors by registering for the free monthly newsletter at orbit-books.co.uk.

if you enjoyed
WHISPER IN THE WIND

look out for

THE HEXOLOGISTS

by

Josiah Bancroft

The Hexologists, Iz and Warren Wilby, are quite accustomed to helping desperate clients with the bugbears of city life. Aided by hexes and a bag of charmed relics, the Wilbies have recovered children abducted by chimney-wraiths, removed infestations of barb-nosed incubi and ventured into the Gray Plains of the Unmade to soothe a troubled ghost. Well acquainted with the weird, they never shy away from a challenging case.

But when they are approached by the royal secretary and told the king pleads to be baked into a cake — going so far as to wedge himself inside a lit oven — the Wilbies soon find themselves embroiled in a mystery that could very well see the nation turned on its head. Their effort to expose a royal secret buried under forty years of lies brings them nose to nose with a violent antiroyalist gang, avaricious ghouls, alchemists who draw their power from a hell-like dimension, and a bookish dragon who only occasionally eats people.

Armed with a love toughened by adversity and a stick of chalk that can conjure light from the darkness, hope from the hopeless, Iz and Warren Wilby are ready for whatever springs from the alleys, graves, and shadows next.

1

THE KING IN THE CAKE

The king wishes to be cooked alive," the royal secretary said, accepting the proffered saucer and cup and immediately setting both aside. At his back, the freshly stoked fire added a touch of theater to his announcement, though neither seemed to suit what, until recently, had been a pleasant Sunday morning.

"Does he?" Isolde Wilby gazed at the royal secretary with all the warmth of a hypnotist.

"Um, yes. He's quite insistent." The questionable impression of the royal secretary's negligible chin and cumbersome nose was considerably improved by his well-tailored suit, fastidiously combed hair, and blond mustache, waxed into upturned barbs. Those modest whiskers struck Isolde as a dubious effort to impart gravity to a youthful face. Though Mr. Horace Alman seemed a man of perfect manners, he sat with his hat capping his knee. "More precisely, the king wishes to be baked into a cake."

Looming at the tea cart like a bear over a blackberry bush, Mr. Warren Wilby quietly swapped the plate of cakes with a dish of watercress sandwiches. "Care for a nibble, sir?"

"No. No, thank you," Mr. Alman murmured, flummoxed by the offer. The secretary watched as Mr. Wilby positioned a triangle of white bread under his copious mustache, then vanished it like a letter into a mail slot.

The Wilbies' parlor was unabashedly old-fashioned. While their neighbors pursued the bare walls, voluptuous lines, and skeletal furniture that defined contemporary tastes, the Wilbies' townhouse decor fell somewhere between a gallery of oddities and a country bed-and-breakfast. Every rug was ancient, ever doily yellow, every table surface adorned by some curio or relic. The picture frames that crowded the walls were full of adventuresome scenes of tall ships, dogsleds, and eroded pyramids. The style of their furniture was as motley as a rummage sale and similarly haggard. But as antiquated as the room's contents were, the environment was remarkably clean. Warren Wilby could abide clutter, but never filth.

Isolde recrossed her legs and bounced the topmost with a metronome's precision. She hadn't had time to comb her hair since rising, or rather, she had had the time but not the will during her morning reading hours, which the king's secretary had so brazenly interrupted, necessitating the swapping of her silk robe for breeches and a blouse. Wearing a belt and shoes seemed an absolute waste of a Sunday morning.

Isolde Wilby was often described as *imposing*, not because she possessed a looming stature or a ringing voice, but because she had a way of imposing her will upon others. Physically, she was a slight woman in the plateau of her thirties with striking, almost vulpine features. She parted her short hair on the side, though her dark curls resisted any further intervention. Her long-suffering stylist had once described her hair as resembling a porcupine with a perm, a characterization Isolde had not minded in the slightest. She was almost entirely insensible to pleasantries, especially the parentheses of polite conversation, preferring to let the drumroll of her heels convey her hellos and her coattails say her goodbyes.

Her husband, Warren, was a big, squarish man with a tree stump of a neck and a lion's mane of receded tawny hair. He wore unfashionable tweed suits that he hoped had a softening effect on his bearing, but which in fact made him look like a garden wall. Though he was a year younger than Isolde, Warren did not look it, and had been, since adolescence, mistaken for a man laboring toward the promise of retirement. He had a mustache like a boot brush and limpid hazel eyes whose beauty was squandered on a beetled and bushy brow, an obstruction that often rendered his expressions unfathomable, leading some strangers to assume he was gruffer than he was. In fact, Warren was a man of tender conscience and emotional depth, traits that came in handy when Isolde's brusque manner necessitated a measure of diplomacy. He was considerably better groomed that morning only because he had risen early to greet the veg man, who unfailingly delivered the freshest greens and gossip in all of Berbiton at the unholy hour of six.

Seeming to wither in the silence, Mr. Alman repeated, "I said, the king wishes to be baked into a ca—"

"Intriguing," Isolde interrupted in a tone that plainly suggested it was not.

Iz did not particularly care for the nobility. She had accepted Mr. Horace Alman into her home purely because War had insisted one could not refuse a royal visitor, nor indeed, turn off the lights and pretend to be abroad.

While War had made tea, Iz had endured the secretary's boorish attempts at small talk, made worse by an unprompted confession that he was something of a fan, a Hexologist enthusiast. He followed the Wilbies' exploits as frequently documented in the *Berbiton Times*. Mr. Horace Alman was interested to know how she felt about the recent court proceedings. Iz had rejoined she was curious how he felt about his conspicuous case of piles.

The royal secretary had gone on to irk her further by asking whether her name really was "Iz Ann Always Wilby" or if it were some sort of theatrical appellation, a stage name. Iz patiently explained that her father, the famous Professor Silas Wilby, had had many weaknesses—including an insatiable wanderlust and an allergy to obligations—but none worse than his fondness for puns, which she personally reviled as charmless linguistic coincidences that could only be conflated with humor by a gormless twit. Only the sort of vacuous cretin who went around asking people if their names were made-up could possibly enjoy the lumbering comedy that was the godless pun.

Though, in all fairness, she was not the only one to be badgered over her name. Her husband had taken the rather unusual step of adopting her last name upon the occasion of their marriage. He'd changed his name not because he was estranged from his family, but rather because he'd never liked the name Offalman.

Iz had been about to throw the royal secretary out on his inflamed fundament when War had emerged from the kitchen pushing a tea cart loaded with chattering porcelain and Mr. Horace Alman had announced that King Elbert III harbored aspirations of becoming a gâteau.

His gaunt cheeks blushing with the ever-expanding quiet, Mr. Alman pressed on: "His Majesty has gone so far as to crawl into a lit oven when no one was looking." The secretary paused to make room for their astonishment, giving Warren sufficient time to post another sandwich. "And while he escaped with minor burns, the experience does not appear to have dissuaded him of the ambition. He wants to be roasted on the bone."

"So, it's madness, then." Iz shook her head at War when he inquired whether she would like some of either the lemon sponge or the spice cake, an inquiry that was conducted with a delicate rounding of his plentiful brows.

"I don't believe so." Mr. Alman touched his teacup as if he might raise it, then the fire behind him snapped like a whip, and his fingers bid a fluttering retreat. "He has long moments of lucidity, almost perfect coherence. But he also suffers from fugues of profound confusion. He's been discovered in the middle of the night roaming the royal grounds without any sense of himself or his surroundings. The king's sister,

Princess Constance, has had to take the rather extreme precaution of confining him to his suite. And I must say, you both seem to be taking all of this rather in stride! I tell you the king believes he's a waste of cake batter, you stifle a yawn!"

Iz tightened the knot of her crossed arms. "I didn't realize you were looking for a performance. I could have the neighbor's children pop by if you'd like a little more shrieking."

War hurried to intervene: "Mr. Alman, please forgive us. We do not mean to appear apathetic. We are just a bit more accustomed to unusual interviews and extraordinary confessions than most. But, rest assured, we are not indifferent to horror; we are merely better acquainted."

"Indeed," Iz said with a muted smile. "How have the staff taken the king's altered state of mind?"

Appearing somewhat appeased, the secretary twisted and shaped the points of his mustache. "They're discreet, of course, but there are limits. Princess Constance knows it's a secret she cannot keep forever, devoted as she is to her brother."

"Surely, you want physicians, psychologists. We are neither," Iz said.

The secretary absorbed her comments with an expression of pinched indulgence. "We've consulted with the nation's greatest medical minds. They were all stumped, or rather, they were perfectly confident in their varying diagnoses and prescriptions, and none of them were at all capable of producing any results. His condition only worsens."

"Even so, I'm not sure what help we can be." Iz picked at a thread that protruded, wormlike, from the armrest of the sofa.

The secretary turned the brim of his hat upon his knee, ducking her gaze when he said, "There's more, Ms. Wilby. There was a letter."

"A letter?"

"In retrospect, it seems to have touched off His Majesty's malaise." The royal secretary reached into his jacket breast pocket. The stiff envelope trembled when he withdrew it. The broken wax seal was as sanguine as a wound. "It is not signed, but the sender asserts that he is the king's unrecognized son."

Warren moved to stand behind his wife's chair. He clutched the back of it as if it were the rail of a sleigh poised atop a great hill. Iz reached back and, without looking, patted the tops of his knuckles. "I imagine the Crown receives numerous such claims. No doubt there are scores of charlatans who're foolish enough to hazard the gallows for a chance to shake down the king."

"Indeed, but there are two things that distinguish this particular instance of blackmail. First, the seal." Mr. Alman stroked the edge of the wax medallion, indicating each element as he described it: "An *S* emblazoned over a turret; note the five merlons, one for each of Luthland's counties. Beneath the *S*, a banner bearing the name Yeardley. This is the seal of Sebastian, Prince of Yeardley. This is the stamp of the king's adolescent ring."

"He identified it as such?" Iz asked.

"I did, at least initially. Of course, I like to believe I'm familiar with all the royal seals, but I admit I had to check the records on this occasion. Naturally, there is much of his correspondence that His Majesty leaves me to open and deal with, but when something like this comes through, I deliver it to him unbroken."

"The signet was no longer in the king's possession, then?"

"No, the royal record identified the ring as lost about twenty-five years ago, around the conclusion of his military service, I believe."

"That's quite a length of time to sit on such a claim." Iz reached for the letter, but the secretary pulled it back. She looked into his eyes; they glistened with uncertainty as sweat dripped from his nose like rain from a grotesque. "What is the second thing that distinguishes the letter?"

"The king's response to the correspondence was . . . pronounced. He has thus far refused to discuss his impressions of the contents with myself, his sister, or any of his advisors. He insists that it is a hoax, that we should destroy it, though Princess Constance won't hear of it. She maintains that one doesn't destroy the evidence of extortion: One saves it for the inquiry. But of course, there hasn't been an inquiry. How could there be, given the nature of the claim? To say nothing of the fact that the primary witness to the events in question is currently raving in the royal tower."

"The princess wishes for us to investigate?" she asked. Though Isolde held little affection for the gentry, she liked the princess well enough. Constance had established herself as one of very few public figures who continued to promote the study of hexegy, touting the utility of the practice, even amid the blossoming of scientific discovery and electrical convenience. Still, Isolde's vague respect for the princess was hardly sufficient to make her leap to her brother's aid.

Mr. Alman coughed—a brittle, aborted laugh. "Strictly speaking, Her Royal Highness does not know I am here. I have taken it upon myself to investigate the identity of the bastard, or rather, to engage more capable persons in that pursuit."

"I'm sorry, Mr. Alman, but what I said when we first sat down still holds. I am a private citizen. I serve the public, some of whom come to me with complaints about royal overreach, the criminal exploitations of the nobility, or the courts' bungling of one case or another. I don't work for the police—not anymore. Surely you have enough resources at your disposal to forgo the interference of one unaffiliated investigator."

"I do understand your preference, ma'am." The royal secretary rucked his soft features into an authoritative scowl. "But these are extraordinary circumstances, and not without consequence. The uncertainty of rule only emboldens the antiroyalists, the populists, and our enemies overseas. You must—"

Isolde pounced like a tutor upon a mistake: "I *must* pay my taxes. I *may* help you. Show me the letter."

Mr. Alman tightened like a twisted rag. "I cannot share such sensitive information until you have agreed to assist in the case."

"There is another way to look at this, Iz," Warren said, returning to the tea cart. He poured water from a sweating pitcher into a juice glass and presented it to the dampened secretary, who readily accepted it. "You wouldn't just be working for the Crown; you would be serving the interests of the private citizen who has come forward with the claim . . . perhaps a *legitimate* one." The final phrase made Mr. Alman nearly choke upon his thimble swallow of water. "If the writer of this letter shares the king's blood, and we were to prove it, I don't think anyone would accuse you of being too friendly with the royals."

Isolde bobbed her head in consideration, an easy rhythm that quickly broke. "But if I help to prove that he is a prince, I'd just be serving at the pleasure of a different sovereign."

"True." Warren moved to the mantel to stir the coals, not to invigorate them, but to shuffle the loose embers toward the corners of the firebox. "But if you don't intervene, our possible prince will remain a fugitive."

"You think we should take the case?"

"You know how I feel about lords and lawmen. But it seems to me Mr. Alman is right: If there's a vacuum in the palace and a scramble for the throne, there will be strife in the streets. We know who suffers when heaven squabbles—the vulnerable. Someone up on high only has to whisper the word 'unrest' and the prisons fill up, the workhouses shake out, the missions bar their doors, and the orphanages repopulate. And when the dust settles, perhaps there'll be a new face printed on the gallet bill or a fresh set of bullies on the bench, but the only thing of real consequence that will have changed is the number of bones in the potter's field. Revolution may chasten the rich, but uncertainty torments the poor."

Isolde patted the air, signaling her surrender. "All right, War. All right. You've made your point. Mr. Alman, I—"

A heavy, arrhythmic knock brought the couple's heads around. The Wilbies stared at the unremarkable paneled door as if it were aflame.

Alman snuffled a little laugh. "Do knocking guests always cause such astonishment?"

"They do when they come by my cellar," Warren said.

The door shattered, casting splinters and hinge pins into the room, making all its inhabitants cry out in alarm. It seemed a fitting greeting for the seven-foot-tall forest golem who ducked beneath the riven lintel.

Its skin, rough as bark and scabbed with lichen, bunched about fat ankles and feet that were arrayed from toe to heel by a hundred gripping roots. Its swollen arms were heavy enough to bend its broad back and bow its head, ribbed and featureless as a grub. The golem lurched forward, swaying and creaking upon the shore of a gold-and-amethyst rug whose patterns had been worn down by the passage of centuries.

"A mandrake," Iz said, tugging a half stick of chalk from her khaki breeches. "I've never seen one so large. But don't worry. They're quite docile. He probably just got lost during his migration. Let's try to herd him back down."

With hands raised, Warren advanced upon the mandrake, nattering pleasantly as he inched toward the heaving golem that resembled an ambling yam. "There's a sport. Thank you for keeping off my rug. It's an antique, you know. I have to be honest—it's impossible to match and hard to clean. I haven't got one of those newfangled carpet renovators. The salesman, wonderful chap, wanted three hundred and twenty gallets for it. Can you imagine? And those suck-boxes are as big as a bureau. I have no idea where I'd park such a—"

The moment War inched into range, the mandrake swatted him with a slow, unyielding stroke of its limb, catching him on the shoulder and throwing him back across the room and violently through his tea cart. Macarons and petits fours leapt into the air and rained down upon the smashed porcelain that surrounded the splayed host.

The mandrake raised the fingerless knob of one hand, identifying his quarry, then charged at the royal secretary, who sat bleating like a calf.